ALFRED

THE BOY WHO WOULD BE KING

BY RON SMORYNSKI

VOLUME ONE
OF
ALFRED THE BOY KING

Thanks to my daughter for listening to me read this with abated breadth.

Thanks to my sister for her dedication in bringing Alfred back from the brink.

Table of Contents
Book One

Chapter One

A Free Computer..1

Chapter Two

Wooly & the Computer...17

Chapter Three

Good Night Mom 29

Chapter Four

The Ghost..41

Chapter Five

A Dark Forest..51

Chapter Six

Verboden the Cleric..62

Chapter Seven

Grotham Keep..76

Chapter Eight

Afraid of Spiders...83

Chapter Nine

    The Wizard's Room...94

Chapter Ten

    Return of the Boy King...................................99

Chapter Eleven

    A Kingly Farmer?..104

Chapter Twelve

    Of Arms and Armour.....................................111

Chapter Thirteen

    Defending the Defenseless................................123

Chapter Fourteen

    Honor the Mother and Father.............................131

Chapter Fifteen

    The Dark Forest..143

Chapter Sixteen

    The Bandits..150

Chapter Seventeen

    Tirnalth's Secret......................................158

Chapter Eighteen

    The Goblins..167

Book Two

Chapter Nineteen

    The Knights..182

Chapter Twenty

    A Loyal Knight..190

Chapter Twenty One

    Loranna..204

Chapter Twenty Two

    The Harvest and Looming Threat....................................211

Chapter Twenty Three

    Goblin Raiders...221

Chapter Twenty Four

    A True Knight..232

Chapter Twenty Five

    Fevers and Fears..242

Chapter Twenty Six

    Gorhogal..251

Chapter Twenty Seven

    A Mother's Weakness...259

Chapter Twenty Eight

Return of Alfred..273

Chapter Twenty Nine

The Return of the Knights..............................289

Chapter Thirty

The Battle Begins..304

Chapter Thirty One

Ratkins..316

Chapter Thirty Two

The Battle Within..333

Chapter Thirty Three

One Last Time...339

Chapter Thirty Four

The Honor at the Field..................................344

Chapter Thirty Five

Alfred Returns Home.....................................353

Book One
Chapter One

A Free Computer

"Mom! Come take a look at my super duper medieval fantasy epic battle mania monster uhh... crazy... game! Woo hoo!"

"I'm busy, Alfred. I have many sewing jobs tonight!"

"Mah!!! If only I could see something like this in real life! Gaah... goblins are uhhh-tacking! Come on knights!"

CLICK! CLICK! CLICK!

"Ah mom, real quick! You have never seen anything like this!! Evah!!!"

His mother came and leaned against his bedroom door.

They lived in a small, one bedroom apartment, so it was only a few steps. She held a needle with thread and some clothes she was meticulously sewing. His mom was a bit strange. She never wore make-up and had long hair wrapped and hidden in an intricate bun. She had a natural young beauty to her that confused him. All the other mothers at school had make up and salon hairstyles. She had none of this, yet seemed majestic to him -- if indeed he knew what that meant.

Maybe the impression of this came from the oddly old fashioned clothes she wore and her sad eyes. He wasn't sure. She kept to herself -- well, except when smothering him. All she did was work at a laundromat and come home at night to do extra sewing jobs. Alfred did not like to ponder this too much. After all, she was his mom.

"I thought you were supposed to be using that for school work -- that com-puting?"

"Com-put-ER mom! You're weird!"

"Yes, well, whatever it's called, Mrs. Kravitz gave it to you for free. That contraption isn't for playing noisy games. She is an old lady downstairs, and to give it to you was very nice of her. But she said you would need it for school."

"I finished my medieval homework! Oh-oh... gotta build more knights! Aaaagh!!... Hurry before they come!"

Click-click-click! GRRAHH!! CLANG!!!

"What do you mean medieval?" she asked.

SCRAWWTCH!!

"Alfred, turn that down."

BUD-DEEP!

"Ah... what?" Alfred asked nonchalant.

"You turned it off?"

"I paused it. What, mom?"

"Why do you call it, uhh... medieval homework? Are you still studying medieval history?" his mom asked.

"Uhh yeah..."

"But why? Why not learn about... you know, something... something happening today?"

"I love medieval history! And my teacher loves how I put medieval stuff in every assignment!"

"Alfred... why? Why not learn about ah... those things of today? You know -- business or that science thing? Or that phone thing everyone carries."

"Seriously mom! Seriously? 'That phone thing'? They're called smartphones."

"I, I don't want you to worry about that place, about those wars and all the horrible fighting," she said, instinctively sewing at the doorway.

"Yeah, okay mom. Sometimes it sounds like you lived it."

"No!" she froze.

There was an odd moment of silence.

"No, I just want you to be happy here," his mom said.

"I am. I got this computer for free! And a cool game!"

"You're happy?" she asked, flinching with each sound.

CRAACK! CLANK! GRRAAAHHHGGG!!

Alfred's face contorted with each clanging sound. "Yes, mom. This is so awesome! I'm the king of all these soldiers!"

"KIIING!!??" she shrilled.

Alfred flinched. He was surprised at the shrillness of her response. "Uh yeah, king. I'm the king who rules over these soldiers and tells them what to do." Alfred motioned to the game on his computer screen.

"Playing a game doesn't make one a king! And ruling

knights and men-at-arms is the least of what a king does!"

"Whaaahhhh???"

"Kings are just warlords with a crown! They are bitter and corrupt, grabbing authority to lord over others and are nothing more than brigands."

BUH-DEEP.

Alfred paused his game again, freezing and staring wide-eyed at his mother. "You studied medieval history?"

"I?"

"Mom, this game is cool because I get to be the king of knights and soldiers and fight monsters!"

She took a deep breath, "Being a king is more than... it is not about fighting!"

"It's just a game! See!? I know how to click on the peasants and make them build things. And then I click on these guys, who are the knights, and they fight for me. So I think I know more about being a king than you do."

His mom made a meek effort to look at the flashing lights on his computer screen. "I hope you never know."

"What?"

"Nothing, Alfred. You are safe now."

"Ohhh-kay?" Alfred rolled his eyes, trying to avoid the loving mom look – the odd gaze she sometimes held him in, as if she had dragged him out of a threatening situation of epic scale. It was kind of like the look all moms give their kids when they feel concerned or worried about them, he figured.

"Well I can't believe Mrs. Kravitz gave us this computer! I've never played this before. Kids at school used to talk about it, but I never got to play it till now!"

THUNK! KLUNK!

With each violent cartoonlike sound, his mom flinched.

"She never mentioned it plays games. She said all the kids used com-put-ers for homework."

"Mom, it's a computer. You can put anything on it -- games, writing programs, anything you want. Don't you know anything about computers? What century did you grow up in?"

"Alfred, I...I..."

GRAGHHH! KLASH!

She flinched with each sound.

"Well..." Alfred said between maddening clicks.

KBLANG!

"...her son..."

THUMP!

"Robert came by..."

FWWHOTH!

"He found the game and gave it to me. It's an old game he played when he was a kid. He said the computer is so old that this is the only game I can play on it."

BUD-DEEP!

"Mom, all the kids use their phones now. When do you think I could have a smartphone!?" He looked at his mom.

"Is it over?"

He rolled his eyes. "I paused it."

Alfred looked up. Subtle wrinkles around his mother's eyes, tautness in her simple yet beautiful face, revealed her anxiety.

"We can't afford that, Alfred. I don't make that much money sewing."

"I know... sorry, mom. Is it too loud?"

"Yes son, just a bit."

"Okay."

She looked at him with a loving glance and then turned to go back to her work in the small living room. As she left, Alfred stretched his foot out to catch the door, to keep it from closing all the way.

Alfred watched his mother. She sat amid piles of curtains and clothes and returned to sewing. He finally let the door close all the way.

BUD-DEEP.

He continued his game.

FWWOOSH! KLINK! KLANK! GRRAAGGHH!!!

The next day Alfred and his mom came out of their apartment and headed to school. He was tip-tapping and skipping along feeling happy and anxious.

The building next to theirs seemed less like a building and more like a giant brick shack. It must have been a city garage or firehouse that was now used as a repair shack by a strange man named Wooly.

"Hi, Mister Wooly!" Alfred yelled and waved as his mom pulled him along.

Wooly tried to avoid looking at them. His face was horrifically scarred. Many kids thought he was a firefighter because of how bad his face looked and because he lived in what looked like an old fire house. The room had many lockers and a pole that went up into the ceiling. Some kids said maybe he was a murderer hiding out! Alfred's mom always avoided looking at him.

"Just a minute, mom." He yanked his arm loose from his mother's grip and turned toward Wooly, who was in the shack.

"I got a new computer! Well it's actually an old

computer that Mrs. Kravitz gave to me!"

"Uhhh," Wooly said. He did not look up but rather stayed seated at his workbench fixing an old metal lamp.

"Yeah and her son Robert, you know him? He and his wife visit with the baby."

Wooly shrugged.

"He gave me an old game he used to play too! It's called 'Grim Wars'! You have to fight goblins and make knights and build farms. It's soo cool!"

"Fight goblins?! You've seen goblins?!" Wooly stood up suddenly, holding his wrench out like a weapon.

Alfred backed up while his mom stepped between them. "Don't bother the man!"

"I'm telling him about my new game!"

"Game? I'm sorry." Wooly sat back down. "It's a game?"

"Yeah, it's such a cool game! Have you heard of Grim Wars?"

"Grim Wars? No, I don't think so."

"Well, I'll show you. It is awesome! I'm so excited! I have to do my homework first. It's medieval history of course!"

"Medieval?"

"Come on, Alfred! School! Don't want to be late!"

"Okay, mom! I'll show you later Wooly, okay? You'll love it!"

Wooly watched at Alfred as he tippy-tapped back out of the garage. His eyes rose to meet Alfred's mother and then he looked away quickly. It was hard with all his scars to look at anyone, especially her. She looked away and then slowly looked back at him, hoping to catch his eye to show her compassion. Alfred pulled her away before she could see.

"You never talked to him before," his mom said.

"I know. But he's been here as long as I can remember, and I'm just so happy!"

"I promise, mom. I'll do my homework before I play Grim Wars. And I'll try not to study medieval history ALL the time!"

"It's okay, Alfred. Just do well and get good grades as your teacher said."

As they neared the school, Alfred took a deep breath. The humming of cars with kids being dropped off tended to rattle him. The kids invariably came out staring at smartphones as they rushed to school.

It was a chaotic hustle and bustle. Impatient and inconsiderate moms double-parked, then other cars honked. Parents opened and slammed car doors. Moms got out wearing bright clothes with crazy hairstyles, dragging their kids to the entrance. Yet plenty of moms stopped in the middle of the flurry and started 'he-said-she-said' conversations with other moms.

Alfred's mom was not like them. She calmly walked through the hustle of the morning drop-off crowd. Other moms glanced at her, wondering what her problem was. They wondered why she wore odd long dresses in earthy tones. She didn't wear makeup or jewelry. If she was trying to look poor and country-like, the other moms agreed that she did it well. But something about her natural beauty made them jealous.

As she kissed Alfred's cheek, he grimaced. Thankfully the other kids didn't seem to notice. They were always looking at their phones as they maneuvered up the stairs and around the other students.

"Bye, mom! I'll see you later!"

That evening, Alfred leapt up in his jammies. "Victory!!! Grryaaarrrhhhgg!!" Alfred pranced around in a tiny circle in his small bedroom. He opened his door and danced out. "Victory!!!" He danced near his mom, who was working on her sewing jobs.

She seemed in a daze but snapped out of it with all his silly commotions. "Alfred? It's late!"

"I won!!! WWWUUUHHHHNNN!!!" Alfred made some muscle poses. The wrinkles in his jammies gave him some muscular definition, sort of.

"Alfred, have a glass of milk and go to bed!" She giggled at his prowess.

"Whhhuuuunnnnn!!! Okay. I just gotta watch the outro! The victory video!!" Alfred skipped back to his room.

His mom stood up, stretched her back and rubbed her hands. She was half awake as she got him a glass of milk.

She went to Alfred's room and saw him leaning down watching the screen. She handed the milk to him and yawned.

He reached for the glass, which seemed suspended in mid air. His mom didn't notice. Alfred turned in extremely slow motion and yelled in a deep monotone voice, "NooooooOOoooOOOoooOOohhhhh!!!"

The glass of milk came splashing down atop the computer case. Its rich creamy liquid splattered and seeped through every slit and slot of the computer, producing sparks and smoke. It seemed almost magical. Almost.

A small flame burst inside the computer box and flickered, decreasing with each drip of milk. Then a small mushroom cloud of smoke floated upwards.

"Is it supposed to do that?"

"G'ah." Alfred looked at his screen as the computer game he loved suddenly blinked out of existence.

"I'll get a towel. We'll just dry it right up!"

She came back with a towel and quickly patted at the computer. Alfred sat slumped, watching the tiny trails of gray smoke. He unplugged all the wires and then put his head on the desk.

"Don't worry. Once it's dry, it will be fine. How does it work?"

"Mom, it's ruined. Any liquid on electronics destroys it! Don't you know that?"

"No, I..."

"Of course you don't! You don't know anything!"

"Alfred, I'm sorry. We'll get a new one?"

"New one!? Do you know how much they cost!? You can barely afford rent and milk. I gotta go to school where all the kids have phones but me! You know why I go to the library and read the three medieval books over and over? So I don't have to deal with the other kids. So they won't make fun of me because I don't have a phone!"

His mom sat silent next to the dead computer. She dabbed it a bit more then stood up and walked to his bedroom door. She turned around with a thought.

Alfred stood up in front of her at the door before she could speak. "Why are we so poor!? Why do we live in such a small apartment? Why do you have a lame job? Why aren't you a lawyer or doctor or someone on TV!? I hate my life, and I hate you!" He slammed the door in her face.

She stood there stunned, looking down at her hand

holding the ragged towel. She trembled. She began to sink. She turned and sat at her sewing table. She wanted to get angry at him. She tried, but all that came were sad tears.

She placed her right fist on her mouth, to muffle her crying. Instead of standing up with anger, she hunched over in pain and hid her face.

"It's okay. We are safe." She put her hand over her heart and repeated this over and over. After a few moments, she sat up calmly. *"She can't find us here."*

Alfred felt bad about slamming the door on his mother and for saying horrible things to her. He didn't know why he said all that. He loved her and was sorry for his outburst. He didn't know how to tell her how bad he felt for his behavior.

She worked as a seamstress at a local dry cleaning store. Once in awhile he'd go by to see her work. She did some cleaning, but there always seemed a line of old ladies wanting her to sew odd buttons or fix vintage clothes for them. She seemed somewhat popular there for her rare sewing skills.

He went to his door to go out and apologize. He hesitated, feeling frustrated at the loss of his computer and game. They could never afford to replace it.

He could hear his mother crying. She cried once in awhile. He stepped back from the door and returned to his desk. He turned on his old TV with an antennae, which he used to get local shows. He turned to a wrestling show. He loved watching big crazy guys wrestle. He knew it was all fake, but he liked all their crazy moves. He found their yelling and screaming annoyingly awesome. They seemed more like entertainers and talkers than fighters. They were loud. And right now, he needed a way to escape, to drown out the sound of her crying.

A few days later after their unspoken vows of silence, his mother announced that he could get a new computer. He couldn't believe it. He wanted to jump up and hug her. He felt ashamed at how angry he had been and for not talking to her. He had not hugged her in days. An eleven year old boy who hasn't had a hug from his mom in days can get very depressed.

As she walked into the room, she sensed his guilt and need for a hug, so she sat down beside him. She caressed his hair. He immediately melted, leaning into her. She hugged him.

"We don't have to get it, mom. It's too expensive." Alfred sobbed a bit in her arms. "I know you work hard and do the best you can for us. I'm sorry."

"It's okay. You are such a good boy, Alfred. You make good grades and will grow up smart. You will live a peaceful life here in America. So I want you to know all there is to know about computers as long as it helps you in school."

"But how can you afford it? Computers are expensive."

"I talked to some of the ladies at work. They told me of places that need special seamstresses like me. I can pick up some extra work."

"What? Extra work?"

"Well, I have already been fixing some people's clothes at work, just little things here and there. They have been telling everyone how good I am. I've been getting more work. They say my sewing is old fashioned and rare. I guess that makes me special."

Alfred was excited at first, but the feeling quickly faded

as he realized she would have to work longer hours. He looked up at her face. She looked tired and worn. Alfred was worried.

She blushed and looked away. "I want this extra work. I want it because if I don't, we won't be able to be part of this world."

"Part of this world?"

"You make good grades and are a good student. You are a good boy and deserve the best."

Alfred felt really bad. He didn't want his mom to have to do more work. She worked so hard. He heard from some boys at school that he might be able to get his computer fixed instead of buying a new one.

The boys told him to get his dad to do it or some adult to show him how to fix it. It was complicated. Alfred didn't have a dad or couldn't think of any adults he could ask, but he nodded in agreement.

Alfred walked home excited, focused on getting his computer fixed. He thought about the kids talking about dads. He didn't know his dad. As long as he could remember, he never met him or knew anything about him. A lot of the kids didn't have dads at home, so it seemed normal that he didn't either. However, most knew their dads. He never knew who his dad was. Nor had he ever seen a picture of him. He had to have had a dad somewhere, he figured. He hadn't really thought too much about it. If he had a dad, he wondered who he was and what he was like -- and why didn't he know him.

He walked by Wooly's shack. He saw Wooly inside fixing things. Alfred wondered if Wooly could help him fix his computer.

Wooly was a handyman that everybody hired because he was good and cheap. And since he didn't talk much, no one ever felt swindled by him. He would go to their house to fix something, or they would drop off items needing fixing at his garage. Alfred could only hope 'Scarface' would fix his computer.

"Hi, Mister... Wooly?"

Wooly was fixing a lamp in the back. He turned to see Alfred.

Alfred cringed and then faked a cough. "Hi... Mister Wooly right?"

Wooly nodded.

"I was wondering if you could help me with my computer?"

"Computer?"

"Yeah... to fix it. My mom said she'd buy me a new one, but they're expensive, and I thought maybe I could just get it fixed. My mom... she... well... I dropped milk on it, and it burned out."

"I don't fix computers."

"Oh. Okay..." Alfred turned to leave quickly.

"Wait."

Alfred froze, gritting his teeth.

"Let me take a look."

Alfred turned slowly. Wooly stood closer than he wanted. "Oh okay. I can bring it down. I just live..."

"I know where you live."

Alfred stared at Wooly's scarred face a bit too long.

"Bring it down." Wooly's eyes seemed warm. His smile showed more teeth than a natural man and looked a bit gruesome. Alfred always thought Wooly was old. Being so close, he realized Wooly wasn't that old. He might even be his mom's age.

Alfred returned something of a smile, mixed with a cringe. "Okay, I'll go get it."

Alfred had no intention whatsoever of going back. He sat in front of his computer and was like, no way -- that Scarface was too creepy. But the urge to get it fixed and play Grim Wars was maddening!

He quickly grabbed the power cord and box and lugged them down to the shop.

"Here it is! I brought the power..." Alfred said.

"Set it there."

Alfred put it on a table filled with broken lamps, vases, and picture frames. He saw broken furniture and kitchen appliances but no other computers. "Have you ever, I mean, do you ever fix computers?"

"No, this is the first one."

"Maybe I should..." Alfred mumbled.

Wooly put down the wire cutters he was using on a strange lamp and approached Alfred. "It smells cheesy."

"Oh, that's the spilled milk."

"No use crying for spilled milk, hey?"

"For spilled milk? No, its uh... crying over... I think."

"What?" Wooly asked, looking at the computer.

"No use crying over spilled milk," Alfred said.

"That's what I said."

"Uh yeah, okay, never mind."

"I will fix it for you, Alfred."

"Really?"

"Yes."

"How much?"

"I don't know yet, maybe twenty."

"Twenty? Twenty big ones?" Alfred gulped.

"What's a 'big one'?"

"I don't know, but it's a lot I think."

"Twenty dollars."

"Twenty dollars!? That's it? Twenty dollars!?"

"Yes, for you, Alfred."

Alfred smiled and hopped and could not care less if any of this made any sense whatsoever. "Okay!" He shook Wooly's oily hand and hopped right on out of there.

Wooly watched him go. "Yes, for you, Alfred."

Chapter Two

Wooly & the Computer

Alfred was beginning to think he'd been had. Maybe Wooly was just a thief. Alfred never got a receipt or anything. The kids at school told him Wooly stole the computer for sure and was gone.

Every day Alfred walked back from school and looked into Wooly's crusty garage, but it was closed.

Day after day he would go by and knock on the door, but there were no lights on. He couldn't see any movement inside. It was closed. Where did Wooly go? And where was his computer! Alfred did not have his computer to play Grim Wars.

"Mom... Wooly stole my computer!"

His mother looked up from her sewing. "What? Who?"

"Wooly, that creepy guy in the garage, he stole my computer."

"What, how, where is your computer?"

"I gave it to him to fix because I didn't want you to have to buy a whole new one, and he said he would, but he's gone with my computer. He stole it." Alfred, sobbing, began to quiver.

His mom looked at him for awhile. She too was about to cry.

"What? Oh mom, don't get upset! It's just a stupid broken computer."

"Oh Alfred, it's so nice that you'd do that for me. That you would try to get it fixed so I wouldn't have to pay for a new one."

"Well ya know... I'm trying..." Alfred sniffed.

"Does he know how to fix computers?"

"I don't know. I don't think so, but he said he would."

"I'll check for you, okay Alfred? Let me go down and see." She began sewing again.

"Can you go now?" Alfred nudged her.

"Oh, now? Alright, I'll go."

"Thanks, mom... please... thanks..." Alfred continued to nudge her.

"Alright, Alfred, I'll go."

She went down and saw that the shop was closed. She knocked, but there was no answer. It was odd. She turned to see a shadow of a man down the block. It looked like Wooly watching her. She wasn't sure. A car drove by, and its lights shined on him and his horrible scarred face. She froze. His look didn't seem evil, though, it seemed almost...

Suddenly, a young mom with a little boy walked by, and the boy dropped a bunch of books. He was carrying a stack almost as big as him. She was jolted by the sound and realized they needed help. She bent down to pick some up. She noticed that the books were used. She glanced back toward Wooly, but he was gone.

She asked the young mom, "Excuse me, where did you get those books?"

"Oh, at the library," the young mom said as she put the books into her bag.

"Library? For children?"

"For everyone. Just sign up. It's free."

"It's free?"

"Of course, all public libraries are free. You just sign up and check out a book. Just remember to return them."

"Oh... of course, return them."

"You can keep each for four weeks!"

"Four weeks!? Wow."

"That's a whole month!" her little boy said raising his books.

"Oh yes it is! What a cute boy."

"Thank you. It's down the street across from the school. Most parents don't even know it's there. Their kids just use the Internet or play video games, I guess. Hah... well now you know!"

"Yes, thank you."

"I'm sorry, Alfred, Wooly was not there."

"Oh no... my life is ruined!"

"It's just a computer."

"Aaaaggghhh!!!"

His mom could always understand her son's disappointments. "Why don't we go to the librarium?"

"The what!?" Alfred suddenly stopped sobbing. "Do

you mean library?"

"Oh, yes, that's what you call it. Let's go to the library!?"

"I am not going to the library! No way! Never ever!"

Alfred's mother pushed him in to the library carefully, avoiding everything from the taped carpet bumps to little kids skipping around with their small stacks of children's books. Alfred rolled his eyes as little kids passed. He stood there and mulled his predicament.

He was so annoyed he strutted down the aisles of books as if he was in a mysterious maze. He made squishy sounds in his mouth to relieve his annoyance. Then he saw it. He froze. He shook. He did both! His eyes widened as he read the label on a shelf, "Medieval History." In the next ten minutes he had ten books he wanted to check out. His mom was happy, and best of all, it was free.

He had books on castles and knights, on what life was like in medieval times, on battlefields and myths and legends. As he looked through all of these, he realized that the people that made 'Grim Wars' must have read the same books. There was all kinds of information about knights, peasants, villages, and castles.

"Mom! Dang... so many cool books. Our school only has a few... Why didn't they tell me about this place!?"

As he pulled out some more books, he saw Wooly through the opening in the next aisle.

Alfred hustled around to the next aisle. Wooly cleared his throat, quickly putting a yellow book back on a shelf.

"You stole my computer." Alfred's face was red, and his eyes teared. "You stole my computer! I want it back!"

Wooly looked at him through his scars. But Alfred was not afraid of the scars now.

A series of "Shhhhss!" echoed throughout the library.

"Alfred?" his mother called under her breadth.

Alfred waved at his mom through the wall of books. "Mom, I'm here! The repair guy is here too."

His mother came to the aisle and hurried down. "Alfred, shhh, not so loud. Whose here?"

Alfred looked back, but Wooly was gone. He must have walked down to the other side and left. That was fast! Alfred was mad, seething mad.

"What's wrong?"

Alfred was about to explode. He was so enraged, but then something caught his eye. He stared wide-eyed at the shelf. He grabbed the yellow book Wooly was looking at.

"Upgrading & Fixing Your... what's that say?" His mom still had trouble with some words.

"Computer."

His mom went by to check Wooly's workshop, but it was still closed. It was a few days since Alfred saw Wooly at the library, and there was no word from him.

Wooly seemed gone. Some of the other neighbors were concerned, saying he hadn't returned this or that, although most agreed that he always took awhile getting things done. Everybody, it seemed, had something in his garage. Most of his work was shining silverware, taking out dents, welding stuff, or fixing furniture and lamps. He was very handy with wood and especially metal.

Then one day the computer was at Alfred's door. First he was excited, but then he was enraged. It took this long, and then he left it outside on the doorstep? Granted, it was in a hallway of an apartment building, but still! Any one of the locals could have taken it and hid it in their apartment. Whatever! Alfred couldn't wait.

He had to make room on his table. He had cluttered the table with all kinds of library books and drawings he had made of pretend villages, castles and battles. He had drawn what he could remember from scenes from 'Grim Wars' and of medieval life. He pushed it all to the floor.

He was so excited. 'Grim Wars' wasn't on the computer anymore, so he had to re-install it. Then he got mad when he realized none of his saved games were on the fixed computer. He got angrier as he realized the computer looked different -- the interface on the screen, that is. Once the game was installed, he calmed down and started a game.

It was as if he was home again, just playing his game. He then noticed something. Everything played smoother, if that was the right word. He remembered that during the big hectic battles with a lot of units on the screen, the computer couldn't, well, compute fast enough. This would cause the units to flicker on screen and their animations to become choppy. Now, no matter how big the battles were, the game ran smoothly. He used to hesitate to start big battles. Hmph! Wooly had fixed his computer all right!

It took a few days before he realized something else was amiss. He never paid Wooly. Oh my gosh! Alfred suddenly panicked. Now he felt as if he was the thief, taking from Wooly. The computer ran much better than before. The colors seemed more vibrant all around. Alfred was quite thrilled.

He rushed down to find Wooly. And lo and behold, the

garage door was open. Wooly was back in business. Alfred looked in. Wooly was tinkering with some other computers. It was like he suddenly had a computer shop.

"Hey? Hello?" Alfred rushed in and came to a stop.

Wooly looked up.

"Thanks for fixing my computer!"

Wooly nodded.

"How much do I owe you?"

Wooly thought for a second, "How about that twenty? I had to replace a thing or two."

"Oh, yeah, right. Uh, I have to ask my mom," Alfred gulped again.

"Oh yes, well, since it took awhile, why don't we say it's free of charge. I had some learning to do."

Alfred nodded happily, "So are you fixing computers now?"

Wooly thought for a moment. There were a few computers in his garage now. "Yes."

"Was mine the first?" Alfred glanced at the other computers.

Wooly smiled. At first it seemed to Alfred a horrible evil smile. Then he realized it was just the scars. He could see that Wooly's eyes were smiling warmly.

"Yes. I'm sorry it took so long. I had many things to learn. I gave you a better graphics card and updated your operating system."

"Uh, okay," Alfred sighed relief. Wooly's disfigured face could look so evil and yet his voice sounded so... actually it sounded gutteral and evil too! But he didn't say evil things, it just sounded that way. Alfred walked backwards, waved bye, turned and dashed off.

Well mom was a bit upset. She wanted to pay for the repair. She would not have it free of charge. Nothing is free. She thought perhaps he was up to something. She was going to pay the price Wooly first quoted. Alfred was dismayed. He shouldn't have told her how excited he was to get it fixed for free. She wouldn't have it.

Though they had little money, this was suddenly a matter of pride or possibly stubbornness. Both were qualities that Alfred had not seen in his mother. He was a bit baffled. She wanted to thank the man and pay for the repair herself. Both of them went down to his shop.

Alfred couldn't help wonder if she was merely going down to size Wooly up, to see if it was even safe for Alfred to be dealing with this stranger.

When they got there, Wooly was working on other computers. Wooly looked up and saw Alfred's mom. He looked away. She looked away too. A cold shiver went down her spine.

Alfred felt as if he was standing between two silent brooding adults. It was typical of adults to say hello or talk about something boring like how each was doing or something. But they stood silent. Wooly watched a blank computer monitor as it restarted and his mom gazed about. She was looking at the mess in the garage. Alfred sensed from the look on her face what she was thinking, that the place was filthy, cluttered, dangerous – and other words Alfred couldn't think of.

She then looked at Wooly's back and saw in the computer screen his gaze, looking at her. Both glanced away. She twirled to see Alfred gaze with big eyes at her, motioning her to pay Wooly.

"Thank you… sir… for fixing my son's computer."

He nodded with his face still turned away.

She pulled out the money to pay him. "May I get a receipt?"

Alfred rolled his eyes.

Wooly focused on an open computer box next to him. He muttered oddly, "Is there something wrong?"

"Well, if I'm paying for this repair, I just want to make sure it works."

"Mom, it works."

"I just need a receipt or ticket. They do that at the cleaners, you know, just in case," she said.

Alfred could hear her dig her nails into her purse.

"You don't have to pay," Wooly muttered.

"Mom," Alfred hissed.

There seemed to be some strange standoff between mom and Wooly. He was generally standoffish. Alfred was sweating bricks. He knew Wooly fixed his computer and made it even better. Now his mom was making things difficult. What if something goes wrong again? Would Wooly be willing to help again?

"Well, here." His mom defiantly put the money down on the table and walked out. Alfred felt relieved but embarrassed. He waved bye to Wooly's back, noticing his shoulders suddenly sag. He followed his mom out.

They walked upstairs without saying a word.

After dinner and homework Alfred sat back down at his computer. He was so excited. He began a new game. His mom was in the kitchen cleaning up so she could begin her nightly work.

"Mom!? Come take a look at my game! Come on, Wooly really fixed it. It works even better!"

"I'm very busy, Alfred!"

"Mom, seriously, I don't think you've ever, ever looked at Grim Wars or see what I love to do! Well, except that last time, but that was BEFORE this awesome computer fix!"

"Alright, just a minute."

...

...

...

...

"MOM!"

"Alright, alright... I'm coming," she answered.

"Come on... gosh, the battle is almost over!"

She walked through the small one bedroom apartment, which consisted of Alfred's bedroom and another room with an open kitchen, a table, and a couch designated as the living room. Since she didn't watch TV, Alfred had all of that in the bedroom, and she slept and worked her sewing jobs around the table and couch.

She came to the door and leaned in. She had to step around behind Alfred to see the flashing screen and hear the sounds of fantasy fighting.

"Now look how awesome it looks. You gotta really focus okay, don't just pretend look!" Alfred said.

For the first time, she focused on what he was doing. He was creating armies to go into battle. He selected a group of knights and men-at-arms and attacked a large army of goblins.

"Look, I'll zoom in so you can see the details of the

units!" Alfred clicked his mouse furiously as sounds of galloping horses, yelling knights, and growling goblins came out of the small speakers.

His mother looked at the game as his knights and men-at-arms were getting overwhelmed. Alfred was gritting his teeth and clicking his mouse furiously to build more units and save the one's he had.

"Grrahh... hold on mom, I'm getting surrounded by a ton of goblins! This mission is tough."

She screamed. It was a loud gasping outcry. She stepped back, tottered and fell on his bed, then rolled off onto the floor. Alfred was stunned by how loud her scream was and then by her sudden fall. He paused the game and looked at her. She looked pale white, lying on the floor. She had her arms raised in helpless defense.

He went to pick her up. "Mom! Mom?"

She looked around as if in fear of her life and grabbed him tight, saying weird things like, "Bedenwulf!!? They've come! ...We're surrounded! ...Secret passage, hurry!"

"Bedenwulf?" Alfred mumbled.

She gasped and twisted in Alfred's arms. "...Beden... wulllll..."

"Mom!? Mom!" Alfred, not knowing what to do, was nearly in tears. His mother was sweating and in some kind of shock. Then all of a sudden she stared up at Alfred, blinking and beholding the room. She held him tight for a long while. Alfred was big, so it was easy for him to hold his dainty mother. He had never seen her like this. She seemed paralyzed with fear.

She sat up and looked at his computer. The image was frozen. She read the words 'Game Paused' in clear bold type.

And the sounds of battle were paused.

"Are you okay, mom?" he asked, still trembling.

She sighed. He sighed.

"Are you afraid of my game? Huh?" He chuckled to shake it off. He lifted her up.

She smiled. "A game? Yes, it's just a game." She stood up, straightening herself. She still seemed beside herself and stood in a way he had never seen before, as if she were summoning courage, trying to be brave. "I'm alright." She put her hands out, to give herself some space.

He shrugged it off and sat back down.

"Just a little fright is all. It's just a game," she said. She patted Alfred's head and slowly began to walk out.

He glanced hesitantly at his mom.

"Are you sure?"

"Yes! Yes. I'm fine. Took me by surprise. It does look real. Too real. I have a lot of work to do. Ah, but I'm glad you are enjoying your game."

"Ohh-kay." He continued the game.

Startled at the sudden sound of clashing swords and grunting beasts, she left the room quickly. Alfred shook off an unsettling feeling. After all, he had a battle to win!

Chapter Three

Good Night Mom

One seemingly magical night when he was working on a paper for school, "Life in the Castle," his mother entered his room with dinner. He was flipping through books, taking notes, and organizing how he wanted to write the paper.

"Your favorite dinner, roast stew and baked bread!"

"Ahh... can't we just have bread from the store sometime?" Alfred broke open the steamy buttery bread made from scratch and ate a delicious morsel. But he longed for the sliced bread like the other kids ate, perfectly wrapped in plastic, all with the same uniform spongy look.

"I love baking bread for you!"

"Just seems like so much work, and you look so tired."

As Alfred stuffed another fluffy piece of grainy goodness into his mouth, his mother gasped and covered her mouth. She couldn't help but smile.

Even so, Alfred couldn't stop picking up morsels of the bread to eat. With each bite his countenance became brighter, his smile larger.

"I am tired, Alfred. But it is a peaceful tired, the perfect kind of tired."

"Okay, mom, whatever you say."

She noticed the books on medieval history. "Medieval times were dark, violent and full of hardship. You should not concern yourself with them."

"What do you know about the Dark Ages? Hah ha, there were knights and chivalry!"

"Knights are big-headed thick-skulled sword-swinging barbarians stuffed into steel cans and adorned with banners to make them appear more than they really are!" And with that she left.

He rushed out. "Whaddaya mean they're big thick steel cans of barbarian banners??" Alfred stopped to think about what she, and-or he, just said.

"I don't want to talk about them!" She plopped down to do her night's sewing.

"Okay, what about castles? Do you know anything about castles!?"

His mother began repairing a worn leather jacket. "Well for one, most women in a castle sew!"

"Wow! Really?" Alfred sat beside her and listened to her story about life in a castle. She weaved a great tale of daily life for the women of a castle. She spoke as if she were telling him things from memory, as if they were her own stories. Alfred was amazed. He listened with gleeful eyes. For the first time he could remember, he saw life spring into her face as she spoke of bygone ages. Alfred was stunned. Where did this come from?

He became more intrigued and began to study more, shall we say, adult books concerning castles and knights. These books had a lot fewer pictures and more writing. Many were dry to read. Still, Alfred was intrigued, especially when he read the stories of knights who would have been mere brigands if it weren't for a supporting lord or king.

Some kings could easily be compared to modern day mafia bosses. Many were ruthless in their rule over peasants and began wars merely to try out their newly formed army. Many kings conscripted peasants, meaning that peasants were forced to fight wars the kings wanted to fight. And it was the knights who carried out their orders and forced peasants onward in battle.

But not all kings or knights were bad. As with people of all professions, there were good ones and bad ones. Many knights tried to uphold a degree of honor, justice, and fairness. Alfred learned that knighthood was mostly inherited, a fact that led to a selective snobbery amongst the nobility. They felt they were better than peasants, and this often led them to be cruel tyrants.

After discovering this colorful depiction of knights, Alfred desired to ask his mom about her lowly opinion of knights. When she came back from work one night, he rushed out to interview her again, as if she were a star witness. "Hey, mom, I want to ask you something."

"Yes, Alfred?" she asked with her weary yet loving voice.

"Remember when I was writing that paper about knights and chivalry?"

"Yes, I remember. How can I forget? You are always writing about the very thing I wish you wouldn't." She unpacked a small bag of groceries.

"Well you have a very bad view of knights, right?"

"Yes."

"Well, why is that? Where did you learn about them? What book?" Alfred was too focused on his questions to help her put groceries away. It wasn't as if she asked for his help. Nor would he even know where things like milk went.

"It was no book." She almost smiled, but then her face became grave. "I must have learned it in school."

"School?" He realized he did not know much about his mom, about where she went to school or really anything. She never talked about herself or her past. "Uhh..., what school did you go to? You know, what middle school?"

"Oh, I did not go to a middle school. I went to a special school." As she was talking, she began to chop meat and vegetables for a stew she was making. She made a lot of stews, roasts and baked hams.

"Well, where did you go?"

"Well, I had some private tutoring. And, well, I, I went to a monastery school. You know, where all the teachers are monks and nuns."

"Oooh! Nuns? Monks? No wonder you don't seem that... educated...?"

"Educated!? I'm very... educated... just in different things!" She waved a washed potato at Alfred that sprinkled a little water on him. He smiled and wiped it off.

"A monastery? Hey! That's like medieval times!"

"No! No it isn't!" She quickly chopped the potatoes.

Alfred stared at her violent chops.

She suddenly stopped and looked at her finger. "Phew, almost." She began cutting again, but this time slower. "Well, a little Alfred, but there are many schools like that now, I think. I went to one like that. And it is nothing like back then, nothing like that place."

"What place?"

"Oh, no place. I mean that place, you know, the Dark Ages."

"Are you hiding something, mom?"

"No, no. Of course not!"

"I think you are. You never talk to me about your family, and you have never told me about how you grew up." Alfred became wound up with how much he wanted to say.

"Well, I will one day. It's not important. Really, Alfred, it's not important. I just went to an old school, and now I work as a seamstress. It is very simple, and there's nothing important about it." She quickly put all the cut vegetables into the pot.

"But, mom... who is my father?" He did not know he was going to ask that, but he did. At school he had learned about how a child was born only after a man and woman came together. So he knew he must have had a father at some point -- unless he was a robot or alien being!? Hmmm...

His mother stirred the chopped meat and vegetables in the boiling water. She seemed to stare blankly at the pot. He couldn't tell if her face was moist from the steam or if she was sweating. She did not reply for some time.

Alfred looked down. He was sad. He finally had asked her the big question. Who was his father? He had expected some sort of explanation. For sometime he had wondered about it but never felt like the right time to ask. So many of his classmates' parents were divorced or having marital problems. Some kids knew they were abandoned by their dad. He didn't know what happened to his.

They all knew something about their father, whether he was around or not. Most loved their fathers, but a few hated them. Fathers seem to come in all sizes and shapes, good and bad – just like knights, he thought.

"Why don't you ever wear makeup?" He did not know where that question came from either, but in after-thought he knew why he asked. She never wore makeup and never went out and had no friends.

Alfred looked at his mother. She seemed a bit crazed, staring intently into the pot and not saying anything. Her eyes seemed to be looking at something far away. Alfred did not want to look, but he was drawn to something in her eyes. Or was it that he had his computer game on his mind? He felt as if he was seeing knights charging with one great knight swinging his sword. There was a dark huge shape battling the knights.

Alfred shivered. The room was warm from the steam of his mom's delicious cooking, and yet he shivered. His mother, however, was still in her zombie-like state, merely stirring and not answering. Alfred, not wanting to push it, not now, went to his room.

That night, after his bowl of stew and reading about knights and mystical creatures, he had a dream of a princess fleeing within dark caves. He had a dream of a knight fighting creatures to protect her. As the princess fell on the ground, he realized that though she looked slim and fair, she was burdened with an unborn child.

As if he were with her on that cold dark cavernous floor, he could see a huge dark beast rear before them. A lone knight was battling the beast. The beast reared up like a dragon as the knight turned toward the princess, toward Alfred. The knight looked over Alfred at her. "Run, Ethralia! Run to the doorway! Now!"

Alfred turned with her and felt close enough to hear her heartbeat, her cries and heavy breathing. Fire seemed to consume the cavern walls, fanning around him. He could hear the princess's frantic cries of horror and panic. And then they heard the cry of the knight in torturous pain.

Alfred awoke in a sweat, gasping for air. He felt hot and frightened. It was the most vivid nightmare he had ever had. He was so rattled that he had to go tell his mother. He couldn't keep it in. He crept out quietly. He wanted to wake her, but he did not want to startle her.

When he opened his bedroom door to look out, he saw his mother standing there with her hair down. She was wearing an embroidered gown and looking out the window into the deep blue night. Alfred slowly walked up to her, wanting to see what she was looking at. As he got closer, she seemed to be looking at the stars up in the sky. Yet she had an odd blank stare, as if she was not really looking at anything.

Alfred began to hear the sounds of music, of stringed instruments playing and laughing, of dancing and joyous singing. He could hear metal cups clanging and people with food in their mouths muttering away. He looked around but could not tell where all the sound was coming from. They were in their small apartment, and he knew the sounds were not coming from their neighbors. With each song he also heard a soft voice humming a soft tune. It was not like any song he had ever heard. It sounded like a mystical wind. He then realized it was his mother singing softly.

Alfred stepped closer, listening to his mother. Where did she learn to sing like that? In the monastery? It must have been. It sounded so beautiful and yet so sad. He could hear soft words come from her mouth. It sounded like English but spoken in a way that was odd and maybe old. He could barely make out the words. She sang so softly that the words seemed to melt or dissipate as they left her lips.

Of western winds and whistling hymns
of green fields and the sun that shines
of love long cast to the rays of light
do not forsake, I will always await.

I sing to thee, my love you are free
and I shall return one time again
there is hope yet kindled
in the fire of youth, to live in peace
to live with truth

I hold my head, to the stars at night
to hear the song, of our last time.
Do not forsake, I will always await.

"Oh, Alfred!?"
Alfred was startled as both jumped at each other's

presence. It seemed as if even Alfred had gone into a dreamlike state – a trance, if you will.

"Mom, what were you singing?"

"Me? I don't know?" She stepped away from the window and into the shadow, immediately grabbing her long shiny hair and wrapping it up.

"What was that song you were singing? Did you learn it at the monastery?"

"No. I mean yes -- yes, I learned to sing there. Many girls sing in churches, you know, even today." She busily bundled her hair.

"Well, can you sing it again?"

"It's late! You should be in bed." She finished winding her hair into a tight bun.

"Why don't you leave your hair out, mom? How come you never show it to anyone?"

Alfred's mom looked at him, her face in the shadow beyond the starlight. Her eyes held a glow like that of the stars.

"If you're not going to show it, why don't you just cut it off?"

"Alfred, my hair is not important. I was just letting it dry."

"But you always bundle it. You never show it to anyone."

"Well, it's long and, and it gets in the way of my work."

"Yah, but you never go out. You never do that, you know, like other moms."

She smiled and came forward to hug him. "I want to take care of you."

Alfred stepped back. His mom hesitated and stood

looking at him with caring but sad eyes.

"I just want you to be happy, mom."

His mother then smiled with tears and hugged him. "I am happy, Alfred. I am so very happy. I am happy because I have a son, a smart strong son. I am happy because you are alive and growing and will one day be a man. You will live in peace and happiness. I know it."

"Mom?" Alfred thought she was a little kooky.

She was swelling with tears. "I did this all for you."

"Mom! I don't want you to do this all for me! I want you to be happy too!"

"I am Alfred! I am."

"You work so hard and never go out. All the other kids have two parents, a mom and a dad, or at least some have boyfriends or stepparents or whatever. But you, mom, you don't have anything, and you don't tell me anything, and I don't know who my father is!"

"Was." She stood back in the shadows.

"What?" Alfred immediately understood but felt disbelief. "What?"

"He is dead. He died before you were born."

"What? Why? What did he die from?" Alfred's heart sank. Though he rarely thought about it, somewhere inside him he always hoped that when he was old enough, he would meet his father. Suddenly this little bit of hope was dashed against a rock.

"He died fighting. He died in a war." She seemed to be carefully choosing her words.

It took awhile for Alfred to recover. He had never known his father. But now, learning that he had been a warrior, intrigued him to no end. "My dad was a soldier!?

Was he a big soldier? I mean was he a colonel or something?"

"Yes -- I mean no." His mother seemed confused, trying to remember or figure out what to say to appease him.

"Yes? He was a colonel?" Alfred asked excitedly. "What war did he fight in? What happened? How long did you know him? Was he really a colonel!?"

"No, he was not a colonel. He was a warrior, I mean." She shook her head, trying to think.

"A warrior? What kind of rank is that?" Alfred looked at her with suspicious eyes.

"No, no, not that, he wasn't that. He was not like the others, I mean. I don't know what I mean. He's gone, and it's not important." With that, she suddenly blurted out, "I mean, it's important but not right now, not here. Don't ask me anymore! I can't say anymore -- please, Alfred. We must not say anything more right now!" She seemed hysterical.

Alfred was astonished. He became angry. It was as if she was taking his father away from him again. He just learned something about his father, something very exciting, and then she became hysterical and wouldn't tell him more. "Mom! You have to tell me! I am going to find out one way or another!"

"No, Alfred, you will not. You will never find out! You cannot know! You will never know!" She gasped at what she said. She knew how hard it hit her son, how harsh those words were. Alfred looked as if an arrow had pierced his heart. He was a strong, smart boy who deserved better than this and ought to live in peace.

Alfred's eyes swelled with tears. It was as if he had nothing, no past and now no future. His mother was the key to understanding who he was, and she was like a ghost –

someone he could chase for the rest of his life but never catch.

Alfred went to his door and then turned to look at her shadowed face. "I don't even know his name. I don't know anything about him."

"You can't, Alfred. You must never know his name. It's dangerous," his mother said softly.

The weight of that was heavier than anything Alfred had ever felt. He leaned against his door, his emotions swelling into tears and anger. He looked at his mother, as if penetrating the dark, when something snapped in his mind.

"Bedenwulf."

"What? What did you say?" His mother stepped from the shadows into the light of the window with strained grievous eyes.

"That's his name, mom, isn't it? You said it the other day when you were delirious, when it seemed you were crazy. That's his name! Bedenwulf!" Alfred shouted at her.

She seemed to grow in stature as she walked up to him. Then she slapped him with such force that it knocked him aside. As his eyes filled with tears, hers began glancing to and fro in the darkness. To Alfred she looked frightened, as if some monster was about to appear. Finally she stopped looking about and gazed at him. As if this crazy behavior wasn't enough, her voice was terrifying. "Do not say that name again, ever!" She delivered the words as if speaking a curse or foretelling doom.

Alfred walked backward into his bedroom and shut the door in her face. Locking it, he wept.

That night, bundled in his bed, he could think only of that name, Bedenwulf.

Chapter Four

The Ghost

Though Alfred tried to sleep, he was wide awake with heightened senses. He could hear every sound outside his window, see every dust particle that floated by, and feel the temperature in his room.

In a big city, cars drove by late in the night. He was used to this. The headlights shone through his blinds causing bright lines to race across his wall. The headlights came in a pattern. Every few moments the bright lines would appear, forming at one side. When a car passed, the lines of light would zip across his wall to the corner, then bend along the other side, glide by the window and disappear.

Alfred was mesmerized by the repeated sound of the

coming cars and the glowing lines of light as they crossed the walls. While watching this, he wondered about his father. He tried to think of which war he could have been in eleven years ago. What war did his country fight that his father could have been a soldier in? Hmmm… He realized that he was not familiar with most modern wars or even the current struggles going on around the world. He could think only of medieval wars, of knights and men-at-arms, of barbarians and monsters.

"Bedenwulf," Alfred whispered. He imagined his father as a knight, a great knight in shining armour charging with his lance and impaling a great beast. Then he imagined him fighting other beasts. And, of course, there was always the dark beast, the great unclean dragon. He imagined that his father was killed by this fire breathing dragon. It was a creature so dark and mysterious that it seemed to melt in shadows. It had long ghostly talons and left wisps of darkness, trails of inky clouds, when it passed.

He saw his father as a knight fighting the dark beast. He could hear his mother crying and screaming in fear. He sat up in his bed.

"Bedenwulf!?"

Alfred wasn't sure if he had nodded off and dreamed. He saw the headlights again, moving slowly across the wall. They glided along to the corner and then raced along the back wall up to the window and zipped out.

Another car went by, but as Alfred watched the lines of light this time, something was different. The lines slowly glided to the corner, but instead of dashing along the wall they seemed to undulate along a bumpy surface and then race out. Alfred was confused. He looked again as more lines appeared from another passing car. They went to the corner and, as before, undulated. He realized that they were not racing along the smooth wall but passing over someone standing in the room, right there in the darkness.

Alfred immediately jumped from his bed, his heart racing. Someone was in the corner! He picked up an old plastic baseball bat he had standing in the corner and raised it to strike.

"Do not be frightened, my boy! Do not be frightened." It was an old raspy voice.

"Who are you!?" With the bat in his hands, Alfred felt strong.

The man came forward. He was an old man bent over with a long white beard and long white hair. He was wearing a white robe that began to glow, not bright like the sun but dim, like distant stars.

"Who are you?" Alfred had never held a bat in defense, but it felt right.

The strange old man paused and thought for a moment. "I, I don't remember." He looked genuinely perplexed. "I don't remember my name. I don't remember anything. I have no memory."

"Well, how did you get in here?"

The man was tall but bent over and frail. With eyes that seemed worn, he blinked and looked about confused.

"I don't remember that either."

"Well, do you live here in the building? There's a lot of old people here. Wait! You don't remember that either, right?"

The old man nodded and smiled. "Yes, yes, I don't remember. I have no memory. I have no memory, and I feel that I have awakened from a long sleep."

Alfred was unsure what he meant but thought of things like amnesia or senility. This old man looked strange. His clothing, a robe or gown, looked as if it would go well in a mental hospital or carnival. As he looked at it more carefully, it seemed to sparkle. The garment had ornate embroidery all around it, faintly colored in gold and silver. It looked like it came from a well-funded mental hospital.

"Let me go wake my mom, and we can help you."

"No! Do not wake your mother! I have come here for you. You have called me. You have summoned me, and I need to take you with me!"

Alfred cringed.

"You cannot tell your mother. This I know... I mean I feel. I don't know because I have no memory. So whatever it was that I did know, I now know, I do not know. You see, very simply, I can't explain a thing because I have no memory to explain why I feel the way I feel, but I do feel that you must come with me in these desperate times!"

"Come with you? Where to? An old folks home?"

"Old folks home? Hmmm, I wonder if I can remember that... old folks home? I don't think I know this Old Folk? Or at least not now. Not now, now that I don't know ...anything."

"What's wrong with you? Are you crazy? Mental?" Alfred kept holding his bat, just in case.

"Hmm? Me? Well? Possibly. I certainly feel crazy... a bit. I feel impatient. I feel I must take you with me, to show you what you must do and to help in any way I can, though I do not remember what it was or what it is you must do."

"Well, I don't think I can go with you, and I think I should get my mother." Alfred went to the door.

The old man sprang between Alfred and the door and

then leaned on it, waving Alfred off. He was waving his hands frantically, putting his finger to his lip to try to remember, rolling his eyes as if searching in his empty brain for something to say.

Alfred's lip curled.

"No, no, do not wake her. Do not bid her to come. For I know, or rather feel, that she has the power to dismiss me. She has the power to end our last hope, which is you, my dear boy. You are our last hope. We need you. I don't know who *we* is, but I feel, still, that I am a part of we, whoever we are? Please! I need you!" The old man wrung his feeble hands.

"My mom?" Alfred was about to call for her out loud.

"The Queen! I think? Or feel or fear? I don't know! I don't know! I don't know!?" The old man beat his own head, albeit gently of course.

Saying the word queen softly, Alfred remembered her long hair, her soft song, her embroidered robe – the image of her standing there at the window singing while gazing at the stars. He thought there was something more to her.

"Is she a queen?" the old man asked, looking up from his gentle self battering.

"My mom? No!"

"All I know, or feel or what have you, is that I need your help. I have finally come. Something has brought me here, and I have come, and now it is time. It is time for... It is time for you! Will you help me? Ah us? Me?"

Alfred was a bit taken by the sudden movements, the desperate cajoling, and the emotional pleading.

"I feel I have come because you are of age! That must be it! You are eighteen years old!? A man!" The old man posed proudly motioning to Alfred.

"I'm eleven years old."

"Oh, eleven? Ooohhh… a bit young, isn't it? Oh well, it will have to do, I suppose – I have no idea!" The old man raised his arms to the ceiling. "Still, I'm here. You are here. We must go anyway!"

Alfred nodded a reluctant okay.

"Good, good, thank you."

"Why don't you want to tell my mom? What power does she have over you?" Alfred crossed his arms with the bat still gripped tightly, of course.

The old man suddenly braced against the door as if it were going to crash in from gushing water. He seemed positively out of control. "I told you I don't remember. I don't know. I but feel what I must and feel that I need you and feel that your mother, the woman on the other side of this door cannot know, not now."

"Why?" Alfred stood firm, bat re-raised.

"Because… there is a great sadness in her. I can feel it."

Alfred stepped back, his stern look lessened. There was something interesting about his robe. It looked similar to his mother's, yet very, very different. Her robe was an earthy green with gold embroidery. His looked more like a snowy hill with twinkling snowflakes on a brisk moonlit night.

The old man closed his eyes as if concentrating on the other side of the door. "She loves you with all her heart. She is willing to sacrifice… everything… for you. She knows the dangers that lie ahead. She won't take the risks, not any more. But you will, my boy, won't you?"

Alfred smiled and nodded, "Yeah. What danger? What risk?"

The old man thought for a split second. "Uh… I don't

know."

Alfred still kept his bat ready but not as high and obvious. He carefully watched the muttering old man. "You can feel?"

The old man nodded, waving his affirmative finger.

"But you have no memory?" Alfred asked.

"Yes, I believe that is right."

"Did someone take your memory?"

The old man froze, "Yes! At least I think so. Though I'm not sure I can think so. I just know I feel so."

"Do you remember how you got here?"

The old man raised a finger in ponderous excitement of having known something, but then said... "No."

"Then how do you know me?" Alfred asked.

"Know you? I don't know you. I feel. I mean I can feel that you are the one destined to come with me." The old man gently poked Alfred's shoulder. "You are the one I need, the one the land needs. I do not belong here, nor do you."

"What? I do not belong here? You mean in this city and country?" Alfred asked.

"No, I mean HERE!" The old man waved his arms about.

"Here as in where?"

"Oh! How can I explain if I don't have any memory... huh?" the old man said.

"Well, if you don't have any memory, how will you take me wherever it is that you want to take me?"

"Good question. I have no idea."

"Where did you want to take me?"

The old man got excited. He opened his mouth to tell wonderful stories about a wonderful place, but then his faced strained in puzzlement. He obviously could not remember a thing about those wonderful places or the wonderful stories. "I can't remember. I have a task. This I feel, and it involves you. This I felt when I heard the name, and now I am here."

"Name? What name? What did you hear?"

"It was… I don't remember. At least I don't remember while I was asleep or gone or what have you." The old man closed his eyes.

"Was it Bedenwulf?"

"Bedenwulf!" the old man's quivering lips finally said. "Bedenwulf?" He stared into the void before him. "It was that name that called me back from my doom – that name that I have waited for all these years, to be summoned, to be awakened!"

Alfred was a bit scared and taken aback by this old man who looked so strange yet acted so familiar. The man looked intently at Alfred, a gaze more focused than before.

"You are the son of Bedenwulf! He was a great... something… I can't remember. I feel very strongly that he was my friend. And he was doomed."

"Was he a great knight?" Alfred asked.

The old man's eyes twitched as he glanced about. Then he gasped for air as if remembering things or at least trying to remember. "Yes! He was a great knight!"

"Wait! Don't we mean a soldier? Right?"

"No, not a soldier who is paid by lords. He was a knight – a great one, one of the greatest! Or so I feel. And you are his son. You must return with me to the land of… of… oh, I can't remember! A terrible curse has been cast upon me! At least, I feel it were so. Something has been taken from me!"

"Your memory?"

"Yes, my memory!" the old man said.

Alfred looked at the way the old man with his long white beard and long white hair stood. Above him there was a shadow against the wall in the shape of a triangle. It was pointing upward like a cone. The old man stood as if he were leaning on something. He leaned against the wall where a shadowy line went down to the floor. Yes! It looked as if the old man had a coned hat and was holding a staff.

Alfred tilted his head to get that image juxtaposed just right. "Are you a wizard!?"

The old man suddenly stood straight with the wonderful thought. "A wizard? Yes. Why yes! That is what I am! It's all coming back to me now!" He danced around the room. "A wizard! That's what I am! I'm remembering! My memory is coming back!"

"And you appeared right there, out of nowhere?" Alfred recalled the man's magical arrival. He most certainly did not come through the door or window. He had to have come magically, somehow. Alfred put down his bat and stepped around the frolicking figure to have a closer look at the corner of the room. Was there a magical portal? Alfred stared intently as the old man did some remarkable dance moves.

"I'm a wizard, yes I am... a wizzy wizzy wizard!"

Alfred saw strange sparkling energies suddenly web along the wall. "He is a wizard! A real one! In my room!"

Alfred turned to the wizard and began dancing with him. They grabbed hands and did some odd footwork, both of them giggling. Alfred looked back at the wall and saw the blue energy sparkle and spread.

"Wow! So you're memory is back?"

The old man nodded briskly, but then thought about it, and stopped dancing. "No… it isn't."

When they stopped and were looking at each other, they realized something was different. They saw that they were standing in a dark forest at twilight.

Chapter Five

A Dark Forest

Alfred and the old wizard separated and rubbed their hands as if something filthy or perhaps magical was on them. The eleven-year-old, in his pajamas in the middle of a dark forest, was afraid. Moonlight shone through the canopy of dark leaves, giving everything except the shadows a dark bluish hue. The magical blue sparks Alfred saw in his bedroom faded away.

The wizard looked around. "Yes, yes, I know this place."

"You do!? Where are we?"

The wizard shrugged. "I don't remember. But I know I knew at one time. Or rather I feel I know this. Hmmm… a new feeling as well."

"What?" Alfred paced with bare feet, tiptoeing on the clammy forest floor, looking around, hoping to find a door or window out of this dark place.

"Danger!" the wizard suddenly said, barely whispering, glancing about with his dancing eyes, grim face, and furled eyebrows.

"Danger?!" Alfred rushed behind the old man.

"Yes, something is here, in the shadows near us." The old man, or wizard as Alfred hoped he was, rolled up his sleeves.

"Can you take me back home? Now!?" Alfred tugged at the man's robe. The forest felt dangerous, whether something threatening was there with them or not.

Then they heard a growl. It echoed in the deep crevices of the bark of the old trees and along the quivering ends of the dark leaves. It reverberated along Alfred's spine and at the tips of the old wizard's hair. Alfred leapt about, causing the old man to falter in his footsteps.

"Now, now, calm down, boy! Calm down!"

"There's something out there!" Alfred pointed hysterically in all directions.

"I know. I can feel it!" The wizard waved his hands as if to prepare a spell.

"Are you going to cast a spell? You're a wizard, right!?"

The wizard waved his hands again. And again. "Hmmm, no. I can't remember how." He shrugged in a hopeless manner.

"What kind of wizard are you if you can't cast spells?" Alfred hopped like a bunny in panic mode.

"I don't know. I don't remember!"

Just then from out of the trees leapt a wolf. It was a

dark huge hairy beast with enormous extended limbs, and its paws seemed much larger than a regular wolf's paws. Man-like fingers landed and gripped the ground, folding in earth and bramble. Terror-struck, Alfred could say nothing.

The animal's growl, a low rumble, vibrated through Alfred, leaving him frozen in fear. The creature stood up like a man on its back legs. It was no mere wolf. Its snout was long and grotesque. An array of thick pointed teeth protruded from its mouth. Its ears were huge and hairy, twitching from side to side.

"Stay close, Alfred!"

Too weak-kneed to run, Alfred clung to the wizard. "Are you going to protect me?"

"No, no, I'm just really scared too!" The wizard tried to give Alfred a comforting smile. Alfred was not very comforted.

The beast growled again, spittle and steam pouring from its snout. Its eyes glowed with blood red hatred and hunger. It took a few heaving steps towards them, its paws digging deep into the soft earth.

"Stay back, dire one!" The wizard bravely stood between the wolf beast and Alfred.

"It's a werewolf!!??" Alfred shook uncontrollably.

"Oh, a werewolf? That sounds apropos!" The wizard gave a smug acknowledgment.

The creature leapt upon the wizard, knocking him and Alfred back. He felt as if he was in a dark bizarre dream, with no will or power to defend himself. Though he had played 'Grim Wars' and fought in imaginary worlds against numerous types of evil creatures, this one was far too real. It brought waves of shivers down his spine and made his whole body limp with fear and exhaustion. He had never felt such a bombardment of sensations. The smell of the decaying leaves, the cold night air, the clammy dark earth, the spidery shadows of the trees, the serenely misty hues of moonlight, and the growling vibrations of the werewolf -- all chilled his bones and weakened his limbs.

Thrown back into the low-lying leaves and branches, Alfred thudded onto the spongy forest floor. The werewolf took to slashing at the wizard, swinging wildly in the air.

Alfred sat up in the bushes, covered in mud and leaves. He could just see the beast through the leaves. The werewolf looked down at its bare claws. There was nothing there or anyone to swing at. It looked slightly confused. The wizard had vanished!

Alfred gulped. The werewolf's ears twitched, and its blood red eyes came to focus on Alfred. With a growl, the creature charged at Alfred, who sat paralyzed with terror.

As the werewolf leapt, Alfred was yanked out of the way, leaving the bestial wolf to crash into a tree. It had charged so hard, its head collided with the tree flipping its body upside down. The werewolf then slid to the ground upon its head. Out came a growling moan, followed by a gurgle of pain.

Alfred landed on roots and stumbled about but was able to stay on his feet. The wizard looked at himself, patting his body and arms. Then he looked at the stricken werewolf. "It can't touch me!... how convenient!" The wizard seemed amused by this.

"Can it touch me?" Alfred asked with hope.

"Mmmm... probably..."

"What? Why?"

"Well, I can FEEL that it can't touch me, see! I feel it. But I can also feel that it... CAN touch you!" The wizard proudly tapped his thinking cap.

"Well, what do I do then?" Alfred continued his bunny rabbit hop.

"Oh yes...yes... Calm down, boy. This is the whole point, right? Heh heh... I'm feeling that our being here is the whole point!" The wizard patted his chest and stood proud a bit too long.

"The whole point is me? Right? You need me for something?" said Alfred, stunned, muddied and sore. "To live??"

The werewolf growled in pain and anger, jostling to get up.

"Oh right! Follow me if you want to live!" The non-spell casting wizard took off through the forest.

"I want to live!" Alfred yelled.

"Yes, yes, of course! I feel it!"

Alfred awoke from his state of fear and raced after the strange wizard. They traveled a good while in the dark.

Alfred was breathing laboriously. He had never run so hard. Though young and healthy, he was not considered much of an athlete. At school, his physical education class was pretty easy, and he never put in the effort to be any better than what was expected. Now he was running for his life, being cut and scraped by branches, feeling the sting of thorns and stickiness of plant sap. He had jabs of pain run up his feet from running barefoot through broken branches, dead leaves and who knows what else on the forest floor. Snails? Worms? Leeches? Spiders? Fungi? Ladybugs? Yuck!

"Hah! The dire wolf could not touch me!" The wizard

breathed heavily too as he hurried through the forest.

"Why?" asked Alfred, barely able to keep up.

"Ah, I don't know why it can't touch me. Perhaps I am some kind of ghost!"

"But I touched you!"

"Because I wanted you to," the wizard winked.

"Oh."

They heard the werewolf howling from a distance. Alfred looked back fearfully but saw only dark shadowy trees and slow rolling mist.

"Come, boy! Hurry!"

Alfred continued to run, but everything in his body screamed with pain. "I need shoes! I'm hurting!"

"Ah hah, there's your answer!"

"What answer?"

The wizard turned to Alfred as they ran. "I don't feel a thing."

"So what's that mean?"

The wizard stopped in the forest, breathing lightly, while Alfred, stopping and bending over, breathed heavily.

"It means, my dear boy, that since you feel pain, thusly, ergo... the werewolf can hurt you." The wizard seemed thrilled by his powers of deduction. He stood tall, arms crossed in satisfaction.

The werewolf howled again, the dreadful sound seemed closer.

"There! Run!" The wizard pointed to a small square glowing yellow light.

Alfred thought that odd to see in the middle of the dark forest. But he had no other choice. He did not know what else to do. His fear shrouded any other thought but to get to that yellow light. He ran as fast as he could through the blinding darkness of the forest. Then he saw another square yellow light next to the first one. He realized they were coming to a small dark cottage lit from within.

Again he heard the howls and growls of the werewolf – this time with the sound of its feet pounding upon the forest floor. Now all he could think of was getting into the cottage. He leapt at its door, banging his tired and beaten body against it. It would not open.

Then he heard the werewolf snarl right behind him. Turning, he saw it leap! The hairy beast suddenly flew by him as if yanked by an invisible leash. It yelped as it crashed into nearby bushes.

"Down, foul beast!" a booming voice yelled, much different from the wizard's. Then a bright searing light blinded Alfred. "The Father of Light repels you, cursed brother! You know its power! Begone!"

The werewolf got up, cowering, and ran off. As suddenly as the light had appeared, it was gone. Alfred's eyes adjusted quickly to the dim light in front of the cottage. A cloaked man stood there with a staff held out like a weapon. He turned to peer at Alfred.

Alfred, breathing hard, peeled himself off of the small wooden door.

"Who are you?" the booming voice asked.

"He is the one," the wizard said, stepping out of the forest.

The cloaked man turned. "Who are you that comes into the night like a ghost!?" The man slowly waved his staff at both wizard and boy. Then he paused, peering closer at them. Alfred winced, shivering in shock and fear.

The wizard smiled warmly. "I know you," he said with confidence. "You were a boy. I knew you."

"Tirnalth?" the cloaked man said, as if expelling years of despair.

"Yes, that was my name! I am Tirnalth, the wizard!" the old wizard or rather Tirnalth said. "But I must warn you that I have no memory. I can not recall who I was. I did not even know my name, until now."

"I am Verboden," said the cloaked man, bowing on one knee. "I was a young servant to you many years ago. I was a cleric in the Order of Light, but now, in these troubled times, I am but a hermit. The last we have known of you is that you were to give up your life to the Dark One to lessen his sway upon Gorbogal."

"Hmmm," Tirnalth nodded. "Dark One? Gorbogal? Yes, those sound important... serious... dangerous. I seem to remember..."

"They are the bane of the land. All has been lost. The people are scattered."

"What? That sounds really serious!" Tirnalth said.

Alfred tried to stand apart from the door but fell back against it. Verboden and Tirnalth looked at him with pity.

"We should take him inside. There we can talk. I am glad, Tirnalth, that you have returned, even if just in spirit. I fear, though, that the Dark One has succeeded." Verboden lifted Alfred in his arms and opened the door.

"Take care of the boy first," said Tirnalth, entering the home behind Verboden.

It was a small cottage with a bed, two chairs by the fire, several pots for cooking, a table and some baskets with mushrooms, wild roots, herbs and the like. There were several walking sticks and staves and jars of stored provisions.

Tirnalth looked about with an old man's smile. "It's a nice little place you have here, Verboden."

"You truly do not have your memory."

Verboden laid Alfred on the bed. Spent and in a hot sweat, the boy fell asleep. Verboden washed his many scrapes and cuts, applying a green paste to them and speaking soft ancient words.

"Tell me, Verboden. Who am I?" Tirnalth sat in one of the chairs and pulled a pipe from a small basket next to it. He looked at the pipe in curiosity, wondering how he knew to pick it up. Then he looked down and saw smoking leaf and a set of long branches. He stuffed the leaf into the pipe, thrust a branch into the fire, placed the flickering flame on the leaf and then puffed at his wonderful little pipe.

Verboden smiled, seeing Tirnalth's old habits. After cleaning and bandaging Alfred's minor cuts and abrasions, Verboden gently placed a blanket over him and then sat down next to Tirnalth.

"Some memories not even the Dark One can take." Verboden nodded to the small stool where Tirnalth acquired the pipe and leaf.

"How was my memory taken and why?"

Verboden looked to the sleeping Alfred and then spoke quietly, "All I know is that you knew you had to confront the Dark One, the one who must not be named. You had to dissuade him from aiding the evil witch Gorbogal. You had to give him something he wanted, and so you sacrificed yourself. You gave him your soul. But I wonder if all the Dark One could take was your memory. After all, you are a servant of the Father of Light."

Tirnalth watched as his smoke swirled up into the small rafters. "The God of Light – yes, I feel that is my salvation. My soul is not mine to give. But my memories are. So I am not completely destroyed. I am not completely gone."

"But you are without your memory, your powers, and your knowledge?"

"All can be regained or relearned or whatever. I am not worried." Tirnalth continued to puff.

"Not worried?" Verboden ignored the smoke lingering about him. "You truly do not have your memory!"

Tirnalth glanced at Verboden, wondering what he would say next.

"Once Gorbogal knows you have returned, as powerless as you are, she will hunt you down as she has all the wizards. Her power is supreme. She destroyed the line of kings many years ago and scattered the people. Men of the Westfold now hide in holes while she curses the land with plague and darkness! What hope do we have in a brainless wizard!?"

"Silence!" Tirnalth suddenly boomed, much as he would have when he was a great wizard.

Verboden looked away. Both men sat in silence, Tirnalth staring at the fire, Verboden looking at Alfred.

"This one is but a soft gangly boy. A peasant you found lost in the woods, I would think, though he looks well fed," Verboden finally spoke.

Tirnalth was deep in thought.

Verboden turned to the wizard, "Tirnalth? Why have you returned?"

Tirnalth finally looked at Verboden, "I can not remember anything."

"If you can not remember, if you have lost all your powers, then we have no one to stop Gorbogal. The Father of Light has abandoned us." Verboden added another log to the fire and prodded it, crouching close enough to see the flames reflected in his eyes.

Tirnalth stood and walked over to where Alfred was sleeping. "I do not even know his name."

Then he turned and smiled warmly at Verboden. The cleric did not look reassured.

"It feels right, standing here, back in this place, with this -- I suppose it is my smoking pipe," said Tirnalth, puffing greedily. "And with this boy here, I can feel it.... the line of kings has returned!"

Verboden's eyes widened in wonder at the remark, but soon the shadow of doubt filled his face.

Chapter Six

Verboden the Cleric

Alfred woke, yawned, and stretched. "What a crazy dream that was!" he thought to himself, shaking his head. He had to tell his mother. He sat up. "Mom!?"

Suddenly, there was the crashing sound of wood banging on the floor. "Oh, my dear boy," Tirnalth said. "Don't call out for your mother!"

Alfred saw that the old man from the dream had just entered the room with some firewood.

Then Verboden rushed in. "Is everything okay?"

"Who are you?" he asked. "Why are you still here?"

Alfred cringed in the bed, thinking it was his own.

"Here?" Verboden smirked. Then he sighed, realizing that Alfred had every right to be frightened and confused. Verboden and Tirnalth pulled their chairs up in front of Alfred and sat down.

"What is your name, boy?" Verboden asked.

"It's Alfred."

Tirnalth nodded assuringly at Verboden. "Doesn't ring a bell."

Verboden sighed and then spoke softly, "Alfred, Tirnalth here is a wizard, a great wizard."

Tirnalth shrugged. "No recollection!"

"He has no memory because he gave it up to save the line of kings. Well, long ago, to save your mother who was bearing you."

"Where's my mom? Where am I? She'll be worried, you know. And she'll call the police." Alfred covered himself more, then looked down at the rustic wool blanket and realized it wasn't his. He glanced about the cabin at all the medieval looking props.

Verboden asked Tirnalth, "Do you know what or who the police is?"

Tirnalth shrugged. "I have no memory."

"Oh yes, of course," Verboden shook his head, then spoke to Alfred. "We will explain everything. If I am right, your mother will know where you are. She... fled... I think to protect you."

"Protect me? Why? From what?"

"To protect you from..." Verboden hesitated, choosing his words carefully, "...from harm."

Alfred eyed Verboden and glanced at Tirnalth, who

kept his old man smile. "Protect me from what? From that werewolf? Was it really a werewolf? Was it really real?" He did not like the idea of being in a place where there were actual werewolves.

"No... Well yes... The truth of the matter, Alfred, is that the only one who knows what happened or why you are here, the only one who really knows what to do, is this man." Verboden pointed at Tirnalth.

"Ha, ha, and I have no recollection, no idea of what that is," Tirnalth smiled and patted the bed, trying to reassure Alfred.

Alfred was not sure whether to laugh like a crazy freak or cry with real sobbing tears. When he did both, Verboden and Tirnalth looked at each other in confused dismay.

"Guhhhar hah... I wanna... guhhh... gooohhh... sniff snorf... home!!! Guhhhh...hahr hahhh...guhhhh..."

"Why is he here, Tirnalth?"

"He is in the line of kings. I feel this. His mother is a queen, I believe."

They looked at Alfred as he continued crying.

"How do you know?" Verboden asked.

"My father's name is Bedenwulf," said Alfred, tapering his hysterics to a sniffle.

Tirnalth nodded in approval. "Yes, that was the word the boy spoke that awoke me from my long lost dreams. It was Bedenwulf."

Verboden, becoming more dejected, stood up and walked away. He leaned against the stone of the fireplace, staring deep into the small crackle of fire.

"If my memory serves me right, this boy is not from the line of kings," Verboden said with disdain.

Tirnalth and Alfred looked at Verboden, both uncomfortable with the tone.

"He is born of a princess, not a queen. And he is not from a Lord Knight. His father was not an ordained knight of the Realm. Nor was he of any royal house. He is... a liability... a shame upon the crown." Verboden's expression was stone cold. "Their love was forbidden!"

Tirnalth looked at Alfred with a compassionate smile. Alfred did not like what he heard. He did not feel welcomed.

Tirnalth looked back at Verboden. "If all I have are my feelings, and no memory, than it is with my feelings I know." He pointed at Alfred. "This boy is to be king."

"The Knights of the Realm will never hear of it. They remember Bedenwulf's betrayal all too well," Verboden met Tirnalth's gaze. "I remember his betrayal."

"Betrayal?" Alfred and Tirnalth asked together.

Alfred looked at Tirnalth for reassurance. Tirnalth smiled and leaned in. "I have only good feelings about Bedenwulf and about your mother," the wizard said. "He was a great warrior and a knight. He was there to the end. This I can feel." Though his words were an attempt to reassure Alfred, they conveyed a sense of sadness and pain.

"You speak of Bedenwulf as if he were a hero," said Verboden, throwing a new log onto the fire, creating a small explosion of embers. "He took the princess as his own when the kingdom was under siege by Gorbogal. He took her and was never seen or heard from again."

"I can not argue with you, Verboden. I have no memory of what you speak of. I know only that this is Alfred and that he is to be king." Tirnalth trembled with wizardly conviction.

Verboden was unmoved. "The Council of Knights will accept only a knight, not a boy, to lead the kingdom. And not a boy of a disgraced line."

Alfred gritted his teeth.

"Forgive me, Alfred. This is not your fault." Verboden finally looked at the boy. "I do not mean to offend you. It is not our way. But I must speak plainly with Tirnalth."

Alfred, his face reddening, nodded.

"The kingdom is in a desperate way. There is no kingdom but in name. The land has suffered since you were taken, and there has been no king. A plague has ravaged the countryside. Foul beasts appear in the forests and take weary travelers. The knights bicker amongst themselves. Most died long ago defending their king. The king knew Bedenwulf took the princess. He knew his daughter was kidnapped."

"She was not kidnapped!" Tirnalth clenched his fists and shuddered, trying to remember, but he could not.

Alfred's eyes were wet with tears. Tirnalth put a hand on Alfred's knee to comfort him. "She was loved."

"And you remember this?" Verboden rubbed his face, trying to soften his clenched jaw.

"I don't know. I suppose I feel it, even now."

Verboden returned from the fireplace and sat down beside them. "You are Tirnalth. I can sense this in your presence, in the tone of your voice, and in your manners. But if you have no memory, then you do not have your powers, and therefore can not confront Gorbogal." He bent over and rubbed his hair. "You can not be exposed with your frail limitations."

Tirnalth took a deep breath. "This all sounds very true – I must be weak."

Verboden lifted his head up. His face was distraught. "You must stay hidden!"

"Yes, I agree. You must take Alfred to the people, to the knights."

"What? Me?" Verboden looked away, rubbing his reddening hands.

Tirnalth puffed his pipe. Alfred was frightened but also in a state of wonderment. Though he kept with the conversation, he couldn't help glancing about. The dwelling was everything he imagined a small medieval cottage would be – the rustic wood, the heavy black iron spikes and hooks, the woven baskets and tapestries, the rough textured linens and clothes, the simple dirty floor with thrown rugs, and the thick blurry glass windows.

"You! Boy! Alfred!" Verboden shook Alfred's shoulder to get his attention.

Alfred leapt to his bare feet and began to pace, weaving in and around Tirnalth and Verboden, mumbling… "I'm in a dream. I'm in a world that is a crazy fantasy place with witches and werewolves and dark ones and wizards! Right?"

Verboden and Tirnalth looked at each other and shrugged. "Yes, of course… it seems so," they said in unison.

Verboden continued, "But it is not fantasy. What other kind of place is there?"

"My place, my kind of place. And it doesn't have any of this -- no magic or weird fantastic creatures, certainly no real ones. We pretend they exist, but they really don't!" Alfred kept pacing. The wizard and cleric followed him with their eyes.

"What kind of a world do you come from?" Verboden asked. "It must be a nice place to be without witches and sorcerers and foul beasts."

"No, it isn't exactly that," Alfred said. "I too live in a harsh world."

"Then why did you go there?" Verboden asked. "Why did your mother go there?"

Alfred did not know. Nor was he even sure who his mother was or what she did.

"To protect him," Tirnalth said, pointing at Alfred.

"I can not conceive of a princess, burdened with an unborn child, leaving us in our time of need and abandoning her father," Verboden said.

"Was it to protect the unborn child, the next king, from your witch, from the dark one?" Tirnalth puffed his pipe. His eyes were wide with fresh insight.

"If it were so, it was a harsh blow," Verboden said. "Her father never recovered. He was slain where he sat. He had not the strength to lead nor fight. That day was the day of defeat for a long line of kings."

"Who was my dad? I mean my father then?" Alfred sat near Verboden on the bed.

Verboden felt uncomfortable having to explain to a possible king, a heathen and an unwanted child, who his father was. "He was a good knight. Really, he was the best knight. Those who did not know him called him the Black Wolf or Black Knight, Bedenwulf. He was incorrigible and contemptible. He was frustrated that he came from a fallen royal house. It had failed the king and was no longer ordained."

"So he was a knight then?" Alfred asked. "He was a real knight in this place?"

"Yes, but not a Royal Knight. In all respects he was a

mercenary. He worked for Lord Dunther, the Baron Knight. In times of war and and in times of struggle, the Royal Knights would seek out and use as many mercenaries as they could, even from fallen houses."

"Fallen houses?" Alfred asked.

"Yes, well, your fath...Knight Bedenwulf was from a fallen house, one where debt or failure to heed the rulings of the king caused them to lose status, land or... or duties. The king, your grandfather, King Athelrod, wanted your mother to marry a merchant lord from the south, to bridge two kingdoms to unite against the Dark Lord. But Bedenwulf was caught courting your mother secretly, and his house was further demoted. The Telehistine emissary to the Merchant Lord ended the fragile allegiance. Our kingdom became isolated."

"What about the witch?" Alfred asked. "Who is she?"

"Her name is Gorbogal. She is a foul abomination, a beast living in a tomb far to the East under the shadow of the Black Spires. They say her flesh is always hungry. She was once a sister to the Royal House, but she turned to sorcery and made a deal with a demon of the Dark One. Now she wants only to shroud the land in darkness and rule it with malice. Many armies, great armies, have challenged the witch, and all have been defeated."

"Hmm... they sound like all the villains I've fought in 'Grim Wars' – my computer game," Alfred said.

Verboden and Tirnalth's eyebrows rose.

"Com-puh-tah game?" Verboden asked, confused. "You have much to learn, boy! You should respect the fallen and leave us to our own fate."

"Now, now, Verboden. It was not his choice that

brought him here, but mine. I feel you have respect for me and some allegiance to me! So respect my... err... notions... " Tirnalth gripped Verboden's shoulder.

There was a long moment of tension. Verboden trembled and finally sighed, nodding in agreement.

"This can only be a dream," said Alfred, holding his head with his hands.

As Verboden nodded smugly, Tirnalth's brow furrowed and he shook his head.

"Then I've been living in a dream all my life," said Verboden, turning his chair toward the fire to attend to it.

Tirnalth began to stroll around the cottage, trying to remember all the knickknacks he saw, puffing thoughtfully on the pipe. "Well I certainly feel that way now," he said.

"This can only be a dream, and I must wake up!" said Alfred with a whimper. Then he pounded his head against the wall.

Verboden stood up, clearly concerned. Tirnalth coughed on his pipe.

"Ow!" Alfred rubbed his forehead. "Dang that hurt!"

Verboden and Tirnalth watched in dismay.

"Tirnalth, this is crazy. Even he does not believe in this land or the role you feel he is fated for." With that Verboden hooked a kettle above the fire.

"I do not have the answers, Verboden. I only feel what I feel. Other than that, I suppose I am quite useless," Tirnalth sighed. His eyes drifted out the window.

Alfred pondered the situation -- sitting down again, standing up again, pacing, mulling, reviewing, considering, reconsidering... "You're a wizard, Tirnalth?"

Tirnalth nodded absently, "So I've been told."

"And you're a cleric?" Alfred motioned to Verboden.

"A cleric of the Order of the Light and a healer," Verboden declared with some contempt, bowing in his chair.

"And there are knights?"

"Yes," Verboden said.

"And a castle?"

"Well, what remains of the castle," Verboden shrugged while packing a small clay infuser with tea leaves.

"No king or royalty then?"

"They have all been hunted down and killed, or have fled," said Verboden, concentrating on pouring hot water through the infuser into a small wooden cup.

"There are lots of peasants or people still?" Alfred asked.

"Scattered, living in hidden squalor and fearing for their lives. Gorbogal has goblin raiders who look to steal farmers' harvests each fall and kill the peasants. She keeps everyone near ruin, starving and disease ridden." Verboden sipped contentedly at his perfect tea.

"May I see the castle?" Alfred asked.

Tirnalth's eyes sparkled. Verboden looked up with surprise, spitting out a little of the tea.

"Are you mad, boy?" Verboden asked.

"Well, it doesn't seem like it could get any worse," said Alfred, pouring himself a cup of tea.

Tirnalth laughed, knowing the idea was utterly appropriate. Then he shook his head in disapproval at his outburst.

Between sips Alfred said, "Let's see now. There are foul beasts in the forests. The knights are all dead or lost. The line of true kings is gone. I am the son of a fallen knight. There is disease and death everywhere. Goblins hunt the humans. A werewolf lurks about in the forest..."

"Alright, alright, let us go to the castle," Verboden gulped his tea and stood up again. Tea dripped down his chin. He wiped it quickly.

Alfred took a long full sip of tea. Tirnalth watched tilting his head.

Verboden put his hand on Tirnalth's shoulder, "You must stay here! If Gorbogal knows you have returned, she will hunt you down. You will have no way of defending yourself!"

Tirnalth nodded agreement, frustration clearly visible on his face.

"But Tirnalth is a wizard and was once a great wizard, right?" Alfred asked.

"Yes, but without his memory he has no powers," Verboden replied too quickly.

"Well then he must relearn his powers. Isn't there some way for him to learn spells again? You know -- memorize them or read about them in a book? A spell book? Don't you have spell books here?" Alfred stood up, wiping tea from his own chin.

Verboden was not impressed with Alfred's youthful impatience. "He speaks with such insolence!"

"But he's right." Tirnalth stroked his beard. "I can relearn. I may have lost my memory, but I still have my mind."

"If there are no spell books here, would there be something in the castle, like a library or something where spell books are kept? Did Tirnalth have a wizard's tower or something like that?" Alfred asked.

Verboden stood a moment, thinking. "Well, yes there

was a small library and resting room for Tirnalth when he came to the castle." Verboden's eyes lit up, and he hurried in donning belts and cloak. "Yes there is! And perhaps there are some books left, if it has not been raided!" Then a weight seemed to lower his shoulders. "Traveling there will be dangerous."

"We could use a disguise? We could dress as peasants or something?" Alfred suggested.

Verboden never had such a thought. Tirnalth smiled in glee.

The countryside of the Westfold, for that was what the land was called, although this particular area was noted as the Northern Kingdom, was dreary at best. A cold foggy mist blanketed the land like a slow flowing river. Grass and dirt were gray. The ground was soggy. Verboden's and Alfred's suctioning footsteps echoed in a hollow wind, and slippery goo thickened on their shoes and the hems of their ragged peasant garments.

Alfred, disguised with dirty rags and a mud painted face, spoke quietly, "Tirnalth, you shouldn't walk so upright."

Tirnalth turned to him. "I don't believe anyone can see me."

"Well I can see you," Alfred said, whispering.

"That is because I wish for you to see me. Here, now, I do not wish for you to see me." And with that, Tirnalth disappeared. "You see, I am a ghost, a former shadow of myself."

Verboden walked up to them, "I do not think that will work with Gorbogal, Tirnalth."

Reappearing, Tirnalth said, "Yes, I believe you are

right. If she defeated this land, then she must have defeated me. I will use discretion with my presence and hide whenever possible." Tirnalth bowed and continued walking, deep in thought, seeming to fade a bit, looking truly like a ghost.

They passed a few farms that were barely noticeable until Verboden pointed them out -- small thatched hutches in the mist. Alfred saw no fields or crops. Verboden said the farmers out tilling the soil would hide whenever anyone passed by. And it was not yet spring. He feared many were starving now for any food stores would be at their lowest.

"Do they have horses to till or plow?" Alfred asked.

"Horses?" Verboden smirked. "They'd choke on the reins. We use ox to till."

"Why not horses?" Alfred skipped along the mud to keep up with Verboden.

"As I said, to yoke a horse would choke it."

"A yoke? What is a yoke?" Alfred asked.

"It is a piece of wood you put on the shoulders of an ox," said Verboden, rolling his eyes. "The yoke is attached to the rake. The ox pulls the rake along the ground to till the soil. The ox has a thick neck and broad shoulders, so it can handle the pressure. The straps would tighten around a horse and choke it. Understand!?"

Alfred thought for a moment. "I read in one of my books on farming that horses are much better and faster at plowing, not tilling. In the dark ages... well in these times... a special sort of collar was invented that rests more on its shoulders. And the plow isn't a rake but is a sort of blade, curved to one side so that as it cuts the ground, the earth is turned over, exposing the roots of the weeds. Plowing the soil deeply is better than just tilling or raking the surface."

Verboden considered what he was hearing as he peered at the barren landscape, at the fields yet to be tilled.

"I also read that they rotate crops," Alfred continued. "Do these farmers rotate the crops?"

"I'm not sure what you mean?" Verboden looked at the barren gray pastures.

"I mean do they, you know, do they plant a different crop in each field each year?" Alfred had to hopscotch along, as the road was pocketed with puddles and coated with slippery mud. "This helps the ground, uh, not get drained of its nutrients by the same crop year after year."

"Noot rey-ents? What is that?"

"Oh, ah, nutrients are what's in the ground that the plants, you know, eat to grow big. I read that cow crap or rather manure is a really good nutrient for crops." Alfred could not really notice Verboden's furrowed brows as he was too busy skipping from dry mound to dry mound and keeping up. "So if you grow, say, wheat in one field, the next year you'd grow oats or peas. Then the next year, you'd leave that field alone and let the sheep or cows graze there and leave their droppings. That way the soil replenishes. At least that's what I remember reading."

Verboden saw Tirnalth's raised eyebrow. "You see, Verboden," the wizard said, "there is hope."

Verboden kept his eyes shrouded in his hood.

Chapter Seven

Grotham Keep

"There is Grotham Keep." Verboden was pointing through trees at a hill in the distance.

The castle on it, abandoned and silent, was shrouded in mist. It was a simple structure, square with thick walls and towers at each corner. As they drew near it, they saw that it was intact and in good shape for a building long uninhabited. To Alfred it was impressive. He could see the inner keep. He read it was the main enclosure that must have housed all the important people long ago.

"It was a modest yet strong fortress for its time," Verboden said as they approached. "It was built by King Grotham of olde, long ago, before the downfall of man."

Alfred breathed excitedly, trying to keep up. "Is there anyone inside?" he asked.

Verboden and Tirnalth began the ascent to the castle on an old road. Verboden looked about. "No, it is uninhabited."

"What about monsters?" Alfred gulped at the thought.

Verboden and Tirnalth froze and glanced at each other. "Oh, I don't know," said Verboden. "I have not been here in years."

"Perhaps I should go first," Tirnalth said. "It does seem I have one power. I am but a ghost." Tirnalth winked and then faded in and out of view. "Nothing can touch me that I will."

Verboden put an arm out to restrain Tirnalth. "I do not wish to take that chance, not with you, not after so many years. I have some powers. I will go."

Tirnalth floated hazily through his arm.

"Could I have a weapon?" Alfred stepped forward showing his small bare hands. "I'm probably not any good, but at least I could help."

"I have none but my staff," Verboden said, lifting the large heavy stick. "Maybe we will find something in the castle, if there is anything left."

"Then let us all go," said Tirnalth, floating forward. "We shall confront together whatever may lurk inside."

"If you are a ghost, Tirnalth, you could be the decoy!" Alfred raised his idea finger, double-stepping to keep up.

Tirnalth chuckled, "Yes, that sounds like a good idea. I will flail about as Verboden dispenses with his powers of conviction!"

"I have more than that at my disposal, old man!" Verboden twirled his staff and spoke magical sounding words.

Strength upon us
Light upon us
O domme rai
Vee bede mohn

"Oh cool! Was that a blessing?" Alfred wondered if anything was different, "Am I glowing?"

"It is a blessing," Verboden said, rolling his eyes, "to give you strength and courage!"

"Alrighty!" Alfred's skip was a bit bouncier. "Now just find me a sword! And a shield! And a rocket launcher!"

"A what?" Verboden's brow furrowed as he marched forward.

"Ah hah!" said Alfred with a crimson blush. "I was just kidding. "A sword and shield would be great."

Verboden and Tirnalth nodded in agreement and continued up to Grotham Keep.

"No... I mean it."

The castle walls were made with large stones. Gray mold had grown up through the mortar in geometric webs. Gray rotted wood beams stuck out from the walls at odd angles. At one time a wooden hoarding or roofing hung atop the battlements. There was an eerie feeling in the air, as though the silent stronghold was anticipating and awaiting their visit.

Verboden and Tirnalth led the way through the decrepit gatehouse, a structure containing a rusty portcullis. This defensive gate was retracted up within the stone wall.

Alfred swallowed and walked slowly under .the

enormous gate. Knowing that it could drop down at a moment's notice, he could not keep his eyes off of it, especially the rusty spikes. He peered up and felt dizzy. The split second during which he was passing under the black pointed spears seemed like an eternity. As he moved forward, his head angling around to keep his eyes on them, he became disoriented. Thankfully, nothing happened.

Blinking and shaking off the shivers and strain, he leveled his contorted face back to normal and looked about. The courtyard was filled with rubble. In the center of it Alfred saw a statue of a king, fallen, lying headless, sprawled across a broken fountain and cobblestones holding scattered pools of murky water. Dark weeds and vines were everywhere, much of them seeming to have grown and died and then grown over themselves again and died.

Suddenly Alfred realized that Verboden and Tirnalth were nowhere to be seen. He spun about, wondering how they could have vanished so quickly. Though the courtyard was littered with stones and broken structures, he could see in all directions. "Tirnalth? Verboden?" he whispered anxiously.

At last he heard their mumbling voices, echoing from a place just beyond the fallen statue and a large pile of rocks. He sighed in relief as he skipped closer. In the countryside he had been curious but safe. Here, inside this precarious place, his curiosity was being undone by fear.

Verboden was pointing out the entrance to the inner keep. Its door was gone, and wood and stone lay about. "When Gorbogal defeated the Lord Knights, she began her siege of King Athelrod's realm," he said. "She besieged this castle with her goblin horde. Most of the knights were gone, so the king's personal guard and men-at-arms defended these walls. It was then that you, Tirnalth, forsook the king. Or at least that is what he believed. His daughter had fled with the renegade knight and... he lost all heart to fight."

Verboden turned to see Alfred standing close and peering down at old dry pieces of gray wood. "Why is the door broken outwards?" he asked.

Verboden and Tirnalth looked at the destroyed door. It had been bashed from the inside out. Most of its pieces lay scattered near their feet.

"That is an interesting observation, Alfred," Tirnalth patted Alfred on the head. "Perhaps there is more to the siege of Grotham Keep than we know."

"Gorbogal is not one to let up on tricks or treachery," Verboden said.

Just then a fluttering of shadows crossed overhead, and wings folded upon Alfred. He felt a painful grip on his shoulders and heard a ghastly screeching sound that paralyzed him. Verboden, unaffected by the horrible scream, quickly swung his staff. A flash of light burst into the air, blinding Alfred and whatever was above him. The talons loosened their painful grip on his shoulders, and he fell to the ground.

"Har!! Hahr!! Foul flyer!" Verboden cried, swinging his staff about as Tirnalth rushed to Alfred.

The boy was frightened and stunned. His shoulders throbbed. "Just some scratches," said Tirnalth, dusting him off. Alfred nodded as a cold sweat flooded his dirty face. Then, unexpectedly, the pain ceased, and Alfred felt able to stand without assistance.

Alfred glanced at a shoulder. "I am glowing!" he exclaimed. The radiance faded as he rolled his shoulder around.

Verboden continued swinging and jabbing his staff upward at a horribly ugly beast. It was a gangly white-skinned gargoyle with long sharp talons on squat, muscular limbs. It had the face of a humanoid bat and was hairless save for a few scrimps of scraggly fur. It screeched a loud wail that brought shivers down one's spine. Alfred would not be surprised if that scream had some cursed properties to cause fear and paralysis. Another winged beast screeched and swooped down just as Tirnalth yanked Alfred to the ground with himself.

"Watch your back, Verboden!" Tirnalth cried out. Then he shouted, "Come Alfred! Let us seek cover!" Yanking Alfred along through rubble with surprising strength, Tirnalth reached one of the towers. A small door led into a tower through thick stony walls.

"We'll be safe in there!" Tirnalth said, out of breath.

Alfred was not so sure. There didn't seem to be any safe place in this land and least of all in a decrepit tower in a keep. He remembered that Tirnalth had no memory. "Are you sure we will be safe in there?"

Tirnalth mumbled, "Oh, I don't know now. I just felt that was the proper thing to say, to comfort you."

"Oh great!"

As they hurried through the tower doorway, Alfred stopped. Tirnalth yanked at his hand, "Now what's the bother!?"

"Ah, I'm stuck! I think!" Alfred was being held just inside the doorway. "Something is caught!"

Tirnalth turned to look. Alfred seemed to be swinging in midair while peering at Tirnalth, who looked oddly veiled or shrouded. Tirnalth looked sideways at Alfred. "What is that? What are you doing?"

Alfred tried to look about, but with each movement he felt restrained. He tugged repeatedly, bewildered, trying to get free, saying... "It's... It's... It's..." Finally he was able to identify the thready creation holding him captive. "It's a spider web! A really big spider web!"

"Oh my! That can't be good!"

Chapter Eight

Afraid of Spiders

"You got me stuck in a spider web! I can't believe this!" Alfred kept tugging to no avail.

"Shouldn't you be quiet and stay still?" said Tirnalth, putting finger to lip and glancing about in the dark.

Alfred froze in fear. His eyes darted around as his body swayed slowly back and forth. The web spanned upwards, receding into the dark tower. The sound of claws scraping on stone reverberated above, as did the twang of the taut web being pricked. These sounds grew louder and louder.

"Tirnalth, help!" Alfred couldn't believe this would be his end. He suddenly felt empathy for bugs.

"I... I... I don't know what to do." Tirnalth shrugged and fluttered his arms.

"You have to cast a spell!" Alfred fought every nerve to not freeze further from utter terror.

"I can't! I don't remember any!" Tirnalth put hand to forehead and squeezed his temple. Alfred again tried pulling at the web to get loose. Then, looking up into the darkness, he saw two large glowing red eyes peering at him. Just below them was the glint of two enormous fangs. Several other dark shapes appeared from various spots along the web work. Oh no! There was more than one!

"Tirnalth, help!"

"Back, you things! You spiders! Shoo!" Tirnalth yelled with an underwhelming aggression.

Several spiders were visible, each the size of a large crab, each carefully feeling its way downward on eight prickly limbs. Tirnalth's yelling seemed to work. The spiders backed away. "Can you get out now?"

Alfred tugged but still could not free himself. His movement was causing its own twanging on the web, as if calling the spiders back. Realizing no harm had come from Tirnalth's shouting, the spiders began to move closer.

"It's not working. They're coming back," Tirnalth said nonchalantly.

Alfred stopped moving. For the last few moments of his life, he could scream till they got him, or he could find a way out. He decided to calm down and think. And then it came to him. "Tirnalth, I want you to feel fire."

Tirnalth, confused, put his hand to his ear. "What?"

"Fire!" Alfred cried. "I want you to feel fire!"

"Fire? I tell you I can't cast spells. I don't remember."

A large spider was just above Tirnalth's head ready to pounce on him.

"Not remember, feel it! Hurry, you must feel it! Think fire! Just feel it!" Alfred gritted his teeth as he glanced up at several spiders carefully approaching him with red glowing eyes. They made a snip-snip scissor-like sound with their fangs.

"Oh right. Okay, let me... feel... fire!" Tirnalth nodded, furrowing his eyebrows. Then the spider above him leaped upon him, swinging in the air, swishing in and out of his ghostly image.

"Hurry!" Alfred cried, trying desperately to pull away from the spiders encroaching upon him.

"I don't think it is working!" Tirnalth moaned. The spider swinging about him managed to pull itself onto the webbing and then leap again, but it caught nothing of the ethereal wizard as it folded its limbs and continued to swing.

"Do you remember the fire at Verboden's cottage?" said Alfred, still tugging helplessly.

"Oh yes, that was a wonderful fire," said Tirnalth. "It's been so long since I've seen or even felt the warmth of a fire." Just then he began to glow.

"Yes! If you could put your hand in and feel it, it would be very very hot, right!?" Alfred did everything he could to avoid contact with the picking, poking spiders.

"Oh, quite so!" Tirnalth said. And with that the spider trying to catch him caught fire and screeched horribly as it fell to the stone floor. "Oh, sorry!" Tirnalth stepped back. The flame, surrounding him like an aura, torched the web and quickly moved upward. The spiders around Alfred leapt from their spots to avoid the fire, but it spread fast like -- well, like wildfire!

Of course, this put Alfred in a worse situation – trapped in a burning web! Thrashing around, he suddenly broke loose and fell to the floor, with small pieces of lit webbing cascading all around him. As Alfred crawled out of the doorway, Tirnalth quickly followed still aglow, bursting spiders and webs in flames.

Alfred freed his legs from the remaining webbing and leapt out as Verboden was still fighting off the pair of gargoyles. Fortunately, with small flames coursing across his tattered garb, Alfred stumbled over the small fountain wall and fell into the pool of murky water. The spectacle of this and the sight of Tirnalth rushing after him, a glowing aura of fire, were more than enough to frighten the gargoyles. They flew off in dismay.

As Tirnalth bent down to raise Alfred from the muddy water, the cloud of fire surrounding him subsided. Verboden gazed behind them at the tower, smoke rising from each hole. "Did you do that, Tirnalth?"

Tirnalth looked back surprised at the plumes of smoke and fleeing spiders. "Oh my! Is that what I can do? I must be a great wizard!"

Alfred rolled his mucky eyes.

From the broken doorway they peered into the main keep. It was dark and musty. Verboden held a torch he created by impaling a glowing spider, courtesy of Tirnalth's conjured fire. It created a warm orange light in the vast space of the inner keep. The large entrance hall was surrounded by a balcony. Columns ran along each side, holding up the balcony walkway encircling the hall. In the back was a toppled throne.

The group advanced further into the Keep to view the rubble, trying to determine what happened so many years ago. Behind the throne was a huge hole littered with rock and debris.

"Something must have come through there!" said Alfred, pointing at the dark ominous hole, tiptoeing closer to look down without getting too close.

"Yes, something came through," Tirnalth said. "So, they were attacked from below as well."

"So that was Gorbogal's deception! She used ratkins." Verboden tipped over a small ratkin skull with his staff, and it fell into the hole. They heard it land quickly, not far below.

"Ratkins?" Alfred asked.

"Yes. Ratkins are vile vermin, the scourge of the underworld! They are large viciously crazed rat men that can scurry through small openings. When enough of them gather together, they can quickly dig their way through anything. Look here. These scratches are from thousands of them that must have poured in." Verboden pointed to what at first looked like foot worn stone. When they looked more carefully, however, they could see that the stone was forever etched with the scrapings of hordes of rat feet.

"Are they still here?" Alfred asked, stepping behind Tirnalth.

Verboden looked about at the multitude of tracks leading to all parts of the Keep. Then he stepped precariously to the top of fallen rocks to peer into the cavernous hole, pushing his torch into the gaping darkness below. "No. This all happened long ago."

Alfred sighed.

"But there appears to be something else down there!" Verboden stepped back as huge black limbs protruded from the opening. It was another spider, the mother of all spiders. Its limbs were as thick as tree branches, and it had the hair on its appendages sticking out like spikes. Its many black eyes were far more evil looking than those of the previous spiders. With each of its steps sounding like a heavy thump, it brushed aside large stones and rubble. As its enormously bloated body pivoted up through the opening, the creature looked ready for a new feast or two or three.

Verboden immediately cast a new blessing upon his friends, pronouncing their resolve while casting doubt into the behemoth arachnid.

Lord of light, give us strength
courage and might.
Lord of light, cast doubt
into the foulness that rises
the foulness within our sight!

The spider appeared poised to pounce. Saliva and froth dripped from its black scissor-like fangs. If it landed upon any of them, it could easily crush them. But it hesitated and retracted for a moment, looking at them with hunger.

Verboden raised his staff, ready to strike. "Its stomach is much stronger than any spell I can conjure to repel it!"

The great beast lumbered forward again.

"Tirnalth, think fire again!" Alfred was unsure if he should run, scream, faint, or all of the above.

"Oh, yes, of course!" Tirnalth furrowed his eyebrows

and made an odd pose. Immediately the aura emanating from his being caught fire, and the flame ran along his silhouette.

"Ouch!" Alfred stepped back, – on the opposite side of the giant spider, of course!

The lumbering beast moved about, striking at Verboden, avoiding Tirnalth's torch-like aura. Verboden used his staff to deflect the spider's strikes and to pivot away from it, rolling and leaping, narrowly escaping the wild stomping of the spider's heavy limbs.

"Tirnalth, charge the spider! Catch it on fire!" Alfred stumbled backward in the rubble, away from the heat.

"Right! Here we go!" At first, Tirnalth hesitated, trying to remember how to charge. He then rushed forward. The spider was surprisingly quick for its size, easily scaling large columns to avoid the flaming aura, yet becoming noticeably frustrated, hissing and chattering. It loathed the idea of expending such energy on what seemed easy prey.

It clambered up on the balcony, crouched and then leapt over Tirnalth. Verboden ducked and rolled, again barely escaping the beast's clutches. The spider landed behind Alfred, who had thought he was standing well away from the danger. Towering over Alfred, revealing its fangs and stinger, the creature extended its four front legs ready to strike.

Alfred ran forward, tripped and fell into the hole, landing on webbing that rolled him to a lower level. The spider lunged after him, leaving Verboden and Tirnalth behind.

When Alfred came to a stop, caught in more webbing, he was banged up and bruised, muddy and dirty, and altogether in disbelief at his predicament. He thought briefly of werewolves and dark forests, of a dark god and a witch named Gorbogal, of spiders in a tower and flying gargoyles. Then his mind focused on the gargantuan spider lurking near in the darkness, extending its feelers for him. He poked about in the darkness with his hands, just glimpsing shadowy shapes of cocooned creatures. "Are they human?" he worried. He wasn't sure, as many appeared to be smaller than humans. Suddenly he felt something he sensed might be useful and grabbed it. It was a spear.

Alfred pulled the weapon up and thrust it forward just as the giant spider pounced upon him. The spear slammed back toward him so forcefully that it caused him to drop to the floor in the littered remains. Unfortunately, he had been holding the spear backwards. When he thrust it, the butt end had only dinted the spider's hard chitin shell. Fortunately, this unexpected contact caused the spider enough pain that it retreated a few paces. Alfred tried to use the spear again but couldn't move it as the head had been jammed into the crusty earthen ground.

The spider, seeing the flames of Tirnalth above at the opening of the hole, had it in mind to steal away with Alfred before the others arrived. "We are coming, Alfred. Hold on!"

Alfred grabbed the shaft of the imprisoned spear and pulled vigorously. The spider saw its chance and leapt at Alfred again, avoiding the spear. It grabbed his leg, pulling as Alfred held on to the spear for dear life, grimacing in fear and pain.

Tirnalth looked down from the edge and again hesitated as he wasn't sure how to dive onto the spider. He shrugged, said a mental "oh well" and leaped like a swimmer doing a cannon ball, holding his nose. It was a direct hit. The spider, exploding into flames, screeched in wretched agony while continuing to hold Alfred in a painful grip. Verboden then jumped in, jamming his staff into one of the spider's leg joints, breaking off the limb. He then pried the spider claw from Alfred's leg and pulled him to safety. The spider quivered in its final death throes as the magical flame engulfed it. Tirnalth stepped out of the fire, a flaming ghost.

"Are you okay, Alfred?" asked Tirnalth, the orange aura subsiding.

Alfred cringed in pain.

"I think he's been through quite a bit," Verboden said. He quickly chanted a calming spell, and Alfred gave a sigh of relief. Verboden quickly went about healing Alfred's leg that had some large scrapes and contusions. He pulled out a small mortar and pestle. He added some dried leaves from a pocket, poured water from a waterskin, and a dash of powder from another vial. Then he spoke some words as he mixed it and applied it to the scraped leg. Though not instantaneous, the healing was very quick indeed. Alfred gazed in amazement. He got up and stood on his leg.

"Well, how do you feel?" Verboden put away his ingredients.

"It feels okay. I still feel it, as if the pain is still there, but it doesn't hurt." Alfred felt his leg gently.

"Your body is telling you that the injuries should still be there. With the grace of Armahn, you are healed," Verboden said.

"Armahn, the God of Light," Tirnalth said softly.

"Yes. Indeed. Do you remember now?"

"I suppose if Armahn is the owner of my soul, he would not allow me to forget," replied Tirnalth. "That is all I remember."

"He may not be thrilled you made a deal with the Dark One," Verboden said. Tirnalth's only response was a raised eyebrow.

Tirnalth's fiery aura was gone, but the enormous ember of the burning spider glowed, giving off a charred, rancid odor. Acrid smoke glided up the tunnel.

The three explorers looked around in the crypt, seeing that it was the lair of the giant spider. Scattered throughout it were the ancient remains and bones of ratkins, goblins and fallen men-at-arms. Alfred was finally able to pull out the spear and gaze at it. Verboden looked closely at it. "It's a ratkin spear, lighter and shorter than a knight's," he declared. "It is an inferior weapon."

Alfred liked the weight of it in his hands. He shrugged. "It stopped a giant spider, so it must be okay."

"If you want to be a king, you can not be armed with a vermin's weapon." Verboden picked out an old rusty sword amongst the debris and tossed it to him. Alfred stepped out of the way of the blade, trying to catch the weapon by the handle. The weight of it nearly flung him off his feet. He fumbled the sword, dropping it to the ground with a loud clang. Verboden observed the mishap unimpressed.

"Sorry, sorry," Alfred murmured as he tried to lift the sword. It was much heavier than he expected. He lifted the spear, then the sword, then the spear, then the sword. Finally, he lay the spear down and tried to hold the sword in two hands, his arms began to shake. He tried swinging the sword, and it ended up swinging him.

"This boy has no strength for a sword. At his age and height, a squire would handle it easily," Verboden said to Tirnalth.

"I am not concerned with his sword-swinging ability. In time, I am certain, he will grow into such skills. I don't believe he used such weapons where he comes from." As he spoke, Tirnalth was looking at the many passageways and doors within the crypt.

"Where did he come from?" Verboden asked, as both men flinched when Alfred banged the sword against the wall. Verboden picked up the spider torch he had used earlier and rolled nearby spider webs onto it.

"I'm not sure. His world seemed different, simpler." Tirnalth watched as the flames from the spider spread along the webs. Tirnalth spread his arms and summoned a concentrated thought. A spray of water burst from his finger tips, putting out the flames. As the water dripped onto the webbings and the embers fizzled, a self-satisfied expression came to his face.

The men turned to see Alfred bumbling around with the sword, pretending he was a great knight.

"I feel I know this place," said Tirnalth.

"Yes, you had a room back there, I believe, through the passageway." Verboden pointed down one of the many hallways to an opening.

"Let's see if anything remains."

Chapter Nine

The Wizard's Room

Alfred gently leaned the sword against a fallen column. Of course, it slid down with a loud clang. He picked up the light spear and rushed over to Tirnalth and Verboden. "What's in there?"

"As you said, Alfred, I need to study some spell books – that is, if we can find any here. I will relearn to control my... ah...great powers." Tirnalth gently elbowed Alfred's shoulder and winked.

They bent themselves through a small doorway to peer into a large room. Though it felt like a crypt, the room was lofty, appearing to rise up into the dark vault far above.

"This must be the tower at the back of the Keep."

Alfred felt along the crude, solid stone.

"Yes, it seems so." Tirnalth noticed an old overturned chair and table. He picked up the chair and set it upright.

"What's that?" Alfred asked, pointing to markings on a stone illuminated faintly by torch light. They leaned in closer to look.

"It says, if you are me, look up..." As Tirnalth read these words aloud, the others slowly gazed up and saw a bit of light filtering through holes. "I see something, up there," Tirnalth said, squinting up into the hazy interior mist of the dusty old tower.

"What is it?" Alfred asked.

"Can't you see it? It's a shelf," Tirnalth said, pointing.

Alfred and Verboden looked harder but saw only a ruined tower with rotted wood floors. Then, oddly, their eyes beheld, hidden under some old wood, a lone shelf with things on it.

"We should..." was all Verboden could say when Alfred tossed his spear up into the dark. It hit the wall and skidded up, sticking with a twang to the underside of the shelf.

"Nice throw," Tirnalth said.

"And now?" asked Verboden.

A cracking sound could be heard echoing from above. The shelf's braces creaked and dust began to sprinkle down. Then suddenly the entire shelf plummeted straight down, falling to the floor at their feet. Several books tumbled out. Alfred rushed to retrieve his wonderful spear. He joyfully posed with it.

Verboden and Tirnalth nodded in smug agreement, the spear was a handy tool indeed.

"Well, are these your books?" Alfred asked as Tirnalth picked them up.

"I don't remember. Remember?" Tirnalth reminded.

"Oh, right."

Tirnalth gazed at a book. Verboden blew the dust off the cover. The dust billowed into Tirnalth's straining eyes. He blinked and sputtered in utter contempt. Verboden shied away, mumbling an apology. Gripped by a horrible realization, Tirnalth was stricken with a paralyzing fear.

Alfred and Verboden approached him cautiously, wondering with apprehension at what Tirnalth was seeing. Was it some kind of evil vision?

Tirnalth let loose a deafening sneeze, which sprayed dust and spittle on both Alfred and Verboden. "Oh, excuse me! Oh my, these are some very old dusty books!" He sniffed and sneezed a few more times.

Already covered with caked mud, web threading, and dried blood, Alfred feebly attempted to brush the spittle off. Verboden stood back and used his cloak as a towel.

Alfred noticed large chunky candles on the floor. He picked them up and set them on the table. Observing this, Tirnalth waved his fingers, and the candles took flame. Tirnalth made a gesture of satisfaction with a quick nod and furrowed brows. Alfred scooted the rickety chair and table together for a grateful Tirnalth. Now, by candlelight, he could sit and review all the books they placed before him. Verboden and Alfred anxiously awaited Tirnalth's comments about each book.

"Can you read, Tirnalth?" Alfred asked.

"I don't know. If I have no memory, would I remember to read? Hmm… The Laws of Fire! A Beginner's Journey. Hey!

What do you know!"

Alfred clapped and cheered. Verboden rolled his eyes.

Tirnalth, as if opening birthday presents, gazed at each volume. He read the difficult runes and scribbles, turning books upside down, and reversing, reading several pages and then going back to the cover, all the while sighing and whistling, rubbing his beard and scratching his head. When he held one book in his hands and read the words on its cover, "*Telekinetia* by Tirnalth the Grand Wizard." He smiled in triumph.

"Yay!" Alfred put another book before him.

"My goodness! You wrote that one too!" Verboden said encouragingly.

"Yes, I suppose I did!" Tirnalth leafed through the pages.

"What does it mean?" Verboden asked.

"I haven't the slightest idea!" Tirnalth said, licking his fingers to turn a dusty page.

"It means floating or pushing things with an invisible force!" said Alfred, pointing his finger upward knowingly.

Verboden and Tirnalth stared blank-eyed at Alfred. Neither wanted to say he did not understand what Alfred was saying. So both nodded okay. Tirnalth turned to another book, "*The Troubadourian Travels of Verboden?*"

"Oh, that one's mine! How did it get there!?" Verboden grabbed it and slipped it under his cloak, never to be seen again.

Tirnalth continued with another, "*Feast and Famine, The Culinary Arts of the Pig*. Well, that could come in handy, I suppose," he said. "And *Illuminatia*? Hmph! Good. *Stone and Earth, The Elements of Foundation*. Very good! *Riddles and*

Poems of the East Passages? I suppose one could use a bit of entertainment. *Apothecary, Oils and Metal Works.* Good. And this one, *Entrance to the Ways of Before, Forget Naught.* Hmm... That reminds me..."

"Of what?" Alfred asked.

"I don't remember," Tirnalth said. "Well, I have these and a few others to study. I suppose I can stay hidden down here and get to work on these. I require naught from you two. I suppose, as a ghost, I will need little. I have so much to do."

Verboden and Alfred blinked and looked at each other. "What do we do?"

Tirnalth looked up, as if sensing something. "There are people above. They have come." Tirnalth seemed to look through the walls. "Go and begin the story of the king's return." Tirnalth's bright hopeful eyes met Alfred's.

"How do you know who is above, whether they are good or bad?" Alfred looked blankly at the dark stone above them.

"I can feel them," said Tirnalth, closing his eyes and smiling.

"They won't believe he is the king," Verboden said.

"Well, not unless you persuade them! They know you. They know Verboden, Cleric of the Order of Light!"

"But I have nev-"

"But no! These people need a leader, and he is the one! I know it. I feel it in my heart!" Tirnalth jabbed Verboden with a long wizard finger. "Now go! Begin this journey out of darkness."

Verboden nodded with a heavy weight, then straightened up and beckoned Alfred to follow.

Chapter Ten

Return of the Boy King

Alfred and Verboden went up a winding stone stair case. Verboden was silent, deep in thought. Before they walked out to the courtyard, Verboden glanced left, right and up to see if there were any gargoyles outside. It looked clear, save the rubble, the broken fountain, and the ruined towers. Verboden motioned for Alfred to follow. The tower that Tirnalth had lit with his immolation was still smoldering. It was sending a thin plume of black smoke into the misty sky as they passed through the gatehouse.

Down the road was gathered a small group of peasants

in gray and brown clothes. They huddled together pointing at the smoky column. An old man hurriedly walked up the road. Verboden went to meet him as Alfred followed behind.

"Hullo, my dear sir," the old man said, bowing to Verboden.

Verboden returned the bow. "Abedeyan, it is good to see you again."

Abedeyan stood humbly in gray-mottled, threadbare garb. His gray skin was visible through many tattered holes. He was gaunt. His body twitched. There was a long silence. Alfred looked anxiously from Verboden to the old man. Verboden looked at the ground near Abedeyan's feet.

"Um," Verboden uttered, clearing his throat. "This is Alfred. He is in charge now." Neither Verboden's expression nor his choice of words was convincing. Alfred's face could be seen growing red, even under all the dirt and filth.

"Ey? What was that Master Verboden? Tis my bad ear. Actually both are bad. Have to speak up, sir." Abedeyan leaned feebly forward, cupping his good ear.

"This boy is in line to be king... He is the king!" Verboden was embarrassed by his own sudden outburst.

Abedeyan, it appeared, did not fully understand. His gaze seemed to come undone. Slowly he turned to look up at Alfred, who was standing behind Verboden. Abedeyan's eyes focused, gathering tears. Verboden stood silent. Abedeyan beheld Alfred with piercing watery eyes. His mouth fell open.

Verboden was going to speak again but stopped, seeing that Abedeyan was hobbling toward Alfred. The old man, fraught with tension, twitched all the more. Alfred was not sure what the old man was going to do. With his mouth still agape and eyes glazed, he reached out to touch Alfred. His eyes brimmed with tears.

"You have your mother's eyes, milord!" he finally said. As he stumbled toward him, Alfred caught the old man. With dismay registering on his face, Alfred looked up, his eyes meeting Verboden's stunned expression.

The old man gently pushed away and bowed. As if there were never any tension or twitching, he turned quickly and rushed down the road. "The king has returned!!"

Verboden looked on with confusion. Alfred stood silently, still looking dismayed.

The people below were huddled together. Abedeyan rushed to gather them around and pointed up at Alfred. While they all listened intently, many poked their heads out to view him.

Alfred stepped closer to Verboden. "Who is he? He knows my mom?"

"He was the Steward and Exchequer of your grandfather's castle," said Verboden, leaning on his staff.

"So he managed the castle?" Alfred stepped closer, leaning in.

"Yes."

"And the other people?" Alfred rubbed his arms, as the misty air was chilly.

Verboden looked at them. There were maybe two dozen people, a few young. "Mostly peasants, I think. Abedeyan will know." Alfred was off and running down the road. As he drew near to the people, they clearly became nervous, shushing Abedeyan and fanning out to stand before him.

"Hi," said Alfred with a quick wave, himself nervous.

A few of the older ladies and some men bowed.

Children gazed in wonder. There was one large boy, bigger and a bit older than Alfred, who looked mistrustful and possibly jealous.

"My name's Alfred," he said, clearing his throat. Verboden came up beside him.

An old lady approached and bowed again. She nodded to Verboden, who returned with a bow. "I am Lady Nihan. I was once Head Seamstress to... your mother and I..." She turned away, overcome with a sudden swelling of emotion and tears. Alfred stepped forward and put his hand on her shoulder. She was taken aback and stepped back, unsure. Some of the peasants took steps forward.

Verboden whispered to Alfred, "A king does not touch his vassals."

Alfred shrugged, "I guess I'm the king or something. I know I will need your help. There's like a bad witch or something, right?" He turned to Verboden for reassurance but caught him rolling his eyes. Verboden stopped when he noticed Alfred looking at him. "You're supposed to help me."

"Right, sorry." Verboden straightened up.

"What is it you want us to do, Lord Alfred?" Abedeyan pushed his way through the peasants.

"Well, help rebuild the castle." Alfred stepped aside and with a hand gesture revealed the smoking barren keep.

Just then, what was left of the wood roof on the burning tower collapsed inward. Alfred shirked. The peasants stared on. Verboden's expression became glummer if that was even possible.

A larger man spoke quickly to Abedeyan.

"Speak up Derhman! Your lord is before you!" Verboden burst out angrily, stunning everyone.

Derhman, a gruff looking farmer, stepped forward. "I am sorry, milord, but we have crops to plant and there are so few of us left."

"Well that's important," Alfred said with a magnanimous nod. "Verboden and I will help you plant your crops. Then, if we can get enough people together, we'll work on the castle."

Taken by surprise, the people glanced at each other and then nodded agreement.

"That is most gracious, milord!" said Lady Nihan, as if speaking for everyone.

Alfred smiled.

"A king will help us plant?" Derhman shrugged.

"Yes!" Verboden stepped forward. "Though don't expect him to be as stubborn as you, Derhman!" A few peasants chuckled. "Or as tough skinned as you, Cory, son of Derhman!" And more laughed. Derhman began to laugh. Cory's face was red, but he smiled.

Verboden waved his staff about in a grand manner. "The king will help, and you'll promise to give him a few blisters on his hands now, won't you?" The peasants laughed, feeling excited and assured. Alfred's eyebrows danced.

Chapter Eleven

A Kingly Farmer?

And so the days passed that Alfred, King of the Westfold, was out in small cluttered fields doing the best he could. He wasn't that much help. Even peasant girls had to take up the slack. The work, harder than Alfred had expected, left him daily with a sore aching body. Still, seeing their king out there in the misty fields with them was a blessing to many – and an odd affair to some.

Alfred spent many moments sitting on a log, resting his aching back and soothing his bandaged hands. The peasants appreciated his willing presence, not minding that he wasn't on a par with their rugged abilities. Some wondered if he was there to spy on them. Regardless, he did seem to know a lot about farming and provided ideas for how to improve what they were doing.

Alfred read about the evolution and use of the plow during "The Dark Ages" of history. He thought it odd that the period was called The Dark Ages, when so many incredible advances were made. For ages, people used oxen to rake the ground to remove weeds and plant seeds. This was slow and arduous. During the Dark Ages, farmers invented several different devices to create a plow. Alfred knew this well because he had drawn a picture of one and its parts for an art assignment at school.

The peasants used crude rakes to plow, which merely dug shallow grooves, leaving many weeds intact. Also, these implements did not loosen and turn the soil. Many farmers would not rake the thicker fields, which have the richest soil because their rakes were too weak.

The peasants shared one measly ox to rake the fields. Alfred realized that the farmers of this land did not yet know of the horse drawn plow, which needed a well fitted collar and a strong pony to pull it.

The people had several small ponies in their small barns, but they did not use them because the simple reins and crude wooden yokes, appropriate for oxen, choked the ponies. Alfred spent time with Verboden and the farmers devising a plowing yoke, or collar, that would fit ponies comfortably. With this correctly fashioned collar the ponies could help pull a real plow. The collar took the pressure off their necks and placed it on their shoulders, distributing the strain.

Alfred showed a farmer handy with metalwork how to make a curved blade for the plow. The farmer's old venerable father was once a blacksmith at the castle. But he was too old to work on anything now. His son did the best he could to make a large curved blade with what metal he had. When the soil was plowed, the blade turned over and uprooted the weeds completely, leaving them to dry in the sun.

The news about the new plow spread, and many peasant farmers came around to see the ponies pulling it. They were shocked at the speed, strength and efficiency of the horse drawn plow.

Oxen were slow and prone to wandering. But the ponies, as if blessed for challenges, loved to pull the plow. Unlike the lazy oxen, the ponies were proud and determined to accomplish their task. The curved blade slid fast, dug deep, and made rows ready for planting much more efficiently than the old rake plow.

As Alfred hiked about, he saw patches of land he knew would be good for crops and wondered why they were ignored by the farmers. He gathered the farmers with Abedeyan and Verboden at one of these pastures, asking why lands like it were not being farmed. He was told these were the king's lands, for hunting only.

Alfred responded, "No, no, no! From now on you will plow and plant on the best land. We can hunt anywhere."

Abedeyan spoke up, "But sir, this land has been part of the King's Royal House for generations!"

"Look, this is clover and there's a stream nearby for irrigation. This is perfect. I read that clover and alfalfa make for very fertile soil."

"Fertile? What's that?" a farmer asked.

"Its soil that is rich with, you know, nutrients, things that are very good for growing crops. If the soil is fertile, it will yield better crops. Cow manure helps make a soil fertile, although we don't have any, right?" Alfred looked about at the farmers present. "Pony manure should be saved and spread on any soil that seems barren. And pond scum or any stagnant water is good, as well as dead fish and rotting vegetables. "

"Rotting vegetables? We stay away from all things foul!" a farmer said.

"No, rotting things are good for the soil," Alfred responded firmly. "You should bury anything rotting, fish and plants that is, and let the crops grow on top. If there's a pond near a field, dig a ditch and drain that water into a field, or at least some of it. Just do not use our waste, you know, our own bathroom stuff... heh heh... because that can cause disease and plague."

A farmer raised his hand.

Alfred answered, "Yes?"

"Ahhh... what's a bath-roohhhm?"

"Oh... ahh... a room where you go..."

"Yesss?" the farmer waited for the answer.

"Go to the potty?"

"Potty?"

"Where you... you know.. poopy dooh?" Alfred's face reddened.

"Poopy dooh? What's that?" The farmers looked at each other. Alfred was unsure of what to say. Someone giggled.

"Hey!?" Alfred suddenly realized.

Everyone began to laugh. "He said poopy dooh!?" The farmers' laughter became uproarious. Alfred's face was red.

"Silence! You are in court with your king!" Verboden hit a nearby tree with his staff. It was a powerful knock that shook the tree. The farmers settled down. Alfred sighed and nodded thanks to Verboden.

Someone chortled. They all began to laugh again! Verboden couldn't help himself either. He tried to hit the tree again but missed. The laughter increased.

Alfred waited.

Finally, they got their breath back.

Nope... they began laughing again. Verboden waved for Alfred not to look at him as he chuckled.

Finally...

Abedeyan was able to bring it back, "Milord, you say our own waste can cause disease to us? Yet you want us to use foul things to add 'nutrients' to the soil?"

"Yes, other animal waste is okay because they do not have the same diseases we do. But our body gets rid of, uh bad things, and our waste can carry diseases. Even if we put it in the soil, it can stay and make us sick through the crops. So our waste must be removed from our water supplies and crops! Plagues in history have been known to be caused because humans did not keep their waste away from their crops and food."

"Makes sense," a farmer said.

The farmers began talking excitedly about manure. They had goats, chickens and pigs and so a lot of manure.

Verboden quickly tapped on the tree again to bring back order.

"Ah, yes... thanks, Verboden. Now where was I? Oh... rotting stuff... yes... the other stuff is good, cow and horse waste, dead fish, pond water, and so on. You see, it's important to fertilize, or give back to the soil, so that whatever crops you grow, they will have nutrients to use for growing."

Abedeyan, Verboden and the farmers gazed at him

with amazement. The farmers seemed eager to learn more.

"Tell all the farmers they can plow any field or patch of land they think will grow crops, king's hunting ground or not!" Alfred declared. Abedeyan wished to speak but merely opened, then closed his mouth. The farmers were already down the road yelling out the news.

The land was alive again. Many, who had not seen each other in years, once again rejoiced to be in each other's presence. There were still many difficulties. Many had not survived the wars, and those who remained suffered from lack of food and disease. There were few elderly left, as they had difficulty surviving the winters. There were fewer women than men, and most of the women seemed sickly and weak. The winter wheat storage was sparse, so all were focused on farming above all else.

One night at a farm while Alfred was having dinner with a few farmers, he noticed how small and gaunt the women were. They tended to have coughs and frail demeanors.

"I remember reading about men and women of the dark ages. The women were known to not have enough iron in their diet," Alfred said.

The farmers gazed at him with confusion. One finally queried, "Iron, milord?"

Alfred realized he had to talk to them differently, not like someone who watches TV and goes to school and has a biology class. He needed to talk to them as if he was talking to a child. "Well, it's a certain thing in our blood that helps give us strength. It's actually iron, very small bits of it. It's dust... iron dust. The way to get it is by eating red meat, you know, cow or rabbit. Women actually need more of it than men. Without this nutrient, this food, they become weaker and sick. I want everyone who wants to hunt to do so wherever they choose, including the king's hunting grounds. So whatever you can catch, wherever, is fine. And make sure the women get plenty of this kind of food."

The quiet farmers gazed at him. Their eyes twinkled with orange stars from the fire. They looked at their wives with hope and love. Verboden sat near the fire, smoking his pipe, staring into the flames. The warmth in the room was more than heat from the fire. The people had hope. Verboden glanced about to see it in their eyes as they talked softly to each other. He looked back into the fire, adjusting his position, clearing his throat.

Verboden was busy each day giving strength and blessings to the people, healing their aches and pains, ridding them of rashes and disease. He saved a young girl from a deathly fever and mended the bones of an old lady. His work was exhausting in a good way. He could not help but smile as he prayed quietly late into each night.

Chapter Twelve

Of Arms and Armour

Alfred resided at the castle. Abedeyan insisted that Alfred, as king, stay there. In his small clammy room, Alfred woke up each day with Abedeyan entering with a bowl of steamy hot water. "Wake up, my lord, my king! King Alfred!"

"I don't feel like a king! I'm just a kid," Alfred yawned.

"You are not a goat! You are a boy whose line comes from glorious kings of old!" Abedeyan said, setting the bowl of hot water down.

"I'm just a kid.. uh boy. I... well I just know a few medieval things. I mean, I know I'm being helpful, but I'm not a king! I don't even know what that is, Abedeyan." Alfred somberly went to the steaming bowl of hot water.

"Most kings don't know what it is! They are born into it, thrust into it, usually at a young age, and die with the crown on their head! And even then, at the end of their lives, they still don't know!" Abedyean said, unwraveling towels.

"Gulp... well..." Alfred scrubbed his face with the hot water. "I don't know. I'm not even sure I should stay here. I mean, what about my mom? She probably misses me!"

"I'm sure she does, Alfred. I miss her. She was a young lady last I saw her, and even then, only at a distance. She was as beautiful as the evening stars and as the morning sun." Abedeyan stood silent a long while, staring out the window as the morning light filled the room.

Alfred's face was dripping wet. His eyes closed as he reached blindly for a towel. Abedeyan instinctively handed him a linen.

"I miss her. How can I see her or visit her or go back to where I came from?" Alfred said, drying his face.

"You'll have to ask the wizard that! I am merely the Steward of this Castle."

"Yes, I should ask Tirnalth!" Alfred said, feeling refreshed.

"Yes indeed you should, King Alfred. If he should ever return!"

Alfred was going to speak but Abedeyan did not give him the chance.

"But before that, we still have much to do here! Verboden is busy rooting out more spiders and those ghastly gargoyles. I'm still sweeping and hiring. Lots of the families, who survived and once served the king and his castle, are returning. They need you now, Alfred!"

"Well, I'll do my best... But I still don't feel like a king."

"Ah hah... tah tah... don't you worry... it will grow on you! Let us begin a new day!" Abedeyan led Alfred out of his small stone-walled room and into a new day of fantastical medieval endeavors!

People all across the land were hearing of the king's return. Craftsmen and laborers came, most living in squalor with local farmers. Many still had their tools though they were dusty and worn.

As they walked out to the King's Hall or Great Hall, Alfred saw a handful of young men and a carpenter. Abedeyan was overseeing the repair of doors, shuttering windows, and replacing floors within the towers.

All were welcome. Families came by the wagonload and were quickly enjoined to become involved in cleaning, repairing or building. A starving stonemason came, remembering his trade only after receiving a warm meal.

Alfred noticed that Lady Nihan had several men carrying out large bundles of strange dusty stuff. They were climbing up from the darkest halls, burdened with tied bundles. Alfred rubbed his eyes and yawned as two were passing. He was still getting used to his bed, which was just hay with a coarse linen covering. They tried to bow, but with their loads it was awkward.

"Ah, carry on," Alfred said, hoping they would.

They heaved to adjust their loads. As they trudged by him, Alfred saw a small, decrepit, clawed hand protruding from one of the bundles.

"Hey, what's that?"

One of the loaders replied quickly. "Lady Nihan is clearing out the dungeon, milord. We are carrying out the foul filth."

"Let me see?" Alfred peered inside the bundle. "I didn't really examine it all before. I want to see it."

Sweating in the early morning, standing in the Great Hall just after a stair climb, both hesitated. As the first loader's knees gave out, his load came down with a crash. All sorts of goblin things spilled out. There were small bits of armour and bone, bows and spears, all darkened from age and dust.

Alfred saw a broken spear. He picked it up. It was similar to the one he had.

"Careful, milord. That could still have poison on it. Goblin spears are also very sharp!" Abedeyan bent over to look at a few items.

"Hey there, men. What is amiss up there?" Lady Nihan climbed up the stairs to see. The two loaders rolled their eyes. The second gently, if one can call it that, leaned his load against a column and then slid it down. Neither man was strong enough to stand with such loads for long.

Lady Nihan with a broom in her hand crossed the hall quickly and peered at the fallen bundles. "Aye, what's this? Oh, hello milord. Good 'morrow. Aye, hey? Don't touch that foul filth, milord. It's goblin vermin! Don't touch! Unclean!"

Alfred picked up an unstrung bow. It appeared to be in good shape, though the string had rotted away long ago. He closely examined the bow's strange black grain. It seemed to be made from strands of thick hair glued together. He bent the bow. It held well. It was light and felt strong in his hands. He imagined it notched with an arrow and aimed it as if about to fire it. The two laborers acquiesced, ducking playfully when his aim crossed their path.

"Milord! Filthy, foul, unclean, pest, vermin!" Lady

Nihan helplessly swept the air with her broom, trying to remove the foul litter's unclean curse.

"What are you doing with this stuff?" Alfred gazed intently on the bow, feeling it with his hands.

"Burning it!" said Lady Nihan, stiffening.

Alfred ignored her and picked up a cruddy curved dagger. "Hmm... how much stuff is there?"

"Oh, there is a huge pile out in the yard!" the second loader huffed, clearing his nozzle with his sleeve, gulping as his eyes met Lady Nihan's cold stare.

"What? More like this? A big pile? Where is it?!" Alfred hurried out.

"But sir! It's foul goblin!" Lady Nihan chased after him.

"Foul goblin or not, if this stuff works, we'll need it!" Alfred, huffing, exited the hall and stared at the pile of ancient refuse in the courtyard. "Do not burn any of it until I look through it!"

Lady Nihan was beside herself but did what any old lady would do under such conditions. She huffed and puffed and went back into the hall to sweep and clean.

Alfred became excited as he looked through the debris. The peasant folk looked at him, with his black greasy face and hands, as if he were mad. Indeed, he looked a bit crazed, giggling with delight while pulling out small spears, blades and bows. Most of the items seemed to be in excellent condition. They just needed a sharpening here or a restringing there. All were of small goblin or ratkin design so they were light and sturdy!

Alfred recalled hearing about the old blacksmith who used to do fletching and archery work. He had shaky hands and a mumbling disposition and now sat next to his son while his son did what smithing work he could. Alfred quickly rushed to find him. The son was busy chopping wood for a new furnace. It was the same man who made the new plow.

When Alfred asked the son about his father, the son reminded him that his father was no good, lame as it were, ready for the next life. In truth the old man, gaunt, unable to control his shaking, looked as if he had seen better days. He was sitting near the warm furnace and appeared to be waiting for his inevitable end.

When Alfred set down a pile of goblin bows in front of him, the old man suddenly came alive. He focused his eyes intently on them and picked one up, bending it with surprising strength and then putting it between his knees. He untwined some rope, cut an appropriate length and re-twined it, adding oil and tightening it further. Then, deftly, almost surreptitiously, with sudden quick movements he tied and strung the bow. He held it up, pulled on the string and sighted it as if he were back on the field of battle. His son, axe in hand, stared with amazement. The old man strung another bow just as quickly. His eyes watered, remembering the glory of days past. He smiled and giggled to himself.

Picking up one of the strong bows, Alfred tried to copy the stance of this old warrior preparing to launch an arrow. The old man slapped at Alfred's legs and pulled him and tugged him into the right position.

His son apologized over and over for his dad's impetuous behavior before the king. Alfred ignored this. He wanted to learn the craft of archery. Many children gathered to see what was happening. Once the old man strung a few bows, Alfred realized that they were much too small for the men to use. He looked at the children, many near his age. When he handed a bow to a girl, she backed away, frightened. Then Alfred showed her what to do. He took a proper stance and pulled on the string. Then he handed the bow to the girl again. She took it with glee. The other children stepped in closer to see if they too would get something from the king.

Alfred and the children found many old and broken bows from the scattered remains of the goblins and ratkins. Taking over part of his son's work area, the old man repaired dozens of small bows for them to use. For the first time in the dreary world they had been exposed to all their short lives, the children were excited and had high spirits. Most had brothers and sisters or other close relatives who had died from disease or famine or worse, goblin attacks. With Alfred the King learning to shoot the bow with them, they were filled with courage and a new spirit of hope.

Alfred sharpened his spear as the children took turns with the small bows. He had found several ratkin and goblin spears. Most of the peasants would not touch them. Alfred noticed that Cory, son of Derhman and busy in the fields, was always watching Alfred when he passed along the road.

One day when passing by Alfred stopped, went out to Cory in a field and showed him a ratkin spear. Cory took it in his hands and thrust it forward as if he were a warrior. He was almost showing off, but in a mean bully sort of way.

Alfred couldn't help but flinch, "Wow, show me how you do that!"

Derhman came up, "Boy, leave the king alone. We have a field to finish."

Cory stopped and handed the spear back to Alfred with

117

disdain.

"It's yours, Cory. I have more," Alfred returned to his traveling cart. Cory looked at Alfred with wide incredulous eyes, then at his glorious spear. Alfred waved goodbye. Cory impulsively waved back.

As time went on, with activity in the castle, Alfred spent less time in the fields. Craftsmen were busy repairing under the watchful eye of Abedeyan the Steward. His raspy voice echoed from sunup to sundown, keeping every able adult in the castle busy. Hammering and sawing could be heard all day long.

Lady Nihan conscripted every able-bodied woman to clean and repair the inside of the Keep. The women spent the evenings sewing. Many farmers' wives had brought gems of fabric that they had kept hidden, considering them treasures too valuable for their downtrodden lives, hopefully awaiting the return of a king to give the cloth a more exalted use. One of Lady Nihan's first jobs was to sew a respectable Steward garment for Abedeyan. It consisted of a clean tunic, tight pants, and a cloak. Abedeyan looked small in it. He brushed Lady Nihan aside as she kept tightening and adjusting while he was still in it. He thought of himself as being too busy for such frivolity. Those two were at each other's throats constantly it seemed.

As much as Alfred wanted to help around the Keep, he found his knowledge of how to do detailed work required in the castle was lacking. Most of the castle laborers would ask Abedeyan for orders. Abedeyan did not ask Alfred for his permission or help. He instinctively knew what needed to be done and where things needed to go. As old and feeble as he looked, he filled his days herding families to appropriate places, pushing workers into assigned tasks, gathering small portions of food from hunts and forages, and giving directions to peasants delivering loads of their goods. Alfred felt more like a symbol of a king than a king.

Alfred regularly visited Tirnalth in the tower to give him updates of the daily events. Tirnalth was always transfixed in his books.

"What you doing, milord? Reading?" Lady Nihan stood at the low entrance, broom in hand, ready to enter and clean.

Alfred looked at her, then at Tirnalth. Apparently, she did not see him. The books were visible, and when Tirnalth turned a page, the Lady saw it. "Oh, a draft! We'll have to get that roof covered." She pointed high up. "And these floors fixed!"

"Lady Nihan, I'd like this to be my reading area. All the books should remain here, okay? Leave everything here as it is."

"Oh, don't you worry about that. This was once a great wizard's room, you know." Lady Nihan swept briskly. "Perhaps one day you'll get to meet him."

Alfred smiled. She smiled, bowed and went on her way.

Alfred became frustrated. No one needed his help, it seemed. He found himself lacking in day to day skills. He tried smithing, hammering away at rings and making nails. Eventually the old man who made the bows and his son took the hammer away from him to get the nails made more efficiently. Alfred also tried tanning, but the steam and stench of boiling dead rabbit and rat skins was too much for him. The tanner was working with what was available.

He tried working alongside Abedeyan. This too was fruitless, as the Steward would wander off to the next task without so much as a word or nod. Alfred would look up from sweeping to see he was in the midst of a bunch of busy peasants bowing each time they passed him.

"I don't know how to be a king," he thought to himself. "I don't even know what it means. I've read about kings and played kings on a computer game, but..."

"Computer game?" Verboden the Cleric muttered. Alfred was sitting with him one evening in front of a small fireplace in the sparsely furnished kitchen. He was sipping a gray soup as Verboden smoked a pipe.

"Well, a game. I don't understand why everyone accepts me as king. I'm just a boy. I can't fight or lead anything."

"King's don't always have to fight, Alfred. That is why they have lords, vassals... knights."

Alfred sat up, mouth agape. Grey soup dripped off his lips. Verboden stared into the fire, puffing his pipe. Alfred, wiping his lips, stared at Verboden. Finally, after squirming, Verboden looked at Alfred, who was mouthing the charmed word... knights.

"There are no knights around? We have no soldiers or men-at-arms. How do we make knights?" Alfred finally asked.

Verboden coughed out a puff of smoke, "Make? You do not make knights."

"Oh yeah, right. This isn't a computer game. Shoot!"

Verboden gently puffed on his pipe. "If there are any still left in the land, sooner or later, they will come."

"And if they don't?" Alfred loudly sipped.

"Then we must arm the able men."

"Able men? You mean the older men? There don't seem to be very many. Most are old farmers and peasants. The craftsmen don't seem like the fighting type." Alfred tipped his bowl up to get every last drop. "There's like hardly anybody here."

"We must do the best we can." Verboden puffed gently, remaining motionless, looking at the small flames of the fire.

Alfred stared at Verboden.

Verboden shifted in his seat and glanced at Alfred.

Alfred continued to stare.

Verboden shifted again.

"I will search the lands, then, to see if any knights or warriors are in need of a king," Verboden sighed.

Alfred nodded a smile and slurped up the last of his soup.

There was a small chapel with a praying room in the Keep. It was up on the balcony overlooking the Great Hall. Its one window, once glazed, was now covered with a worn tapestry. Verboden lit a small candle and prayed, "Father of Light, I know we forsook you long ago, but many of us have tried to keep the Light. Many of us have tried... and when you left us, never to return, we kept the faith... so few... so few... I pray you give me, give us, this Land... this.. that... king... a chance... a ray... of your great Light..."

The next day Alfred saw Verboden off. He traveled on

foot, for the few ponies they had were all needed for plowing and hauling loads. As Verboden passed out of sight, Alfred felt profoundly alone.

Chapter Thirteen

Defending the Defenseless

One day, Alfred stood in the tower gazing across the once barren land. He saw plowed fields taking shape and peasants building small hutches along hillsides. He sensed that hope was filling the realm. Lives were being remade, souls rejuvenated. To Alfred this was overwhelming joy. He felt content in helping these people – a sensation he relished.

Then something hit him in the side. He felt a pain. Turning, he saw several young boys and girls playing and giggling. One had shot him with a padded arrow from her small bow!

This enraged Alfred. He picked up the arrow and broke it. Then he rushed at them. As he chased them down the stairs and around a corner, a young girl shot off another soft-tipped arrow. It hit him squarely in the stomach. Ouch! Now he was really angry. The girl giggled and ran off.

He picked up the arrow in anger. Before he broke it he noticed it was a small stick with chicken feathers fletched at one end and cloth padding on the other to soften the impact. It was a toy! Days before this he had shown the children how to make these harmless arrows. He made a few of the arrows and tried shooting them at a target but kept missing. He then tried to run around with the children pretending there were goblins about and shooting at make believe targets, but the children became scared and ran away. So he reluctantly put the bow and arrows away, ashamed of his idea. They must have gathered up enough courage to steal the bow and arrows and figured out the game themselves!

He found them huddled inside the Great Hall behind the rubble, laughing hysterically. Several popped up and shot more arrows at him. On the one hand, he was very annoyed because most of their shots hit him. On the other hand, he couldn't help but smile since it was an enjoyable idea after all.

Several of the larger boys had his spears, the ratkin spears. "How dare they go through his stuff and take things?" he thought angrily. As he approached, all the children cowered in the rubble surrounding the giant spider hole. The larger boys held him at bay with the ratkin spears, jabbing and hollering. Alfred tried to get through but could not. They poked at him while arrows kept popping off of him. His initial annoyance turned into admiration for their tactics and coordination. The boys were able to keep him at bay as the girls launched arrows. The children were having a great time at this new game.

Alfred suddenly stopped and looked down. "Do you all know what that is!?" He crouched in mock fear and pointed to the large tunnel behind them. Many froze, while others ducked down and peered back.

"Ratkins came through there! Rat critters rushed in and took the castle while the knights were defending the castle walls!" Alfred projected his booming big boy voice.

The children jumped from their side of the rubble to Alfred's side and set up a defensive perimeter with the larger boys encircling Alfred. That gave him an idea.

He stood upon the rocks above the children. "Do you want to defend this castle from the onslaught of the rats!?"

"Yes!" they all shouted.

"First, you must train like a knight trains!" Alfred posed with an imaginary shield and sword.

The children stood, lowering their weapons and, like sponges, absorbed whatever Alfred said.

"We must set up some sort of classes," he declared. "You know, training." Alfred strutted about in the rubble. "What I want is for you to set up targets and practice firing arrows at them. And you big boys, find more of those spears and get other boys, like Cory, to come here. Wait! Okay!" Alfred rubbed his hands. "First, the girls with the bows, find as many arrow heads from that pile of goblin debris as you can. Take them to the old man and have him make us arrows. Then bring all the bows and arrows here into the hall. This will be our practice or training place. Okay? And I will make all of you warriors of the king!" Alfred lifted up his fist. It glowed in a ray of sunlight slanting through the boarded windows.

The children, stunned, frozen in awe, had never heard of such a thing. As a matter of fact, they never heard much of anything. To hear this boy, said to be the king, though they had heard of him only in legend, connect and interact with them in this way astounded their little grimy young ears. They screamed and hollered, creating an uproar heard throughout the castle.

Lady Nihan noticed Alfred and several children dragging old wood barrels, boxes and buckets into the castle for target practice. She immediately ordered them to clear it out. "This is the King's Hall! It is for the king! There will be no frolicking in here!"

"Well, I am the king!" Alfred stepped forward into the hall carrying a wooden box. "I want this stuff in here."

Of course, this stunned Lady Nihan. She immediately left and returned shortly with Abedeyan the Steward. "Kind sir, tell our king that this is most improper behavior for a king, – to frolic with the children!"

Alfred and several of the smaller children had already begun target practice and were shooting arrows. Arrows bounced off stone walls and rubble with a few hitting their mark. Alfred, the least skilled, was impressed that the children took to the endeavor so wholeheartedly.

Abedeyan stared wide-eyed for a moment. Lady Nihan

nudged him. Then he cleared his throat. "Sire, you are king of Grotham Keep. There is no need for this activity, especially in the Great Hall or King's Hall."

Alfred shrugged his shoulders, fired a shot, and missed.

A sudden bustle of noise came from the makeshift front door as more boys entered, Cory in the lead.

"What is this!?" Lady Nihan fluttered about, lifting up her dress so she could more easily hustle from spot to spot. "What are you boys doing here!?"

"Ma'am, the king sent for us." Cory raised the spear Alfred gave him. He looked to Alfred who nodded in return.

"Sire, this is most inappropriate." The Steward sighed, cringing at the twang of fired and ricocheting arrows.

"I don't care!" Alfred pointed to the Steward and Lady Nihan. "You fix the castle. You clean the castle." He pointed to himself. "I will defend the castle."

"Knights defend the castle, my Lord!" Abedeyan proclaimed, straightening and facing Alfred head on.

"Well, where are they?" Alfred asked.

Abedeyan and Lady Nihan looked at each other. The lady had pleading eyes. Abedeyan looked away, rubbing his scrunched up chin.

"We don't even have a garrison," Alfred said.

"You expect children to fight?" Abedeyan shouted in dismay.

The children all stopped what they were doing to look. They had been running about the rubble, gathering their spent arrows.

"I expect everyone to fight," Alfred said, "including me, including you. Don't worry. Everyone will have an opportunity. I have figured this all out – well, sort of."

Initially the farmers did not understand why Alfred and Abedeyan were asking for their children from ages six to fifteen to come to the castle. There was still much to do on the farms. Many of the children cried out of fear. When they saw the group of children already with Alfred, all sporting bows or small spears and looking rather dashing, they wiped their tears and ran after them.

Alfred was amazed that both the old smith and his son diligently worked on arrows, spear shafts and small shields. The old man was alive again, barking enthused orders to his smithy son. Both worked late into the night, each and every night, as if they had a purpose. And they did, Alfred realized.

Alfred rewarded them with fresh rabbit. He and the kids had advanced their skills such that now they were hunting in the nearby forests where rabbits were plentiful. Both the boys and girls had become skilled at using the goblin bows. They were made for small hands. Practicing diligently, the children became stronger and stronger and more accurate.

The hard working fathers and mothers would hug their children as they left for a few days to the Keep and to their king. Parents eagerly waited for their return. A few complained to Abedeyan, but when their children returned with rabbits, pheasants, squirrels, and other roasty type critters, complaints ended – with a feast, that is!

The old man and his son were called the weapon makers, for they made all sorts of tools for war using what they found in the pile of goblin scrap metal. The old man took the goblin daggers and blades and added elongated wooden handles so they were more like small halberds, great at keeping enemies at bay. He started making bowstring from the wild game. The gut and sinew of the animals the children brought made for stronger string than what the goblins used. Alfred loved every weapon and shield the pair made. They armed the farmers with small swords or spears and shields and commanded them to participate in practices with him twice a week.

Alfred finally knew why he was there. With all of his computer gaming and knowledge of medieval times, he could help the people rebuild and defend themselves. While they were bolstering their farms, he realized they needed also to rebuild the Keep's defenses as well. It was just a matter of time before they were attacked. Ratkins would attack from under the Keep. Goblins would soar in from the outside.

Once the farmers and their children had become skillful with their weapons, Alfred began focusing on defensive tactics, especially in repelling ratkin attacks. He spent many hours with the boys exploring the lower dungeons to learn the layout. The room that Tirnalth was in was off limits for now. He told them he had a secret weapon in there that could not be revealed.

"Why can't you reveal it?" Cory asked.

Alfred shrugged, "If I told you, it wouldn't be a secret weapon."

The boys were curious, but Alfred kept them busy enough that they did not ask again. They found many corridors and passageways in the dungeons, many paths ratkins of the past could have taken to dig up and collapse the floor in the King's Hall. They found more spears and weapons throughout the passages. Standing over the spot where the spider's burned body once lay, the boys stared in awe at the size of the smudge.

Examining the dug holes, claw marks and trails, Alfred began reconstructing how each ratkin wave came through the dungeons and how they attacked. He found a few dried carcasses, old and decrepit, which still looked menacing. Just as he imagined, they were small with humanoid shapes but rat snouts, teeth and claws. No doubt they were agile and vicious. The young king contemplated many ways to try to defend the castle, thinking through scenarios as if he were home playing his computer game – except that here he knew the concentrated effort was no game.

Upon King Alfred's orders and standing over the hole, Abedeyan recounted in a soft voice what happened. The children listened intently. "Because the few remaining knights held the goblins off at the doors, the ratkins came out of that hole in the floor. When they broke through the floor, a river of them flooded into the hall. Though the knights fought valiantly, swinging their swords and smashing with their shields, the numerous ratkins surrounded and overtook them. They had no chance."

Abedeyan bowed his head in silence. The children looked about, now knowing what caused their kingdom to fall before they were born.

Chapter Fourteen

Honor the Mother and Father

Mothers would often come to visit their children in the Great Hall or King's Hall – whichever you pleased. It wasn't much of a surprise when they would see their children eating cooked rabbit or wild pig or wild goat, as the children were very successful on their hunts. Still, some, especially mothers of girls or the younger ones, asked for their children back. Alfred would convince them to let them stay to train. He felt a gnawing sense of urgency to have everyone prepared. It

131

wasn't as if he kept them like prisoners. They were always free to go home if they wished. Alfred was puzzled by the worried looks on these women's faces. The children were eating better, getting stronger, and having a lot of fun with each other.

Derhman, the parent most angered and so objected to Alfred's conscripting of his son, burst into the Hall and took Cory back by force. Derhman stopped short of pushing Alfred, the King, out of his way. Cory merely snuck back each day. Derhman came to get him several times in this manner.

Then one day, to Alfred's surprise, several of the castle laborers, the cook and a stonemason followed Derhman into the Hall. Instead of helping Derhman, they stopped him from taking Cory.

The portly cook waved his portly arms about. "Just look at the children! They are getting stronger! Let him stay!"

"He's my son!" Derhman said, yanking Cory along as the children rolled their eyes, continuing their training. Cory, resisted but only a little, holding in his anger.

When the cook and mason approached, Derhman's face reddened and he released his boy, producing fists.

Alfred stepped forward, hands raised for calm. "Ah, guys, it's okay. Thank you for your help." The cook and mason raised their hands and stood back. Cory was nearly in tears, holding his spear tight as he stood at a distance from his father.

Alfred spoke, "Derhman, you may take your son."

"Thank you, your sire, that's all I've been asking, as his father!" Derhman said, not so politely.

Then Alfred turned to Cory, "And you may not return until your father allows it."

The cook and mason sighed loudly. The children gasped and stopped what they were doing to look one last time at Cory, whom they held in high esteem.

Abedeyan and Lady Nihan came in from different doorways to see what was amiss, showing looks of disdain at the whole matter.

Cory looked at Alfred with dismay, as if his heart were crushed by an invisible hand.

As Derhman went to take his boy, Alfred turned toward him. "Derhman, do you know of any great spear men or warriors? Know of any knights?"

Derhman mumbled as he pulled his son away, "No, milord, I know of none."

"Well, you can take your son, but you'll have to replace him with a knight," Alfred said.

Derhman stopped. His crazed eyes beheld Alfred with contempt. Cory's spirit was in ruin. Derhman grabbed the spear and tossed it to the floor at Alfred's feet. The cook and mason advanced in anger, but Alfred signaled them to stop.

"Well, Cory is the best fighter we have," Alfred declared. "He is training the rest of us on the spear. Look what he showed me." With that, Alfred thrust and parried with his spear. "So you can take him, but the only person that could replace him, his pride and his skills, would have to be a knight. In this hall, only a Royal Knight of great skill could replace your son." Alfred posed with his spear.

Derhman was stunned. Perhaps it was the dust in the hall or his anger that caused his eyes to water and his face to turn red that day. Visibly shaken, standing still and quiet, he looked at his growing boy, pondering the words he had just heard from the king. Cory's eyes met his father's.

The cook and mason looked at each other and smiled. Abedeyan glanced at Lady Nihan, they shrugged and looked on with a less stern look.

Derhman rubbed his son's hair and gripped his shoulder, tears flowing more freely now.

"You'll have him and all of us to help for harvest," added Alfred. "That I promise."

Derhman's pride was evident. Joy swelled in his heart as he nodded acceptance and walked away. With what emotion he had left, Cory ran after his father, and they embraced.

It was late spring. The castle was as busy as ever with people bustling about. Many came to practice in the field with Alfred. He had all the men and women practice too. At first, the women were meek and hesitant, fearful of their husbands' jealous eyes. When Alfred reminded them that their children would be the first targets of evil creatures, that the young are always taken first – well, no one could imagine the ferocity of these mothers' protective anger!

All learned to thrust a spear, to charge and swing, to block and roll. Alfred devised all of these movements. The first few times were awkward. Many seemed dismayed. But as Cory and the other boys showed how to do these motions over and over, even Cory's mother got into the right rhythm. Derhman joined in as well, leading the men in formation. Clearly, he had set his pride aside to support his son and the larger endeavor.

It seemed what the folk really came for, though, was to see their children practicing their marksmanship in the King's Hall. Their high hopes were not disappointed. On the other hand, it was a bit surprising for them to see their girls handle the small bow with such ease. They fired with great skill into targets newly sewn by Lady Nihan and her seamstresses. The young maidens were stronger and stood straighter than anyone expected. They were quick to smile and spoke without hesitation. Indeed, they spoke with conviction, and Alfred encouraged each and every girl and boy.

He had the boys, handling spears and shields. They spent many hours in the crypt and dungeon. Alfred had Derhman's son, now called Sergeant Cory, devise defensive tactics against ratkins, as these nasty critters would invariably dig their way in and try to overtake the lower passages.

Alfred discussed with the old smith, Broggia, and his son, Boggin, the many drawings of shields and spears that he felt could work well against such an attack. The bucklers were designed with a pie-cut hole for the spears to go through. And the surfaces of the shields had small protruding nails. Based on the evidence in the castle, Alfred believed the ratkins were strong with large clawed hands. He designed the spears to have jagged teeth just under the head. If a ratkin were to grab any of the boys' spears or leap upon their bucklers to take them down, they would be instantly wounded.

Alfred wanted each fighter to have a light buckler shield that could block many of the smaller corridors. The boys spent many hours with the old man and his son, getting instructions on how to hammer in nails and make holes in the material to create the shields. Broggia and Boggin got to know the boys well.

The boys then practiced blocking a corridor from a potential onslaught of ratkins while jabbing their spears

135

through the holes in their shields. Cory taught them to yell and scream, more to summon their own ferocity and tenacity than to intimidate the ratkins. Alfred knew that the boys needed to be strong and capable, trained as mean fighting machines.

They did not know what a machine was, but they liked chanting the phrase "Mean fighting machine!" Alfred told them stories of large fighting machines, which men made of metal, with no souls, lumbering forward, swinging huge mauled fists and firing big rockets.

"What's a rocket?" Cory had asked.

"Oh, it's a big stick that fires off, kind of like a wizard's magic. You know, it has a fire at one end which pushes it into the air, causing it to fly fast like a giant arrow!"

Just before bed time, late into the night, Alfred would describe many such things to the boys and girls, their eyes wide open with wonder. In the mornings, when he sent them back to their families, they would have scratches and bruises from their time at the castle. These were healthy "in training" type wounds. Wanting to be sure they stayed strong, Alfred ordered each of them carry his or her weapons as well as a bundle of firewood and food for their families.

Alfred had the girls concentrate on archery. Broggia and Boggin spent many hours making arrows and simple bows. Alfred made sure the children helped. Broggia was amazed at how quickly they learned to make their own arrows, helping with fletching and fixing up the old goblin bows. In case you didn't know, the word fletching means to attach feathers to the end of an arrow to make it aerodynamic and help balance the shaft with its heavier arrow head. There was more than enough work to keep each girl busy.

The older girls spent much time caring for the younger ones, especially in bandaging blisters and picking out splinters. Alfred was impressed by all the children's abilities and strength. He could see a change in each one. They practiced tirelessly all day, even on their days off at home on their farms. All across the countryside there were makeshift targets with children's arrows stuck in them. The peasants became jumpy, flinching at the slightest movement of a sparrow or rabbit. You see, the children were everywhere, with their arrows flying at any moving target!

There were some problems, however. One day a farmer came to the castle to drop off firewood. When he put down his huge load, the backside had six arrows stuck in it. Lady Nihan fainted right there! The other seamstresses had to cool her poor head. The farmer stared in disbelief while the smiths laughed a bit too much. Realizing that he could have been seriously injured, the farmer became angry and complained to Abedeyan, who in turn told Alfred.

Alfred knew this was serious. The girls were just practicing but should not be shooting at farmers. They needed to understand and respect the fact that their weapons were not toys. So Alfred gave them all a serious speech about the importance of training and showing respect for their elders by not shooting at them or even near them. He was firm but not harsh. The children listened and agreed. Later a young girl came to him to confess that it was she who had fired at her uncle's large load. She cried. Alfred told her he was glad she owned up to this and cautioned her not to do it again. He then made her run a lap around the castle. Twice.

Alfred got them organized into squads made up of eleven girls -- one older girl as leader and ten archer girls.

They learned to fire in unison. Then he had each squad fire with other squads, each taking turns.

Alfred paced the stony hall, chewing some hay. "Okay, so now that you are in squads and know how to fire together, I want you to get into three squads and then fire in turns. Any of you see the movie Zulu?" In that old movie about a colonial battle, British soldiers with single fire rifles lined up in three rows, each shooting in turn while the other lines loaded their weapons. He had forgotten that this was a medieval world, one of fantasy, not a modern world with televisions and old movies. Most of the children shook their heads no to the question, but one of the younger girls nodded yes. Alfred pointed at her and then looked about the medieval stone hall. "Wait a minute!"

The young girl giggled.

"Sorry, I forgot. You guys don't have TV!" Alfred bellowed.

"What's a tee vee?" asked Loranna, a girl Alfred's age. She was strong and fast and very pretty with long bushy brown hair. Once when they were eating, Alfred, joking around, tried to wrestle a piece of moldy bread away from her, but she evaded him deftly and twisted his arm. He was a bit shamed by this but also happy to have her on the team. And the incident gave him the idea of having all the children learn some wrestling moves. This was a beneficial break from archery and from the boys' shield and spear maneuvers; they would all grapple each other outside along the hillside.

There was some discomfort in this – boys and girls wrestling! But alas, it was an order from the king. As dismayed as the peasant folk were at what their children were being forced into, they could not ignore the fact that they were becoming stronger and for the first time in their lives were filled with confidence and pride. They even worked harder and faster when they were at home, helping with daily chores.

The farmers now found plenty of time to visit each other and talk about their children and what was going on. Though there was plenty of complaining, they knew their children were healthier and happier because this new boy king had come. These conversations generally ended in a quiet warm feeling of contentment and hope.

Back at the King's Hall, Loranna yelled "Fire one!" From a line of girls, arrows flew to their targets at the other end. "Fire two!" Another line of girls let loose. "Fire three!" A third line fired. By that time the first line was loaded and ready again. Alfred clapped politely. Loranna turned and leapt in front of him. "What's a tee vee again?"

It was difficult for Alfred to explain this. He would need to tell the history and culture of his land, his time and place. He had to keep it simple. He puckered his lips, fluttered his eyes. "Ah! You know about puppet shows, right?"

Most of the children shook their heads. Alfred was bewildered. These children had not even seen a puppet show? Hmm... so from that moment he decided that in the evenings after sharing their meals, they would put on puppet shows. Better yet, he wanted them to put on a larger show, a theatre production for the people of the castle. In the evenings, after chores were done, there wasn't much to do. Everyone prepared for sleep, bundled in itchy wool blankets on piles of straw. It was quiet and somewhat lifeless. A stage play would be just the ticket to liven things up.

Alfred tried to explain what theatre was. He pranced and danced and sang, but this was awkward. The children

139

looked perplexed.

Loranna stepped forward and said, "I know a bit of dance. Perhaps we could have a dance?" She twirled on her feet, swirling and waving her hands in the air, looking beautiful even in her tattered dress.

"We could show our maneuvers!" said Cory, rising with shield and spear and beginning to chant commands. The boys quickly took formation and chanted various howling responses to each of Cory's shouts. It was almost like an Indian dance, Alfred thought, very impressed. Some of the kids clapped.

"Yah, we could have a variety show," Alfred said. "That would be a nice starter. We could show off each of the children's skills. Cool."

So each night Alfred would get the boys to practice chants. He became so excited that he began drumming his own spear and shield, stomping his feet, and creating a rhythm that led everyone to clap and holler. So emerged a percussion type ensemble, the boys banging their spears on their shields, jabbing the butts of their spears onto the stone floors and stomping their feet. It took them a while to get this perfected. Laughter erupted whenever someone would mess up. Alfred would sometimes have to yell, "Stop laughing so much! We're trying to have fun!" The girls would dance about and periodically form a line and then weave in and out of the boys. It was all good natured and merry.

"What is all this?" asked Abedeyan as he entered the Great Hall one evening, wearing an odd looking oversized bed robe and carrying a small lantern. Lady Nihan was right behind him with her own fancy lantern. She appeared to be the instigator of this inquiry. The children rushed about to hide, but Alfred stood with his spear and shield in hand, smiling, sweating, exhilarated.

Abedeyan hobbled jerkily up to Alfred. "What's all this noise in here each night, keeping us all awake!?" he demanded to know. Lady Nihan stood tall behind him, eyeing Alfred over an upturned nose.

As the children ran to their appointed cots or piles of straw, huddling together, Alfred began his little spear and shield jib. He was quite good at this. He then began dancing around Abedeyan and Lady Nihan. Abedeyan crossed his small arms and rolled his eyes. Lady Nihan gasped and flung her lantern about like a disco light. Then Alfred stopped and drew himself up proudly in front of the Steward.

Abedeyan had held a stern grumpy face throughout the performance. Lady Nihan breathed heavily, leaning on him. The children remained deathly silent as they watched from afar. Abedeyan set down his lantern, raised one hand and stood still. All wondered if he was going to slap Alfred. Lady Nihan smiled in an assuring way. Then Abedeyan clapped the raised hand with his other hand, again and again, slowly but firmly. Then he hummed a strange yet lyrical old tune and began to prance with great conviction yet light as a feather. He tapped his toes softly, stepped to and fro, circled Alfred and Lady Nihan many times, and sang a wonderful old song.

Tis mired of old, this land we know
Tis a spirit roaming, like ghosts of old
Our fathers shall warn in dream and song
One day we share the same fate be told
And our children be us, as they grow.

Abedeyan paused and glanced quickly about...

Tis mired of old, this land we know!
Tis a spirit roaming, like ghosts of old.
We lost the light! We lost our souls!
One day we share... the same fate be told...
And our children be us, as they have grown.

The children raised their heads, watching and listening in wonder, experiencing for the first time an old tradition nearly lost. Were it not for Abedeyan's magnificent performance, it might well have been lost. The Steward stopped in front of Alfred, ending with a gracious bow. Clapping echoed throughout the hall. Lady Nihan applauded. Then from the passageway came the delightful sound of seamstresses, cooks and laborers, all cheering and clapping too. Everyone in the castle, not awakened by the children's noise, was now sitting up and alert, enraptured by the sound of an ancient yet familiar song.

Then, clearing his throat and picking up his lantern, Abedeyan became the official Steward again. "Here here, we all need rest now," he said. "Keep it down a bit, Alfred. King or no king, I am the Steward here, and we all need our sleep! There is still much to do!"

Alfred nodded.

As Abedeyan walked out of the hall, pushing his way through the crowd of happy onlookers, he kept a stern look on his face. But when no one could see as he exited, there slipped a smile.

Chapter Fifteen

The Dark Forest

One day after returning from a hunt, Alfred realized that they had done so well in the fields around the farms and Keep that not many wild rabbits, pigs, and goats remained. They had been hunting in the neighboring hillside and patches of trees for some time now, seeing few game animals. Most were small rabbits and pheasants. The farmers had the same diminishing luck. They were setting traps that caught little and admitted that they used their children to hunt whenever there was time. Alfred smiled at this.

However, he was concerned about food shortages. If they ran out of game to hunt, they wouldn't keep up their strength.

More crops sprouted this year than in the past, but harvest time was a ways off. The few stored provisions were running low. More lost folk were coming to the castle, many hearing that the king had come. There would be more mouths to feed.

Alfred decided to ask the castle folk about the surrounding forests. Everyone warned him about a vast wood to the north, a realm of the goblins and foul beasts. Alfred wondered about this. Would it really be a problem taking his kids there after all their training? He couldn't get the idea out of his head. He wanted to explore the forest and see how his children would fare against real enemies. Also, he could hear the echoing voice of Abedeyan discussing their meager storage of moldy breads, dwindling game meat, and worm-ridden grain. Supplies might not last until the harvest. Alfred knew he had to do something.

Verboden had not yet returned from wherever it was he went off to, and Tirnalth was but a muttering bookworm, grunting only a few syllables at a time whenever Alfred tried to speak with him.

After a few days of fretting and thinking about it, Alfred finally decided it was time. They must go. He did not tell anyone what he was doing.

"I have an idea," he said with enthusiasm. "We shall go on a field trip!" Alfred thought this was a pleasant way to explain that they were going somewhere new. The boys and girls looked quizzically at each other, not sure what a field trip was. Children of peasants in dark times did not go on field trips.

Abedeyan must have surmised what was happening when he saw the boys and girls all fully armed. Three squads of archers and three dozen of the boys with spears all marched out of the castle. The local peasants looked on as if this was a parade, all nodding with agreeable expressions.

Abedeyan chased after Alfred. "You're not going to the dark forest, Danken Fuhrs, are you?"

"Why not? We need food." Alfred had to skip a step to keep pace with the marching children.

"It is dangerous! Goblins reside there!" Abedeyan shook his hands and hobbled alongside Alfred. He didn't yell too loud as he didn't want to upset the castle workers.

"Well, what do you think I've been training them for?" replied Alfred, motioning to the boys and girls.

"This is child's play. Goblins are for real!" The Steward leapt in front of Alfred.

Alfred stopped and looked angrily at Abedeyan. The Steward was taken back. "Child's play? Oh, so let me get this straight. We have no garrison and no food. There is a good chance of being raided by goblins once we make it to harvest time. And you say this is child's play!?"

As Alfred continued his tirade, Abedeyan shook his head and turned around, regretting his incompetence in not preparing better for this eventuality. He ambled back up to the castle.

Danken Fuhrs was a dimly lit forest veiled in a gray mist. Its thick gnarly trees, dense with dark leaves, threw jet-black shadows on a muddy ground. Because of the density of growth, everything retained its moisture and thusly had a dark wet look. Alfred surveyed the edge of the forest, noting its foreboding appearance, and thought to himself, "Dark Forest indeed, even the shadows are really black!"

Just as he was beginning to wonder if going into the wood was a good idea, some girls saw mushrooms at the edge of the forest and rushed to gather them.

"Stay together!" Alfred yelled under his breath. He rushed everyone closer to the girls. "Give me a perimeter," Alfred whispered. Sergeant Cory and his boys fanned out in a wide circle, and the archers set up behind them in a smaller circle.

"Okay, Loranna, your squad can pick the mushrooms," Alfred said. So Loranna and her group quickly shouldered their bows and pulled out sacks to harvest the big mushrooms.

"Are those safe to eat?" Alfred asked.

"Of course they are," said Loranna. "They are Branstools. They have healing powers. These are much bigger than the few found around the farms!" As she spoke, she picked at the forest floor, collecting as much mud as mushroom.

Alfred peered into the forest mist as he moved from spot to spot among the groups of young soldiers. "See anything?" he asked Cory.

Sergeant Cory shook his head. Alfred noticed that it was a quick nervous motion. For some reason Alfred sensed something. Perhaps it was just the rustling of broad dark green leaves. In most places and further in, the thick mist shrouded the forest. It was called the Dark Forest for a very good reason. When the mist thinned enough, the sun would send shafts of light through small leafy openings.

Suddenly, all heard a thundering crackle of wood from

within the forest. The sound came from a tree falling and crashing to the ground not far from them. Everyone froze in fear except Loranna. Muddied, she motioned for her squad to drop their harvest sacks, pull out their bows, and retreat into the circle. Alfred motioned to tighten up the formation.

Then they saw it, a large bear-like creature with a huge beak and oversized claws. It had toppled the tree and was tearing at its bark. It looked ferocious yet busy. Then it stopped and began snorting, its attention turned toward the hunkered down group of children. It stood up on its hind legs and let loose a long ferocious howl. Several of the children dropped to the ground, grabbing their ears. Others rose to dash off. Loranna and the other older girls grabbed the runners and yanked them back in line. Alfred was proud of her, for even he was shaking. The hairy bear-beast with a beak for a mouth advanced like a bull, stomping and raking the ground with each step of its huge mole-like digging claws.

Alfred yelled "Spears forward!" and ran to the front of the group, going down on one knee to brace himself and his spear. Sergeant Cory rushed to his side, and the other boys came up as well to reinforce him. The creature faced a wall of spears.

"Archers ready!" Alfred shouted.

Loranna and her squads rushed up behind them in rows. The first squad was on its knees, the second crouched just behind them, and the taller ones stood in the back.

Undaunted, the beast lumbered forward, bitter bile seething from its mouth and steam spewing from its nostrils.

"Row one, fire!" Alfred yelled. A volley of arrows shot at the beast. Most hit their mark though many bounced off its coarse matted fur and thick hide.

"Row two, fire!" Alfred yelled. Another volley fired with some arrows sticking while others bounced off. The beast seemed annoyed but undeterred.

"Aim for its head, for its eyes!" Alfred hollered. "Row three, fire!" Arrows converged on the beast's ferocious beak and small beady eyes. It was now only a few paces away, ready to swipe its huge claws at Alfred and the boys' small spears.

Arrows pierced the animal's head, with many landing in its gaping maw. The beast emitted choking sounds along with snarls. Other arrows skidded along its large beak, piercing deeply into its face. It contorted with fury at the pain, stopping and gurgling, desperately clawing and snapping at the arrows in its bloody, slobbering mouth.

"Row one, fire!" Alfred yelled. Arrows flew. "Row two, fire!" More arrows flew. "Row three, fire!" Yet more arrows flew. "Charge!" Alfred shouted. The boys yelled and made a great howl as they rushed toward the beast. Clamoring to pull out the arrows in its mouth, the beast left its underside exposed. The boys converged there with their spears, handily piercing its soft underbelly. It fell dead.

Everyone stood silent in utter amazement and shock. They stared at each other, sweating from the fear. The children ran up to collect their arrows and look at the beast. Alfred put his hands out to stop them and then carefully stepped around the beast. It did not move. He poked at it. Nothing happened. He poked again and again. Nothing. Then he raised his arms and cried out, "Yeah!!!" Covered with dark cold mud, they all yelled and cheered, lifting their weapons in victory.

There was a huge feast in the hall that evening.

Makeshift tables were set up, and a fire raged with large chunks of sizzling meat. The children seemed like children again, huddling around the blaze and watching the biggest piece of meat they had ever seen bubble with delicious juices and smoke with wondrous aromas.

It had been a chore to carry the great beast back to the castle. Each kid had to shoulder a large chunk of meat, but it was all worth it.

Alfred and the children rose after the feast and put on a dance for all, from farmers to castle keepers. For the first time in a long time, the adults watched their children dance and sing. It was not a primitive chaotic dance, but a well timed rhythmic display, where the boys were the anchor with percussion and boisterous booming voices and the girls floated light-footed about them, jigging to each new beat. The younger children were like fairies prancing. Much to everyone's surprise, Abedeyan, the farmers and the castle men joined in, demonstrating the traditional dance of Thanks and Merriment. It was a wondrous occasion. Nothing like it had taken place in many long years.

After the great meal and dancing, Abedeyan sat among the children. He looked up at King Alfred, wordlessly expressing, in his watery eyes, his joyous gratitude. Alfred smiled back, holding in his own surge of celebratory emotions. Abedeyan then turned back to the children and began telling them the tale of a beast they had killed. It was a story of magical heroic times in the past when knights used to hunt the beast called a Bikehnbahrt. Abedeyan had no idea that he was telling them of heroic experiences yet to come.

Chapter Sixteen

The Bandits

Verboden walked along a dark road. Alone in a veiled forest, he shrouded his face with his hood while his eyes darted to and fro. His knuckles were white from tightly gripping his staff. Though he saw no one, he felt the presence of others in the dark mist. It was a night on which others would not dare to travel, not at this hour and not in these dark and terrible times.

He stopped and leaned against his staff. The crunching of dirt and bristling of grass echoed as dark shadows rose from the surrounding foliage. Sensing that he was surrounded, he softly chanted words to himself.

"Quickly!" said a voice from the dark, gruff with the sound of spitting. "He is a sorcerer casting a curse!"

A shadowy figure notched an arrow and fired. Verboden ducked as he flung his staff out, deflecting the arrow. It spun off into the night. A shadow rushed from behind him screaming, flailing an axe and shield. Verboden rolled and twirled his staff, hitting hard upon the shins of his assailant. The ruffian went airborne and landed hard. Verboden quickly leapt up and stepped over him. The downed man, though alive, wasn't thrilled to get back up.

The others were cautious but quickly ran up to the fallen man. "Hedor! Did you catch something!?"

"Aye, a sorcerer!" Hedor, the big one, sat up rubbing his pained shins.

"I am not a sorcerer! I am a cleric of the Order of Light!" Verboden stepped back from the ragged armed group.

"Bah!" said Hedor with vile contempt, emitting phlegm and sweat. "The church is dead! Look around you! The land is dead. The people are dying, and you dare come through here in the middle of the night? I don't think so, my foul enchanter. Take him!"

The bandits stood still. They seemed too tired to rush. Verboden could see in their eyes and filthy faces that they were worn and gaunt. Many were half naked, torn and tattered clothes hanging on their frail forms. They held rusted and dented weapons. All appeared to have diseases, aches, and pains.

"I said take him now!" Hedor advanced, swinging his heavy axe. Verboden caught it with his staff and used the momentum of the axe to twirl it around, tumbling Hedor to the ground again.

Hedor had rage in his eyes as he rose and pushed his ruffians forward. "Get him! We are many!"

Verboden noticed that a few of the bandits were younger, barely in their teens. He rushed forward as they huddled with raised weapons and closed eyes. He ably pole vaulted over them, dashing into an area of scattered trees and high grass. The group blinked and looked about confused. Hedor huffed and pointed behind them. They turned to see the cloaked cleric sprinting away.

Verboden entered a dark thicket, its thick bramble and twisting thorns slowing him. As nimble as he was, he could not get through the dried overgrown bushes before the bandits caught up and circled him again.

Hedor, huffing and gruffing, had had enough. "Finish this vile sorcerer," he rasped. "He brought the plague upon us and doomed the land! He is one of them, the vile enchanters! Finish him! Let loose your arrows. Throw your spears! I will hack him down!"

As the bandits raised their bows and spears, Verboden went down to one knee as best he could in the bramble and chanted a sonorous song. The bandits lowered their weapons upon hearing it, as it sounded familiar. They had not heard such ethereal music in a long time.

Oh Creator of all,
hear my call
bring me strength
before I fall.

"You fools!" yelled Hedor, sweeping thorns aside. "He is casting a charm! Now shoot!"

The bandits raised their bows. With his eyes closed, Verboden raised his hands out, reaching toward the sky. Something round dropped from the trees, landing firmly in Verboden's hands. The bandits scrambled away. One fired an arrow wildly, almost hitting another bandit. Hedor fell back and got stuck in some thorns. With a painful grimace he chopped at them to get up again. Still, he was paralyzed with fear, breathing hard, and feeling the doom of a demon presence. His companions were similarly stricken.

Verboden held the ball close to examine it. It was large, brown, grotesquely wrinkled and lighter than it appeared. Verboden exerted no effort in holding it. Digging his fingers into it, he heard a cracklng sound, like that of dry leaves being crushed. The sphere split open, revealing a pattern of small squares of clear six-sided cells. From this set of hexagons, a honeycomb, oozed the shiny syrup of honey.

Verboden looked up and broke off a piece of the comb, raising it to a young quivering bandit who had his bow taut. The archer, mishandling his weapon, twanged the string, causing the arrow to fall from its notch. Yet he reached hungrily for the glistening morsel.

"Don't do it!" cried Hedor, trying to wrest himself free from the thorns. "It's foul sorcery!"

The bandit boy touched, with trembling fingers, the oozing parchment of honeycomb. In a brief moment, his filthy fingertips were covered in the gooey syrup. He retracted his hand and suckled his fingers.

The bandits leaned in to witness what they felt for sure was the boy's demise. Instead, he grabbed the piece of honeycomb from Verboden and hungrily suckled it. He giggled like a child with, well, honey. His friends immediately began frothing at the mouth, each begging for a piece. Verboden complied as quickly as he could.

"No! He is putting a curse upon you! It is a charm that will damn you!" As he yelled, Hedor continued to twist and turn in the thorn bed.

Verboden saved a piece for him and tossed it on his lap.

"Damn you!" Hedor said.

Raising his staff high, Verboden spoke more words of enchantment.

Oh Creator of all,
hear my call
bring me strength
before I fall!

Hedor tried to raise his axe with one hand but was filled with fear and went limp with exhaustion. With the last word, Verboden swung down hard with his staff. It met the earth with a great cracking sound. Hedor closed his eyes. The bandits peered wide-eyed with syrupy drooling mouths. Hedor opened his eyes, expecting to die. Instead he saw Verboden lift his staff from a hole and pull out a big fat rabbit, dead, and ready to be cooked. Verboden spoke again in chant form, raising his staff and whacking the ground with it. Out bounced another big fat juicy dead hare. In no time the makings of a fire were laid and a spark struck.

"If this is a sorcerer's curse, Hedor," mumbled a large greasy-mouthed bandit sucking on a tiny rabbit bone, "then damn me to hell, I say!" Others laughed in unison with him as

Hedor himself chewed on a bone and merely shrugged.

There would soon be nothing left but bones as ravenous young ruffians licked and gnawed their way through the two rabbits. Then all sat about a warm fire. Verboden stood in the shadows.

"Why aren't you eating, sorcerer?" Hedor asked. "Are we all to fall asleep after our meal, never to wake?"

Verboden walked into the crowded circle and crouched, reaching into his cloak. This dismayed a few of those huddled near him until they saw that what he pulled out was an old piece of bread. Verboden tore off a small fragment and dabbed it into a nearby piece of honeycomb. He brought it close to his mouth and then prayed a silent prayer of thanks. Hedor vaguely remembered such an act, from long ago, when gratefulness once existed. Verboden chewed the morsel slowly.

The bandits shrugged and continued gnawing tiny bones and sucking on the honeycombs. After all the food was eaten, most fell asleep and began snoring, especially the older ones with their sonorous noses.

As drowsy as he was, Hedor held onto his axe and leaned against it while staring at Verboden. He seemed drunk on the first wonderful meal he had had in ages.

"Foul sorcerer, leave us to die," he mumbled.

"I am a cleric, not a sorcerer, and I need your help."

"Help!? Hahr hahr hahr!!!" Hedor roared, awakening some sleepers from their peaceful slumber. "Look at us, ruffian rabble! We have nothing left but our broken weapons, our broken backs, and our broken spirits."

"We are rebuilding Grotham Keep."

Hedor's eyes widened, "Grotham? Who?"

"The king has returned. People are gathering. We need men, fighting men such as you. With food in your stomach I'm sure you'll be impressive."

"Impressive? Well sorcerer, if you would be so observant as to notice we are starving young and old, and sick and in dire need. We are not warriors, sorcerer. We were once farmers and laborers. We merely lived longer than our wives, and children, and our souls." Hedor sat quietly for a long while. He longed for a deep sleep he hoped he'd never wake from. "I hope you are a sorcerer.... to end all of this."

"Where is he going?!" a young bandit asked, jumping up and down in the morning mist, racing back to the others. The bandits lay sprawled around a small spent campfire.

Many woke with soar stomachs, headaches and such. They were gaunt folk who had just eaten too much. Some puked while others let loose foul excrement. That would be 'poo' to the younger ears! To be fair, descriptively speaking, they went out into the tall grasses for such business. The sounds of flatulence or 'farting', moaning, groaning and burping echoed throughout the meadow. Pee-yew!

"The sorcerer! The cleric! He's leaving!" the young anxious bandit said, wakening the others.

"He cursed us with foul food!" moaned one.

"We are doomed!" groaned another.

"I'm going to see my Bessy soon!" squealed one.

"Oh, the curse!" barfed another.

"I actually feel pretty good as it were.... ooohhhhh... That was a good expelling!" busied another.

"Where is he going!?" the young bandit frantically asked.

Hedor harshly poked the young bandit with the end of his axe. "He's going to Grotham! They're rebuilding the castle."

"Grotham?" an old bandit spoke with sadness. The word spread through the two dozen bandits. The younger ones only knew about Grotham's glory days from stories of the elders.

"Rebuilding the castle?" another bandit asked.

"Then they are rebuilding the land?" another said.

Hedor's eyes widened as he shook out of his sleep. "Yes, to Grotham we go!" He leapt up with such nimbleness that the others gave him room as he pranced down the road to follow after the cleric.

"Well, the sorcerer's curse looks like it's wearing off," someone said.

The others smiled and ran after him.

Chapter Seventeen

Timalth's Secret

Alfred had many sleepless nights worrying about his mother. As time passed, his uneasiness about her, especially since he was gone from their apartment, increased. The peasants, workers, Abedeyan and Lady Nihan were busy building, cleaning, restoring, farming, hunting and the like. Loranna and Cory kept the children active with archery and combat practice.

Setheyna, the youngest archer, was Loranna's

messenger and aide-de-camp. Each morning when she came to the castle, she would rush up to Loranna to get orders for the day and then assemble the children. In running around the Keep ringing a bell to wake everyone, she made sure to ring twice as loudly and twice as long when she got to Alfred's sleeping quarters, as he seemed to be a deeper sleeper than the rest. Of course, the early morning was when Alfred dozed off after his restless night of worry.

On many occasions, Alfred went into Tirnalth's tower to talk. Tirnalth always seemed possessed, chanting and mumbling. Alfred would sit and wait. It took a great while for Tirnalth to notice him. When Tirnalth finally smiled and nodded, Alfred took that as confirmation that he was free to unload his concerns.

He was worried about the farming and the ever short supply of food. He was concerned about the dirt and filth and no running hot water for baths – oh, and about the toilet, a mere chair with a hole to a pan for private matters. And Lady Nihan carrying it away. Blech! What else? Oh, why couldn't Alfred just say it!?

"Tirnalth, I, I, I, don't know if I can do this. I don't know if what I'm doing will really help the people. I mean, I don't know anything about farming and all this stuff. It's so dirty here, and I have rashes and flea bites and sores. I just want to go home. I miss my mother. I mean, she must miss me and must wonder where I am, and the police must be looking for me. I don't want her to cry or be sad because I know she would be sad." He paced around the room.

"She does everything for me," Alfred continued. "Maybe she does too much. But still, I love her so much. I want to make a lot of money and buy her a big house and all

159

that. If I'm here, then she has no one. I mean, I know the people need help, but wouldn't it be better if you were in charge?" He paused to look at Tirnalth, who was still smiling and nodding.

"Well, I suppose maybe you are not the right person to lead them if that Gorbogal witch knows you're around. What about Verboden?" Alfred looked at the oblivious wizard with sudden hope... which fled from his face as fast as it came.

"Hmmm, he gets worn out every time he casts a big spell to heal someone. That won't do. No, that won't work at all. And we have no knights, no lords and no vassals. Will Verboden ever find any? Will he find any knights in time? I still don't understand what it is to be king!"

Alfred emitted a long sigh and shook his head. "Okay, I know I have helped out. I know that I can help, like when I went around to all the peasant homes. Do you remember me telling you about it?" Not waiting for a response, he plunged ahead.

"I know! You don't remember. Anyway, I stayed with them overnight, sleeping next to their pig and sheep and with the whole family. You know, I just wanted to see what it was like, to see how they were doing and how they lived. I saw how the women took the pots of pooh and stuff to the stream and dumped them there. They waited for it to run downstream, and then they filled their buckets with water. This all seemed fine until I realized that all the farmers lived along that small funny smelling stream. I was like, no, no, no, no, no! Man, was I like no! That was so vile! Oh hey! I used the word vile. Hah-ha! Mister Nord, my teacher, taught us that as a vocabulary word, and I was like, when am I ever going to use that word? Boy, does that word work here! Man, that stuff was so vihhhhhh-el!"

"So, I was like, okay, okay, people, no dumping pooh in the stream. No, no, no! Let's see. Find a tree area or patch of forest that is used for chopping wood or something. Dig a big hole, and then each morning, dump your pooh in there. Cover it a bit each time, and when it's …well…vile enough, cover it completely and dig a new hole. Abedeyan made me declare it a law! To think, my first King's Law was about pooh. The people were a bit upset because the men had to now dig holes for the pooh, I guess they dig a lot of holes. I was like, no way are you dumping pooh in the water we drink. It causes disease and stuff. Verboden said a prayer chant thing while the peasants all waited. I was like, what is he doing? Then he woke out of it and was like, 'King Alfred is right. The water was causing all kinds of maladies. By making this change, everyone will feel better.' At first all the peasants gasped at this new information. Then they began clapping."

"Suddenly," Alfred continued. "I spurted out more rules and stuff. I was like, take water out of the stream to bathe in, but do not bathe near or in the stream. Do not put anything dirty in the stream, not even the bath water. Let's keep the stream clean. And let's use some soap. I couldn't believe it when they asked me what soap was. I was like, oh man, no soap! You don't know what soap is? I couldn't believe it. I'd been wiping my sweaty armpits with water from a bucket wondering when they'd be able to start making soap, not knowing they don't even know what it is. And I don't know how to make it. Shoot! So I said never mind about that."

"I mean, I guess I'm getting used to the dirt and oiliness. If I sit and think about it, I suddenly feel totally covered in dirt and oil. Blech! And my hair! I wish I had shampoo."

Alfred sighed again.

"I guess Abedeyan is handling all the taxes and stuff. I did tell him to keep them as low as possible because everyone was starving and it was tough on everyone. And I told him that anyone who wanted to stay in the castle could. Abedeyan seemed a bit bummed about it. We have plenty of room, and there's like not that many people there anyway. I also said that anyone who wants to farm near the castle can."

"So I dunno, Tirnalth. I guess I'm helping out. I guess the farmers and peasants are happy, and luckily nothing bad has happened. We don't have men for an army. Thankfully, nothing has attacked us yet. I've seen all the ratkin and goblin weapons but never seen them. I don't know if we can even fight them. What if I have to? I am just a kid from a city who likes to play computer games. I'm not a king! I just wish I could see my mom. I wish she knew that I was okay and that I was coming home."

Alfred was tired. He had spoken more than ever in his life. It was the first time in a long time that he had poured his heart out, disclosing everything he was thinking and feeling. Looking up, he realized that Tirnalth was mumbling to himself, still in his own world. Alfred grew angry. Tirnalth was unaware of Alfred being there and everything he had just said. Alfred stood up and began swinging his fists at Tirnalth. "Why did you bring me here?" he cried. "Why don't you listen to me? I hate this! I hate you!" His fists went wild, flailing through Tirnalth's ghostlike aura. Exhausted, Alfred fell to the ground and began to cry.

Still mumbling to himself and unmindful of Alfred's swings at him, Tirnalth heard something vaguely nearby. This brought him out of his trance. He blinked, looked about and saw Alfred on the ground sobbing. Alfred was crying, holding himself, alone in the dark crypt. "My dear boy, what is the matter?"

Alfred looked up, filled with relief and surprise. "Tirnalth!" He leapt up and hugged the wizard, who now was fully formed. Alfred could feel him.

"Alfred, my dear boy, my dear boy, whatever is the matter?" At first surprised by the feeling of the hug, Tirnalth warmly returned it.

"I'm scared, Tirnalth and I, I, miss her." Alfred sobbed with a blubbery face.

"Oh, Alfred, do not cry. You can see her whenever you wish."

"What? I can?" The tears stopped flowing.

"Yes, of course, it is within you," Tirnalth whispered with enthusiasm. "Your love is the key."

"Well how? When? How, when?!?"

"Well now. And, uh… how? Well, I don't know."

Alfred backed away and crossed his arms.

"I have been studying who I am, and I know much now. I know that I left these books here to help me find my way back. I left them high up on the wall there, veiled as stone for thirteen years, only to reappear when the blood of a king was near. Alfred, you brought them back. Somehow I knew back then what to do, well I suppose, because I'm a great wizard! Oh, shhhhh, don't tell anyone. I'm not all back yet. Look at this, look at what I left. These books are not even spell books. They are a gateway!"

Tirnalth stood waving his arms in a grand fashion. "*Kurehnde, buht-thaguhm, muhrathum!*"

And with that a spell book opened, shining light into the shadows of the tower walls. The light illuminated a wall of books, all wrought with gold leaf and some woven with silver string. They were all bound in rich red, brown and black leathers. Many were secured with metal brass clasps and lockets. It was a wondrous vast magical library. Scrolls were stuffed in many crevices and corners, as were candles of all sizes and shapes, many burnt down to piles of wax.

"As you can see, I have much yet to learn. I hid my library of knowledge so that at the right time, I could use it again to relearn all that I knew before. I sacrificed myself to give your mother time, Alfred."

"Time?"

"Yes, to give her time to escape. I knew all was lost. And I knew that the Dark One had aided Gorbogal. I broke that bond by offering him myself, my knowledge, my mind. And he took it, abandoning Gorbogal, weakening her powers by indulging in his own selfish needs. Somehow, I knew he could only take my memories and my skills of magic, and not my spirit. For my spirit is owned by the Father of Light and it is not mine to sell, trade, or bargain." Tirnalth smiled with relief.

"Or sacrifice?"

"Yes boy, yes. I left myself clues, and this library. All of this is my memories, a copy for me to regain. It is my secret place!" Tirnalth stepped aside, stretching his arms out to reveal more. Beyond the grand wall of books, as if in another dimension twinkling through, was a great hall with a vast library. It was so vast that it went beyond their vision, into bright rays of sunlight.

"How is that possible? It's huge!" Alfred gasped and

stared at the immensity of what he was seeing.

"It's a portal, a doorway. I hid this hall of books somewhere, not even I know. I suppose one of these books will tell me." Tirnalth gazed in wonder at it. He had been in its presence this whole time.

"It looks like it will take a while for you to read them all," Alfred sighed.

"Well, I'm a fast reader." Tirnalth looked at Alfred's wonderment and could also sense his concern. "But yes, I suppose it will. I think I know what book I will read next."

They looked at each other. Tirnalth patted Alfred's shoulder. "I'll read about how you can get back to your mother."

"It's been so long. She must be devastated that I'm not there."

"Oh no Alfred, this magical portal isn't just a doorway through space, it is also a doorway through time! You can return to her and it will seem as if only a moment has passed. It is all up to you!"

"What? You mean no time has passed?"

"Well, not ...'no time', but more like stretched time. These two worlds are linked, through space and time, but they are also linked magically. And magically isn't the same as reality. My boy, time passes based on what it is you want as the traveler. I have a feeling your mother will see you... shortly."

Alfred smiled and looked down sadly. "Won't the people here need me? As their king? Not that I even know what that is..."

"Oh, I suppose we can find another. There are kings everywhere, at all the shops. You can get one nowadays for a low price." Tirnalth's attempt at humor did not cover his sad expression.

"No, seriously," Alfred said, "I don't want to abandon them."

"Well, that is the difficulty of being a king, Alfred. Your people need you and you can not abandon them. I don't think you have to. Come, don't worry about the magic portal and departure until I learn it fully. And fully I will. For now, help them as best you can and keep a good face about it all. Soon enough, I will learn the way that got you and me here, and how you can take yourself back. Deal?"

Alfred nodded agreement. Tirnalth patted Alfred's head. Alfred smirked.

"Sorry, old habit. Now run along king! You have much work and leading and inspiring to do!"

Chapter Eighteen

The Goblins

Alfred was happy that the bear creature they had killed in the Dark Forest had provided much needed meat. But Abedeyan was annoyed that Alfred shared it with the peasants and workers. He had wanted to make salty pork and bacon and jerky to store away for future use.

"Abe," said Alfred, using the name he had begun calling Abedeyan, much to his annoyance. "There is no tomorrow. We have to feed everyone now to make sure everyone is strong and able. I'm not going to hide away any of the food for later. And soon will be the harvest. Besides, we're going out again."

"What!? Milord? This is dangerous. We do appreciate the success of your hunt. But it is only a matter of time before you meet up with goblins, and they are not so easily shot down. They are themselves hunters of the Dark Forest. They are raiders of the land. They are vicious, I tell you!" Abedeyan warned.

"Well, I am king, and whatever that means, what I say goes," Alfred said.

"That is not how a kingship works!" Abedeyan replied.

"What do you mean? I can do anything I want! Isn't that how a kingship works?" Alfred said.

"No, Alfred. No. Not at all! You can't just do whatever you want as king!"

"Abe, seriously, I don't even know what it means to be king. I've helped in so many ways. The farming is done faster and better. I trained the children! I got us armour and weapons from scraps!"

"Alfred, what is amiss here? Why are you questioning what it means to be king?" Abedeyan said with restraint.

"Silence, Abe! I can do that too, right? As the king, I can silence you! I guess it means power," Alfred said coldly.

"Buh..." Abedeyan was stunned, if not hurt.

Alfred raised his hand in a kingly manner, giving the humble Castle Steward an awful egotistical glare.

Abedeyan looked down, sighing, as if decades of servitude had returned.

Alfred shrugged with an upturned look. "Abe, we have to try. We need more food. The forest is the best place for us to find it, so that's where we are going. We've trained enough. Going out like this is important, dangerous or not. I don't know what it means to be king, and I don't care anymore. All I know is what we need. And what we need is more food. And if I can get it, I have to try. We are going."

They once again entered Danken Fuhrs. The children crept along in the dark misty woods, quietly looking for anything to hunt. They heard a few scattered noises, rustlings fairly close and howls in the distance. Alfred hoped for another of those bikehnbahrs.

As they walked, the children were able to stay quiet for the most part. The few times someone began to speak, Alfred stopped and glared at them. He was very serious now and did not want any frolicking from the kids. He wanted true huntsmen, with stealth, discipline and focus. This was difficult for the younger children, but the elder ones kept the younger ones in line.

The shadowy forest had difficult terrain. Many gnarled roots stuck out from the damp earth. The children could easily get their feet stuck. Some did on several occasions whispering loudly for help. Others hastily pulled at the roots. It seemed as if the roots tightened around their feet as the others struggled to free them.

Cory resorted to beating the root, which seemed to make the trees groan. Loranna lit a torch and waved it nearby. That worked best at releasing shackled feet, but it caused odd creaks and moans to echo from the trees.

Alfred began to fear this forest. There was an unease rising amongst the children. Last time they were lucky, as they came upon the bikehnbahr on the outskirts of the forest. Now they were deep within.

"I think we should go back," Cory whispered.

Alfred nodded with a quiver. "Yeah, we'll try along the edge, not so deep in like this."

There were many sighs of relief. Suddenly Alfred's shield jerked and hit him in the head. He fell down and shook his head. A small black greasy arrow had lodged in his shield.

"Perimeter!" Alfred cried, hurriedly getting up, shield raised.

Everyone knew what to do, but in the gnarled roots and uneven earth it was a scramble. The boys with spears and bucklers crouched low. Everyone peered into the mist.

"Loranna, your torch!"

Loranna quickly thrust the torch into mud, it hissed out. The darkness that surrounded them veiled the forest and anything that crept.

Alfred looked at the black arrow again. It was nothing other than a goblin's arrow. It was black, not from paint but from filth and dirt, oil and grease. The feathers used, from a brownish gray bird, were matted and oily, as if rotting and leaving a residue of black ick.

Movement could be heard. It reverberated across the leaf canopy and resounded off the many thick squat trees. They could hear many footsteps and grunts, the scrapes of metal and swishes of leather. Then shadows appeared before them. An arrow twanged and hit Cory in the shoulder. He yelped and fell. Alfred bent down to help him, but Cory waved him off.

They were alone in this dark forest, cut off from Tirnalth their wizard, from Verboden their cleric, from anyone anywhere. Alfred felt paralyzed with fear.

"Alfred, fire back!" Cory grimaced.

More arrows zipped by, hitting wood and shield. The children cowered for cover amongst the roots. Hissing growls echoed from distant shadows. Alfred was in a hot sweat, momentarily paralyzed. The girls cried and held each other. The boys trembled with their spears. He could see shadows of goblins flanking them on either side.

"Fire!" Alfred yelled, or tried to. Hoarse with a gut-wrenching terror, he barely had a voice.

"One ready!" cried Loranna, aiming her bow. Girls scattered about raised their bows in her direction. Alfred looked back at her in fear. She showed none. Cory pulled him down. "Fire!" Arrows flew over them into the mist.

"Two ready!" Loranna pointed to the shadows. A new set of girls knowing their number rose. Their bows creaked. Their strings tensed. "Fire!" Howling anguish from the goblins in the dark pierced the air.

Cory lifted himself up. Alfred saw the arrow and blood streaming from Cory's shoulder. He had never seen anything so horrid. Now he was even more terrified.

"Pull it out!" Cory begged.

Realizing what he had to do, Alfred snapped the weak goblin arrow and pulled it out from each side. Cory screamed, and his face grew pale as if he was going to faint. As sweat, dirt and blood dripped from the wound, he gritted his teeth. Alfred and several boys held him up.

He was as pale as a ghost. "Much beddah..."

"Three ready!" Loranna looked frantically for the grotesque shadows scurrying beyond the forest mist. Foolishly, several came too close.

"Fire!" Loranna pointed, and the girls cut loose their

171

arrows. They were definitely hitting goblins as many yelps could be heard in the shadows and tangles of tree limbs.

"We have to leave. Now!" Loranna pulled Alfred up. The boys held their shields up as a few arrows came in from the distant goblins. As they began to retreat, Alfred in his feverish state could see the shadowy figures of goblins rushing alongside them, ready to pounce.

Alfred pointed with a trembling finger at the passing shapes.

Loranna glanced at Alfred then leapt around with arms raised. "Two! Look to our left! Three! Look to our right!" The archers immediately split up, crawled over the roots and aimed their bows to either side. There was a sudden stillness and no sound. The young children had their bows notched. The children were starting to tire from the adrenaline caused by fear. They were barely able to hold up their weapons. Their hearts beat furiously. Fear clawed at their spirits.

"Vigilance, everyone!" Loranna said. The steadiness of her voice calmed them to focus on the here and now, not the evil spirits of cowardice and panic.

One young girl accidentally shot an arrow blindly into the mist. It hit something, as there was an unexpected guttural moan. A large goblin, as big as a burly man, suddenly fell through the sheet of mist toward them. It carried a fearsome scimitar and wore scaly hide armour. Even so, it had an arrow in its neck. It was more hideous and ferocious looking than Alfred imagined. His heart sank.

Growls erupted from all sides as goblins angrily and nimbly leapt along the roots, coming toward them.

"Fire at will!" Loranna yelled. Alfred looked up at her in awe. She had such passion and bravery. He gulped. Then he felt a surge of energy and stood up next to her with his spear and shield. Looking to one side, he saw several large goblins swinging axes and crude blades, leaping in fast.

"Spears on me!" Alfred yelled, and the boys did as best they could to point all spears toward the leaping goblins. One leapt into the sudden raising of spears and was skewered, knocking back several of the boys. Alfred and the rest closed ranks.

The goblins paused at the demise of their lead. That was opportunity enough.

"One! Fire!" Loranna pointed her arm straight at the goblins.

All bows turned toward the attackers. They yelped and tried to retreat but were shot down. With many arrows piercing them, they fell like rag dolls between the thick roots and muddy earth.

This gave the children repose, a moment, a breath, as more goblins halted in the shadows. They were not so keen to charge in after seeing their brethren pin-cushioned with arrows.

"Quickly, we have to leave this place!" Alfred ordered. They began to back up. Several helped Cory. He grimaced in painful anguish with each move. They moved out as best they could. The younger ones were getting the hang of traversing the roots as the goblins did, lightly stepping on them. A few were quite good and kept arrows notched.

"Number One, hold your fire and be ready," said Loranna. "Two and Three, fire at will, even if you don't have a target, it will slow them down."

The archers nodded agreement and fired their arrows at anything that moved. This worked to slow the goblins' attempt to regroup and make chase, at least for a while.

This went on for some time. The traversing of Danken Fuhr was difficult at best. There were many strained ankles from the roots. There were many cuts and bruises from the gnarly branches. Alfred wished he had listened to Abedeyan. The fighting, only lasting a few minutes, seemed to take years off his life. His heart was beating so fast, his breathing could barely keep up. He felt on the verge of hyperventilating. Panic was on the verge of over taking him. He felt as if he was struggling to keep above water. He was shaking all over, as were the others.

Finally a beam of light broke through the distant wall of trees. He felt a sudden calming of his spirit. He could catch up on his breathing. They reached the open pasture where Alfred had hoped to make a hasty getaway, but everyone was exhausted. Try as he wished, since his legs felt like rubber, he could barely move. Everyone was breathing hard and limping. Many dropped and had to be helped up quickly.

A few of the younger ones held their own well and kept a rear guard, shooting arrows back into the forest. Some had to borrow arrows from others. The larger girls had carried extra, so at the moment there were still plenty of arrows.

They reached a small hill when the goblins poured out of the forest. There was a large group of them, maybe thirty or forty. Alfred gasped when he saw how many. They appeared faster and more vicious, now that they were in the open and could easily see their prey.

The thick mist that emanated from Danken Fuhr created a cloud over the land even in daylight, allowing these sinister creatures of dark to rush out on the unsuspecting.

The goblins were not much taller than the children, but

they had the gait of large strong monkeys. Alfred recalled from his biology class that monkeys could be twice as strong as men, if not stronger. The goblins had large black frog-like eyes and long black stringy hair, greasy and matted to their green lumpy skin or tied back in coarse lumpy ponytails. They wore various tied and sewn together animal skins, all layered, grimy, hard and worn. Their weapons were crude leather-bound axes and hammers or cut iron blades. Many had significant apparel and weaponry scavenged from fallen men, perhaps even knights.

Alfred wanted to run or give up. He wanted this to end. He was tired and looked to see if they could hide. But there was no place to go. He was shaking all over from the strain of such intensity, of fighting and surviving. He didn't like this. It wasn't like a computer game or story. This was real, and there was no break, pause button, or time out. There was no rest.

"Archers, hold your fire and be ready!" yelled Loranna.

Cory pushed Alfred with a grimace and pleaded, "Get the spears ready."

Alfred shook himself awake but was trembling tremendously. He and the other boys formed a line in front as the girls grouped into three rows of archers. Cory angled a spear as best he could while in such pain. His wound was ghastly. He was pale. Alfred could see the pain and strain in his face, realizing again that this was no game.

The goblins fanned out, advancing up the slope.

"One fire!" Loranna yelled. The arrows went wild in all directions, trying to hit different targets.

Feeling a surge of anger at the goblins, Alfred rushed to the front. "Wait!" he shouted. "Whichever goblin I point at, you fire there!" Crouching low, he pointed at one goblin whose dark furrowed brow suddenly widened. "Two fire!" A volley of eleven arrows showered him. He fell like a pin cushion. The other goblins screamed in anger and charged more furiously.

Alfred pointed at the nearest big brute who hid behind a shield. "Three! At his bare feet, fire!"

The large goblin fell and rolled down, arrows puncturing its feet. It yelped with each roll as the arrows broke off.

Alfred pointed again. A fast goblin was almost upon them. "Fire!"

A volley pierced the goblin. He stood for a moment with nine arrows in him, slashing at the air, then fell dead.

Alfred pointed again. "Fire!" Another goblin fell. "Fire!" Another slumped to the ground. But there were still more, and they were frothing with anger. They were now upon the small group of children. The boys jabbed out their spears to repulse the goblins, as the creatures swung fiercely with their weapons. One caught the jagged end of a boy's spear and yanked it down. The boy fell forward hitting the ground hard. The large growling goblin lifted his crude blade to swing down at the boy. In the nick of time, he was brought down by many arrows.

Another leapt in, swinging his heavily armoured limbs, pushing aside the boys' spears, throwing many off their feet. He swung down at a girl who tried to notch another arrow. The blade cracked through bow and cut across her forehead. She fell.

"No!" Loranna cried and fired an arrow point blank. It did not penetrate deep enough, and the goblin pulled it out.

He let loose a hot steamy spittle-filled roar and raised his blade to strike. But just then he arched in sudden paralysis.

Alfred yanked him down with his spear from behind. "Form up! Quickly!"

They lined up as they saw a few straggling goblins retreat to the forest edge to regroup. The boys would have cheered if not for the sheer exhaustion and fear. Several lay on the ground crying with bad cuts or battered limbs.

Alfred looked to see Loranna cradling the youngest girl, Setheyna, the one with the horrible cut on her forehead. She looked alive but in shock.

"No!" Alfred shuddered and fell to his knees. Loranna cried out.

"I'm sorry. I'm so sorry, Loranna!" Alfred cried.

In a desperate attempt to keep from hyper-ventilating, Loranna gasped air. Tears flowed but she did not sob. She finally began to exhale and calmed.

"Alfred? King Alfred?" Cory mumbled as he prodded Alfred.

Alfred stood, peering along the edge of the Dark Forest. Out swarmed fifty or sixty goblins with three huge ones holding large wooden bramble as makeshift shields. They were forming up to charge. Alfred looked at the boys and girls. None stood straight. All bent or kneeled or huddled in pain or exhaustion. None could flee. Even at full strength the kids could not outrun a goblin.

"I know what it is to be a king. I understand now." Alfred wiped away the mud and tears.

Loranna looked up at Alfred. He looked down at her. She stood up next to him.

"I'm sorry, Loranna. I didn't understand before. But I

know what it is to be a king, to make mistakes like this and cost the lives of those around me. I'm sorry. I wish I would have known before. I wished I would have known what it meant to be king. But now I do, and I guess it's too late. I'm sorry I made such a mistake."

"No Alfred, this is not a mistake. I'd rather die here, fighting than hiding away to die in fear, as many of our friends and family have before us. Each harvest we hid in fear, hoping goblins wouldn't find our home. Each year they took a family or two, and we hoped some harvest would be left. We lived like slaves to fear. And we were going to die as slaves. But not now, King Alfred, you've taught us to be free of fear, to fight. We've never had a king before. We were all born after the kingdom fell, when there was no king, just tales. None of our families would fight. We didn't know how. I know what a king does. He leads his people, to protect them and to give them hope and freedom. A good king does that. And Alfred, you are a great king! You are my king!"

Alfred faltered. Loranna held him up. "I am proud of you, King Alfred, my king! I'm proud that I will go down killing goblins, fighting this evil!"

"I'm proud too, King Alfred," said Cory, managing to stand, trying to keep upright and hold his spear.

"They're coming!" a boy cried out.

The goblins traversed up the hill, lining up behind the bramble shields.

Loranna stood tall, "Archers up!"

What girls could, stood and tried with what strength they had to ready their bows. All were exhausted and quivering from the shock of battle and the sight of horrible evil creatures about to brutally end their lives.

"One fire!"

A weak volley of arrows flew into the goblins. Only one dropped as the attackers hid behind the bramble shields, howling like crazed monkeys, speeding up their advance.

"Two fire!"

Another spattering of arrows sunk into the goblins with little affect.

"Three... fire."

Again, one dropped, merely holding his legs as a good fifty neared the small group of trembling kids.

"For King Alfred!" bellowed Cory, raising his spear. The boys felt a surge of strength and lined up with just a few dozen. They were smaller and weaker than the goblin force.

"King Alfred!"

"I know what it is to be king," Alfred said to himself. He raised his spear, ready for the end. "I know what it is to be king!"

"One fire!"

The volley seemed more potent. Goblins dropped.

"Two fire!"

More fell. The goblins began tightening up behind the three leaders. A few tried to rush headlong but met their end with arrows.

"Aim for their feet!" King Alfred shouted.

"Three fire!"

Two of the large goblins dropped their shields as arrows pierced their feet and calves. They barked furious pain.

"One fire!"

Arrows easily shot into the masses, taking out a few more goblins. The steady advance turned into a frantic mess as the goblins knew they were close. They suddenly charged with a howl, only a dozen paces away.

"Hold your spears up, boys!"

"For King Alfred!"

"Two fire!"

The archers were renewed, but was it too late? The goblins were upon them. Some fell, but many reached the spears and leapt right at them. Several fell right there but opened the way as goblins leapt in and swung furiously, tossing spears aside and smashing shields. Boys whimpered as they retreated and rolled away in pain and exhaustion, fearing that a goblin scimitar would suddenly swing down upon them.

"Three fire!"

Up close, a few more goblins fell, but more leapt in and easily broke the spear wall. The next wave of goblins rushed in to finish the children.

"King Alfred!"

The goblins were fierce and easily breaking the grouping of spears, swinging with their strength, throwing the boys and their spears aside. Alfred knew they could not match their strength and ferocity. He knew all was lost. There were too many of them.

Then the goblins froze and stood. They howled and gritted their sharp teeth. They stepped backwards.

"Gaargh!" a large goblin yelled. It was not a roar of ferocity but one of panic. He kicked a boy down hard, raising his curved scimitar to strike, but was knocked back by another goblin. They began to back-pedal and run away down the slope, screeching and yelping.

Loranna wanted to fire but wasn't sure. So she held her

hand steady.

Nearly forty goblins retreated, most in good fighting condition. The larger among them hobbled back with arrows in their feet. They fled into the forest, one by one. Finally, the last, a formidable creature, looked back and roared in frustration as he entered the forest.

Alfred could not believe it. He must be dead, in a dream just before dying. He was stunned, sweating and filthy. He glared at the blood on his hands, Cory's, his own from gashes, and the sticky black blood of goblins.

The children began to cry. Boys lay stunned and shocked in the mud, knowing that a heavy crude blade was about to descend on them. Girls lay strewn about with broken bows and crushed fingers, hugging and shivering.

Alfred looked at the children he led into this horrific nightmare. He gritted his teeth in his muddy, sweaty, cold exhaustion.

One of their youngest and most brave girls was lying pale on the ground. Her head had a huge gash in it with blood trickling out. Loranna knelt down to cradle her and cry quietly. Cory fell down so weak from the loss of blood. It was as if all their spirit had left them.

Bewildered by the goblins' sudden departure, Alfred slowly turned around, struggling to focus. He gazed at the next hillock. Three horses were standing there, and upon them, three knights.

Book Two
Chapter Nineteen

The Knights

Alfred wiped aside his matted hair. Dust and sweat trickled into his eyes, causing them to sting. His hands were filthy with dirt and blood, he couldn't clear his eyes. He tried to look at the knights as their horses trotted slowly down toward him. He was sure they were knights by their helmets and tunics and the chain and plate mail they were wearing. They carried lances, spears, swords and shields, and they looked magnificent. They were true knights.

As they got closer, he could see that they were worn and tired, not at all what he thought he saw a moment ago. The children scooted in behind him.

The knights' mail was rusted and grimy. Their tunics were tattered with holes and filth. They were hunched over and frail. One had a small metal cap on his crusty head with tattered, dirty hair.

"We need help!" Alfred cried out regardless.

The knights did not answer. Keeping their lances ready, they reached the small knoll that Alfred and his group stood upon. Their horses were gaunt, with ribs showing, and there were many sores and growths on their tangled hides.

"Are you knights?" Alfred trembled. The calming of nerves as the goblins retreated had been too brief, and now he was seeing these strange, weary-looking men.

The knights did not answer.

"They are the witch's own. Gorbogal must have sway over them!" Loranna cried out, holding Setheyna.

"Dare thee say that name in our presence? I shall hew thee down now!" It was a guttural voice echoing from one of the crusty helmets.

One knight hit his horse several times with his spurs. The horse lumbered forward slowly. The children sat in the mud in front of them, and the horse did not seem inclined to walk over them.

"Are you hungry!?" Alfred asked.

The knight stopped. The other knights made their first sudden movement since Alfred spotted them, turning their full attention on Alfred.

"We have food," Alfred said nervously, turning to

Loranna and pulling dried meat and stale bread from her pack.

The second knight, with his helmet still on, came off his horse. The first knight, with his lance still pointed at them, though its point had long ago been sheared off, warned, "Gorham, stay!"

But Gorham walked past the first knight's lance and pulled out a rusty dagger. He made his way to Alfred, who barely revealed the food before Gorham took it and pushed Alfred aside. He pulled off his helmet and ate it greedily, keeping his rusty dagger pointed at the children.

"Gorham!" the first said, thrusting his lance at him.

Gorham grabbed the end of the lance and pushed it aside. "I am your servant, knight, but not on an empty stomach! Not to the brink of death!" He ate greedily, eyeing the stale bread as a treasure.

The other two could not control themselves much longer. The first knight dropped his lance and slid quickly off his horse. Alfred got out more food.

"It's all we have," Loranna said with tears, holding the girl's wound to slow the bleeding.

Alfred paused and looked at Loranna with her moist reddened eyes. His focus went to Setheyna, who was barely breathing. Loranna's sleeve and dress were filthy and stained in Setheyna's blood.

Alfred turned back just as the first knight threw off his helmet, grabbed the food, and walked back eating in small bites. His gums were rotten. Each bite looked painful, but he was too hungry to allow that to stop him. The third knight, the one with the cap and the oldest, came up and reached out his hand for food. His eyes were forlorn.

Alfred gave him the last of it. The knight bowed and took the food. He ate it with much care as his fingers trembled.

"Alfred, she is dying," Loranna said. Others sat down by Loranna, crying.

Alfred looked at the children.

"Why are you here, boy?" the first knight asked, "with your bows and arrows fighting goblins?"

"Can't you see, Lord Dunther?" said the sad elder knight. "They are hungry. They are hunting. They have no men to feed them."

"They're doing better than us!" Gorham said, swallowing before he had fully chewed his food. Nearly choking, he coughed his food out and had no shame in picking it up off the wet earth and continuing to chew on it once again.

They were filthy and vile looking, with tangled hair and wrinkled coarse faces. They did not look much better than the goblins.

"Boy, answer me! Why are you here?" Lord Dunther said with his mouth full of food.

"We are hunting. That meat you're eating is a bikehnbar we killed in this forest days ago. We came hoping to find more."

The knights paused for a moment. Then Gorham and Dunther burst into laughter. It was a difficult laugh, as if they had not laughed in many years. It sounded more like a cough, with food falling everywhere and them greedily picking it up.

"I don't know why you two are laughing," the sad knight said. "The proof is in your hands and bellies."

The others shrugged. "Don't lie to me, boy," Dunther

said. "Where are your men? Who gave you those weapons?"

"He did," said Cory, crying out in pain and pointing to Alfred. "He is our king and lord!"

Alfred flinched, feeling incredibly uneasy about that claim in front of these decrepit knights.

Dunther and Gorham were now ready to laugh fully, having cleared the years of phlegm and feeling moisture in their dry throats once again. And so they did.

"Well, that explains it then," Gorham said. "A boy is claiming to be king. Well, why not? There is no one here, the land is lost, and the witch rules over men. Why shouldn't a lost boy make such a claim? It makes perfect sense!"

Lord Dunther eyed Alfred. "Boy, are you king, hey?" Then Dunther approached him. The mildewed leather and cloth he wore crinkled and his rusty chain and plate echoed with each step.

Alfred staggered back in fear. Dunther was big. Though sallow and gaunt, though sagging and tattered, he still seemed huge. And now with a filled stomach, he seemed alive.

"Well, are you king? Huh, boy? King?" Dunther pushed Alfred's lanky shoulder and it gave in easily. The children did not like this. Many stood up with bows and spears at the ready. Despairing as they were, no one was to push their king.

"Maybe you should be king? Hey Dunther? And you could rule over these grand people." Gorham laughed at his own joke.

"Not a bad idea." Dunther smiled, revealing swollen gums and blackened and brown teeth.

Much to Dunther's surprise, Alfred pushed him back,

catching him off guard. But even with as much force as Alfred used and as worn as Dunther appeared, the Lord Knight immediately gained the upper hand and twisted Alfred around, using momentum, and tossed him aside. Ripe with tears and spittle, Alfred fell to the wet muddy earth.

Dunther tramped after him and easily picked up Alfred by the shirt. "I will put you in your place, boy!"

"You are Lord Dunther, Royal Baron Knight of King Athelrod!" Alfred yelled.

Dunther dropped him and seemed dizzy. Gorham was silent. The sad knight walked over to Loranna and looked at the wounded girl.

"Who told you this!" Dunther hissed.

"Verboden!" Alfred said. "He went out to look for you, to help us."

"The cleric?" Gorham asked. "Did you hear that, Gylloth? Your cleric friend has returned."

Gylloth, the sorrowful knight kneeling before the girl, spoke, "Perhaps, he never left, and it is we who have returned, or wandered back into our homeland."

Dunther looked at Gylloth with vicious eyes. Gylloth returned Dunther's gaze, and then both turned away.

"She is gravely wounded," said Gylloth. "I have a salve that may stay the fever and blood loss."

"Nay, Gylloth. That is the last of our medicine!" Dunther said.

Alfred's eyes widened and met Loranna's, "You must help her!"

Dunther swatted Alfred with sudden harshness, driving Alfred's face into the mud. "Dare tell us what to do, boy!"

"Dare you to touch him again!" Cory yelled in anguish. Dunther turned to see a dozen bows aimed and many spears pointed at him.

Gorham drew his rusty sword, ready to attack on Dunther's command. Gorham was the tough fighter, always ready to do his lord's bidding.

Lord Gylloth, the kind, older knight, spoke softly, "If I were to have such loyal servants, I would certainly feel like a king." Gylloth approached Cory with open hands. Cory was faint, pale from blood loss. His shoulder was swollen and black from the arrow wound. Gylloth moved slowly due to his age. As he neared, he smiled gently and nodded reassurance. Cory leaned in as Gylloth examined the wound.

"Help him down quickly," Lord Gylloth said to nearby boys. Gylloth searched within his many tattered clothes, belts and pouches. Several tore off from rot. "No, not that one."

"Don't waste it!" Dunther said. The children kept their bows taut even longer than they did in the Dark Forest. Many had determined faces. "Easy now."

"Dunther, he's using our salve!" said Gorham, waving his sword at the children, ready to strike.

"Gorham, you make things harder than they really need to be. Do not interfere." Gylloth administered the green pasty salve with his dirty fingers on both Cory and Setheyna. "Sorry for the filth," he said gently to Loranna. "This will not heal them, but it should give us time."

Gorham simmered with rage. He wanted to strike out.

Alfred finally stood up, wiping blood from his nose. "You must have many aches and wounds, huh Dunther?" Dunther met Alfred's eyes, as they both shared a hatred for each other. "Verboden will help you. And we can mend your armour and weapons back at the castle."

"Castle? What castle?" Gorham wiped his nervous brow, still pointing his sword at the armed children.

"Grotham Castle, I mean Grotham Keep," Alfred said.

The knights looked at him in unison.

"I am Alfred, son of Bedenwulf and Ethralia, grandson of Athelrod, and King of Grotham Keep," Alfred said. No one responded. Alfred walked around his archers and spearmen to help Gylloth with Cory and Setheyna. Dunther wanted to follow him and cause more harm.

"If this is true, Dunther, then you struck your king," Gylloth said.

"That is but a bastard boy!" Gorham pointed his cruddy sword at Alfred. More children stood with their weapons ready, enraged at both knights.

"Put your blade down, Gorham," Dunther said.

"What!? You believe him!?"

"It does not matter right now." Dunther eyed the children. They have kept their bows taut for some time. He could see the strain on their angered faces. "Now!"

Gorham sheathed his sword and spat. Dunther walked back to his horse, gripping the reins to hold it steady as he leaned on it. He began to think in silence.

Chapter Twenty

A Loyal Knight

The knights followed at a distance behind the children, behind Alfred. When Grotham Keep was in sight, activity upon the walls and smoke from chimneys could be seen. Gorham and Dunther galloped ahead, not looking at the tired and worn children. Gylloth walked among them, having Setheyna and Cory ride on his gaunt horse. Cory held her as best he could, still struggling with his painful wound.

"Do you know Verboden?" Alfred asked Gylloth, who was walking beside him.

"Yes, a cleric of the Order of Light, having status of a friar at one time, as I recall." Gylloth thought of distant memories. "Long ago, though he was a cleric, he was servant to Tirnalth, a great wizard and counsel to the king—a counsel to many kings, they say. Verboden was young when I last saw him and if I recall correctly, a very quiet fellow. I'm glad he's still alive. I remember..." Gylloth looked at Alfred, who couldn't help stare at the knight's ragged appearance. Gylloth didn't mind.

"You have your mother's eyes," Gylloth said.

Alfred looked away but then at him, and they both smiled.

Alfred entered the castle amidst a busy affair, but everyone went silent and crowded around Dunther and Gorham. The steward, Abedeyan, who had been trying anxiously to convince people of something, grew silent when Alfred drew near.

Dunther and Gorham did not look pleased. Dunther opened the way for Alfred and looked at him with disdain in his eyes. "Even if he is of the line, he is tainted. He isn't even a knight! Look at him."

The people's faces turned down. Alfred tensed and then bowed to one knee. "Then, Lord Dunther, I ask you to make me a knight. I care not for your mercy, but only to be given a chance."

Dunther stood back and shared a confused look with Gorham. The people swelled together to see what would happen. Gylloth walked in with the children. Lady Nihan, caring not for such feuding, rushed to help the wounded.

Alfred slowly looked up, wondering what Dunther

would do. Dunther pulled out his sword and pointed it at Alfred.

"You are not worthy of knighthood. You are not worthy of kingship. And I shall never knight a tainted boy such as you." His words dug deep into Alfred. Dunther strode off. "Servants, I need a bath and meal. Now!"

Alfred rose with weak knees as Abedeyan caught him. "King Alfred, I shall throw them knights out. They don't belong here. How dare he insult you! He is as brazen as ever. The suffering of the people, the fall of the kingdom, and the plague of the land has not affected his stubborn idiocy! Why did you kneel to that toad?!"

"I saw it in a movie once and thought it might work." Seeing Abedeyan's confused expression, Alfred tried to explain, "A movie is like theatre, you know. But never mind, Abedeyan. Let them stay whether he believes I'm the king or not. Even I'm not so sure I am. I just hope he'll help us." And with that, Alfred fainted.

Gorham and Dunther showed no care for those around them, but they still expected much care from them. They sat chewing on more salted meat and dry bread then was worthy of their share and motioned for the servants to wait on them. Lady Nihan directed the workers, rolling up her own sleeves to help.

They began by untying the straps that held the armour. Their knots tied long ago, merely crumbled or broke as they were pulled off. The outer wear was like onions. The servants peeled off each layer, revealing a grotesque layer underneath. The rusty plates came off, exposing a layer of rusted chain mail, all of its rings broken into sections with holes filled long ago by dirt, grime and rust. When the chain came off, it tore away padded clothes that seemed to have grown into the iron mesh.

As Lady Nihan and a servant pulled away the conglomeration of chain and clothes, exposing skin, a foul stench came out, setting both back for several moments. Flies and gnats flew out or fell out as did the larva of various insects. The skin would have been the palest white were it not for eruptions of red rashes, purple boils, yellow pustules and green abscesses. Lady Nihan had to summon all her strength to pick with a knife at the flesh eating larva that squirmed amongst those boils and rashes, abscesses and pustules. One servant fainted.

The knights merely twitched with each knife poke or pulling away of tattered clothes and disintegrated skin. They kept eating as others stood around hungry. All of what they had been wearing was boiled or burned. Boggin, the armourer was not sure he could repair anything. He banged a breastplate on his knee, and it cracked in two.

Their bodies were gangly and not much larger than those of peasants, but their arrogance and snobbery relayed that they were royalty. That is, this was the manner of Gorham and Lord Dunther. Gylloth was polite and seemed to have less of the royalty affliction.

They spent several days in hot baths. Gorham and Dunther sang song after song, ordering the poor servants to scrub their bleeding and puss ridden backs. To the knights it seemed as if they had an itch or two that had not been scratched in twelve years and now, finally, they were getting their satisfaction.

They had only begun to display their snobbery. Once

they were clean and well fed, all other important work had to stop so that their armour and weapons could be repaired or, if not repaired, then replaced. Broggia the smith tried to tell them that nails and tools were still needed by many in the castle and on the farms. Abedeyan supported him, attempting to persuade the knights that other work was crucial, but Gorham pushed the old steward aside, and Dunther declared to all within earshot that their foremost duty was to the knights. He warned that any who didn't obey, would be cast out.

Broggia and Boggin began the long tedious task. In days gone by, this work would have been done in a timely manner. But now, with the quality of workmanship the knights expected, with limited materials and with the realm's only two smiths taxed already, it would take weeks if not months to refurbish or remake their suits of armour.

A few days after their arrival, Verboden arrived with the two dozen hungry bandits. Immediately he went to heal Setheyna and Cory. When the knights found out about this, they yelled at him, saying that their aches and pains were more important. By treating someone else, they argued, he had done them a great dishonor!

Also, they wanted to hear Verboden's views on the boy's claim of kingship. Verboden spoke to them in private, doing his best to support Alfred, but to everyone's dismay Gorham and Dunther still were not convinced.

And they went on enjoying themselves at everyone else's expense. They expected ale and wine. They told ladies, boiling water for laundry, to begin making ale for them immediately or they would cut their throats. Perhaps this was a mock threat, because they laughed. But their deranged looks were quite awful to the ladies.

Abedeyan knew this was going too far. Verboden was called on to speak to them repeatedly about their behavior. In these hard times the ladies should not be required to undertake such a time consuming process, especially as they had little barley and oats These knights' threats left them distraught. Yet somehow the two received mugs of ale and were showing them off as they got drunk.

Verboden slept for many days after healing Setheyna, Cory and the knights. Rumors had it that he himself cast his spells of sustenance—not for the hungry and needy but to cater to the selfish knights' need for drink.

Alfred finally recovered from a fever that kept him bedridden for days. Abedeyan went to him and told him that the knights were acting as warlords, taking over the castle with fear.

"Where is Gylloth?" Alfred asked.

"He is in the small chapel. I reckon he is praying for the last twelve years of his life, the many sins, I do not doubt, he committed with Gorham and Dunther."

"What of Broggia and Boggin? I hear they are laboring over the knights' armour."

"Yes," said Abedeyan. "The work is too much for father and son, the crazy goons! Neither was trained for such master craftsmanship, and making these repairs is a sheer waste of their valuable time!"

Alfred was beside himself with anger, pacing, thinking. "...And who are these other men that came with Verboden?"

"They are bandits he met on the road," said Abedeyan. "He fed them, and now they are willing and able to help. They are good men. Most were farmers in the surrounding country just west of here. They experienced much loss..."

"Are they warriors? Can they fight?" Alfred asked, pondering.

"Well, they are bandits and lived in dangerous lands all these years. I reckon they have some skill..."

"Let's go meet them!"

The bedraggled bandits lay in the half built stables where a few goats were tied. The men were snoring, resting peacefully with their tight shrunken stomachs full of a farmer's meal. Hedor was awake, sitting quietly in the back shadows as Alfred and Abedeyan entered.

Alfred walked around them, looking at them. The weariness of this life was on their faces, from the very young boys to the old feeble ones. All were gaunt, dirty and ragged. Alfred picked up a weapon. It was but a hoe wrapped with rotted leather and a stone added to give it weight. He put it down and picked up another implement, a small wood axe that had been repaired with additional branches to reinforce the broken handle.

"They're not much of warriors, just thugs," Alfred said quietly to Abedeyan.

Hedor spoke from the shadows. "Deagle, Snig, most were farmers. Gjorg and Smillin were carpenters. Ruig and I worked in the king's mines long ago."

"Mines?" Abedeyan asked. "We are in need of ore. We have a little that we've scavenged off of dead goblins and ratkins."

"Forget it, old man," said Hedor. "The caves haven't been mined since the fall of the king. There's no telling what lies within those dark tunnels."

"We'll worry about that later. First, I need your help, the men's help," Alfred replied.

"How can we be of service?" Hedor leered with rotted gums.

"Watch your tongue, commoner. This is the king, and what he says is law." Abedeyan stepped forward, sternly pointing an old wrinkled finger.

"Naw, you don't have to listen to me if you don't want to." Alfred crouched near Hedor to speak quietly.

Hedor shirked back. Alfred seemed a bit too close.

"We're in trouble. I have two knights that are creating problems. They don't like me as the king. They're eating all the food, making everyone work for them and..."

Hedor stood up. "Just tell me where they are."

Alfred and Abedeyan were impressed at first. However, that faded as they saw Hedor more clearly. His visage, viler than the meanest of Gorham's looks, was not all that comforting.

"Uh, wait, I don't want to kill them or anything." Alfred stood up and smiled meekly.

Abedeyan nodded in agreement. "Yes, no fighting."

"Oh?" Hedor sighed.

"Let's just kick them out," said Alfred. "Maybe that will change their attitude."

Hedor spat on the ground. "Knights changing their att-i-tude? After twelve years of death and famine, goblins raiding at will, killing fathers of wives and children, and all the knights can do is whine and complain about themselves? If that won't change their minds, I don't know what will."

The mood was somber. Hedor must have suffered greatly. Alfred stood next to Hedor. "Well, I know what you mean. But we can't go about fighting each other when we have so much building to do. I just want to show them force, you know, that we're united and can push them out. Maybe when they're standing out there, they'll realize something or go away. I don't care. I don't want to kill them. We have a chance here of doing something good for everyone."

Hedor, with the weight of his memories, shrugged. "What's your plan?"

"To rid us of those idiots!" Alfred smiled.

"Give us a look, hey?" Gorham said to a young lady who dropped off more food. Drunk to the gills, he was trying to fondle her. His rotted teeth and gums were not too enticing. Nor was his countenance. In a land struggling to survive after so many years of turmoil, this knight seemed less concerned about the troubles of others than his own pleasure. Dunther sat across the table, drink in hand, waiting for his turn. The young lady was red-faced and fearful. She tried to leave but with each attempt at departure was pulled back in.

"Come on, you haven't finished yet, have you?" Gorham chuckled.

"I think she has, Gorham," said Alfred, walking in and motioning to the lady that she could leave, "and I think you have as well!" The lady left with great relief, thanking Alfred on the way out.

Gorham and Dunther had holed up in one of the towers, making it their lair as it were. They had kicked out the three families who were residing there. They still had the keg of ale that Verboden created for them. Alfred was furious with him for making ale when many were starving. He spoke to Verboden angrily about it as the cleric was woken from his

198

long sleep having used up too much of his powers.

"They are the Royal Knights," Verboden had said. "They are second to the king."

"I don't care! They are worthless to us! They're just drunks and jerks who act tough and probably are, so they bully everyone. That's all a knight is, a bully! That is probably all a king is too, just a gang boss, a warlord. I'm not going to be like that, and I'm not going to let them bully everyone. We have too much to do, and too much is at stake!"

Verboden, lying quietly under comfortable covers, had turned to Alfred and fixed him in a drowsy gaze. Before lapsing into a long deep sleep, he said, "I'm sorry."

"Well, what do you want, boy!?" Dunther said, waking from his drunken stupor.

"I want you two out of here. I want you to leave us. We'll give you food and water and your horses and armour. Then leave."

"Our armour is not done!" Gorham thundered, waving his finger, sipping from his mug.

"Your armour will never be done, not the way you want it to be. We have cleaned your old armour as best we can. Take it and your arms and your horses and leave."

"You don't tell us what to do, boy! How dare you!" Dunther rose from the table, lifting his dagger to point at Alfred.

"Then, we do it my way," Alfred said.

Loranna and her archers appeared from above with all their arrows pointed down at them.

Dunther and Gorham looked up perplexed. Alfred stepped back. "I will have them shoot if you do not drop your weapons and come out."

The knights, fully loaded, gazed vacantly at the girls. To see them poking their heads through the upper balcony railing, looking down at them, was amusing at best. Ignoring drawn bows, the men laughed raucously, clicking their mugs in toast, slapping their small table with uncaring hands.

Alfred did not know what to do. This was too confusing. Some of the girls started to giggle. More upset, Alfred lifted his arm as if to order arrows to be fired. Loranna and the girls nervously aimed. Hedor grabbed his arm from behind and tugged at him to leave.

"No, boy," he said. "Let them laugh."

"Girls?!"

"He brings little girls with toy arrows?"

Throttled in this way, Alfred was further perturbed. Hedor could see this. "Leave it to me, young king. Drunken brutes like that have a pattern. I know."

Alfred nodded, still worked up. He waved at the girls. They climbed down from the tower, some giggling while others elbowed them to be quiet. Alfred looked at them all sternly and motioned for them to leave.

"Come the morrow — you'll see, boy," said Hedor. "Go and get some rest. We'll take care of this." His mates in crime smiled with pleasure, many with black gums and missing teeth.

"No killing," Alfred said.

"Oh no!" they all said in return. "Not a hair!"

Hedor kept his word. Alfred woke to distant echoes of laughter. He dressed quickly and ran out to find Hedor and his men on the wall facing outward, laughing. The peasants and workers were there too, but they looked forlorn. Alfred clambered up the stone stairs to look over the wall.

There in the field, waking up and dressing themselves in the cold, were Dunther and Gorham. Both looked terrible, and of course, they were angry. Beside them, along with their horses, was a pile of their belongings.

"Now run you off, maggots!" Hedor yelled.

Alfred looked closely at him and his friends. "You're drunk!"

"Oh, 'tis okay, I'm a good drunk!" Hedor said with a laugh. His men next to him all had mugs or bowls of ale.

"That is so lame!" Alfred said.

"Don't worry. We are just finishing it off. Besides, it's a meal in a mug! Now come on young king, we did what you asked. They've been taken care of, and we're not rude like them. We're simple folk."

"Bandit folk, we are!" said a younger man, flashing a drunken, evil-looking grin.

"Well, we are in times of need — in times of need only," Hedor said. He tried to be somber, but as he met the eyes of his fellow thieves, he let out a laugh with them.

"Hey you, who put us out!?" Gorham yelled from the field.

Hedor and the crew began their laughter anew, pointing derisively at the two abandoned knights. Dunther sat dressing in his armour, fully aware of his predicament. Gorham was still unclear as to what happened.

"Who are they laughing at?" Gorham asked.

"At you, Gorham, at us." Dunther put on his old worn clothes.

"What do we do?"

"Get on your armour."

Once the knights were somewhat dressed and somewhat armed, they mounted their horses and stared up at the walls of the castle, at Hedor and at Alfred.

"I don't know why you gave them their weapons, sire," said Hedor to Alfred. "They are much too dangerous."

"Well, there are goblins about, and I want them to be able to defend themselves."

Hedor and the bandits gave signs making a mockery of the knights. Alfred noticed. "Stop it! All of you, stop it!"

"Hey, we're just having a bit of fun," Hedor said.

"I don't care. Just go. And—and thank you." Alfred watched the knights. He expected to feel satisfaction. Instead he felt sadness.

Some of the younger bandits wanted to continue the fun, but Hedor pushed and herded them down the stairs. One became belligerent, leading Hedor to knock the bowl of ale from his hands. The young one shoved Hedor back. All were stunned and fell silent.

Hedor threw down his own ale and begin knocking down the rest of their mugs and bowls of ale. "Now, do as the king says and go and clean yourselves up! Now!"

As they left, Alfred looked at the peasants and workers to gauge their reaction. They looked forlorn at the knights' predicament. With tears in their eyes, they looked at the knights. Alfred walked up to them. "What's wrong?"

"We've abandoned the knights, milord," a lady finally said.

"What do you mean? They were mean to us."

"Yes, that is true. They were. But they also protect us

and are our champions."

Alfred shook his head. "No," he said. "We will protect ourselves. We will be our own champions. If they want to join with us, then great. But if they're going to oppress us and take everything and tell us what to do, then forget it."

The peasants and workers listened to Alfred with a sense of wonder and perplexity. Many nodded. All remained silent and somber. The lady nodded, wiped her tears and went down the stairs. The others followed.

Alfred was alone on the wall. He looked out at the two knights. They were mounted and motionless. Gorham looked from Dunther to Alfred and remained silent.

Alfred and Dunther looked at each other from a long distance. Alfred felt as if Dunther was shaking the very foundation of his resolve. He began to shiver. Fear, doubt and uncertainty grew within him. As if all else did not matter, he wanted to open the gate and let them back in, with their might and strength. He turned to go down the stone stairway.

"Don't you let him do it to you, boy king. Don't you let Dunther have his way." It was Gylloth, dressed in a simple robe with a belt and sword, looking up at Alfred from the lower steps.

Alfred took a deep relaxing breath, as if releasing a ghost. He stepped back up to the wall and looked out at Lord Dunther again. Gylloth came up and stood beside him.

Dunther was visibly upset now. He turned on his horse and rode off. Gorham, sharing one last glare with Gylloth, turned and followed.

Chapter Twenty One

Loranna

After Cory's wound healed, he and Alfred focused on toughening up the boys and improving their spear skills. Remembering the ferocity of the goblins, the boys learned better ways of protecting themselves from goblin attacks. They rushed about the tunnels below the Keep, wrestling and screaming and yelling. Alfred and Cory decided to look and behave like goblins. They told the boys, "We'll be right back," and rushed away. They put on goblin helms and dirtied their faces with mud. Then they rushed in screaming and yelling. A few of the boys fled. The second in command, Wilden, quickly formed up a wall of spears and had the remaining boys jabbing at Cory and Alfred.

Both backed away, swinging wildly at the boys. The younger boys, remembering the goblins' viciousness, would pull back as Alfred and Cory swung. But then they would move right back in to fill the gaps and prevent a charge. The boys who fled returned and joined the lines, encouraged by the braver ones. Wilden and the boys then advanced. Alfred and Cory quickly surmised that they had been beaten back and took off their goblin helms and rubbed the mud from their faces. There were great cheers from all the boys as they passed the test.

There were many such drills, including having the boys with large shields charge the archers. Loranna got the girls to form three lines of archers with their small goblin bows. Loranna then yelled, "One fire! Two fire! Three fire!" A hail of clay and cloth tipped arrows flew at Alfred, Cory, Wilden and the boys. The drill was to ensure that the archers would be able to fire under pressure as an enemy charged. A few boys in the lines, using sticks as spears, held off the charging boys. The exercise was a great success. All gained valuable experience along with many bruises.

From time to time Alfred or Cory would get through and swing their sticks at the archers. Each day someone would cry from an injury, bruise, cut or just plain aches and pains. Alfred established that anyone who got hurt would receive immediate attention from Loranna and several of the older girls. He decided to have a few classes on first aid, as he called it. Whenever there was an injury during the practices, the children would cry out "Medic!" The worst incident was when a little girl got her eye poked by a stick and her eyelid began to bleed. Many of the children fainted and after that, were reluctant to continue with training.

The girl got better after a while, though her eyelid had a small scar. The whole experience had Alfred worried. He was constantly reminded that this was dangerous and not at all a game. With spears, arrows and fighting, he had to take the training seriously and be careful. He had to make sure all the rambunctious children understood the dangers as well.

All the training weapons were modified with some kind of padding, a wrapping made of old cloth or leather bits on each end. Many children fashioned their own helmets and skull caps from the pile of goblin armour that Alfred collected from Lady Nihan's cleaning. Every other morning they paraded out of the castle and onto fields for military exercises. Many of the farmers, most being parents, would come to watch for a few moments during their hard working days.

Cory and Alfred devised better weapons for the tight corridors in the dungeon. They received the shields with spikes and a pie-cut hole to jab a spear through. The smiths had added small nails on the sticks of the spears, below the heads. These hurt the ratkins when they grabbed at them and hopefully dissuaded them from trying to grab again.

The shields were large enough to be held by one boy to block a dungeon corridor while another boy jabbed a spear through. There were many corridors with most ending at the doors that led up into the Great Hall. These were the strategic points where the boys needed to hold off the ratkins if Alfred's plan was to work.

One day as Alfred was on the wall of the Keep, leaning on the battlement, watching the sun go down and thinking of his mother, Loranna climbed up the steep stone stairs. "Alfred? Milord?"

Alfred turned toward her. Her presence comforted him in his loneliness. His frustrations seemed to diminish, if but for a moment, whenever she was near. She had her bow and quiver of arrows with her.

"Are you practicing?" Alfred asked nervously.

"Always milord." Loranna smiled, walking close to him.

"Uh, that's good. I, uh, I'm sorry about that swing. Are you okay," Alfred asked.

Loranna showed a small bruise. "It's just another small bruise. How are you feeling from all those shots you took?"

Alfred pulled his shirt up to reveal several bruises where arrows had hit him. "Oh, uh, sore but I think it will be okay. Hey, don't touch it!"

Loranna smiled, lightly punching Alfred on the shoulder. "I came up to say thank you. You've done a lot for us, King Alfred. And I'm glad you forced those rude knights to leave."

It seemed to Alfred that with each sentence, she moved a little closer to him. She leaned against the wall, looking out onto the land, as if unaware of how close she was getting with each sigh or stretch.

Alfred stepped aside slowly. Still, each time she told him something new she drew nearer.

"The girls and boys are coming along nicely. Broggia has figured out that the goblins string their bows wrong. They don't use all the bow's strength. We're bending them backwards, against the shape, and it is making a big difference!" Loranna slid closer.

"Oh, that's great." Alfred leaned away, just a bit.

"And we're getting stronger too. We can shoot twice as fast and twice as far. Look!" Loranna showed her muscular young arm, flexing the small yet strong bicep. She leaned in. "Touch it! Go on!"

Alfred meekly pinched the bicep, gulping.

"Still, I think you showed the bigger boys what was missing. They do a lot of huffing and puffing and gallivanting about, but they still need to learn to be strong, to be courageous." Loranna leaned in close, looking straight into Alfred's eyes.

Alfred blinked... and then blinked some more.

Loranna seemed to notice something on his face and she picked at it gently. She rubbed whatever it was nonchalantly. Alfred backed off, rubbed his own face and looked to see what it was. Loranna began sighing with the evening breeze and smelling the air.

"I can smell it, Alfred. I can smell what you've done."

"What I've done?" Alfred was confused. She was silent, taking in the scents and smells, breathing in and lifting her arms to the cool summer breeze. Alfred was curious. He stepped close to take in what she was sensing. "What do you smell?" He lifted his arms to smell his pits. His face was not so keen after that.

But Loranna was talking about something else. She twirled and then stood as if ready to dance. Her eyes were closed, and she was using her other senses. She turned on her toes and landed close to him, opening her eyes and looking at him sweetly. "Life!" She kissed his cheek and backed off.

Alfred was stunned, paralyzed actually. While he stood still as a stone, she moved about him, dancing with the breeze and twirling in joy. "I smell life, Alfred. For the first time, I feel this land has awakened and is alive."

She ended her dance close to him, arms spread out as if ready to accept his embrace. Never has anyone seen a boy in such terror and fright. A horde of goblins or a giant spider could have been rushing at Alfred, or evil darkness closing in on him, but none of that would have frozen the young king with such terror as this young girl standing open armed before him.

Embarrassed, Alfred turned and looked down at the workers and peasants. Abedeyan and Lady Nihan, from the inner ward, were looking up at them. As Alfred met their gaze, they immediately turned and began arguing about something, as if they were working and had not noticed. Both suddenly became angry at each other, huffed, and turned to go about their business.

Alfred blinked and turned to look another way. He saw Cory and the children staring up, but when their eyes met Alfred's, they suddenly turned away and began wrestling and tumbling and rolling. Cory was barking out odd orders and cheering them on. Soon they scattered out of view, heading back inside the Great Hall. Alfred blinked again. His gaze drifted out into the hills, dotted with farmsteads and fields of rich green crops. The scene was illumined by a warm crimson sunset. Farmers strolled about, talking with each other while smoking pipes. Sheep grazed in pastures.

"Uh, how's your mother and father?" asked Alfred, feeling a bit crowded.

"Oh, they are fine!" Loranna said, twirling again as she glanced at Alfred. "They're happy and in love. They're working hard on the land and have strong, growing children."

Alfred wiped his mouth and loosened his already torn and loose collar. "Yeah, that's good."

"Tell me Alfred, what would make you happy!?" Loranna asked, spinning blithely again.

Alfred didn't know it would happen, but it did. It came out so suddenly that he could not contain it. "To see my mom." And with that he began to cry, nearly falling as he folded to hide his face.

Loranna, being so close, caught him and hugged him. He was embarrassed again and wanted to turn away, but Loranna would not have it. She held him quietly for a long time.

Chapter Twenty Two

The Harvest and Looming Threat

Alfred felt better. His mood improved every time the children were near. He felt part of a family and a greater cause when the children came to the castle. There were sounds of laughter and talk about what was in store each day. Loranna's presence was comforting to him. She would touch his shoulder or give him quick hugs. They were kind and gentle, almost motherly. He knew there was something growing between them that was difficult to explain, even in this story.

Loranna kept everyone's spirits up. She would say encouraging words. "The harvest will be soon! We'll have plenty to eat! All will be good and fair!"

"Yay! Woo hoo!" the children would sing out.

Alfred found his shyness around the girls his age perplexing. He couldn't stop sweating and gulping.

The girls were practicing archery at one end of the Great Hall. They moved in formation, firing at the targets. The boys were taking a break. They had climbed out of the great hole with their spears and shields and were sitting around. Alfred and Cory sat at a bench, drinking herbal brewed water.

Loranna often danced around Alfred, and today was no different. Cory and the boys rolled their eyes and giggled, elbowing each other. "There will be a great feast, a fall feast at harvest," she sang as she circled Alfred. "I think this will be the grandest one of all. Many farmers have returned to the land. Many crops are full and ready to be harvested. The sheep, goat and pigs are bearing young. All is growing again. Love is in the air."

Cory and the others stared wide eyed and open mouthed at her.

She stopped her dance, curtsying in front of Alfred. "How old are you, Alfred?"

The boys looked at each other.

"Me!?" Alfred gulped his water, trying to make it seem as if his throat was dry, very, very dry. "Uh, I'm eleven."

She shrugged, "Me too." Loranna danced slowly, humming as she drew ever nearer.

Cory could not help but jab Alfred.

"Wait, what did you say?" Alfred straightened up.

Loranna stopped and smiled. "Yes, Alfred?"

"Harvest?"

"Yes, King Alfred, harvest," she chimed.

"Harvest? When? How soon?" Alfred stood up.

"The harvest will be at the end of this month. After the

hay has been cut and dried, we will harvest all the food!" Loranna continued dancing as she spoke.

Alfred paced in front of everyone, "I remember something about harvest—that, well... that is when the goblins raid. That is when they come to take the food!"

Loranna stopped dancing. Cory stood next to Alfred.

"Is this right?" Alfred asked.

Loranna and Cory looked at each other. Both nodded.

"That is when our fathers take us to hidden caves with what food we can carry, and we wait in the darkness hoping not to be found." Loranna and the rest bowed their heads, as if remembering a distant nightmare yet from not so long ago.

Alfred walked off.

Loranna went after him. "Not this time! Now that you and Verboden are here, things will be different. Not now! Things are better!"

Alfred looked into Loranna's eyes. "I don't think so. This is the first harvest since I've been here. We don't know what will happen. I must go talk to Verboden."

Verboden was in a white robe, kneeling in the small chapel, a small stone room at the rear of the Keep. A servant was patching one of its walls when Alfred hurriedly entered.

"Verboden, harvest is soon," he blurted out.

"Yes, I know." Verboden kept his eyes closed, praying.

"Didn't you say that the goblins raid each year after harvest?"

The servant looked up from his work and gulped.

"Yes," Verboden said while continuing to pray.

Alfred stood before him. "Well, what do we do?"

Verboden opened his eyes, reached up and grabbed

Alfred's shoulder. Then he pulled him down to the bench. "We pray."

The servant set his trowel and pot down, and began praying too.

Alfred imitated Verboden, praying to the Father of Light, his eyes going to Verboden and then the altar. He was not sure what Verboden's beliefs were or what sort of god this Father of Light was.

The altar, a simple post with a small wooden loop at the top, looked like a magnifying glass. It bore a resemblance to the Christian cross in where it was placed and how simple it looked. There were no statues or figurines. He recalled seeing churches with simple crosses on the altar at home. He also recalled other churches with angels and a mother named Mary. He wasn't sure what it was all about. They prayed to the son of God, Jesus?

He was not familiar with this kind of worship. His mother kept away from churches and the like. Most of what Alfred knew about religion was from his fellow students and what was taught at his school. Most teachers were of the opinion that religion is based on fairy tales, oppressive and not to be trusted. They said it was old fashioned and not necessary for a modern world. Of course, Alfred was not in a modern world now. The people here seemed more alive, under such fear and hardship. Religion and fairy tales were quite true, and necessary. He shrugged out of his thoughts.

"What do the goblins do?" Alfred asked in a whisper.

"The goblins will raid. They attack, take the food and burn all else." As he spoke, Verboden kept his eyes closed as if still praying.

"Well, what do we do?" He glanced over to the servant,

who had one eye open and was staring at them through it. He quickly closed it when he realized Alfred was looking at him.

Verboden prayed for a long while. Finally, he stopped and said, "We will gather as much of the harvest as we can, store it in the castle and have everyone stay there. We will defend the castle and survive till spring so we can plant again."

"What about the farms and people's homes?" Alfred squeezed his praying hands.

Verboden opened his eyes and looked at Alfred. "They will be destroyed."

Alfred's jaw clenched. He knew how important the farms and homes were to the people. He stood up and left. Verboden watched as he went, turning back to prayer but not closing his eyes. Instead, he gazed at the symbol on the altar for a long time.

Then he spoke aloud in frustration. "Why have you abandoned us? Why have you let the dark magic and powers unleash? You know all things and must have a purpose that I do not understand." Though spoken with intensity, his last words had a tone of obedient acceptance. "How do I remain faithful?" he added.

Alfred found Gylloth, the only knight left, sharpening his sword on Boggin's stone wheel. Alfred nodded to young Boggin and Broggia, the venerable old smith, each busy as ever.

"Gylloth, did you know the goblins will raid soon—that they'll raid the harvest?" Alfred stood very close to the man, leaning in to hear his response.

"Yes, milord, I did." Gylloth raised his sword, a motion

that led Alfred to step back. Gylloth tested the sword's sharpness with his fingers.

"Well, I don't want the farmers to lose their homes."

"Well then, if I understand you correctly, you want me to go out and protect the dozen or so farms spread out along the hillsides. Is this correct?" Gylloth peered down the length of blade.

Alfred thought for a moment, hands on his waste and tapping his foot. "No."

"As soon as harvest is done, everyone will come into the castle, and we wait it out till spring. Raiding goblins will not attack the castle." Gylloth turned the blade to look down the length of the other side, shaking it to sense its strength and balance.

Alfred thought a moment while looking at Gylloth's unconcerned expression. "When did you and Verboden and Abedeyan decide this?"

Gylloth's eyes widened and finally met Alfred's.

"I'm the king," said Alfred. "Why are you guys deciding things behind my back?!"

Broggia whispered to his son. "Sounds like a king alright."

Abedeyan rushed in. "Milord, milord, what is all this fuss?"

Alfred turned his gaze to Abedeyan, who suddenly stopped and chose his stance carefully. He tried the obedient stance first, bowing his head and clasping his feeble fingers. "How may I be of service, milord?"

"You all have gone behind my back to decide what to do about the goblins! Why didn't you talk to me?!"

When Abedeyan tried to steal a secret glance with

Gylloth, Alfred noticed. This angered him all the more. His face reddened. Now Abedeyan became defiant. Standing straight up and crossing his arms, he spoke boldly, "Well milord, if you are going to continue to play games with peasant children and gallivant around with a commoner's daughter, then as adults we must take it upon ourselves to make decisions to protect us all."

Stunned, Alfred said nothing. With anger dissipating instantly, he hid his new feelings. His eyes stared at nothing. Abedeyan and Gylloth glanced at each other with knowing eyes. Then, seeing Alfred slowly walk away, they became unsure.

Alfred walked around a corner and saw the children, all of them, including Cory, Wilden, Setheyna, and Loranna, huddled together. Loranna ran off with tears in her eyes.

There was a strange tone, hushed, hurried and apprehensive, to the harvest time. All were busy with scythes and sickles, cutting and bundling wheat, rye and barley. The men cut and hacked, the women followed behind to gather and bundle, and the children picked up any leftovers that were missed by the women. Abedeyan had the castle workers carting as many bundles as they could to the castle, returning quickly to get more.

In peaceful times, before Gorbogal, it was said that harvest was a time of celebration and much merriment. The fields, towns and castles were alive with joyous festivals. The crops were distributed as part of an orderly business arrangement passed down from generation to generation. The king would get the lion's share, dukes or lords would get their cut, and farmers and peasants, would have the rest to live on, sharing some of it with the local church. Even with large portions going to their feudal lords, there was enough for everyone.

This harvest was different. There were no festivities. With the foreboding of goblin raids in the air, everyone was in a secretive rush. A few yelled out or barked orders. Most talked in whispers and under their breadth. Though the sun was out, the clouds were ever present. Many days were gray with fog, and mist rolled in early each night. People moved about in fear, flinching at any sound from the nearby shadows and dark forests. Even Loranna, eager to dress and partake in celebratory harvest activities, was constrained by her folk. Alfred was in a somber mood as well. He sensed everyone's fear.

Alfred was hurrying along a road one day when he came upon Gylloth. He was fully armed on his horse on a hill overlooking the hard working farmers harvesting the crops. "Where are you off to, milord?" he asked.

"What's it matter to you?" Alfred said as he passed by him.

"I am your knight, milord. It is my duty to know where you are to protect you and the land." Gylloth had a polite if dull demeanor.

"Well, I don't need your protection. I am your king, right?" Alfred paused only a moment.

"Yes, milord."

"Then mind your own business." Alfred continued on his way.

Gylloth's left eyebrow rose. Under his breath he said, "You are my business." His horse snorted. He kept his eye on

Alfred as long as possible from where he was.

Alfred darted through hedges and came out on the other side to see Derhman and his son Cory. They were busy with their harvest. Alfred rolled up his sleeves and began to work along with them.

"Is all ready?" Alfred whispered.

"Not yet, milord," Derhman replied. "Harvest is hard work. I don't know if we'll have time for what you wish."

"Do you want your farm saved?" Alfred's question reminded them of the purpose of the plan.

Derhman bit his lip.

"Well then, you must do as I have ordered as soon as possible! Hedor and his men will help. I have ordered it so. And Derhman, you must not tell the others."

"Others?"

"Gylloth, Verboden and Abedeyan. I don't want them to know."

Derhman tied down bundles of wheat. "But they are your servants, milord. They are wise and knowledgeable."

"I don't care. I don't want to talk about it. Just do what I say."

Derhman gulped while looking helpless at his son. Cory shrugged, piling wheat bundles onto a small cart.

Hedor and his bandits carried shovels and the like out of the castle. There were now many farm folk and peasants huddled in all the corners of the castle, all with as much as they could carry from their homes and what would fit. They didn't have much. Blankets, clothes, a few pots and pans, candle sticks and the like were all they had. The women were making the best of any spot they could find to make their temporary abode. Abedeyan and Gylloth noticed Hedor and his men.

"Where are you off too?" Abedeyan asked.

"Oh, me? Us? We're off to finish up any last bits of harvesting." Hedor smiled with a bit too much skulduggery! Yep, he looked a little too underhanded!

"I have taken care of that, so there is no need for you to go out. You are needed to man the guard posts," Abedeyan said.

"King's orders," Hedor began to pass. A staff was placed in front of his path, halting him.

"The Exchequer, the Steward of the Castle... Abedeyan has not finished talking to you," said Verboden.

Hedor and his men looked at the staff, not out of fear but in annoyance.

Abedeyan moved closer to them. "King's orders? He would give me any such order to give to you!"

"Apparently not, old man. Alfred told me and my men directly."

"What orders!?"

"King Alfred told me not to say, sworn to secrecy, and so I won't. Now, if you don't believe me, that's your problem. You think I can gallivant about this castle lying about whether a king gave me specific orders? You want the truth, go to King Alfred yourselves. My men and I have urgent business, king's orders!"

In so saying Hedor lay heavy emphasis on the word king. Then he slapped Verboden's staff away with his shovel and continued out.

Abedeyan yelled after them, "Where is Alfred!?"

Chapter Twenty Three

Goblin Raiders

In the moonlit night on a far hill, a farm lit up the sky, flames engulfed it. A farmer, on the castle walls holding a rake, pointed and gasped. Many others rushed up to the wall to see.

"Tis our home!" one man gasped. His wife clutched him and cried.

"Goblins! They have come!" another said as he shuddered.

Dozens of shadows snuck along the hillsides and down

dark empty farm roads. The goblins looked like dark ants roaming beneath a dark blue sky, searching fields, expecting to find hiding peasants.

The War Chief, a larger creature, rode a huge black greasy boar with thick curled tusks and a foamy mouth. It leapt about, prodded by smacks of the War Chief's blade or pokes from his spiked boots.

Goblins would form up near a farm and then rush in growling and howling. They banged in the door and leapt through windows, smashing anything inside and taking whatever loot they could. Then they rushed out and headed for the next farmstead. Their archers grouped around a torch bearer, lit their arrows and fired at small hovels. Thatched roofs readily ignited.

The attackers showed no secrecy, skill, tactics or invention. Groups of them scattered about the hills and took the same approach over and over as they rampaged the land.

From the castle walls, the marauders were now easy to see -- torchlit groups of dark figures racing from one homestead to another. They could also be heard yelling and howling, growling and yelping. The farmers watched with horror and fear. Gylloth, smoking a pipe, sat below the wall by the smith's fire tended by Boggin and Broggia.

The War Chief and several goblins neared the castle's walls and noticed it was inhabited. They sniffed the air and pointed, knowing their prey were locked up inside. Many came close, howling goblin insults at the farmers on the walls. In fear, the farmers backed away from the walls, ran, ducked or leapt into the court area.

Gylloth sensed something and stood up. "Where are Hedor and his men?"

Abedeyan rushed over, "They did not return."

"What about archers? Do we have any?"

"Some of the farmers have skill with bow and arrow." Abedeyan motioned over to farmers, fathers huddling with their wives.

"Where are Alfred and his archers?" Gylloth asked.

"The children?" Abedeyan said with a smirk. He looked around. None but the youngest of children were present. He started feeling uneasy. "They must be in the Keep somewhere."

"Then go get them," said Gylloth, gritting his teeth.

Abedeyan looked at Gylloth and then turned.

Crashing through hedges, a group of goblins came upon a farm untouched. They howled with enthusiasm in discovering a new target. Rushing forward, they began to race, each trying to knock others down so as to be first to arrive. Goblins are nasty, bitter, jealous and foul, hating everything including each other. Their bitter rivalries were obvious even as they worked together to ravage the landscape.

Before they got too close, the farmhouse's tattered cloth windows opened, and children peered from them. The goblins stopped, staring in surprise. Then they howled in joy and renewed their charge.

The door opened, and to the goblin's amazement more human children appeared. But something was different. The children crowded at the windows and doorway had their arms stretched with bows and notched arrows. In heightened chagrin, for goblins are chagrined about most things, the children were using goblin bows and arrows—and they let loose.

A good dozen goblins fell. All bent over, grabbing at arrows stuck deep in their tattered bodies. Many had two arrows drawing blood. One had three! All but one dropped, and he stood there unsure of what to do. More arrows flew at him. He looked like a pin cushion, finally falling amidst the pile of dead gobs.

Several smaller goblins by the hedges, witnessing the surprise defense, hissed in shock. They had torches and bows. One quickly lit the others' arrows, and they fired at the farm, yelping with joy.

All of their arrows missed except one that hit the roof. The goblins leaped in joy, each proclaiming it was his that hit its mark. The flame went out rather quickly. The goblins pointed at it in dismay and confusion, huffing, unsure of what was amiss. Again they fired a volley of flaming arrows, and again the one or two that hit thatch sputtered out.

Unbeknownst to the goblins, the roof was reinforced with wood and bramble, and all of that was caked heavily with clay and mud. The children had poured water on the roof earlier in anticipation of this battle. There were small peep holes in the roof where several boys were ready with ladles of water.

Disappointed, the goblins howled eerily into the night. Other goblins from across the hillsides turned from their own wanton destruction and focused on the unique pitched howl. Hearing this instinctual warning, the War Chief turned from the castle wall and growled with a deep rasping voice. He and his bodyguards gathered and raced off.

When he heard the excessive howling, Gylloth rushed up to the walls just as the War Chief and his group were leaving. Abedeyan clambered up the stairs behind him, huffing and puffing. "Gylloth, I did not find the children or Alfred. They are missing!"

"I know where they are."

Goblins gathered along the hedges near the farm where the children were. Surrounding it was a harvested field, now an open space. In the middle of it lay a dozen dead goblins in a pile. Seeing this, the goblins leapt and howled with anger. A group rushed forward, driven by murderous revenge. As before, the windows and door opened. Out flew a shower of arrows. Most found their mark. Goblins fell to their death.

A silent grumbling permeated the remaining goblins. Then they renewed their guttural growls and howls of anger. More charged in and were themselves shot down by several arrows. Goblin archers fired repeatedly. Most seemed unskilled, as only a few arrows actually hit the farmhouse. The flames at their tips went out quickly. The place seemed impervious to fire.

By the time the War Chief and his group arrived, many goblins lay dead in the field. He looked at the frustrated and hesitant goblins still remaining. He bent over and pushed a nearby goblin forward, wanting to see for himself what had happened. The goblin roared with enthusiasm and charged.

It got about half way in and then retreated. The War Chief saw that it had an arrow in its neck. It hobbled a few paces and then fell down dead, revealing several more arrows in its back.

The uproar was stupendous. All around goblins yelled and screamed. The War Chief raised his huge scimitar and let loose a horrendous howl. Then he lowered the sword and pointed it at the farm. The large group of goblins charged from all sides, issuing a thundering chorus of howls. The War Chief moved in last, whipping his fighters forward.

Goblins fell everywhere. Arrow after arrow flew at them, but they kept charging. With so many of them in force, they were bound to reach the farm and gain the upper hand. Collectively the pack held onto this notion as goblin after goblin fell gurgling or grunting its last breadth.

When the goblins closed in on the farm, many suddenly fell into a ditch encircling it. It was hidden with grass and bramble. Each falling goblin yelped in pain, breaking a bone or, worse, stepping onto a wooden spike with shoe-less feet. The goblins behind them surmised the situation and paused in confusion. These made perfect targets for children shooting arrows. Row after row of attackers fell, creating a wall of dead. This slowed the bewildered goblins behind them.

There was now a pile of goblins moaning and groaning. The War Chief saw that all was lost. The remaining goblins dispersed in utter fear. He turned his wild boar to retreat. But it was too late. The door opened and children rushed out, forming a line and firing at him. His boar fell from many arrows. It landed on the War Chief's knobby fat leg, pinning him to the ground.

Hedor and his men then rushed out from the cabin. On his way out, Hedor slapped Alfred on the back, shouting "Well done! Hahr hahr!"

The bandits rushed about the fallen goblins and dispensed with any still alive.

Setheyna began to rush out, but Loranna held her back. "What are you doing?"

"I want to get m'arrows to kill more goblins!" she said

with pride.

"Nay, young warrior, we brought plenty. Stay back!" Loranna commanded, much to the chagrin of the smaller children.

Hedor and his men were judicious and quick. There were only a few goblins still alive. They tried to jab at Hedor and his men's feet. Hedor and his band were experienced at this and used their spears to strike from a distance. A few goblins got up but were quickly shot in the back by the waiting children and fell back down. Hedor gave the thumbs up many times.

From near the dead boar a raspy bellowing sound erupted. Alfred immediately dashed over, leaping across the ditch and goblin corpses, climbing atop the boar, and saw the War Chief blowing on a tusk horn. Alfred speared the War Chief, ending the goblin signal. He expelled a sigh and retracted the spear. He cringed at the site of such a horrid creature. His relief was short lived.

Far off in the distance another horn blew. It was another War Chief. And from a different direction, another horn blew.

Alfred rushed back. "More are coming!"

"We should get back to the castle! Now!" Hedor commanded.

Alfred looked at the men and children. He was tired and had had enough fight for one night. "Okay, let's hurry!"

But it was too late.

"Look, over there!" Wilden yelled. He was one of the boys on the rooftop of the farm.

Along the ridge lit by the moonlight, at least a dozen goblins on boars raced their way. They were all the size of the chieftain Alfred had killed.

"Back inside! Quick!" Hedor yelled.

The children rushed back inside the farm. Hedor and his men followed, quickly killing any moving goblins they saw as they went. Wilden and the other boys atop the roof, having wet it with more buckets of water, slid down and leapt inside.

It took only moments for the goblin riders to reach the hedges and see the field of dead gobs. They growled with moonlight misty breath and spat frothy saliva. One was foolish enough to ride forth and was shot down by many arrows.

The others raced along the perimeter screaming and hollering until the rest of the goblins that were on foot arrived.

"There are so many of them," Wilden said anxiously, peering through a window.

Loranna and Setheyna unbundled another bunch of arrows, quickly leaning them in choice spots along the walls under windows for easy access. Many children huddled on the floor, tired.

"Your archers are very skillful, Alfred. You've done well by them, but I'm afraid they are still children," said Hedor. "I do not think they can last this fight."

Alfred looked down. He too felt exhausted. "Let them rest. When the goblins attack, we'll wake them."

"They could attack at any moment," Hedor growled.

The goblins gathered. Several riders took it upon themselves to keep their fellow goblins in some order until more had arrived. Their horns bellowed in the night, and more horns answered. Soon dozens of goblins turned into hundreds, as dark figures swarmed in from across the hillsides.

"They will be cut down!" Abedeyan said in a panic from the castle wall. "There are too many!"

Gylloth pulled his armour tight.

Abedeyan looked at him. "And what do you propose to do?" he asked.

"What I can."

"It is too late. Alfred made his choice." Abedeyan sunk below the wall. "You cannot save him. You cannot save them."

"It is my duty to protect the king," declared Gylloth, adroitly clasping buckles.

"He is king no longer. He abandoned his castle." Abedeyan sat stoically still, staring blankly.

"I beg to differ!" interjected Lady Nihan, standing below them on the stone stairs. "A castle is nothing without its people, and its people nothing without their homes!"

Abedeyan rolled his eyes. "Hush, Lady! This does not concern you."

"Does not concern me? How impudent! King Alfred has helped rebuild this land and given hope to the farmers and workers. He has given hope to us all. And now he is out there fighting for their farms, for their lives. He is fighting the evil that has cursed us for so many years. And he is using children to do it!" Unable to speak any longer, Lady Nihan rushed down the stairs and out of their sight.

Abedeyan looked up at Gylloth, who was staring out at the forming goblins. "Shall I get Verboden?"

"Please."

Abedeyan rushed off.

The goblin horde was now in the hundreds, surrounding the whole of the farm. They were at least two, maybe three goblins deep. A shower of flaming arrows flew wildly at the farm. The only flame that held was that which remained on the shafts of arrows landing in thatch. Damp mud prevented them from igniting their target.

The riders moved forward along the advancing perimeter, each in turn raising its scimitar or other malformed weapon. Each signaled to the others that all would attack in unison. They met each other's big black eyes and growled until a tumultuous howl from several hundred goblins rose into the air. Then they charged.

Goblins fell to the left and right as arrows flew from every window. Goblins rushed in, undaunted by their falling comrades, quickly leaping and climbing over the many dead and fallen. Some fell into the ditch, grabbing their punctured feet in pain, while most climbed over mounting piles of dead.

Arrow after arrow flew from the children, tired or not. Goblin archers fired back, but their aim was so bad that the best merely hit the farm. It had hundreds of goblin arrows stuck to it. Very few flew through the windows, most were lodged in the frame or on shields. The archers were guarded by the spear boys holding up their shields at the various windows. The boys were also ready with their spears.

The goblins slammed against the farmhouse door and windows. The boys thrust their spears furiously, sticking and cutting at the dismayed goblins. As Hedor and his men held the reinforced door, they felt the bang and hack of goblin axes.

Alfred yelled, "Fight them! Fight!" He did this to encourage himself as much as anything. Some of the boys and Cory and Wilden jabbed their spears through their windows with shields held up high. They kept up a furious attack as goblins pounded against the shaking farm. Would it hold?

Goblin arms pushed through the windows, swinging black blades and axes. Hedor swung violently to hack an arm off. A goblin squealed in pain, falling back as another replaced it.

Hedor kicked and hacked. "There are too many, Alfred!"

Chapter Twenty Four

A True Knight

Oh Father of Light,
Give this land, this King his might
Empower then, and bring forth
That will rise, a powerful Knight!

    With this blessing, Verboden opened his arms toward Gylloth, who raised his sword. A streak of light shone down and encompassed Gylloth. He glowed with a great aura.

    "Go, knight! You are endowed with his Holy Light!" Verboden stepped back.

    "For the king!!! Heeyah!" Gylloth commanded his horse to gallop. He charged from the castle and raced down the hill along a farm road. As he neared weary goblins, they became blinded by the great light and fled with fear into the darkest parts of the forest.

Gylloth arrived at the farm and came upon the swarming goblins, swinging his heavy sword into their backs, hacking and hewing. Goblins fell in pairs and triples. Limbs flew everywhere. Goblins turning to see this new danger were blinded by holy light. In fear, many took flight, climbing over the dead, grasping and choking and scratching each other to flee. Even as Gylloth made his way through the unruly mass of vicious goblins, many more were still fighting at the farm, bashing in the door or trying to climb through windows.

"There! Take them!" Hedor yelled as his men scrambled to stop the goblins from rolling in. The fighting was close and furious. Hedor and his men were more ferocious than Alfred realized, more so than the boys could be at their age. Even so, Cory and Alfred had trained the boys well. They held together a wall of spears that stopped the goblins countering Hedor and his men. Goblins would fall from spear wounds, blocking the window they were trying to climb through, restricting the space for the others attempting to break in.

All of a sudden a mighty light shined upon them.

"It's the sun! Goblins can't handle the sun!" Alfred shouted.

It seemed true. The attack weakened, and goblins fell from the windows, replaced by the bright light.

"How can it be the sun?" Hedor asked. "It rises from the wrong side!"

Alfred and Hedor shared glances and then cautiously looked out the window. Before them was a great radiant armoured knight and his horse, trampling and scattering the goblin army. He was a lone figure, huge compared to the three to five foot goblins. He towered over them, smashing all who haphazardly came within his path. The mounted knight's only difficulty was steering his horse so as to not break a leg on the unsure footing of so many dead goblins.

"Woooohooo! It's Gylloth! I know it!" Alfred yelled. The children, though weary, got excited and cheered with great relief. Loranna leapt upon Alfred and kissed his lips so fully and for so long that everyone including Hedor stopped in shock. Many of the exhausted children suddenly erupted with giggles.

Loranna backed off. "I'm sorry. I'm so sorry, milord." She was genuinely embarrassed and ashamed, almost to tears.

Alfred stood up a little dizzy but shook it off. "It's okay, Loranna. Don't worry. Come on! We must help Gylloth!" Alfred rushed outside and yelled, "Spears forward!"

The boys ran out and made a line of spears.

"Archers! Form up!" Alfred yelled.

Loranna and the other girls rushed out to form their lines behind the boys. "One, fire!"

Arrows flew at nearby goblins. Most were disoriented by the brilliant light or were trying to clamber out of the wretched mound of fallen goblins.

"Two, fire!" Loranna yelled as the few remaining goblins fell by arrows, even before Gylloth could get to them.

The goblins were scattered across Derhman's land. Many riders regrouped beyond the field and the bright light. They yelled out with howls of anger and blew their war horns. There were still many left, rushing about the fields and in the dark forests. They gathered around the half dozen goblin riders. Though worn and tattered, they were the toughest of the lot and still had fight in them.

Gylloth came before Alfred and lifted his helm visor. Alfred returned the visor salute with a modern salute of a bare hand. Gylloth noticed the array of spearboys and archer girls. He then quickly glanced at the massive spread of goblin dead. He smiled and nodded one last time to Alfred.

As he turned, Gylloth yelled "For the king!" and then charged headlong into the gathering goblins.

"No! Gylloth!" Alfred cried and ran after him.

Hedor rushed up, stopping Alfred. "We must go, sire! He has given us a chance! Everyone, to the castle!!!"

Hedor did more than insist. He stared defiantly, almost with vile contempt, at Alfred. Hedor understood the severity of the situation and would use whatever means necessary to get Alfred and the others to go, as it was their only chance to survive.

He pushed them with much force, knocking them over and picking them up again, tugging and pulling them, exhorting them to leave immediately.

Molger carried two of the smaller exhausted ones. Other bandits carried or pulled whomever they could, running through the forest and along the farm roads toward the castle.

Alfred cried quietly, hobbling along as best as he could, frustrated by each thrust Hedor committed upon him. Alfred glanced around at everyone and realized, more fully, how exhausted and injured the children were. His adrenaline began to decrease as he considered how terrifying the goblin army trying to reform still was and how far they still had to go to get to safety. He knew Gylloth was charging alone to save them, charging to break, or at least slow down the goblins' resolve before they could muster their forces. He knew Gylloth was sacrificing himself for them, to give them as much time as possible to escape. After surveying their group, Alfred feared they had little chance of making it back to the castle several miles up the road. He began helping to push the children forward, not daring to look back toward the howling goblins.

Peering from the castle wall, Verboden could just see the faint light of his spell upon Gylloth and hear the distant sounds of a horse galloping and a knight yelling and goblins screeching. Verboden yelled from the wall at the people in the castle, "He rides his last ride! Get as many carts and mules as you can down that road!"

"Are you mad? Has casting your spell enfeebled your mind?" Abedeyan responded.

"Nay, old warden," said Verboden as he rushed down from the castle wall. "He is giving Alfred one last chance to escape!"

Hedor and the bandits, though physically fit, were worn down from carrying and pulling the wearied children. There still had a few sloping hills to ascend to get to the castle. Though utterly exhausted, the bandits trudged along, breathing heavily. They pushed on by sheer will, knowing they must save the children's lives and their own. They would fight with everything they had till their last breath.

Loranna and the girls were quite skilled, more than Alfred could have imagined. Using the goblin bows, they continued to outperform the goblin archers. Periodically, a few came out of the forest to attack them. Somehow the goblins chose the wrong night, for the moon glowed much brighter then even on a full moon, making them easy targets for Loranna and the girls. Goblin archers would miss and quickly find themselves being fired on, meeting their end.

Loranna glanced up at the moon and saw a face within the glow, an old bearded face that seemed to be looking down upon her with tenderness. She knew not who it was or if it were a dream brought on by her exhaustion. She had no time to think on it as she saw shapes moving within the shadows of the forest. The goblins were catching up to overtake them as the men and children hobbled toward the castle.

Alfred noticed a few other untouched farms. "We could hide in there!"

"No, don't stop! To the castle! It's our only chance!" Hedor spoke with heavy breath, carrying one of the younger boys.

A small group of goblins rushed from nearby woods. Loranna and her girls fired just as they drew near. All but one fell. Cory and Wilden rushed with their spears. The goblin turned to flee but was killed where he stood. So fatigued, Cory and Wilden began using their spears as walking sticks.

Gylloth charged around and around, hacking at groups of goblins, throwing many into the air with his powerful swings. Though his blade became dull and though many arrows were stuck in his back and in his horse, he felt no pain. All he felt was the warmth of the light. The goblin riders were enraged by his strength and the brilliance of his aura of light. As soon as Gylloth charged one side, the riders would yell at the fleeing goblins on the other side to resume attacking him.

Most of the goblins that were left were archers. They fired more arrows into Gylloth's back with seemingly no effect.

Eventually, however, the light faded from Gylloth, and the pain of death came. He fell from his horse, as it had one last neigh before it died. Gylloth tumbled to the ground, arrows snapping as he rolled to stillness. Goblins rushed up. Gylloth hacked one impetuous rider and its boar as they neared. The rest backed away in fear. Then another rider, the biggest, came up with his spear and thrust it from a distance, finally ending the life of the fallen knight, Sir Gylloth.

Hedor and his men had managed to get them halfway, but even they could not hold up much longer. Several were lagging, holding children up as best they could. Many began falling from pure exhaustion, no longer having the strength to stand, let alone walk. They had worked all day preparing defenses and had fought many goblins. Now, after several miles running up a long slope and carrying children, the bold effort had become too much.

Hedor turned to see a long line of his men with children. They were spread out down the road with some stopped and others hardly moving. He tried in vain to lift some up, but all were utterly drained.

"Go, Hedor. Go on," one bandit exclaimed with heavy hoarse breathing.

"Come on! Come on!" Hedor tried to push them on, but he too was losing the will to press forward.

Alfred sat on the ground, leaning against his spear. Loranna and the other girls came up. She tried to lift Alfred, tears streaming down her face. She had no strength and so huddled beside him, holding his arm.

Goblins mustered along the road. They pointed at the weakened bandits holding the children. They howled to alert the rest. A few goblin archers shot wildly, arrows landing near the bandits and children. Many of the wearied children cried, huddling within the feeble protection of the arms of the bandits.

The remaining goblin riders on their boars rushed up to the front of their advancing group. They roused each other in the perverse joy of blood lust, each slapping and cajoling the other. Who would be first to charge? Who would be the first to kill? It didn't matter. They just wanted to finish off the group. As soon as one kicked his boar forward, the other two would quickly catch up. Yelling in glee, the goblins came in for the final kill.

Their enthusiasm quickly faded. "How could it be?" they wondered. Racing down the road was that horrible knight on his horse—the one they just slew. He was advancing at an incredible speed, coming straight at them. They shrieked in fear. One panicked and turned his boar, only to crash into the other, causing both to go down. The third stopped and reeled about riding his boar over goblins. In a panic, they all began to flee, scattering into the nearby forest.

Alfred gazed with wide eyes, pointing, lifting Loranna up to look. "It's Gylloth! He's alive!"

Hedor looked up. The glowing knight's speed was so fast that he was already upon him. Hedor fell to the ground, trying in vain to avoid the inevitable trampling. But Gylloth and his mighty horse merely passed through Hedor and the rest of the group. It was as if he were but a vision.

Alfred, very near the fallen Hedor, saw that Gylloth was translucent. He was a ghost of his former self. Alfred realized this was not Gylloth, or at least not the one Alfred had hoped to see.

Verboden, whipping a mule, came quickly down the road on a cart. He leapt off when he was near.

"Quickly, help the children get on! Quickly!" Verboden helped the bandits carry the children to the cart.

With renewed strength from the hope that they might make it to safety, Hedor lifted many, piling them haphazardly into the small cart. Verboden gave the reigns to one of the exhausted girls and slapped the mule into action. Up the hill it went.

A larger wagon appeared with Abedeyan driving it. "Come on, men!"

Alfred, Loranna, Cory, Wilden, Hedor, Molger and the rest climbed in with what strength they had left. Abedeyan turned the wagon around and, as quick as a farmer's wagon could go, went up the hill to the castle.

Verboden stayed for a moment watching. "The ghost of Gylloth! Never did I think I could call such a spirit. Holy indeed was he, a true knight!" He then ran to the castle.

Though Gylloth's ghost swung madly and raced after the goblins, hot on their tail, driving them into sheer terror and panic, it could not actually harm any of them. They did not understand, caught in such fear. When he swung, they fell as if cut or sliced. But they would slowly get up, realizing they were unscathed, concluding that they had been lucky and ran off. It never occurred to them to report their good fortune to each other before they fled.

Gylloth's ghost galloped into the dark forest where the goblins hid and scattered them further. His glowing spirit passed effortlessly through the thick trees and bramble. This went on until the sun rose, when Gylloths' ghost faded at the first rays, far from any man's eyes, far from Verboden or Alfred's eyes, deep within the dark forest beyond the hills.

Chapter Twenty Five

Fevers and Fears

Though all were safe, fear still permeated the group. They were surprised that so many goblins had come in this raiding party. How many more would there be when an army of goblins came?

The sun rose as they reached Grotham Keep. Caring for the wounded was a somber affair. Though the bandits had many gruesome cuts and bruises, the children's wounds were more frightful. From large gashes to vast skin scrapes and piercing splinters, the children felt the pains wracking their fatigued bodies.

Not realizing it, one boy had nearly lost a finger. He was drenched in his own blood and never realized how deep the cut was because of his sheer exhaustion. Lady Nihan stitched it up and secured it with bandages so quickly that the brave boy whimpered only once. Lady Nihan and her seamstress maidens tore cloth and cleaned wounds, bandaging them as fast as they could. All had a wound or two. All were bruised, scraped and utterly worn.

"Children fighting? What will become of us?" Lady Nihan said under her breath.

Their mothers and fathers were frightened for their children and angry at Alfred. They could not fathom why he had placed their children in front of a goblin horde where they could have met a most horrible death.

Alfred was unaware of the tumultuous uproar of the parents, for he lay in bed with a heavy fever. Loranna, weak and bearing several wounds herself, sat beside him and dabbed his face with a wet cloth.

Abedeyan tried to appease the angered farmers and peasants, but eventually he grew angry too – outraged at their impudence. He lost control. "What insolence! This is your king! He gave you refuge in his castle! Stop your crying! Stop this nonsense!"

This further enraged the farmers and peasants. Lady Nihan came and pulled Abedeyan away. The air was full of defiance this cold brisk morning.

Verboden did what he could to heal the children and bandits. He was already weak from the events of the night, from the holy prayer for protection that he bestowed upon Gylloth the Knight to the subsequent summoning of the knight's spirit, which allowed the group to return safely to the castle.

Verboden, weary, stood outside the Great Hall staring up into the dim morning sky. Above, at a distance, hovered a cloaked figure. It was not frightened by Verboden, as it waited patiently in full view. It was Death, floating in tattered black robes, veiled, with a great black crusty sickle.

"You have Sir Gylloth. Take no other," Verboden whispered. Death was patient, floating high above, silent and foreboding.

Abedeyan came out in an angry huff. As he pulled out his pipe and began to smoke it, he noticed Verboden and walked to him. "Well, how goes the healing? Are all going to make it?"

Verboden did not answer as he stared intently up into the sky. Abedeyan looked up and saw only dark gray clouds. Abedeyan blinked, unsure of what Verboden was looking at.

Death slowly moved, turning. Verboden uncrossed his arms and put them down. He stood like a soldier ready to face an enemy. He alone knew the enemy was Death, and he was prepared to meet it head on. But Death did not come down. It turned slowly and floated away, gliding into the mist. Verboden gave a sigh of relief and then noticed Abedeyan standing next to him, looking with trepidation.

"Yes, Abedeyan, all will make it."

Abedeyan took the news well, puffing heavily on his nicely carved wood pipe. "Good, good."

When the fog and mist rolled out that morning, the farmers went to see what was left of their farms. To their amazement and wonder, all but four were intact to some degree or another. Derhman's farmhouse where the battle took place, though severely battered, mauled, stuck with hundreds of arrows, and surrounded by hundreds of dead goblins, was still standing.

Derhman clambered through the dead, rotted, piled carcasses of steaming goblin goo and ooze to his farmstead. Goblin dead in the sun did not fair well at all. Seeing all that had transpired there, he was as proud as ever and full of glee. He was in awe at all the cuts and hacks upon his home and all the arrows and spears scattered about. He stood in the doorway, turned to face the dazed onlookers and slapped the frame of his doorway with prideful joy. A split second later the house crackled. Then came moans and groans from creaking wood. Like a house of cards with hundreds of goblin arrows in it, the farm came tumbling down.

At first Derhman was shaken by each loud creaking. Then, when the farmhouse fell, he was completely dismayed. In the end, though, he was proud that at least the door frame, which he had made all himself, still stood. He smiled as he brushed off a bit of dust from the frame.

Broggia and Boggin, standing in front of the crowd of astonished farmers and peasants, were amazed at Derhman's wonderful attitude. They smiled and clasped hands and leapt in jubilee about the vast mounds of dead goblins.

Eventually they settled down and picked up goblin weapons and armour to take back to the castle. The farmers stayed away from the goblins, fearful that there may yet be a live one that could leap up and attack.

As the sun continued to shine bright that day, the dead goblins melted and shriveled up. Putrid steam and vile liquids oozed from the piled carcasses. Big nasty flies swarmed and larva spewed forth from rotting flesh.

Young Boggin quickly got sick from the stench. It didn't bother old Broggia at all. He cackled with joy as he pulled out weapons and armour, piling them on a cart.

"What a treasure — goblin armour, goblin bows and swords, blades and axes! Look here, you bickering cantankerous fools! You've got axes by the scores, good light axes that even the children could wield for cutting wood and bramble! And here are some other good sharp ones. They are made crudely, and yet, made very well! Just a bit of sharpening and better than new!" Broggia easily used a goblin axe to hack at the rotting flesh of the goblins' limbs to get to more armour, metal caps and weapons.

The other farmers gasped and choked in dismay.

"And this!" Broggia pulled forth a curved metal plate. "It could be used as a shovel or hoe, a plow or bowl! It is stronger than anything Boggin or I could smelt!!"

"What you saying? I do the best with what I have!" Boggin said, busily examining the treasure of steel.

"My point exactly!" Broggia replied. "Goblins have vast bloomeries, great furnaces deep within their caves. Some say they use hot lava pits, hotter than any fire man can make! And what's down in those vast caves of theirs, hey? Iron and black rock! If anyone knows how to make strong steel, that's right, 'tis goblins, and 'tis goblin steel we have here! Dark magic they use! Sorcery! Mix iron and black rock in a hot furnace, then pull it out and hammer it while it cools. It is not just for armour and sword but for shovel and spade! For plow and rake! And scythe and sickle! 'Tis your children and King Alfred who begat this for you! 'Tis their fighting and bravery and sacrifice that brought this to us! They lay stricken with wounds and maladies that will heal as you bicker and argue about the king's choices! Foolhardy!? Bah! What one of you won't take as much as you can carry off this field?!"

The farmers and peasants bowed their heads in shame. Recovering from the fall of his home, Derhman walked up to Broggia as best he could through the maze of slippery carcasses. When he reached him, he was tottering from exhaustion. Broggia caught his arm to keep him from falling. They held each other firmly. What started as a smile of thanks turned into gleeful proud laughter. The other farmers nodded their heads in agreement and joined in laughing. After a few moments, they all busied themselves gathering up the treasured steel.

The goblin armour was not full plates of metal like that of a knight. They had many pieces of metal, large and small, tied or wrapped into the folds of their tattered clothes. They used their own long wiry black hair, bound together in small ropes, to tie and wrap things together, adding some sort of sappy sticky filament as the bond. The smell and rot was no matter to Broggia. It was the metal, the iron and goblin steel that mattered most to him. The wealth in this kill was daunting.

The metal was black and ugly, without design. Many pieces were bowl shaped with punctured holes, cracks and uneven edges. Each was invariably a strong piece of metal and therefore used as a shoulder piece or tied to the goblin's chest or as a greave along the arm. The metal looked black because of the goblins' dirty conditions. Broggia scraped a piece of metal on a rock a few times and showed them how shiny the steel actually was. There was growing excitement as the pile of armour, blades, spears, and bows grew very large indeed.

"Now all we need are brave souls, and we will have a

mighty army!" Broggia bragged to the busy farmers and peasants.

That night, after a hard day of gathering, cleaning and rebuilding, the farmers and peasants returned to the castle. There was still fear about the goblins' return.

Alfred's eyes opened. He was with fever but had such a terrible nightmare that he shuddered himself awake. Or perhaps it was the pounding in his head that awoke him. He could not tell, as all was painful. He sat up and felt pain in his ribs. His eyes slowly adjusted to the evening light. He had slept all day. Loranna lay in a deep sleep huddled in a chair beside him. She was heavily bandaged.

He moved his feet to the floor and found strength to stand. He kissed Loranna on the forehead, then slowly walked out.

In the hall sat Lady Nihan, keeping cool the foreheads of the children, all of them, girls and boys, big and small. All were sick and injured, exhausted and worn.

Lady Nihan saw Alfred and rushed over to help him. "Milord, you should not be up! You must rest!"

"Are they... Is everyone okay?" Alfred said with a moan.

"Yes, king, everyone is okay. Many are still very weak, some with fever. With so many wounds and cuts, fever has set in. It is a malady of war, just as cuts and bruises. By the blessedness of the Father of Light and by our own skill, King Alfred, none have died." Lady Nihan gave Alfred a wonderful gaze.

"Gylloth, he died." Alfred looked down.

Lady Nihan had Alfred sit on a bed where Setheyna lay. She was with fever and slept uneasily. She was having a nightmare not unlike the one she just survived.

Alfred looked away.

"Yes, Gylloth died. He died saving you, saving all of us. He died a noble and honorable death. No man, not even a knight, could ask for more. He goes to the Halls of the Kings and will be welcomed there. Verboden and the men have buried him in a grove not far from here."

Alfred nodded. "I saw him again. His spirit saved us, I think." .

"Yes Alfred," said Verboden, who was now standing there before them. "But do not disregard all that you have accomplished for us and for the noble Knight Gylloth."

Alfred looked up, tears swelling in his eyes.

Verboden touched Alfred's shoulder. "I will not doubt you again, King Alfred."

Alfred smiled. It was a humble smile, laden with tears and emotion, fraught with guilt and fear.

"You must rest, King Alfred. You must," said Lady Nihan.

"Verboden!" Abedeyan yelled from the door to the outer ward.

Alfred, Verboden and Lady Nihan looked at him.

Abedeyan bowed. "Forgive me, King Alfred. I did not know you were awake. If you have the strength, both of you must come quickly!"

Alfred, helped up by Verboden and Lady Nihan, quickly followed Abedeyan's bidding to the outer ward and up the stairs to the wall.

"There!" Abedeyan pointed.

Visible in the evening light upon the ridge, sitting atop several crushed trees, was a giant vulture. And mounted atop it was a dark cloaked figure. Though it looked like Death, with the dark cloak, tattered black robe, hood and shadowed face, it had more accouterments, belts and scaled armour, and a mighty sword at its side. The sword had jagged teeth and looked the size of a man.

In the outer ward were crowded all the farmers and peasants, all the sheep and pigs, all their belongings. They were fearful of this new dread, this new terror.

"What is it? Who is it?" Alfred asked.

"It is Death, come to take the dead!" Abedeyan said.

"No, it's not Death," said Verboden. "It is dressed to look like Death to cause fear amongst men. It's a Dark Servant, the eyes and ears of Gorbogal."

"Oh great," Alfred said in feverish delirium. "Why do they always have black robes? The bad guys always look like that! Typical!"

Verboden and Abedeyan shared a glance and shrugged.

"So now Gorbogal knows we are here?" Alfred asked.

"Yes, or will soon enough," Verboden responded.

The giant vulture lifted and flew off into the night.

Chapter Twenty Six

Gorbogal

Alfred awoke from another horrible dream. He looked about in the dark. He was in a hot sweat and pulled off the covers. Beside Loranna, who had stayed by his side and was sleeping, there was a pitcher and cup. He got up and poured himself water and drank it quickly. He then noticed a rat scurrying along the floor. It was a furry white rat, spotted with gray. All the other rats he had seen thus far had been black or brown. It came up to Alfred's bed. Alfred sat down and pulled up his feet. He was afraid of the rat. It stood up on its hind legs, looking as if it was begging Alfred for food or something.

"I've fought monsters and goblins, and I am freaked out by a rat?"

"Alfred" Alfred heard from somewhere. It was a high pitched plea, but from where?

"Alfred! Down here! It's me!" Alfred looked around and then down at the rat.

The rat's mouth was moving as if it spoke. "Alfred, pick me up. It's Tirnalth!"

"Tirnalth!?" He bent down to look more closely but kept his legs on the bed.

"Well, pick me up!"

Alfred complied. He opened his hand so Tirnalth could hop on it.

Alfred looked at Tirnalth, the cute and cuddly rat with a curl of the lip. "Why are you a rat?"

"I'm not a rat! I'm a mouse! To alert you, Alfred, danger comes!"

"What danger? The goblins are coming back!?"

"No, worse. Do not panic! This danger cannot kill you, but it will be far worse if you are not careful."

"What?"

"Gorbogal comes."

Alfred was paralyzed in fear.

"She comes in the mist, not to attack, but to pry and peer, to seek and perceive. Look!" Tirnalth looked up to the small window above.

Alfred was too afraid to go to the window so he stood on his bed to look out. Down the slope, by the edge of the trees, forming, then slowly seeping forward, was a green mist. It had a faint glowing aura with tentacles like spider limbs feeling their way down one slope, then up another, and slowly creeping up toward the castle. Once in awhile it would stop at a farm, surround it like eddying water, seeming to pause with its eerie mist, and a scream would be heard.

"No, the farmers!"

"She cannot kill with the mystifying cloud, only torment and frighten one in a nightmare," the small humble mouse spoke.

"Can you stop it, Tirnalth!? And why are you a mouse?"

"I cannot stop it. I am in disguise. She would perceive my presence, my form, even in spirit if I remained myself. So I will dash about as a mouse. It is not me she seeks."

"What then? What is she looking for?" Alfred pleaded.

"You. She seeks you and the cause of this uprising. She does not know what is amiss and will soon find out using her veil of shrouded mist."

The mist finally came to the castle, easily floating over its walls and spilling within. It caused a frightened stir amongst the sleeping peasants.

Alfred, ridden with fear, leapt down from the bed and accidentally dropped Tirnalth. He tried to wake up Loranna, who was in a deep sleep.

"No Alfred, you must not awaken anyone. The mist is already holding sway over everyone. It is already seeking within their dreams what it wishes."

"What do I do?" Alfred said, so wrought with fear he shook.

"You must not think of yourself or your plans. I have

awakened you so you can direct your thoughts before she comes. You must think of something else, something she cannot fathom or see through! You must misdirect her perceptions!"

"Huh? What?" Alfred did not fully understand. He was wounded, with fever and exhausted. Just then the mist began seeping into the room from the doorway. It slowly poured in and fanned out. Dozens of small tentacles reached Loranna and felt all around her. She stirred as a nightmare began taking over her dreams.

"You must not think of yourself as a king, not of your plans for defense, nor of the land. You must think of something else, anything else. Alfred, are you listening to me? Do not reveal anything!"

With this, Tirnalth suddenly scurried away.

Alfred mumbled, stumbled and fell to the floor by his bed. The mist scattered for a moment, then seeped back in and curled about Alfred, covering him fully in a shrouded nightmare.

Alfred awoke in pure blackness. He stood unsure, looking about, reeling in a void of black. He then looked down and saw the glowing green mist all around his feet. Indeed, he was knee deep in it.

There, before him, stood a bent figure in tattered clothes. She looked like a peasant woman, with her back to him. She was old and hunched over.

The woman spoke with an echoed raspy voice, "Where is milord? Where is the king? I have come to find my king? Do you know where he is?"

Alfred stiffened with fear, for the old voice was louder

than anything, taking over his ears and all his senses. She was close but did not look at Alfred. She looked through him, as if walking blindly. She made a sound he did not recognize and then it became more apparent to him. She was sniffing for a scent.

Alfred tried to remember something. He heard a faint voice, an echo, saying, "Think of something else!"

The old lady stopped, as if having been interrupted, and looked up listening, unsure if she had heard something. She then put forth a hand holding a gnarled short cane. The hand seemed to be a thousand years old, with wrinkles and warts and black talons. Scrawled along it were dark green tattoos, covering all the skin and giving her flesh a horrible green hue. Protruding from her skin were many black grisly barb-like hairs.

This hand stopped, and the other came forth. It was not human, but a three pronged and cloven-like hand, like that of hairy black goat. It clasped the sleeve of the first hand, pulling the sleeve of the lady's robe down to cover it. Then the cloven hand disappeared under the veil of its own sleeve.

Alfred felt faint and was too fearful to move.

"Where is the king, young boy? Is he here? I have to talk to him. They all say he is here. They say there is a king now in this land. I need only a word. Have you seen him, boy?" The witch's voice was raspy and horribly insidious.

"No, no!" Alfred swayed.

The ground bubbled, spewing forth more of the foul mist.

"Speak the truth, boy! Where is the king!?" the voice boomed. "Everyone says he is here! Where!? I don't see him!"

"I am the king!"

She cackled, and the dreadful sound rose into laughter so shrill and loud that Alfred reeled on the spot, holding his ears in desperate pain. He tried to scream as the cackle piercing derision was too much to absorb. Blood dripped from his ears.

Then there was silence. Alfred remained frozen as the old evil lady that stood next to him revealed herself. Her cloak opened. Out protruded a ghastly face lapped with thick folded wrinkles. From within those folds stuck out black barbed thorns, warts and pustules with oozing discharge. The worst to behold were her eyes. One was black and spider-like with smaller black eyes surrounding it, and the other was like that of snake, a black slit within a yellow scaled iris.

"You are not the king!" she rasped under foul misty breadth, with bilious spittle dripping on each syllable. "You are just a boy!" She paused and began looking more intently at Alfred. She saw his wounds and his frail quivering body.

Alfred's legs gave out, and he fell down. He was in a hot sweat of fear succumbing to her presence, succumbing to the nightmare.

She came closer, sniffing and prodding. "Curious, you are a boy. Why would they pick a boy? Why you?" She squinted her snake eye, angling her face closer. She switched from eye to eye, using the black orb and its many smaller ones and then switching to the snake eye. A forked tongue shot out once and awhile. She had black greasy hair that dangled, swaying with each head turn.

Alfred gasped, taking in a deep breath. Above and around Gorbogal he saw a goblin army scrambling over hills and through valleys, forming a vast horde. And then he saw hundreds of rats, no thousands, scurrying forth. Even in his hot sweat and panic attack, he could focus now and saw scrambling amidst the flurry of rats a very large rat. It stood on its hind legs and was wearing tattered, threaded leather pieces and carried a small spear. It was a ratkin scurrying through a dark tunnel. It commanded the others to follow. Alfred looked up through the tunnels to see the castle crumbling on top of him. Was this happening for real? Or was it a nightmare?

Alfred was so frightened that he yelled, "Mom!"

Then he saw his mother sewing quietly in the apartment.

Gorbogal spoke, "Who is that woman? Who is before me? Who is it? Is that all you have to think about, frightened boy?"

Alfred felt peace at seeing his mom and was able to focus even more, if one could do such a thing in a nightmare that has fully taken you over. "Mom, mom!"

"Your mother?!" Gorbogal smiled, if you could call it that. Her large mouth was filled with sharp teeth and on one side revealed the mandible, a lone black crusted chitin armoured mandible. "Run to your mother, hey boy?"

She turned away from Alfred and peered about, pushing her hand out to spread the green foul mist. "No, no, seek, seek, I want, I want!"

Alfred, hardly able to breathe, suddenly felt strength as he kept his focus on his mother. He saw her. She seemed so large, filling the void as she looked down at him with comforting eyes.

"What?" Gorbogal turned to Alfred once again, her slit eye narrowing. "Wait, I know that woman, don't I? Where are you going? Come back!"

His mother reached for him. Her face seemed calm and caring, unaware of the danger.

Alfred shuddered, "Mom, mom, mom."

"No!" Gorbogal reached out with her hand and grabbed emptiness.

Chapter Twenty Seven

A Mother's Weakness

Alfred sat up. A wash cloth slid down his face.

"Alfred, you have a fever. Lie back down."

"Huh? Whuh?"

In the morning light Alfred could see his mother was smiling lovingly at him. She was wearing her work clothes. "I have to go to work. I will come back at lunch to check up on you."

"Mom!" Alfred choked. He hugged her tightly.

She gasped. Though it was painful, she couldn't help but smile at his strength and unexpected burst of love. "Okay,

Alfred, okay..." she tried to pull away gently.

When he lay back down, she realized he was crying. She leaned in, returning his hug and comforting her boy.

"I don't have to go to work. I can stay home."

Alfred held her for a long time, sobbing silently. "I missed you."

"Okay. I will stay."

Alfred finally released her and wiped his tears. He looked around his room. All seemed as it was, as if... nothing had changed.

"Mom, how long was I gone?"

His mother looked at him oddly. "Gone? What do you mean?"

"I mean, how long was I gone? I think it was like a year, winter, spring and then harvest."

His mother looked at him with affection and concern.

He looked around at his room, and his shoulders sagged. "It was a dream?"

His mother tilted her head. "Ahh, a dream? Of spring and harvest? Sounds like a wonderful dream."

Alfred smiled and then had a sudden flash of Gorbogal. "No! It was a nightmare!" He shrunk back into his bed, cowering a bit.

His mother grabbed him up again, holding him. "Oh, there there, my boy, my dear Alfred. All is well. You just have a minor fever."

"So I was never gone? I wasn't missing or anything? I went to bed last night, long ago, and woke up... this morning?"

"Long ago?" his mother, still cheery, looked sideways at him. "I was here all the time. You were here. Nothing is the matter." She ran her fingers through his hair and noticed that something was different. She brushed the thought aside.

"Then all that time, all that time was a dream?"

"It's okay. I'll stay here with you if you want. You certainly don't have to go to school today. I'll call them.

"No mom, you can go to work. I'll stay home and take it easy. I'm okay now. I just woke up kind of weird is all." Alfred lay back with a dazed look.

His mom stayed next to him and looked at him. Alfred was in deep thought. She hummed something like a song, an ancient song of spring and sun, of life and love, and of a son. She sat looking and humming for a long while. He finally looked back at her and smiled.

"Okay, Alfred, I'll go now. I'll be back at lunch and bring some medicine, just in case."

Alfred held her one last time as she bent to rise. He held her tight again. She was amazed at his strength. She held him and caressed his hair. "I don't remember your hair being this long and scraggly!"

Alfred sat up suddenly, fully awake. He looked wide eyed at her. Then his eyes slowly turned to one side to see that his hair was indeed longer than his usual buzz cut. He remembered Lady Nihan trimming his hair with scissors.

"You'll need a haircut soon."

He nodded. She nodded, kissed his cheek, rose and walked out.

As soon as he heard several doors open and close, he knew she was gone. He leapt from his bed and rushed to the mirror. He looked at himself, at his grown grisly hair, and couldn't believe it. He then raked his hands through it and had this new sense of strength. He felt his arms and pulled off his shirt to see he had muscles and scars and several large ugly scabs.

"Oh my gosh! I've been wounded!" He twirled about trying to see all his sides in the mirror. "It happened. It really happened!"

He danced about doing kung fu kicks and punches. He flexed his bicep and looked for his reflection in anything that would provide it.

He leapt into a hot shower. Ohhh, the feeling! He stayed in there for a long time, just feeling the hot water clean his worn medieval skin. He had really missed taking showers. He had also been missing the toilet and enjoyed flushing it so much. He just sat afterward and flushed again... and again... ohh... the feeling! He smelled the toilet fully. "Oh fresh clean chlorine water!"

After awhile, exhausted and still with a little fever and headache, he laid down on his bed. He rested for a moment, breathing and meditating as best as a kid could do. Then he had a thought and sat up. "Tirnalth? Tirnalth?"

He looked around the room, even under the covers and under the bed, but there was no Tirnalth. He puckered his lips.

"How did I get from here to there? Here, to there? And back again?" He motioned with his hands, totally unsure of how teleportation or any form of trans-dimensional or time travel or inter-planar wormhole travel worked.

"How do I? Tirnalth!?" Alfred had no idea. He paced and searched about his room but found no answers. Before he knew it, his mother had returned at lunchtime and found him upturning his entire room.

"Alfred!? What are you doing?" His mother gazed at

the mess.

"Oh, I'm, uh, looking for something," Alfred said with a shrug.

"What!?"

"Something I lost." He kept peering about.

"Well what is it? I might know where it is," his mother asked in her assuring mother tone.

"An inter trans-dimensional time traveling wormhole, I think."

"Um, worms?" his mother asked concerned.

"No, wormhole."

"We have worms?" His mother tiptoed into the room over the piles of clothes, books and the like. "You need to keep your clothes..."

"No, no, not worms. I'm looking for a parallel universe or alternate reality or something." He felt along the corner where Tirnalth, the ghost, first appeared.

"Oh, so no worms? Or holes?"

"No, no worms or holes... a wormhole! It's magical!"

"I'll heat up the soup, okay? And I have some medicine too," she nodded, backing out of the room. "And tidy your room."

"Okay," Alfred looked intently at the wall for any subtle cracks in time and or space.

Alfred healed quickly and felt great. He would pose in front of the mirror a lot, even in front of his somewhat concerned mother. He walked about with a newfound confidence. Every day, he came home after school and would immediately begin working on homework.

His mother was proud of him. Each night she brought

him dinner as he studied. She would then stand over him a moment, caressing his newly cut hair or touching his shoulder. She did not look at what he was doing but at him, as if she was looking through him.

"Mom, that's creepy," Alfred would finally say, awakening her from a dream.

"Oh, sorry, I did it again." His mother retracted her hand and left him to his work.

One day, Alfred was watching TV, relaxing and enjoying himself. He was eating potato chips and sipping on a coke, something his mother would not normally buy. Usually he had to use his small allowance on such indulgences, but this time his mother treated. He was relishing the simple pleasures of this life, not taking them for granted as in times past.

On TV was a crazy wrestler, dancing and prancing about, posing and over acting. Alfred was thoroughly entertained. Two smaller wrestlers would leap on him, and he would roll and tumble and smash each in turn. Alfred sat up. He began to ponder something.

The wrestler stood up and yelled into the camera, "Bring 'em on. All of your little rat fink buddies can't stop me!"

"That's it. That's how we beat them!" Alfred got up, rushed to his desk and began drawing. He drew a knight— only it was an odd looking knight in armour. He had big mauled fists and posed like a wrestler. Then Alfred drew smaller figures surrounding the knight. The smaller figures were obviously ratkins.

"That's it!" Alfred surmised, looking at his drawing.

"We don't need big heavy swords. Ratkins would easily overtake a knight with a heavy sword, but wrestling and..." Alfred's tongue stuck out, like a snail peering from its shell, as he drew..."Spikes!" He drew lots of them protruding from the armour. Then he drew a ratkin trying to leap on a fully spiked armoured wrestling knight. He was so pumped. He took his drawing and rushed out to his mother. She was sitting in the main room, repairing warn embroidery on a lavish curtain. She had many curtains to finish.

"Mom, look!" He showed her the crude drawing of a knight adorned with spikes and the ratkins all around him.

It was so crudely drawn that his mother merely glanced at it and then smiled. "That's nice, Alfred!"

He looked intently at his mother. She smiled warmly and then went back to her work.

"Can't you tell what it is?"

"Well, no." She finally put down her work to look more closely.

"It's a knight! Look, he's got regular armour on, and I added spikes!"

"Oh yes, I see the spikes," his mother nodded.

"The spikes are on his armour so he can fight a lot of ratkins."

His mother suddenly froze. She slowly looked at him and then at the drawing. "Ratkins?"

"Yah, mom, they're going to attack the castle. That's how they took it over last time! They must have overtaken the knights because knights didn't know how to fight such an overwhelming horde! The ratkins were then able to open the castle gate!"

His mother almost swooned. "Castle? What castle?"

Alfred suddenly stopped. He gulped, realizing he had said too much. "Uh, just a castle—you know, from one of my games."

His mother gained her composure and then looked up at Alfred and at the drawing of an all too familiar knight. She looked at him with an expression he'd never seen. He quickly retracted the drawing. She looked straight into his eyes and did not stir. Alfred looked away.

She stood as she kept looking at him. "Look at me, Alfred."

He did, but it was difficult to look into her eyes, especially when her eyes were so piercing.

"What have you done?" his mother said under her breadth.

"Nothing, mom," Alfred said looking away.

His mother's posture softened. She moved in closer. "How do you know of such things? Of ratkins?"

"I told you, my computer game, Grim Wars."

"You're lying!" his mother shrieked. She grabbed his shoulders and with her stare, she put more fear into him than he'd ever known, even from Gorbogal.

"Tell me the truth!" Tears swelled in her angry eyes.

"I don't know, mom. I don't know," he said, looking away, verging on tears himself.

"Did he find you? Or did she?" She faltered, falling back onto the sofa, on her sewing work. She gasped in fear, convulsing with utter torment.

"Mom, who?"

"You know who, don't you?" Her lips quivered.

"Tirnalth?" Alfred said softly.

She let out a long moan and turned away. Then she

stood up and paced about the room. She stared out the window into the night. She was swaying, as if stricken with a delirium. She remained silent, holding in many tears, many emotions and many memories. Alfred watched her for a long time. She would not speak. Each time Alfred approached her, she stopped him with one hand and walked away within the small confines of the room.

Alfred, tiring of her strong feelings, went to his room. He took his drawing and laid it on his bed and then lay down next to it. After a long sigh, he fell into a deep sleep.

Alfred woke up standing in the castle courtyard. "So that is how you return!" He was happy to be back. He looked about and saw that the stone walls were different. They all looked new and fully repaired. There were many banners hanging from the walls, and there were many new wood structures, from wall attachments to tower roofs. He was impressed at all the work. He heard and then saw many well armed and obviously well trained men-at-arms rushing along the walls. They were equipped with bows and swords of human making. They were not the hastily garbed look of the bandits and children with their goblin gear.

Horses rode through the courtyard right at Alfred. He rushed out of the way just in the nick of time. Then he found himself in the company of knights on their horses. He gazed up at the magnificent men in their gleaming armour.

"The goblin army musters along the northern road!" one knight roared. Alfred did not recognize him even though the knight's visor was up. All the faces, young or old, were fresh.

Then he recognized Lord Dunther. How could he not?

Dunther was obviously the lead, as all were looking at him on his horse. "The princess is at the monastery! We must protect her!"

Another knight reluctantly answered, "No, Bedenwulf has gone and taken his men."

Dunther hissed, pulled down his visor and reeled about on his horse.

Sir Gylloth held out his hand to stop him. "Lord Dunther, we need to defend the castle!"

"We need to defend the king and the virtue of his daughter from this traitor! We will seek justice on this renegade! My company of knights will go with me. The other knights will defend the castle."

"Our duty is to the king and to his castle," Sir Gylloth responded.

"Your duty is to me!" Lord Dunther yelled as he galloped away. "I will worry about our duty to lord and castle!"

Several knights followed him, including Sir Gorham. Sir Gylloth looked back at the other knights, who looked dismayed at their departure. He then turned to follow Lord Dunther.

Lord Dunther galloped headlong at Alfred, who tried in vain to run out of the way. It seemed that with each scramble, each turn, Lord Dunther turned to ride straight through him. All grew dim as Alfred fell into a kind of darkness. Lord Dunther became shrouded in shadow. Darkened by shadows, the eyes of his horse and his own eyes veiled in his visor glowed with an eerie crimson fire. Steam and mist rose about his darkened visage. His blackened armour seemed to have a crenulated edge of ragged bumps and spikes. Lord Dunther was on Alfred like a malicious evil — not like a knight but like a malevolent spirit spreading, growing larger. He had risen in the shadows of the underworld and was now ready to strike Alfred down.

The evil spirit's mighty blade suddenly appeared. While swinging at Alfred, it split into three blades resembling talons. Then, suddenly, Alfred saw a small sword being thrust upward. It seemed insignificant but clanged against the descending weapon of the beast, stopping it with a shattering sound and breaking into pieces.

Next Alfred heard a familiar man's voice shouting, "Run!"

Then he saw a knight wearing black armour. It stood between Alfred and the horrible shadow. Its armour shone, revealing leaves and vines of wrought silver, sculpted upon the armour as enchantments or signs of strength and honor. The Black Knight stood with his shattered sword.

Alfred thought he recognized him, but he was not sure. He could see parts of his face under the visor. The face was fare and young, strong and sure. Wooly's face flashed in his mind. But then he reasoned that it could not be Wooly because he was strange, had a disfigured face and lived a quiet life down the street back home. He fixed things for people, even for Alfred.

Whoever this knight was, he did not fear the great darkness before them, even with a splintered sword. The knight dropped his sword and pulled out a long dagger. "Run, my lady! To the gate! As Tirnalth said, trust him! Run, milady! Now! Or all is lost!"

Alfred did not know who he was speaking to or what was happening. The dark shadow was re-emerging and reforming. Time was of the essence.

"I love you!" a fair young lady's voice proclaimed from nearby.

The knight paused, as if all the days to come were of gleaming sunrises. "Then go, milady. I have lived a thousand lives in you, and I will always be with you! Now go!"

Alfred seemed to be carried along as she screamed in horror. The shadow was forming itself into a great dragon that encompassed the span of the underworld they were in. Now that it was fully formed, he could see that it was an enormous black creature with glistening scales. Before it stood a small knight. Then fire erupted everywhere, consuming them all. She screamed as she suddenly seemed to float far, far away.

Alfred awoke in the dark again. He was in a hot sweat and truly felt as if he had been consumed by fire. He sat up and pulled off his fully drenched shirt. A glass of water was by his bedside. He drank it down with heavy gulps.

Then he saw her. She was sitting across from him and watching him, his mother. Only she did not seem like his mother, but a shadowy ominous figure.

She was gazing with intent at his chest. At first shy, Alfred looked down at his bare skin. He realized what she saw, the scars. His wounds were nearly healed.

"Do not go back there," she said.

"I, I, have to mom. They need me."

"There is only death. There are only the dark shadows. There is only war."

"We have wars here. There are wars everywhere. There isn't peace anywhere."

"This land has a chance for peace. It has a chance. Only

men are here to choose our fate. There is no choice like that there. Dark magic reigns there."

"What?" Alfred wondered. For the first time, more than just those few words, she opened up a whole world of mystery to him, even more than what he had experienced.

"Mom, they need you. The people need you." He knew saying that drove an arrow of sorrow straight to her heart.

Her emotions swelled, weakening her resolve. "I have not the strength to sacrifice anymore. You are all I have left, Alfred. Let them take whatever they want, the land, the people. I will give it all up for what I have lost. I only want you. I only want peace for my son, a chance at peace here in this world."

She looked down at her hands for what seemed an eternity. "It's a peace that was given to us by the great sacrifice of… others…"

"We are fighting and winning. We are rebuilding. There are people there, children, and all are full of hope. Tirnalth is there, and Verboden, and Sir Gylloth. He stopped the goblins!" Alfred became excited, sitting up and pulling on a dry shirt.

"Gylloth? He is alive?"

"Well no, not any longer. He fought off the goblins for us." Alfred bowed his head.

"You see?" His mother's voice became bitter, heavy with affliction. "The land of the West is no more. The men of that land cannot defeat the Dark One."

Alfred's eyes widened.

"That's right, Alfred. Do you think it is Gorbogal whom you should fear?" She looked at him with such eyes, crazed and glancing about, as if looking not just at Alfred but at some dark scene before her, as if the world of men were before her, as if she were a dark god looking upon a piece of property to do with as she pleased. "Do you think my sister is all that lies before you? Do you think the scattered realms of men can withstand an evil abhorrent witch, who was given her powers by a god, to be unleashed for him?"

"Your sister!?"said Alfred, shuddering. "I must go back!"

"That is a land of magic and powers beyond the ability of man! It is a place where gods still live. Those of light abandoned men, not to their own fate but to that of the dark god that remains! The Deceiver!" His mother spoke as if possessed.

"I must go back, mom! I must! I must help them!"

"You must stay here where no magic can come, where the gods do not come. We are safe here, and the fate of men is decided only by men! Here is where you must stay. Here is where destiny hath no power."

So pleading, his mother fell to the floor.

"The same can happen there, mother, the same!" Alfred bent down and took her hands. He looked into her eyes to reassure her. "Now I know my purpose there, mom. I know why I must go back."

He looked closely at his mother. She was drenched not only in her emotions, sweat and tears but in the love she felt, however lost, for her son and for her land. She was beside herself at what he had learned and what he wanted to do. It was her weakness.

"No son, no," she said softly and closed her eyes.

"I'm sorry mom, I can't help it... I have to..." the darkness shrouded Alfred. He blinked but once and was gone.

Chapter Twenty Eight

Return of Alfred

Alfred sat up in bed and looked around. He was back in the castle. From his old flea-ridden cot he could see cold stone walls and the simple basin that held water near his bed. He got out of bed, stood up and stretched. His modern pajama shirt and pants were gone or magically replaced with his medieval tunic and pantaloons. "Hmm... I wondered about that, about changing, and it worked!"

He bent over the bowl of water to wash his face. He placed his hands in the bowl and threw water on his face as he had done many times before. But this time, all he threw was air. He blinked and was shocked that he felt no cold water.

He looked at the empty basin. He lifted it and turned it over, thinking that water would suddenly gush out. But none did. He set it down and wondered. He looked out the window. It was night, quiet and dark. A sliver of yellow appeared on the horizon. The sun was rising. A ray of light shone on the window and Alfred's face. What joy he felt from the warmth! He just felt great.

Then he heard the door open and turned quickly to see Lady Nihan, who seemed in a trance as she entered. She went to the bed and patted it as if she was making it. She then lifted a pitcher of water and tilted it to pour its contents into the basin, but nothing came out, as the pitcher was empty. Was she a ghost or in a strange dreamlike state or under a spell? Alfred was not sure.

He went up to her and touched her shoulder. She turned to see him and suddenly gasped, screamed and fell back upon her bottom.

"Oh, Alfred! Oh, Alfred!"

"Are you okay, Lady Nihan?"

"Alfred, are you a ghost?!"

Confused, Alfred asked, "What's wrong?"

"It is you! You're back!" She became emotional from the joy of seeing him again with wonderful emotions of hope rising within. She hugged him tightly.

Having been awakened by her scream, Verboden rushed in. He saw Alfred and leaned against the wall as if he was about to faint.

Alfred smiled. "Hello, Verboden."

"Beyond all hope," said Verboden, glancing up.

Abedeyan came in carrying a thick candle. "Hey, what is amiss here?"

Upon seeing Alfred, he looked him up and down. "Are you a ghost?"

"I don't think so?"

Lady Nihan looked at Abedeyan with disdain.

"Can't be too sure," Abedyen said with a grimace towards Lady Nihan. "Well then, good to have you back. We have lots of work to do today. Since we are up now, might as well get started."

Verboden shared a smile with Alfred as Abedeyan left. Lady Nihan, bowing many times as she left, rushed out and proclaimed the good news down the halls and outside the Keep. All were awakened to the news that Alfred had returned.

"How long was I gone?" Alfred asked Verboden.

"One hundred and four days," Verboden said rather hastily. "Though no one was count..."

"One hundred and four days!?" Alfred gulped with disbelief. "Well, the timing sure is off from... well, what have I missed?! What of the goblins!?"

Verboden stopped Alfred with his hands. "All will be revealed. Come, let us get some morning meal in us and speak."

So over bread and cheese and with a warm fire, Verboden spoke. "Since your sudden departure, winter set in. All that was once on the move had come to a standstill. Even in winter, the powers of evil cannot move. Spring is now near. We were beginning to think we were alone and all was lost. Even Tirnalth has been in hiding. When Gorbogal came in her shrouded mist, many became sick. Even though her powers are great, she was not able to use them fully here. Word has reached us that her armies are in the South, that she was in need of her powers against revolting kingdoms in Telehistine. I have spent my time fighting the evil plagues of her mist. Not a life was lost to her vile presence, but I am also not my former self in strength yet."

"Alfred, soon, when the frost seeps away and the sun is strong in the sky, her army will come. If she considers us a pest, a few ragtag people inhabiting a ruined castle, then hopefully she will only send a small... horde. Though our harvest was good and our wants are little, we are only a few compared to those under her command."

Verboden sat silent. He really was a shadow of his former self. He looked gaunt and older, as he had seen the darkness of Gorbogal and been weakened by it. When Verboden met Alfred's concerned look, he smiled back with warmth, revealing that his spirit was still ever strong.

"We must prepare for battle against an army of Gorbogal's," said Alfred. "We should assume an army of greater size than before."

Verboden nodded.

"Good, then I have a purpose." Alfred stood up.

Verboden was surprised at his calmness and determination.

"Where are the children, my archers and spearmen?" Alfred asked.

"They are at their homes, most likely," Verboden replied. "Shall I call for them?"

"No. I want to go visit each and every one myself."

"Wear warm clothes. It is still bitter cold out there. I

will get my cloak." Verboden stood up with some effort.

"No, Verboden, you stay and rest. I will go alone."

Verboden sat back down and smiled. "I'm glad you're back, Alfred. And, I'm sorry I doubted you before."

Alfred waved his hand. "Ahnnn... forget about it!"

Alfred walked on the frosty ground making crunching sounds. In some places the ground was muddy from the sun melting the frost whenever its rays poked through cloudy skies. A cool mist rose from the warming ground. Drips of water trickled from thick oak branches. Alfred liked the bitter cold feel of the land. He liked the fresh clean air that came from the mist. Whenever the vast northern winds shifted, he would get hit with the smell of dung coming from farm livestock. Phewee! Mmm... a smell that is a sign of a healthy farm. Then the winds would shift, and the air would be fresh again.

Picking up an odor, Alfred looked up. A big orange furry bull was looking at Alfred with bored eyes. Behind it, sloshing through the mud and forking out hay, was Cory. He had grown a bit, or at least his hair had. Cory looked at Alfred, not recognizing him for a moment. Then his eyes suddenly widened with joy.

"Alfred!" Cory sloshed through the mud, leapt over the small fence and rushed to hug Alfred. "Verboden said you'd return! He did say it, and I believed him!"

They hugged tightly. "I'm sorry I was gone. I did not know the time. I don't know how the space time continuum warp thingamabob is..."

"It's that magic, isn't it?" Cory said.

"Yes. And if I could explain it to you, I would." Alfred

smiled.

"It's okay. My father tells me stuff that I don't understand. He tries to tell me stuff about your mother and the brave knight."

Alfred's eyes widened. Cory tightened his lips. He put his hand on Alfred's shoulder.

"Alfred! King Alfred!" Cory's father Derhman yelled as he rounded the bend. He gave out a deep resonating laugh and opened his arms. Alfred felt odd but slogged through the mud and cow dung to reach and embrace Derhman.

"You must come inside and have some morning meal!" Derhman said.

"Oh no, I already ate back at the castle. I want to see everyone and let them know I am back. I must let everyone know that we must prepare. All who can fight, all who can help, must gather at the castle tomorrow."

This dampened the mood. Derhman and Cory shared a sad glance. Derhman gave a deep sigh.

"It is good to have you back, King Alfred," Derhman said. "You have done us all well, and we will all do our part. As is likely that war is upon us, I will assemble the farmers. After that great victory at harvest, the goblins will surely come in the spring to disrupt our planting and try to starve us out. I guess it is better to fight them as soon as possible."

Alfred nodded. "Thank you for your support. I must go. I will talk to you again soon."

Alfred trudged along small roads to each thatched farmstead and was heartily greeted by each family. The children, many grown strong, danced about him. They had all kept up their archery and spear skills and were ready to return to the castle. They were so happy to lead Alfred into their small cottages and show how busy they'd been all winter. There were bundles and bundles of arrow shafts with goose feather fins. Everyone seemed to have become a fletching master.

"Wow," is all Alfred could say.

Setheyna and her mother had made the most, for they stood in a sea of them, bundle after bundle. All the geese of their farm shared nests inside the cottage to keep warm since none had any feathers.

Alfred was most anxious to see Loranna. He was walking up the lone country road to her father's farm on a hill when he saw her. She stood with a bow in hand, practicing on a target in a grove of trees. They stood and looked at each other from a distance for quite some time. The sun shone on Loranna. The tears upon her face glistened. Alfred came up, wiped her tears away and hugged her. She hugged him back. Though she wanted to speak, overwhelmed by her emotions, she let it all out as muffled cries and a great sigh of relief.

He had lunch with her family. He didn't speak much. Loranna's younger sister and brother, Niranna and Noren, spoke the most. Niranna was an archer under Loranna, and they were the best in marksmanship and speed. They bragged to Alfred about their skills and how much each practiced over the other and how each was so much better than the other. Loranna and Niranna giggled with each boast. Noren reminded them of his spear practice. The parents were a bit uncomfortable about their children being skilled at fighting. Regardless, they did their best to show pride and appreciation. After all, the king was in their home eating a fine porridge from their wooden bowls.

Loranna's father finally said something to change the subject, bringing a serious disposition to Alfred. "So will Lord Dunther and Gorham be in charge of defenses?"

"What? Who? What do you mean?"

Loranna's father Doren looked a bit worried. "Well uh, they came back when winter set up on us. Quite starving, they were. Brought some other knights they found."

Alfred's eyes widened, "Verboden didn't say anything!"

"Ah well…" Doren gulped.

"Tell him, father!" Loranna said.

Doren shirked. The wife smacked him on the head. "Well, now you've gone and done it. Go on and tell him everything!"

Doren gulped again. "Well, they were quite starved and meek looking. So us farmers figured it may not be such a bad idea to have them around. So Dowuhr took them in. We all shared in feeding them. They're quite nice now, you know, for knights. And they could come in handy in a fight. It's too cold for them to cause any trouble, I think."

"They're nice because they're starving and too weak to take what they want! Knights are brigands wearing banners!" said Loranna's mother. "They're gluttonous sods with no respect for hearth and home!" She was in such an upset state that all froze in various positions of eating until she finished talking.

Alfred finally broke the silence, "Where are they? At Dowuhr's, you said?"

"Well, I think so. There is not much elsewhere to go in this weather," Doren replied.

Alfred said his goodbyes to them and gave Niranna and Noren a hug. He looked at Loranna and then gave her a long hug, longer than each realized until the mother and father cleared their throats, and the children giggled. Alfred's face was exceedingly red. He hoped they thought it was from stepping back out in to the cold. He left.

Being late in the afternoon, much of the frost had melted, and the sun shone with a bright glistening aura. Alfred quite liked it, but he knew it meant the armies of Gorbogal would come soon.

Dowuhr's place was a quaint little farm. He lived alone after his wife died during the dark years. Alfred never really got to know Dowuhr for he was a quiet, old farmer. Alfred approached the door and knocked.

Now to Alfred, it was normal to walk up to a farm. But to Dowuhr, the visit was a big thing, as it was the king himself at the door knocking. Dowuhr knew the king had cast out the Knights and considered any who harbored them as outlaw. So after lifting the window cover and gazing wide eyed at Alfred, who smiled back, Dowuhr ran back into his cottage and hid under his sheets, pretending nothing had happened. Nothing at all.

Knowing Dowuhr was there, Alfred was a bit dismayed that he didn't open the door.

"Dowuhr? It's me, Alfred. I've come to see the Knights!"

"You don't need bother him," a gruff voice resounded from the adjacent barn. There, standing in a tattered blanket, was Lord Dunther. He held a sword in his hand.

Alfred backed away, realizing he was not armed. Dunther walked up to Alfred, gazing at him with gray eyes set deep within sockets surrounded by a sallow gaunt face.

Several other men emerged from the barn blinking their eyes. All were aged and worn. They looked like bandits — far worse than Hedor and his lot ever looked. All wore remnants of their former royal tunics and banners, worn and torn, dirty and stained, wrapped like beggar blankets. None wore the group's burdensome filthy rusted useless armour. Each had a weapon at hand.

"You've come to the right place, though, boy," Lord Dunther said under his breath. "I have returned to make my claim."

Alfred backed away from Lord Dunther and his blade.

"Put that down, milord," Duwohr said from his doorway, holding a rake.

Dunther paused and looked at Duwohr, the feeble farmer. He then looked down at his blade, which he sheathed. "I wasn't going to do any harm," he said, smiling with rotted teeth and gums. Alfred was not sure if it was an evil smile or one of assurance.

"I've come to ask for your help, Lord Dunther," Alfred said.

"My help? You hear that, my fellow brave Knights!? The bastard boy king needs my help!" Dunther hissed.

Duwohr stood by Alfred's side with his crooked wooden rake in hand. He nodded reassuringly to Alfred. Alfred did not feel so assured. A half dozen ragged gaunt ugly men, well armed and vicious looking, stood before him. Gorham looked the worst with bleeding gums and a grizzled visage. By the mad look in his eyes, he did not seem all there.

"Well, well, so this is the boy, hey?" another knight said, poking at Alfred with a crusty rash-ridden hand.

"Back off, Murith. I fed you all winter," Duwohr said, pointing his bent rake at him. Murith waved it off. His long hair, scraggly and greasy, hugged his face. His deranged eyes showed a young knight with impudence.

"I am Lord Tahnwhithe," said another knight, bowing as nobly as one could bow. He was taller than the rest, with a hawk-nose and what was once a majestic moustache and goatee, now curled and badly cut with a rusty blade. "I am at your service."

"Don't be so hasty, Tahnwhithe," said Dunther. "You still follow my orders."

"And you follow the king's," Duwohr said.

Alfred was stunned, as Duwohr said more in the last few moments than Alfred recalled the old farmer ever saying.

"And you best hold your tongue or I'll cut it off!" Murith said to Duwohr, leaping in with aggressive energy. He was skinny to the bones, but in a goblinesque ruffian way.

Duwohr stepped back flinching but kept up his bravery as best he could.

"It's okay, Duwohr," Alfred said to him. "These knights are here to help us. I know that."

"And how do you know that, boy?" Lord Dunther hissed. "I came to reclaim what is mine. No bastard child is going to take over this realm."

"You had twelve years to reclaim it. Now I am here. We are rebuilding, and we are making a stand," Alfred said bravely.

Murith pulled out a dagger and began to pick his nails. Two other knights stood near the barn and peered at Alfred from down-turned heads. There was Lord Byrom, easily the size of two men, with raging red hair and forearms that could wrestle down a bull. And there was Lord DuLocke, an elder knight, worn and obedient, barely carrying on in shape and form, as if all spirit had left him.

Dunther paced. Clearly he was pacing between war and peace, between outright killing and biding his time. Something besides hunger gnawed at his gut. He could not place it. The young rascally knight Murith was ready to impose the will of Dunther in a split second, killing both Alfred and Duwohr, dispensing with the problem once and for all.

"I need good knights," Alfred said. "The land and people need you."

Murith eyed them with the conviction of a vicious weasel. Tahnwhithe's countenance was the most revealing. The tall honorable hawk-nosed knight feared imminent bloodshed. The gentle red-haired giant Byrom, unspoken, stood uncaring, as he never knew the boy and had been living as a hermit in a bear's cave for years. Old DuLocke looked as if death and despair were all around him, and he was just waiting for the former. He was short but seemed to have a solid build. And his long white moustache and beard seemed to give him a dwarvish look. Gorham had a strange despondent look, gazing with bloodshot eyes at nothing. Dunther, rubbing his cheeks, grew tired of what little conversation there was.

"I feel like conversing no more," he said, waving his hand, as if that was all that mattered to him. The dispensing of a boy's life, along with that of the farmer who fed them all winter, was worth that much to him, a wave of his hand. Murith quickly leapt at the unarmed Alfred, his rusty yet sharp blade flashing at the upstroke then the down. Alfred's stunned eyes teared as he mentally tried to retreat back home to his mother.

A sudden blur of motion surprised them all. It was Gorham grabbing and twisting Murith's wrist before he could harm Alfred. Murith let out a shrill cry. Gorham, Dunther's trusted second, with a crazed look defended Alfred! He twisted Murith such that he reeled into the mud, landing face down, nearly choking from the suctioning goop.

Dunther stood frozen. Gorham faced him with his blade drawn. Gorham was a larger man, well built and an obvious choice for second in command. However today, after a winter of repose, he looked sallow and defeated.

Loranna and several children appeared from up the road. They ran with bows drawn. "Alfred!" Loranna yelled as her eyes swelled with tears, fearing she'd lose Alfred again.

The knights, in their own dilemma, weren't bothered by children with toy bows. The children were still far away, running as fast as they could. Farmers began appearing on the horizon as word spread that Alfred had gone to seek out the knights. They feared a possible confrontation. Hedor and his men were also running along distant roads to save Alfred. They had snow to plow through and would be exhausted by the time they arrived. Word had spread even to the castle. Verboden and Abedeyan were well on their way. But would any arrive in time and be able to save the king?

"Gorham, you vex me to no end. You, of all souls, want this the most," Dunther said.

"Do I, Lord Dunther? I've been starving for twelve years, rotting in my armour. Gylloth made the right choice, not us."

"How ridiculous! Gylloth is dead! You fool!" Lord

Dunther laughed, pointing at Gorham and holding his belly in because of the pain of such wretched laughter. Dunther did not last long before he was coughing, then bending over in pain, spitting and hacking up blood.

Gorham responded, "How ridiculous? We are always on the brink of starvation, eating rats and grubs. We terrorize those who do not obey us, spreading fear like the darkness we have been fighting. I have followed you my whole life. I have been a part of the choices you made. And it has all come down to this—starving to death, acting like brigands for scraps, standing before a boy who many call king and you wish only to slaughter. Lord Gylloth chose to stand with this boy and died fighting the goblins, fighting for king and country! How ridiculous indeed, for a knight to do such things."

Dunther froze, looking up at Gorham, trying to ignore the heavy truth of his words. The other knights, even those who had heard so few words in many years, understand well Gorham's reasoning and stepped away from Dunther.

"I will never follow a bastard boy! His father betrayed the king! He took our beloved lady as his own!" Dunther said, wavering in strength, spitting saliva and blood, tears streaming down his dirty face. He pulled out his sword and waved it around, ready to kill anything that came near.

Gorham stood between Dunther and Alfred. Murith was still stuck in the mud and seemed to be dying, unable to pull himself out. Knowing when something was near death, Lord Byrom grabbed what torn cloth was left on Murith's back and pulled him up. Murith coughed and spat as he was set down. He shook his head to gain composure and gave Gorham a vengeful look.

Byrom slapped Murith several feet back. "Stay out of

it."

"Lord Dunther, if Gylloth chose this boy as king, then so should we," Lord Tahnwhithe declared.

"Never! Idiots! Don't listen to Gorham. He is sick. We are the rightful rulers of this land. I will lead these people. Now move aside!" Dunther waved his sword at his fellow knights.

"I will end this now!" Gorham moved in to kill Dunther once and for all. Murith leapt past Byrom toward Gorham.

"Stop! No! Dunther, you can be king!" Alfred ran between them.

Dunther's sword was raised such that he could cut Alfred with one motion. Murith came in behind with a blade at Alfred's back. Dunther stepped toward Alfred, whose face grew pale. Yet Dunther swung at Murith. It was a skillful cut that merely threw Murith off, having him gasp with pain from a scratch as he held his arm at his side.

Alfred stood a head below Dunther and stood straight as Dunther bent over him. "I will support you as the king if you wish. You can have anything, but no killing, not each other. We have bigger threats than each other, than who is king or not. I don't care. The land of men is in peril, all of us. My aunt! My mother's sister Gorbogal musters an army of goblins and ratkins!"

Loranna, the children, and the farmers gasped. Lord Dunther looked at Alfred and then at the other knights.

"He knows, Dunther!" said Gorham. "No one but the king and we knew of the witch's past! Even Bedenwulf, the Black Knight himself, knew. We all carried that burden. Only royalty knew, it was our terrible secret."

Alfred continued, "She will come here to finish us. She

will bring an army in the spring, now, as soon as all the frost is gone. It could be a matter of days. I don't know how much time we have. We need you, Dunther. We need all of you. War is upon us. So if you want the kingship, if you really want it, you can have it, as long as you fight for us! As long as you stay and fight!"

Dunther wavered, gazing at the knights, the children and farmers... then at Alfred. He blinked his tearful eyes and then fainted.

Chapter Twenty Nine

The Return of the Knights

Alfred sat at Dunther's side as he lay in Alfred's bed. Lady Nihan and Verboden came in to care for him as best they could. Dunther, battling a strong fever, had languished in bed many days, muttering to himself, carrying on about the past and the fall of the land and the king.

Each day Alfred strolled around the castle thinking of

many things. To everyone returning after the long winter, Alfred's behavior seemed odd. He was silent and solemn. He was clearly absorbed in thinking and planning but gave no clue about what.

"What is on his mind?" Verboden asked Abedeyan after a few days.

"War, my dear sir. He is preparing us all for the coming of the horde." Abedeyan smiled reassuringly.

When Dunther woke, Alfred was asleep in a chair nearby. It was in the middle of the night, on a night with a full moon. Dunther looked at Alfred sleeping there, and he almost smiled. Almost.

Alfred suddenly awoke.

Lord Dunther was standing at the window looking at the moon. He had a look much different from that of the other knights. He was more gaunt and scruffy, even when fed well. He always had stubby facial hair. Yet he had a inner strength, and when he was at peace, his ghoulish features somehow took on the aspect of a gentle, austere monk.

"I loved your mother, if I even knew what love was," Dunther said in a soft voice. "I suppose that is what eats away at my heart. Not even the doom of the land affects me as much as the treachery your father committed upon my lordship and my claim to her. He was one of my knights, the best. He was young and brave. His father, your grandfather, was a great lord. He left on the Crusade of the Silver Age, and the family lost everything. I took them under my protection. Bedenwulf grew to be one of the greatest knights and was like my own son."

Dunther confessed what he didn't realize had poisoned

him so long.

"When the time came, when the king needed me most, I abandoned the castle to go after her. She needed no protection from me, nor did she want it. And to this day, my greed and lust for kingship and for her has darkened me to my very soul."

He gasped for air, having to expose his face, his eyes, and his shame.

Alfred walked up to Dunther and put his hand on his shoulder. "We need you, Lord Dunther. We need you now."

Dunther wiped away his tears. He looked at his hands, saddened by their very presence. "These hands have oppressed and were harbingers of doom to anyone who dared question me. And in time of starvation and sorrow, they only knew violence and tyranny."

"Dunther, I think all have done things to survive that they now regret. It seems everyone became a beast in one form or another during these hard times. Hedor and his men were once farmers and then became bandits on the road. They were hurt and hungry and became violent. Verboden fed them and was kind to them. Now, they are decent men once more. We are all, I hope, coming out of dark times. The time is now to join and fight. There is a castle being rebuilt. It only needs great knights to defend it for the sake of the people, the farmers, workers and children. It is springtime again, with hope for a better life. We all look to you to help us fight for this newfound hope." Alfred gasped at such a long winded and almost kingly speech.

Dunther could not help but smile through his tears. "For king, for country."

Alfred smiled.

The children had returned. They gathered in the courtyard, hugging each other and seeing who had grown to what height. All wondered who grew the most. They compared their bundles of arrow shafts with feathers. Each had all winter to think of the coming battles, and each was required to make as many arrows as possible by order of Broggia.

"Hope you don't mind, milord?" Broggia said to Alfred.

Alfred was completely surprised by the number of arrow shafts the children had made. Shocked would perhaps be a better word. Broggia too had kept busy, sharpening the old goblin arrowheads as well as crafting new ones. All were made of goblin metal. It was strong and light, just not well utilized by the goblin's themselves. Broggia's son Boggin was busy fixing many of the goblin spears and shields, knowing the boys would need them.

Alfred was happy that they had stayed busy during the winter preparing while he was gone. He now needed to help them finish getting ready. As cheery as they were at this quaint reunion, a dark cloud hovered over all of them.

"Okay, let us go into the Keep. I have much to say of the coming battle."

"We have knights now too, right Alfred?" said one of the younger boys, leaping about excitedly.

"Yes, yes, I believe so," Alfred smiled.

The group of children, the girl archers and the boys with spears and shields, entered the Keep. The knights were already there. Rascally Murith was pacing, holding one of the goblin spears that had been left for practice. The red-headed giant Byrom sat on the floor, looking blankly at nothing. Hawk-nosed Tahnwhithe was sitting at table, curling his trimmed moustache and sipping water from a goblet, a nicety he had not known for some time. Crusty Du Locke stood in the shadows, an old man, a faint remembrance of his former self. Gorham and Dunther were not present.

Alfred knew Dunther was still resting in Alfred's room. Gorham had not been seen for some time. Alfred finally learned that he was sick and remained in one of the towers.

"Well, if it isn't the boy king and his school children," Murith said with some mirth.

Lord Tahnwhithe stood up out of respect. Du Locke remained in the shadows. Byrom merely glanced with his big bear eyes.

"Shouldn't these children be at their farms, shooting crows while the farmers plow the fields?" Murith asked sarcastically.

"We have a lot of work to do," said Alfred, ignoring the young knight's foul temperament.

"Work? Here? I don't see any crows in here," Murith chuckled. Suddenly he turned and threw the goblin spear. It hit one of the targets the children used for practice. It hit dead center. The children gasped with amazement.

"Wow! That was awesome, Lord Murith," Alfred said.

"I'm not a lord. I'm a knight!" Murith said.

"You're a squire. Only a king can make you a knight," Lord Tahnwhithe reminded him.

Alfred gulped.

Murith's eyes narrowed. The children stood in awe, knowing Murith must have great skills.

"Can you teach us that?" Cory asked, walking up to

him.

"Go home to your common father, peasant boy!" yelled Murith. "Get out of here!" Cory flinched and then raised his spear instinctively, as if to ward off Murith.

"Look at this farmer's boy, Tahnwhithe!" Murith said with snide arrogance. "Do you see that? He's pointing a spear at me!"

Cory gulped and stepped back. Murith approached him. Alfred watched, intrigued. Cory looked to Alfred for help, but Alfred only smiled. Cory knew he was in for the lesson of his life.

Murith reached out, grabbed the spear's tip and pulled, thrusting Cory to the ground, face flat. Murith laughed and grabbed the spear so he could jab a painful prick into Cory's back.

Before he could, he looked up to see three dozen young girls with bows and arrows aimed straight at him and a dozen big boys rushing him with spear and shield.

Though Murith would have liked to teach them all a lesson, it was he who learned one. He poked and jabbed at a few and then backed off in anger. When he began his infuriated awkward wild swings and thrusts, Alfred knew it was time to quickly end the lesson.

"All back!" Alfred yelled, and the boys immediately retreated into a defensive wall around Cory. He stood up behind the circle of spears, ready with a new spear in his hand.

Murith was reeling and fell, even though no one was around him. He jabbed blindly like a frightened boy thinking he was still in danger.

Tahnwhithe stood still in silence with a smile. Byrom's

deep baritone voice gave a boisterous laugh. Du Locke chortled, his eyes seeming to move with life in them.

Finally Murith realized he was in the clear, got up and tried to act as if he hadn't fallen. He brushed his hair back and tried to provoke the boys to come at him again.

"Murith, you don't even know that you've just survived that one, now do you?" Tahnwhithe asked.

Alfred walked up to Cory, grabbed the end of his spear and pulled. Cory tugged back but got off balance again. Alfred said, "That's what they'll do."

"Yah, that's what I'll do to all of you!" Murith was yelling with feeble anger.

"Not you, the ratkins," Alfred said.

Everyone, including Murith's eyes widened.

Alfred walked up to him and motioned for the boys to follow. "And you, Murith, the ratkins will do that to you," Alfred said.

Murith, at first defiant, leveled his spear and then realized that a dozen spears were coming at him. He backed away with unsure footing. He panicked, slapping away at spears that came too close. Yet others filled the void. In sheer terror he fell back into the great hole in the back of the Keep, the huge opening Alfred fell down the first day he set foot in the King's Hall. That great hole where Alfred had encountered the giant spider, and it is that very hole that leads into the dungeon floors below.

Murith didn't fall far. He merely went limp and got caught in the rubble as a dozen spears angled down upon his meek self.

"How did a bunch of small vermin ratkins kill a knight?" Alfred asked.

"It was Dunther's fault!" screamed Murith. "Not mine! He abandoned the castle! He's the traitor!"

"Hold your tongue, squire!!" Lord Tahnwhithe yelled.

"No! Not even Dunther and his great sword could defeat the ratkin swarm! Not him and a company of knights fully armed could defeat the ratkins," Alfred said.

"What talk is this? No ratkin is better than a knight!" Lord Tahnwhithe said.

Alfred turned to Tahnwhithe and responded, "You're right. No ratkin is better than a knight, and that is why ratkins never attack alone. They only attack when there are thousands of them, swarming around you, poking with spear and stick, clawing with teeth and talons, easily climbing your armour and toppling your weight to the ground!"

Tahnwhithe seemed quite intrigued by the observation, especially since all the boys began to surround him with their goblin spears. "Then if this is true, we cannot defeat such a swarm of ratkins."

"Yes, we can," Alfred replied confidently.

Murith climbed back out of the hole and mocked, "What, with a bunch of children!?"

All were silent and looked concerned. Alfred turned to Murith and shot back with fierce impatience. "Are you done? Is that all you have to say 'a bunch of children'?" The bravado confused Murith.

As Alfred raised his hand, the boys converged their spears on Murith. He flinched a little too much.

Alfred continued, pointing with firmness. "No! We will not fight with just a bunch of children. We will have well trained archers there along the perimeter, and the boys will be below in the dungeons with their spears."

He then turned. "Cory, I want you to get Boggin to finish spiking the shaft of your spears. Murith has shown us that ratkins will definitely grab and pull on them." With that comment, even the silent giant Byrom couldn't help but chuckle and smirk.

"What is it you speak of?" Lord Tanwhithe asked.

Alfred went on, "We have spears with small razor sharp blades along the sides, so when the ratkins try to grab them, they'll get cut. Oh and we've added small spikes to the shields."

"You're no king," hissed Murith. "You're an insane little boy."

Without a word, Lord Tahnwhithe walked briskly up to Murith and slapped him on the cheek. It was no ordinary slap. It was one given by a knight and thus carried a special insult with it. Murith fell several feet back near the hole, tottered on the edge and slipped again. Down he went.

Alfred rushed up and put his spear in the hole. Murith rejected it and held on to the rough hewn edges of the hole to try to climb out, with no success.

"Grab on!" Alfred commanded.

Murith grabbed Alfred's spear and climbed out with an embarrassed look on his face. Murith glared at Lord Tahnwithe but Alfred ignored the tension.

"The ratkins will come up through here. Hundreds then thousands will come," Alfred said.

"Then we should cover it," Lord Tahnwhithe remarked.

"No, this is where we want them to come. If we force them to find other ways out from the dungeons, they will come out and spill into the courtyard and attack everyone. It is here that the boys with their spears shall lead them. The boys have already been training in the dungeon corridors and know which areas to block to direct them to this great hole."

"That is folly," said Murith. "Even if we could arm everyone, even if we had our old armour and swords, we would be overrun. It is just as you said!"

"Yes, even long ago when the ratkins made this hole, whether Lord Dunther was here or not, you would have fallen," Alfred said. "They'll surround you from all sides and easily kill you, Sir Murith. Small little ratkins can do this. But you won't be surrounded. They will. Loranna and all the archers will be up there along all sides surrounding them. They are great archers. They are! However, that is not all we will need. We will need you knights here as well."

"Even if these young children are good archers, the mass of ratkins that would pour through this opening would eventually overtake us," Lord Tahnwhithe duly noted.

"Have you guys ever heard of pro-wrestling?" Alfred asked.

"Yes, of course, we are well trained in the art of wrestling," Lord Tahnwhithe said with pride.

"You expect us to wrestle a bunch of armed ratkins?" Murith asked.

"Yes," Alfred said, pausing a moment to let it sink in. All of the knights raised their eyebrows, including Lord Byrom and Du Locke. Unbeknownst to them, Gorham had joined them and stood above in the shadows just beyond the balcony wall. "Only, your armour, mailed fists, small shields, boots, backs, helmets and knees will be riddled with protruding spikes."

Lord Tahnwhithe and Murith shared an amused glance. What Alfred was suggesting had never been done.

Everyone found it intriguing.

"Every move you make, every swing, roll, fall, climb, jump, clamber and tumble will be a deadly strike on numerous yet far inferior and weaker creatures than yourselves. Every leap and climb they attempt on your armour will only bring pain and death to them. Every attempt to bring you down will only bring down a wall of spikes on them. – This is our time."

Byrom stood up. He was nearly twice the height of all and definitely twice the girth. Du Locke came from the shadows, his eyes glistening with vengeance. Lord Tahnwhithe's eyes gazed with bravery. Murith smiled and licked his lips.

Then they heard resounding applause from above. Gorham walked out from the shadows, standing above them on the balcony and clapped. "Well done, King Alfred. If there is any chance at all, that may be it."

"Well, here it is, the 'proto-type' as Alfred put it," Broggia said as he showed the knights the new armour. It was made of goblin pieces with spikes of various lengths poking out from many sides.

"I kept the spikes short and more dense where I suspect you may fall or roll. I don't want them all breaking off at once. The longest spikes are here, along the maul, the shoulders and helmet."

"It looks a bit ugly. It is not really noble-like, now is it?" Lord Tahnwhithe remarked. Broggia huffed.

Murith touched the armour with keen interest.

"Would you like to try it on?" Broggia said with excitement.

Murith nodded. As Broggia and Boggin tightened the straps, Broggia had to calm Murith down so as not to be killed by him. "Not the slightest move, please, milord." Before long he was fully suited.

Murith waited patiently, barely, but as soon as they were done, he moved about with wrestling moves. He rushed about the ward scaring everyone and hitting things he shouldn't. He rolled onto one of the looms where the weavers had done work and obliterated it. Everything he came into contact with was utterly destroyed.

In his excitement, he leaped at the door and got stuck there like a helpless ornament. "Help!" he yelled.

Broggia and Lord Byrom rushed up and carefully pried him from the door, both reacting several times from repeated pokes. Murith, in his forgetfulness, reached out to hug Byrom, who screamed in utter pain as he backed away.

"Squire, I'll get you!" Byrom grabbed up several large pieces of wood and tossed them at Murith. Each piece knocked Murith back and stuck to him as well.

"Oh, I'm sorry! Sorry, Lord Byrom! Truly, I'm sorry." Murith cried.

Lord Byrom was bleeding from many small holes. He and everyone present couldn't help but laugh at the absurdity of his wounds caused by a squire's hug. Their mirth increased when they saw Murith lying there, stuck with large pieces of lumber he was trying to remove.

Lord Dunther stood in the outer ward. He stared at the awesome display of knights before him, each fitted in spiked dark goblin armour. Each looked like something out of a nightmare, like terrible demons in shadow armour. Lord

Tahnwhithe looked embarrassed. He knew this was not proper attire for a noble knight. Deep down he was hoping Lord Dunther would not approve.

"Well, what do you think?" Alfred asked.

Dunther blinked slowly. Gorham came out in his attire and looked the most ferocious. He carried a spiked mace, with spikes all along it and a spiked shield.

"Hey, where'd you get that?" Murith asked.

"I made it!" Gorham said. He held it up to Murith and then tossed it at him. Catching it in the wrong place, Murith grimaced. Then he carefully removed it from his hand. Once he held the spike-free grip, he forgot his pain and swung the mace.

"I want one. Can I have one?"

Gorham laughed, "It's yours. I'll make some more."

Broggia joined in. "My son can make some more, if you like."

Gorham looked at him. "That would be an honor."

Broggia bowed.

Dunther smiled and then looked at Alfred. "Well, where's mine?"

Murith rushed at the boys, not in his spiked armour, of course, but wrapped in many wads of leather with two big triangle cut pieces that looked like large ears. He almost looked like a rat as he rushed about the dungeon corridors. He yelled and screeched and leapt at the boys. He knocked many over and pulled and tugged at their spears and shields. He finally got several boys stacked in a pile, put his foot on them and raised his arms in victory, yelping and hollering. Several other boys rushed in from all sides with their sticks pointing at him. Murith leapt about but knew he was trapped. He raised his arms in surrender but was given no quarter as the boys continued to poke their wooden sticks at him.

He laughed with each poke, "Alright, alright, I surrender!"

Gorham entered the area. "Good, you helped your fellow men. But you men cannot let the ferocity of the ratkins overtake you."

The boys stood up from their fallen positions. Alfred, Cory and the rest listened intently. They were all especially dirty and tired looking. Murith stood behind, readjusting his ratkin-like costume and protective pieces.

"Right, let's do it again!" Gorham said, clapping.

The boys moaned and groaned, but Gorham would have none of it. "Move soldiers!! Move!!!"

Hedor stood atop one of the towers, looking into the night sky. He had a small oil lamp to keep his hands warm.

"You should not have that lamp lit," said Dunther, slowly ascending the small wooden ladder.

Hedor stood still. "Milord."

"It is much harder to see in the darkest nights when your eyes grow lazy by a fire," Dunther said. Hedor nodded and blew out the lamp. The cold blue light of night seeped in.

"Alfred told me of your stand with Gylloth, fighting off the goblin raiders," Dunther paced along the tower parapets, looking at the quiet dark landscape below.

"Yes, milord, he fought bravely." Hedor rubbed his hands in the cool night.

"So did you."

Hedor kept a smug look.

"And so did your men."

Hedor nodded.

"You were all farmers once?" Dunther inquired.

Hedor nodded. Since Dunther was looking down, he did not see his response. So Hedor stuttered a reply, "Yes, farmers, but we have no farms now."

"All of us have lost something," Dunther replied. "Now King Alfred is helping us to get something back."

Hedor nodded, knowing that this time Dunther's gaze was upon him.

"I need good men, good fighting men," Dunther said. "When the knights and... children... are fighting for their lives in that Keep, we will need men out here holding back the goblins, holding back Gorbogal's horde."

Hedor looked up to meet Dunther's gaze.

"I need a captain. I need a man-at-arms up here," Dunther said.

Hedor mixed a shrug with a nod. Or was he just responding to the chill in the air?

"Good," said Dunther with a nod, climbing back down the ladder. "Good night, Captain Hedor."

Chapter Thirty

The Battle Begins

Farmers hurried into the Keep. Dunther, Tahnwhithe and Murith rode on the three remaining horses to help peasants get to the castle. Goblin scouts had appeared. Groups of them spread across the land, creating panic and fear.

Farmers and castle folk stood on the walls. Each time they saw a new column of smoke rise in the sky, they would speculate on whose farm it was. The goblin raiders were burning whatever they found standing. Farmers and their wives cried when they realized which column of smoke seen must be coming from their very own farms.

They had prepared for this moment. All the seed and

fruits of harvest were in the castle as well as important tools, livestock and belongings. Each family had a designated area within the walls where they could put up makeshift tents and store their belongings. They hugged each other for comfort and for hope.

In their traditional though minimal armour with sword and shield, the brave knights galloped across fields and pastures. The goblins hurried through the darkest patches of forest, trying to ambush fleeing farmers along narrow roads. The knights were well prepared. Dunther, Tahnwhithe, and Murith quickly dispensed the scattered raiders. These short-lived creatures never saw such defiance in men, especially men with well fed horses and sharpened lances. They expected an easy slaughter of struggling peasants. Instead, it was a slaughter and routing of goblins.

"All are accounted for, and all are well!" Abedeyan yelled from the gate. Alfred, Gorham, and Verboden were helping families with their goods. It was a prodigious affair. Chickens flew. Cows mooed. Pigs snorted. Gorham rushed to the gate, peering across the land. Alfred hurried over. Abedeyan was at the wheel, making sure it was ready to lower.

Cory rushed out from the Great Hall. "All the boys are in, sir," addressing Alfred. "We are setting up our defensive positions in the dungeons."

"Good! Make sure everyone is well fed. Then establish patrols and rest times. Everyone must be ready when the ratkins attack," Alfred said.

Cory saluted Alfred and left.

Gorham and Verboden could not help but smile. Alfred noticed and asked meekly, "What?" Even in such circumstances, both tried to nod away their affection for their king. Who happened to be a boy.

Alfred walked through a dark corridor with a candle as his only light source. He entered the tower hall where Tirnalth once resided. It was empty. He sat at the table. "Tirnalth, where are you? I hope you are okay. We could use you, your help."

Verboden entered and sat next to Alfred. "He's okay. I feel it."

"I'm wondering about Gorbogal's mist. Do you think she found him?"

"No, I don't. But I am not sure. If she did, I would think something more grand would have happened, even more grand than a few ratkins and goblins attacking. She would have come herself."

"Is he hiding at his place, in that great hall of books?"

"I am not sure. I will pray for him, and I will pray that he returns."

Alfred put his head on the table.

"You have done well, Alfred. I can see why Tirnalth risked so much to bring you here. Even without his memory, he knew in his heart that we needed you. You are a great king. No matter what happens, you have brought back the light and restored hope in all of us. No one would begrudge you for bringing joy to us this moment, even with evil knocking at the door."

The sun was setting and darkness seeping in. On the horizon all manner of poles and banners appeared.

"Here they come!" Lord Dunther bellowed.

"Why haven't the ratkins come?" Alfred wondered aloud.

"Don't worry, King Alfred. They will come! The goblins will make one meek attack upon these walls to get us focused and worried about our outer defenses. Then the ratkins will strike from within. They will think we are vulnerable, having made the fatal flaw of looking out instead of being ready to defend within. But we will not make that mistake, – because of you King Alfred. Indeed, we will not be vulnerable at all."

Lord Dunther could not help but smile at Alfred. "Murith," he said, "make sure Broggia and Boggin have that *pro-wrestler* armour ready!"

Murith nodded and leapt down from the wall in regular knight's armour with sword at hand.

"Pro-wrestler armour?"

"Well, that's what you called it. Didn't you? Pro-wrestler!"

"Well… sort of…"

As his eyes gazed at the horizon, Alfred went quiet. The sun was nearly gone. Besides banners and flagpoles, he now saw a mass of spears appearing among the hills.

"A goblin horde indeed," Dunther hissed.

They could faintly hear the drumbeats. It seemed there were hundreds of drummers. At first the sound seemed chaotic, each drummer beating to his own rhythm. Soon enough they were in unison, making one thunderous beat after another. Goblins on boars raced about, barking and roaring orders to keep others in line. The goblins formed groups, covering the slopes of the hills and valleys. They waited for their order to charge up the slope to the lone keep.

Captain Hedor rushed from wall to wall to encourage

his two dozen men. They were spread out along four walls and four towers.

Abedeyan slowly climbed up the stairs to where Alfred and Dunther stood. "How is it going?" he asked. Upon reaching the top and viewing the immense field below with goblins filling every slope and patch of green, he answered himself, "Oh my!"

Captain Hedor came up to where Alfred and Dunther stood, passing the paralyzed Abedeyan. "We have only a few men on each wall. If they attack us from all sides, we will easily be overrun! I hope this is only meant to be a distraction. We won't be able to hold them back!"

Dunther and Alfred were clearly unsure of what to do. The immensity of the situation, regardless of any planning or strategy, was just overwhelming.

"If any one of my men are lost, the essential defense of these walls is doomed," Captain Hedor said.

Abedeyan bowed silently and hurried away.

"We will be here as long as we can," said Lord Dunther. "The knights will have to retreat into the Keep to change armour quickly before the ratkins arrive. I don't want to expose the new armour or our plans of defense to them. It may look like there are only goblins out there, but I'm certain Gorbogal has eyes here somewhere. I know it!"

"Look! Up there!" someone yelled out.

All looked up and then ducked as something huge swooped across the dark sky, blotting out stars as it passed. The wail of a giant vulture screech could be heard across the valley.

Alfred ran to the boys in the dungeons. He was already

prepared with small armoured pieces on his shoulders, elbows and knees, and he had on thick leather gloves. As with all the boys' spears, his was a goblin spear designed for battle against the ratkins, with spikes protruding outward from the upper shaft.

Each boy also had small shields with spikes, and each shield had a round hole to shove a spear through. The boys were separated into groups and placed in specific corridors with metal gates hammered into place. All the gates also had protruding spikes. The boys stood behind them for protection. The smaller boys rushed about laying caltrops — twisted metal stars placed on the ground with one end sticking up.

Alfred rushed from group to group, encouraging them and seeing that all was made ready. He gave Cory the thumbs up and then rushed up to the Great Hall.

Loranna and the girls were placing their bundles of arrows at choice points along the balcony. All were aiming and testing their bows. Each had two or three bows and piles and piles of small arrows ready.

Alfred stopped and gazed at Loranna for a long moment. Their eyes met, and there was a shared sense of joy. The noise from the girls with their bows and arrows and the distant sound of booming goblin drums brought them back to the task at hand. Loranna adjusted a pad on Alfred's shoulder to get in close. She hugged him. He hugged back as best he could with his spear and shield in his hands.

They nodded, as there were no words to speak. Loranna wiped a tear away and turned to give orders, to make sure all was ready. Alfred rushed out to the walls.

As he sprinted, he ran into Abedeyan, who was leading the peasants. Broggia and Boggin rushed about giving out their load of goblin swords and axes, shields and pot helms. "Take one. Take all! Come on! We're all in this together!"

"These are a bit small," a farmer said.

"They're sharper than your rake or hoe!" Boggin said.

"Smell odd?" another farmer commented.

"With goats all day and you're concerned about the smell!?" Boggin retorted.

Broggia noticed Alfred and bowed as best he could given he was carrying a handful of goblin accouterments. Peasants, men and women who were strong and could fight gathered what they could. The youngest of children and the oldest of peasants cried and held each other in the shadows of the walls and towers as their fathers and mothers, or sons and daughters, prepared themselves for the fight of their lives.

Abedeyan led them to the walls, separating them into groups to ascend stairs on each side.

Lord Dunther and Captain Hedor turned to see the peasants coming forth. Dunther advanced to stop them but was stopped by Hedor. "It's our only chance. It's their only chance."

With the weight of the situation on his heart, Dunther knew it was not his pride being hurt. He was worried for these people as they passed him and took up positions along the walls. He shuddered when a farmer's wife, weighted unsurely by metal, passed him.

Abedeyan was breathing heavily when he came up. "Some are good shots with bow. I'll send them up to the highest towers. Many practiced with their children, you know!" That brought a smile into Dunther's heavy heart.

The goblins were spread out across the countryside and

wasted no time. They knew they had to attack before the sun rose, or they'd be in for it. It was a difficult season for goblins to attack. The darkest night lasted less than the day, and the full sunny days would blind their eyes. They knew they were more vulnerable to counterattacks from humans if they could not find the darkest of forests to retreat into at dawn. And there was no dark forest near this castle. They were not in the least worried about humans putting up any sort of fight while it remained dark. Goblins do not live that long or have a great memory. It had been a long time since men had put up any sort of fight in these parts.

With a rising crescendo of drumbeats accompanied by barks from larger goblins on heavy spittle-breathing boars, the goblins advanced. Group after group moved forward from various spots. As they came, they became a sea of goblins converging on a simple yet stout castle with thick walls and thicker towers.

It was the darkest of nights and difficult to see. The peasant bowmen atop the towers peered out. Though they could see the tide of goblins moving, they could not pick out single goblins in it.

"Fire at will!" Dunther yelled up to the towers. The peasants nodded and let loose arrows. The handful of arrows were swallowed up by the dark waves of goblins.

As many as the goblins were, arrogance was their undoing. As they got closer, they made a mad dash toward the castle, screaming and hollering with an uproarious clamor of battle rage. The front lines began to fall, literally. They tumbled into pits filled with spikes. Row after row fell into the pits until they were full of spiked, crushed and bone broken goblins. The fallen yelled in panicked torture as their brethren unwittingly stumbled onto them. The goblins were like water filling and then overflowing the pits. They found themselves climbing a pile of their own kind.

"Fire! Keep firing!" Dunther yelled up to the towers at the peasants. Because of the height of the towers and the speed of the arrows descending, each shot was deadly. Yet there were too few arrows as the goblins kept moving forward, angered at their slow and crowded assault. Many died merely tumbling and being crushed as others ran over them.

As a dark shadow loomed over one of the high towers, a great gust of hot air knocked down peasants. All looked up and suddenly felt terror and stopped shooting. They screamed as a giant vulture with a Dark Rider hovered above. The vulture splayed its great talons, ready to grab up a cowering farmer.

From the trapdoor, Murith, the knight, leapt out with his lance in both hands. He yelled with desperate bravado and jammed the lance as fiercely as he could into the belly of the giant beast. It croaked and flapped its powerful grotesque wings, grabbing instinctively at the pain in its stomach. Murith yelled and pushed, twisting his lance to afflict the most damage. Peasants scrambled for cover, crawling toward and then falling down the ladder at the trapdoor. One hung desperately on the outside of the tower screaming. Peasants nearby quickly went to his aid.

Gorham climbed the ladder as fast as he could and caught a farmer sliding down. He quickly tossed the peasant safely to the next floor so he could keep going up. He reached the top just in time to see Murith carried away from the tower, hanging onto the lance.

"Murith!" Gorham yelled. Murith looked wide eyed and confused at his situation, hanging high up above the castle. It was his fortune that the vulture, in such pain, flew back to the castle tower, bashing against the wall. Murith let go and crashed through a wooden hut far below. Cows screeched and pigs squealed as Murith shook it off and rolled away from the panicked animals.

Unsure of Murith's predicament, Gorham had only a moment of respite before the Dark Rider was in motion again. Unperturbed by the awkward flying of his foul beast, the rider moved the beast closer to the peasants, coming only a swing away from the knight. Gorham was not one to miss a chance. He swung at the Dark Rider.

The sword scraped the black armour of the foul rider, bits of armour flew off. Gorham had his chance and thrust fiercely. The rider was attempting to control its mount but he still had powers beyond that of Gorham. He emitted a foul green gas from his clawed hand. Gorham was knocked back by the burst of poisonous hot air. His helm began to smoke from the acid. He quickly pulled it off, falling back while coughing and choking. The beast reeled back, banging the Dark Rider's leg against the tower.

The Dark Rider was not one to tarry above the Keep with an injured mount. He pulled at his giant bird, forcing it to fly off with the lance still stuck in its belly.

Murith shook off his haze as farmers rushed in not to help him but to calm their favored beasts. He glanced and shrugged. Then he climbed back up the tower to find Gorham.

"Gorham! Sir Gorham!" Murith scrambled along toward the pale looking knight.

Gorham gasped for air.

"That was a dirty trick!" yelled Gorham, infuriated. "I had him with my sword!" Even with the severe situation, Murith couldn't help but laugh. They both looked at the melting helm, however, and the laughing stopped.

Goblins reached the castle wall. With their tiny claws and nimble fingers, they could easily find the cracks and crevices of any stone wall and scale them quickly. They were known for being good at this. But this wall was different. It seemed to bite back at them. Unbeknownst to them, it was littered with metal nails and spikes. The first row of goblins got stuck to the wall as their brethren pushed up against them.

The spikes were oily and slippery, so when enough goblins were skewered and new ones grabbed onto them, they'd slide off as a whole. More would push in and get impaled. A vicious piling began to take place.

The farmers and bandits stared down. Many fired arrows haphazardly, easily hitting the crowded goblins

As vast as the initial attack was, it was nearing an end. And Dunther and Hedor could see this. They noted the ranks of dead swelling in piles at the pits and in the field. Many were hit by the descending arrows, and some were crushed on the walls trying to climb them.

"Alfred, that king of ours, is brilliant," Dunther said under his breath.

"I'm inclined to agree," Hedor said with a stunned expression. Not a weapon had been swung when the goblins lost their momentum. No human blood was spilled inside the walls.

The peasants hurled hoots and hollers down at the failing line of goblins. "Stand back, fools," cried Abedeyan, rushing along the wall with his pot helm on and holding a goblin spear. "That will only spur those vile pests on, dead or not!"

Alfred rushed up to Dunther and Hedor, shouting "Ratkins! We can hear them!"

Dunther turned, "Good knights, with me! Captain Hedor, you must hold the walls!"

Captain Hedor looked down at the piles of dead goblins and the retreating stragglers, some being picked off by the peasant bowmen on the towers, "I think we have."

Dunther smiled and leapt down from the wall, peeling off his traditional armour as he went. Alfred hurried back to the dungeon corridors below.

Chapter Thirty One

Ratkins

Alfred rushed from corridor to corridor to check on each group of boys, to encourage them as best he could. All were shaking, knowing this was their moment.

At first, the sound was subtle. They heard a few screeches and scurries. Then a ratkin would pop its head out from one of the many smaller tunnels. It would look around, see the boys and their torches, and then quickly disappear. These were clearly the scouts.

At first glance, the ratkins looked like rats as they poked their heads into the tunnels. That is where the similarities between rat and ratkin ended. Their heads were the size of a dog's head—a small mangy dog, that is. Their noses had the hectic sniffing twitches, and their whiskers fluttered. Their fur was black, greasy and clumped. Their black beady eyes never focused on anything, it seemed. Their brows furrowed in vile anger at the very presence of the boys. They snarled with dirty yellow teeth and pink and black gums.

One could say they were dressed in clothes—if you could call it clothes. They wore dirty leathery straps tied together and wrapped tightly around their limbs. These straps were adorned with small bones or trinkets scavenged from human, goblin or nastier critters. They never took them off. Their garb was greasy and blackened from grime and mildew. From it protruded small knives of bone or wood. Many had sharpened sticks or had stolen arrows, which they reinforced with wrapped leather to make spears. Some had blades they'd stolen from a kitchen or armoury or off some bedside table in the darkest nights.

They also wore stolen belts, buckles, hoods, torn pieces of cloth, strings and pouches. As if to copy those they scavenged, they looked like miniature brigands, bandits and cutthroats but with greasy matted fur and grotesque, long-ribbed tails.

More ratkins appeared and scurried from hole to hole. They leapt about to avoid the light and were inevitably pushed forward by more ratkins coming through. As their numbers increased, there was a flurry of them crawling over each other and forming a mass. The whole looked like a giant furry beast with many grotesque pale white-ribbed tails squirming.

Right away the boys noticed a great stench that came with the arrival of the ratkins. They seemed to wet and stain everything they crawled over or slid against. Their screeching and squealing grew louder and peaked as they began their attack. Within the hall their quick advance was halted by the mere presence of the light and the surprising presence of defenders.

Several ratkins moved forward and noticed the spiked metal gates. They sniffed along the gates and grew angry at the boys they could smell beyond them.

Their ranks swelled as they gathered in force. Several at the front frantically felt along the gate with their large gnashing teeth, searching for any area to chew through, finally resorting to their instinctual method of digging. Soon enough, a small metal spike or nail would cut them and send them squealing back into their fold.

Their purpose was to take over the under realm of this castle and pour onto the castle grounds. To be held up by defenses was unexpected and infuriating. The ratkins gathered in groups to begin their attack. They pounced upon the gates, shaking the hinges and large iron spikes that held them in place.

Cory was the first to yell and rush forward, poking his spear violently through the gate. He poked and cut many as they swirled amongst themselves, screeching with rage at the pain. Other boys came up and did the same, poking furiously through the gates. The bigger boys attacked from above, and the smaller boys poked from crouched positions. They yelled loudly at the squealing ratkins. This gave them courage amidst the terrifying screeches. Within moments the ratkins were backing off from the gates in utter anger and confusion. A large one rushed up with rodent impatience and grabbed Cory's spear, only to have its thin fingers severed. It squealed in pain and disappeared back into the fold of ratkins.

Alfred was with several boys at another gate, poking furiously.

"Back, you foul vermin!"

The ratkins became tormented by the blockade and the pressure of more and more ratkins pressing in from behind. A sense of impending doom was felt by the hundreds of ratkins trapped in the corridors against the gates. Alfred knew they would soon swell to thousands pressing forward. The ratkins at the front were desperate to break the blockades.

Many ratkins found other small holes to rush through and quickly squealed when they hit the traps placed within. Small nails and spikes were in abundance at this castle in many spots. When the ratkins would find a wide open corridor to rush down, the caltrops did their part to slow them down or route them back. The forward ratkins would grab up their feet in utter pain only to be trampled by brethren coming behind them. They would desperately try to advance by turning into a new corridor. Inevitably, they would slam against another heavily spiked gate and be crushed against it by those in the rear pushing forward.

To explain the amount of poking and prodding and violence that was inflicted upon the ratkins would be unwise. The vicious disease-ridden vileness of the ratkins, which have infected, maimed and killed many, was finally returned on them in the corridors below Grotham Keep. Throughout the lands of the Westfold and beyond, a great sigh of relief will be had by many if these ratkins are stopped here and now. The boys held off the ratkins in all the corridors, thrusting their spears into the vicious gatherings. The stench and foulness were unbearable, but the boys kept yelling and screaming in support of each other. Several smaller boys rushed about peering into smaller tunnels to find ratkins trying to sneak through. The ratkins would quickly meet their demise and block the area for a little while.

The boys held up their spiked shields in defense and guided their spears through the pie-cut holes, thrusting violently in and out with a sawing motion. Ratkins would either be killed outright or cut and mangled such that they would attempt to flee. But with their own rushing up from behind, they found themselves unable to squirm away.

The strategy of these horrendously vile rodents was to swarm and overbear the foe by sheer numbers. If the swarm was unable to advance due to spiked gates and poking spears, they would get bottle necked into certain corridors and then the swarm became its own trap. It would cause them to be crowded and crushed by the waves of all those in the rear trying to advance. It brought their onslaught to a standstill.

Alfred knew the dam, as it were, would eventually break, and the floodgates would open. On this occasion, at all the gates there were ratkins, most piled dead, crushed up against the gates and strained to their limit. The boys knew this was it, that they had prevailed. They could hear a few muffled cries of dying ratkins as more beyond were still trying to push their way through. The distressed ratkins kept pressing on, ordered forward by some evil force, which could only be Gorbogal.

"Gates one and two!" Alfred yelled. The boys nodded,

knowing the plan. Cory pulled a chain from one of the gates, releasing several strong supports. The gates buckled rapidly and finally fell through. Hundreds of impaled and crushed ratkins fell forward. Cory and his boys rushed out of the way and set up positions along the side corridors.

This was no matter to the angry and confused ratkins. They sensed the opportunity to unleash themselves, and this spurred them on. Two more gates fell as such, and the ratkins, like water, rushed through the corridor, many fanning out and taking side corridors, only to be met by shield and spear. These were small losses when compared to the greater rush of rodents that now began to climb to the surface where they would kill everything in sight. Finally, they would be able to overtake all within!

The ratkins poured out of the great hole into the Great Hall, the swarm finally unleashed. But to their surprise, row after row fell.

"Fire one! Fire two! Fire three!" Loranna yelled and repeated. Three dozen girls, in three rows, fired arrow after arrow, never missing given the multitude of ratkins that climbed up and poured out of the opening. The first row of girls fired from one balcony, the second row from another and the third from still another—a flurry of arrows shot in unison taking out group after group of ratkins. Loranna's coordinated orders made the volleys seem like a constant stream. None of the ratkins expected volley after volley, row after row or group after group to be eradicated in a shower of arrows. The girls didn't focus on aiming. Instead, they focused on speed and strength, quickly firing volleys of arrows into the oncoming swarm.

Even so, more and more ratkins kept coming up, fanning out in the hall. All the windows and doors were heavily barricaded with wood and metal. There was one door at the end, the great door, and it was open so the river of ratkins flowed toward it. They sensed that that was their way out, to spread and swarm onto the castle grounds. Though many fell from the arrows, many more of the foul creatures, oblivious, swarmed ahead. What did they care if many died by spear or were crushed in the corridors below or felled by arrows? The ratkins reveled that they now saw the opening that would end this siege.

Suddenly, however, they found themselves thrown, crushed, squished, splattered and impaled. Giant black creatures leaped out from behind columns near the exit. They came out swinging with horrifying strikes of death like none they had ever seen. Ratkins died by the dozens from each beast as they swung spiked fists and kicked with pointed boots.

Ratkins tried to discern what these creatures were. They had expected weak humans and clumsy knights who would be easy prey. They knew how to climb on humans and pry and prod for weak points with their fast and furious arrow-sized spears, vicious teeth and claws. These were not weak humans. The ratkins were being crushed and impaled again and again by giant black furious creatures they had never seen before. The ratkins never had a chance to defend or attack them. What maddening horror was this?

As they neared the open door, the ratkins focused all their energy on breaking out. They were halted as the knights in their full 'pro wrestler' black goblin-like armour riddled with spikes and nails pounced from all sides, swinging and kicking. Lord Byrom, the biggest, with mighty bashes, splashed the squealing ratkins to and fro. He squashed or flung them by the dozens at a time.

Lord DuLocke, the old dispirited one, was the most nimble and craftiest attacker of them all. He twirled and rolled with each vicious thrust, crushing and piercing ratkin after ratkin. Tahnwhithe held his ground at the door, swinging with both arms in orderly controlled death spirals. Ratkins would leap on him from all sides, then screech in pain as various spikes poked them.

The ratkins seemed to have no ability to harm the rolling, leaping, jumping, swinging knights. Wherever they tried to leap on them, they were met with pain and mutilation. They screeched in fury, spurring more to advance and attack.

Dunther leapt into the fray, swinging a spiked mace, yelling, "For King and Country!" He created a wide berth as ratkins flew from his deadly strokes. Each knight leapt to where the ratkins were thickest, easily clearing that area of the vile vermin. The ground was covered with the filth of many dead or crippled ratkins.

Finally, a larger ratkin boss appeared to figure out what was going on. It was the size of a large man but with fur, thicker skin and muscular limbs. It emerged from a swirl of ratkins. It had a few arrows in it but was able to reach Sir Murith, who was busy fighting many smaller ones around him. Sir Murith was unaware of the great rat behind him. It raised a large fat cleaver that looked like it could cut through metal and limb.

Loranna saw this and immediately responded. "Concentrate all fire on the big one!" she yelled. The girls from all three balconies turned their bows towards the ratkin leader.

"Row one fire!" Loranna yelled.

The shower of arrows littered the ratkin's bulbous back. This stopped its impending swing.

Sir Murith easily swatted ratkins away as he twirled around. He was stunned at the behemoth before him.

"Row two fire!" Loranna yelled.

Another shower of arrows pin-cushioned the beast. It wavered as it tried to swing its giant cleaver.

"Row three fire!" Loranna yelled hoarsely, unleashing her own arrow.

The arrows shot true, with hers piercing its head, popping out a black orb of an eye! Yuch!

It fell before Sir Murith! Standing behind it, as if waiting to see the outcome, were more ratkins, not in the least delighted by this outcome.

Sir Murith saluted up to the girls and leapt into the fray, swinging and bashing and splattering ratkin after ratkin.

Loranna and the girls looked wide eyed at each other, almost giddy. Loranna shook out of it quickly and yelled, "Keep firing! Keep firing!"

Their arrows hit easily in this mess of ratkin swarms. As the mass toppled over itself to move forward around the deadly swirl of knights, a wall of them would come crashing down with a dozen arrows in them. The girls rushed along the balcony, many just firing arrow after arrow. Others gathered around Loranna and began volleys at choice spots. This gave the knights time to clear dead rats off their spiked maces and spiked armour or kick and punch their way out from under piles of the dead.

Though the knights caused much devastation, the girls'

arrows frustrated the ratkins to no end. The ratkins used their own dead to leap upon the knights, who could still be overwhelmed by them. As they toppled a knight and were getting the best of him, at much cost, a sudden continuous volley of arrows would weaken their resolve giving the knight his chance to leap up, pull off the spiked dead and begin anew. The knights continued their pummeling and kicking at the thwarted ratkins.

Some ratkins, perceiving the ambush and seeing the girls above, tried to scale columns to get to them. Loranna pointed at the ascending ratkins and had the girls fire at them. The knights knew this was their chance to repay the girls, so they leapt on the columns, smashing into and yanking down ratkin after ratkin.

Tahnwhithe still defended the door, but many managed to crawl around him to get to the opening. Alfred had foreseen this and had placed Broggia and Boggin there behind a metal gate that ran across the doorway. They jammed their own spears into the mass of desperate ratkins trying to get out.

"I don't think so!" Boggin yelled fiercely, pushing his spear in. Broggia grimaced at first nervously but then became incredibly virulent and somewhat vicious. "Okay pops, okay, don't have to get vicious about it!"

It was truly a slaughter. Thousands came, and thousands died. The floor was covered with puddles of ratkin blood and spittle and bile along with many crushed ratkins in heaps and piles. The knights stood atop the biggest piles so as not to slip continually in the mess of filthy blood. Lord Byrom was unfazed by it. He simply trudged through and bludgeoned his way forward towards the gaping hole to stem the ongoing tide.

Knights are well trained in wrestling and combat. They are the best and the strongest of men. Though each maneuver, each tumble, roll, jump, leap, kick, bash, smash, crush, twirl, head butt, grapple, and so on resulted in many deaths, more ratkins poured in.

Even at their best, which these knights were not after many years of deprivation, their energy could not last much longer. Their attacks became awkward, in some cases dizzying, as they flailed with waning strength. Each began to show wear and tear and breathe heavily. For each moment given them before the next swelling of ratkins, they would kneel to rest in utter exhaustion. For each new attack wave their swings were a bit wilder than the last. No man could last this long. The knights had gone beyond their breaking point. Du Locke, the eldest, showed the most endurance. He pulled back knights and leapt into the fray to give Murith, Gorham and even Dunther a moment to breathe.

Loranna and the girls worked hard to keep firing non-stop. Eventually, all had bleeding fingers, some had raw skin. They became so weary they could hardly pull their bow strings back far enough to fire. Some resorted to throwing their arrows, but saw that wasn't enough force to cause any injury.

All the knights and the girls were overwhelmed—and stunned that ratkins kept coming. Even down in the dungeon corridors, the boys were doing their part, killing many and piling the dead along the side corridors while herding the rest up to the ambush in the hall. Cory and Alfred were fighting with such ferocity to hold them off that they too were weakening, both physically and mentally. Yet they tried to be aware of any weak points where the ratkins were crawling through to attack.

They wondered how much longer they could keep this up. All had many cuts and wounds, with many boys falling back in pain from a deep scratch or cut or bite. They didn't know if they could keep up their fight. The insurmountable odds of defeating the ratkins were starting to take hold in their minds.

The knights began to retreat, each picking others up while smacking away ratkins with exhausted limbs. They held their ground at the door, surrounded by what seemed unlimited numbers of the gathering foe.

Verboden came to the gate and ordered Broggia and Boggin to open it. They did and peeled away at the dead ratkins to allow him to pass. Many ratkins leaped at the chance to run out in the open and advance the killing spree. They were frothing for the chance to bite. Broggia and Boggin immediately closed the gate once Verboden was through.

Verboden had prepared for this moment with all his spirit. He pushed forward his staff, and a light as piercing as the sun and as white as the moon burst upon the ratkins. It caused them to retreat and topple upon one another in fear. The light blinded many. Accustomed only to the darkest of realms, they screamed and fell, clutching at deadened eyes.

Verboden slipped often on the gruesome rat-filled floor but kept moving forward. It was his moment to give his all to help in the fight. The knights fell back exhausted, trying to hold each other up, feeling as if every muscle in their bodies were paralyzed. Verboden thrust his staff into a pile of ratkins, where it stuck. The ratkins climbed back atop each other, unable to penetrate the incredible aura of light to attack the knights.

Then Verboden turned toward the fallen and weary knights and waved his hand.

Utter light, utter soul,
give them hope, give them might!
Purity of strength
wash over them!
Purity of will
lift them up!
Purity of heart,
Give this day, to the knights!

With each incantation Verboden clapped his hands, creating a booming noise above the shrieks of ratkins, which were piling up like a swirling wall of flesh. The knights felt their spirits lift and found a renewed surge of strength. They lifted their heads, then got to one knee. Then slowly, painfully, they stood up tall. The six black knights with spiked armour – Lord Dunther, Sir Gorham, Lord Tahnwhithe, Lord Byrom, Lord DuLocke and Sir Murith—stood side by side. They raised their fists. Lord Dunther yelled, "For the King!"

And the others responded, "For the King!"

And Dunther yelled, "For Country!"

And the others yelled, "For Country!"

Dunther looked up to the girls. They looked down at the spiritual magic of Verboden, smiling and tearing with a renewed sense of hope. He yelled to them, "For the People!"

And the knights yelled, "For the People!"

Then they charged into the massive wall of ratkins.

Arrows flew past them to knock down the first row as the knights dove into the mass, almost disappearing when the wall of ratkins toppled over them.

Verboden stepped back as his light waned. He grabbed his staff, easily leapt over the barricade and ran along the stairs that led up to the balcony. Many ratkins tried to follow him but got stuck in the barricade of spikes. Verboden turned and used his staff with fury, knocking back ratkin after ratkin.

The ratkins finally realized that this was the way to the girls, to stop them from firing arrows. But it was too late. Verboden was there now, swinging his staff in quick jabs and swats. A meager touch of his staff thrust the ratkins back into their own.

Lord Byrom, the first to break out of the mass, heard the desperation of the boys below, screaming to each other to fall back.

Alfred and Cory could barely hold their positions as boys fell back behind them with cut hands and feet. As blocked up as each corridor was, the frustrated and enraged ratkins began to break open the gates or squirm through bent bars. At this point, more boys were hurting on the ground than standing. Alfred knew they could hold no longer. He had them back away together as the wall of dead ratkins gave away to furious live ones. Many were suffocating due to their masses, but many more were still able to push aside their dead and the gates to get to the boys.

Alfred hurriedly yanked the boys away. They had to retreat out of the tunnels, as they had done all they could do in those tight confines. "Up! Up! We must go!" he yelled above the maddening squeals.

Just then many gates began to buckle, and ratkins

poured in after the fallen boys. Seriously weakened, Alfred and Cory stood to protect crying boys too wounded or weak to flee in time. Ratkins swirled to the openings, ready to exact vengeance on their tormentors.

All of a sudden, Lord Byrom dropped down and squashed the incoming tide. He leapt from the top, bulldozing his way from the great hole. "I have you, my king!" he yelled as he leapt through, rolling down upon the forming ratkins. With each roll he crushed scores of ratkins, and he banged against the tunnels and gates, yanking ratkins away from Alfred and the boys.

"Hurry, my king! Save them!"

Hurriedly and with renewed strength, Alfred and Cory pulled the boys away to narrow stairs that led up to the hall.

Within the tight confines, even after crushing a mass of ratkins against the walls, the space became so constricting that Lord Byrom became exhausted and was overwhelmed. The rats with their tiny spears were able to find their way within his armour. He roared from the pain and had to summon all his strength as he continued the crushing fury. Then he yelled out one last gasp, "For the King!"

The other knights fighting furiously in the Great Hall heard.

"Hurry, up, go go!" Alfred screamed at the boys, pushing and yanking them on.

"Lord Byrom, my friend!" Lord DuLocke yelled his first words in years. He leapt into the tunnel, killing dozens upon dozens as he skillfully slid down. He grabbed Byrom's hand as he became fully covered with motionless dead ratkins. A second and third layer of ratkins leapt upon him. He worked with fury to try to save his friend, knowing he was too late. He began to slow, as exhaustion and fate overtook him.

DuLocke did his best to clear the ratkins. In his haste he did not see the large one rearing up behind him, having come from another tunnel. In the tight space it was still able to swing its heavy cleaver down onto DuLocke's armour. The ratkins then jumped on DuLocke. In DuLocke's last stand, gurgling in pain, he leapt upon the huge ratkin, spiking and bashing it. He died next to Byrom, under a massive swirling of vicious rodents.

Due to Lord Byrom's and DuLocke's efforts below, the Great Hall finally thinned of more swarming ratkins. Dunther, Gorham, Tahnwhithe and Murith, having a moment to breathe, found energy to fight the few stragglers remaining and pull ratkins from each other's armour. Those few brief moments helped them regain focus from the chaos of battle.

Loranna and the girls quickly wrapped cloth, torn from the skirts, scarves and the like, on their hands.

Verboden nimbly leapt on a heap of ratkins and endowed the knights with what blessings he could muster.

Once their strength was somewhat renewed, Murith remembered, "Byrom and DuLocke are down there!" He climbed atop the ratkin piles. The others followed but quickly stopped as they saw Alfred and the boys coming out of the rear of the Hall, as all knew the various corridors to retreat.

"What of Byrom and Dulocke?" Murith asked.

Alfred, in his grime and filth, carrying up a younger boy whose arm was dangling with blood, shook his head, "No."

A buildup of chattering could be heard from below.

"We make our last stand outside!" Dunther said. "Come now, come all of you."

With that and with what energy they had left, they crawled their way out. The girls followed, carrying as many arrows as they could.

Broggia and Boggin pulled open the front doors as the knights fell out into the cool air. The boys and the girls staggered out, wounded, cut, and exhausted. Peasant women, many the mothers of blood drenched boys and girls, rushed up in horror, taking their children to care for them and love on them this fateful day. The air was cool, and a breeze helped clear away the stench of ratkins. They knew the battle was not over, but they had renewed energy and strength within. They now believed that it was possible to defend the castle.

Dunther stooped over with hands to knees and breathed heavily, coughing up blood and spit. The women poured water over the knights to cool them and clear out the ratkin blood and goo.

Captain Hedor approached them. "Lord Dunther, the goblins have not attacked. They are obviously waiting for the fall of the defenses from within. It looks like they will be waiting a long time, thanks to you."

They shared what smiles they could. Dunther looked gruesome and quite evil in the black spiked helmet covered with ratkin blood. Between coughs he managed to say, "It's not over yet."

Chapter Thirty Two

The Battle Within

Broggia and Boggin secured the door leading out of the Great Hall. Upon hearing the screeches of ratkins emerging from within, they rushed down the few steps to the courtyard. Lady Nihan and her ladies quickly passed around water to the remaining knights, Dunther, Gorham, Tahnwhithe and Murith. The knights quickly removed their black blood-ridden helms. They gulped greedily from ladles. Loranna and the girls carried their bundles of arrows and set up behind the knights.

Much to everyone's surprise, Lord Dunther took a ladle of water and offered it to Loranna.

She yelled to the girls, "Archers, set up on the walls, have arrows ready."

"Drink water first!"

All the girls paused in confusion.

With not a moment to lose, Loranna took the ladle from the Lord Knight and thanked him with her eyes and a nod. Little did she know, this interchange would be written in song and lore. She drank heavily, then passed it on. Never had anyone seen a Lord Knight hand a young maiden a drink of water, ever, let alone during a pause in a great battle that enlisted the girl's help. The girls set down their gear and quickly came to get water. Rehydrated and energized, they gathered up their arrows and rushed to the walls.

Alfred and Cory and a few of the older boys drank water and readied themselves for the next battle. They stood beside the knights. "We are here, Lord Dunther. We are ready to fight!"

Lord Dunther and Gorham could do nothing but smile. Dunther looked at his spiked helmet as they put them back on, and then at Alfred. "You've done us wonders, King Alfred. You've done such wonders for us all, no matter the end."

Alfred focused on the Great Hall's gate and the oncoming tide of ratkins. He paused for a moment and looked into Lord Dunther's eyes, beyond the black spiked helm and gruesome dripping blood, into the deep wells of hope and glory.

Verboden passed amongst the girls, healing all that he could and giving them resolve to continue their fight. Some were just too weak and collapsed where they stood. The older peasant folk carried them to a safe place to rest. The hard working farmers and wives came down from the walls. They lined themselves next to the knights and boys. They took up goblin weapons in their unsteady hands. They knew that if there was any chance to survive, it would take every able-bodied person to fight.

Lord Dunther nodded to each one. They looked down, away from the lord, partly afraid of his visage and partly out of respect for royalty and fear of his rule. Dunther looked away. There was no time for thoughts. The peasants gathered in groups with their weapons as ready as could be. Sir Murith stood in front of many, ready to take on the first wave and to die for them.

Captain Hedor and his men were still on the walls. He looked out into the darkness. The remaining goblins stood several hundred yards off, beating their drums and waiting patiently. There was still a massive horde of them to deal with. He shook his head. Abedeyan stood near. When Hedor met Abedeyan's eyes, he handed him his extra blade. "You must man the walls."

"Me? But..." Abedeyan fell silent. He looked out into the darkness, out at the multitude of goblins.

Hedor waved to his men, and all rushed down to the grounds. They stood with the peasants and knights, ready to fight.

The new ratkins came in to the Great Hall yelling and screeching. Never had they seen so many mounds of dead ratkins. The ratkin cared for no one, for each was always hungry and always in bitter struggle with every life form including its own. They were chattering in anger and madness. There was such a mess of bodies and blood, and the mounds of piled carcasses were unsteady, making it difficult for them to swarm.

They were equally frustrated that there seemed to be no way to advance out of the hall. Soon enough, a few found the locked doors and could smell the fresh air and scent of humans. They gnawed at the thickset doors. More came up and joined them, gnawing furiously. The screeches and gnawing reverberated, announcing to all the rest that this was the way forward.

The ratkins chewed at the wood frame of the door, the doorway finally buckled and with a loud clang broke out. A few came out at first, looking about and sniffing the open air. Then more ratkins began to pour through the opening and fan out onto the castle grounds.

Lord Dunther yelled with renewed vigor and charged at the massive swarm. Ratkins met him head on, not knowing the capability of a knight in such armour. Their strength somewhat renewed, Loranna and her girls fired arrow after arrow into the mass. Hedor and his men stood their ground, swinging violently at the stragglers Dunther missed. Alfred, Cory and the boys formed a wall with their shields and stabbed outward to any that passed. Peasants stood at their side, swinging as best they could. The ratkins seemed to fill every gap and opening on the grounds, biting ferociously at anything that moved.

Swinging and crushing many with his spiked fists, Sir Murith fell down by the opening, facing the Great Hall's doorway. He expected more to burst out at him but was stunned when none came. He stared wide eyed for a moment and then realized there was still much to do. So he turned back toward the remaining ratkins. He yelled out as best his hoarse, weakened voice could, "There are no more! There are no more!"

In a moment of hopeful wishing, Dunther looked up at the door and was astonished at the silent emptiness. He bellowed a war cry of hope, which renewed the strength and bravery of those around him. What started as the attack of the ratkins now turned into their panicked flight. Hundreds still raced about the grounds of the ward, but the attacks of knights, girls, boys, bandits and peasants quickly eliminated them.

Ratkins are ferocious and attack in number, but when there is no greasy ratkin on either side, they feel vulnerable and immediately turn into frightened, shivering, over-sized rodents. The ratkins realized all was lost, their kin were decimated. Only a few were left, scattered and retreating from charging farmers and children. The rats fled, scurrying back into the dungeons, then down into the Underworld never to return.

"Milord, milords!? The goblins! They're coming!" Abedeyan yelled.

Dunther looked up. Though full of vigor and spirit at having defeated the ratkins, he was reminded that the real battle was yet to come. He looked at the dirty worn state of his few knights. He knew in his heart there was little hope they could defend against a fresh goblin army. He was grateful no one could see the loss of hope on his face within his helm.

Alfred fell down, unable to go on. Cory tried to pick

him up but did not have the strength. Seeing Alfred down, Dunther did not feel bitter at him, for all had fought as much as they could. And though Dunther wanted to lie down and give up as well, he trudged as best he could to the walls, to look out to see the goblin horde amassed, ready to attack.

Chapter Thirty Three

One Last Time

Loranna rushed down to Alfred. She knelt beside him and held him. Hedor and his men rushed back to the walls. Hedor carefully helped Dunther up the stairs. The knight was completely exhausted and his armour still very pointy! At the top Hedor stepped past Dunther, braced himself and reached out with his spear. Dunther grabbed it. Hedor pulled him up the final steps. With wobbly legs Dunther leaned against the battlements and stared out.

The vast horde of goblins marched slowly in a V-formation with the point coming straight to the gate below

Dunther. He looked down, focusing his mind on the fact that they were not charging.

"They are expecting an easy entry through the gate!" He turned to the inner ward, to all who were fallen in despair. "Archers!"

Loranna looked up at him. The girls were all sitting or lying down. All looked up at Lord Dunther, hearing his shouts.

"To me! Now! Quickly! One last time!"

Dunther waved at the girls. Something was odd in his stance. He seemed excited, almost giddy.

"ARCHERS!!"

Loranna stood up and was able to help the other girls. Alfred also got up and helped, his curiosity overtaking his weakened state. The archers rose and gathered on the grounds just below Lord Dunther. He pointed to the massive force gathering at the castle wall.

"Fire at will!"

From the ground the archers took up their bows and arrows as best they could and unleashed arrow after arrow over the wall. They fired through bleeding fingers and raw skin. The farmers joined in, as most had decent skills in archery. They didn't have to aim, just fire their arrows over the wall. Thankfully, there were plenty of bows and arrows left!

"Broggia!" Dunther hollered, running about with renewed vigor. "Bring bows and more arrows! All who can fire come up now! Come with bow and arrow! All of you! Now!"

Alfred took up a bow from an exhausted girl and began firing arrow after arrow. This piqued the girl to action. She showed a burning desire to help. Alfred winked and gave her bow back as he grabbed an extra one and arrows from Abedeyan. There were plenty to go around. Alfred, Cory, Wilden and the peasants came up. All fired arrow after arrow.

Goblins fell, dozens upon dozens. For a long time they were unaware of their coming demise. They kept beating their drums and howling. They expected the gate to open, giving them an opportunity to rush in easily, raiding, pillaging and taking what they wanted. Instead, they fell by the silent arrows striking them down. Though many died, many more filled their spots. Eventually panic began to rise within their ranks, as they saw many goblins falling at their feet and the gate still had not opened.

The goblins at the gate panicked first. They realized the gates were indeed not opening and saw archers amassing on the wall, firing at them. They began to push back but were crowded in on all sides. This lead to a more densely packed crowd of goblins making them easy targets for arrows headed their way. Most landed on exposed necks, shoulders, throats and of course various parts of their goblin faces.

As feeble and fatigued as the people were, they were united and able to keep firing rapid volleys of arrows. Every able-bodied person on the walls and grounds was firing away! It was literally raining down arrows.

They didn't have to aim or worry about the onslaught of goblins. Since there was no ducking or hand-to-hand combat, they were able to use all their strength to fire at their own unhurried pace. The sound of rising panic within the sea of goblins grew and grew. Howling fear spread like fire from the front line across thousands of unwitting goblins further back.

Dunther watched as goblins began spreading out and fleeing in all directions. There were a few islands of staunch stubborn leaders, the larger goblins on their boars, yelling and barking at those fleeing. They were surrounded by their bravest and most ferocious, but eventually they too were soon met by a volley of arrows. As half a dozen of their own fell, including leaders and boars, the rest realized the futility in standing against the tide.

Still, a few foolhardy goblins, in either hatred of men or utter fear in failing the witch, came forward. They mustered what few they could to head to the gate, to hack at it with axe and hammer.

Unexpectedly, the gates opened. The goblins became excited. In their greed for pillage, they advanced without calling back to their fleeing brethren. They were met by the spike-ridden black-armoured knights. For a moment, recognizing the armour as goblin style, they thought they were seeing some of their great warriors. Or perhaps the witch had provided powerful forces to aid them. But no matter, the goblins rushed in, looking for the easy kill, the easy plunder.

They were stunned when the knights with spiked maces and shields began hammering at them. The hundred or so goblins and boar riders that advanced were suddenly and quite thoroughly annihilated. As tough as goblins are, there is nothing more ferocious than a prickly armoured knight leaping at them and hugging them with dozens of spikes and nails.

The victory was complete. The ratkin swarm was nearly wiped out, and the goblin army decimated and routed. The dead of the enemy was in the thousands upon thousands.

Never in these lands had such a battle been waged, nor had any opposing force so thoroughly routed the armies of Gorbogal. She had defeated many armies of men, dominating the lands of the West and South. She had ensured that all lived in fear and oppression. It was inconceivable that such a defeat could happen so close to her home — or some might call it a lair.

And though Gorbogal would have desired to eradicate this inconsequential kingdom that she had known and destroyed long ago, though she could have easily razed it with her magical powers and greater armies, she was now prevented from doing so. When word spread of the demise of her ratkin swarm and goblin horde, the free peoples of many lands found the courage to gather their forces and revolt against her. Gorbogal now was under siege on many fronts and once again had to contend with the bravery of man.

But that is another story.

We are focused on this small, lost kingdom of the Westfold and on a tired worn boy who, holding a goblin spear and wearing a small spiked helmet, became a warrior king. Who would have ever believed that peasants and common folk, bandits and children, would unite behind and follow this strange boy into battle? Or who could have imagined seeing royal knights bowing before a youngster because his clever ideas for defending a castle, a fortress they had lost, were successful? They called this boy a monarch... King Alfred, the Boy King.

Chapter Thirty Four

The Honor at the Field

The next day while all were still weak and wounded, the people walked down a path near the Keep. Their eyes were downcast and weeping was the only sound that could be heard. Sir Gorham, Sir Murith, Lord Tahnwhithe and Lord Dunther walked aside a small cart with the covered beaten and broken bodies of their brothers-in-arms, Lord Byrom and Lord Dulocke. They were buried with identical simple stone markers next to Lord Gylloth in a grove near the Keep.

While all were in the grove mourning their loss, Alfred stepped forward nervously and spoke suddenly. "We all live, while the knights die."

Dunther covered his eyes.

Sir Gorham wept openly.

Sir Murith kept the stern face of a proud young warrior, wiping only his nose.

Lord Tahnwhithe stood as still as a statue.

"Thank you" echoed softly in the grove that day. Verboden, weak from healings, leaned heavily on his staff and helped by others, spoke a soft blessing of sending. Sending them away.

In the days that followed, the people of the Westfold spent time bandaging the hurt, resting sore muscles and aching bones. Many of the children had come down with feverish conditions as they healed from their wounds and strain. Verboden, looking near catatonic, kept up his healing spells even as he needed rest himself. The peasants began clearing out the massive mounds of dead goblins and ratkins in and around the castle. A mountain of the dead was made outside the Keep. Alfred and Cory helped, resting often, as they were still weary. Hedor and his men stacked dead bodies high on the ghastly pile. Every able body helped in this gruesome yet needed task to minimize the stench and prevent disease from breaking out. Strong women, as well, dragged dead goblin after goblin, ratkin after ratkin, to the pile. The only two that seemed energized were Broggia and Boggin. They picked greedily through the dead, collecting all sorts of metals and scraps as well as blades and arrows.

Over the coming days, Lord Dunther and his knights roamed the fields and farms, rooting out any goblin stragglers. Though the battle had ended, there was still anxiety that goblins and ratkins would regroup and return. But none came. The knights found a few squealing frightened critters hiding here and there and killed them.

Slowly, the heavy atmosphere turned to cheer, and the people worked with a renewed sense of pride in what they had endured and accomplished together.

The men brought in loads of wood to use for a fire on the great mound. Loranna and the girls collected bramble and kindling.

It was on this day, amidst carnage and decay, that a song would be made of a moment not yet fully understood. The moment would change many people in the days to come. Many small and unimportant beings and peasant folk across the land would speak of this day as a day for all.

Lord Dunther and the knights returned and rode up to the tired common folk who labored slowly on the great mound of the dead goblins and ratkins. All were dirty and worn. All were covered by filth from the fallen. Somehow this did not matter to Lord Dunther and his knights. As they rode up, the people stood aside, concerned about the disposition of such powerful and dominating men.

Alfred and Cory were resting on a rock near a stack of goblins they were intent on carrying. Broggia and Boggin were still scavenging arms and armour in the filth. They stopped as everyone looked up to see Dunther and his knights dismount.

The people stood back. Tired and begrimed, Loranna and her girls stood near their parents. Some huddled under the arms of mothers or fathers. Lord Dunther walked up to Loranna's quivering parents and extended an open hand to Loranna. She hid behind her mother. Dunther motioned for her again. She looked pleadingly at her mother, but the size and shape of a fully armed knight with a great sword crusted with the blood of many goblins was too overwhelming. She stepped out, toward him.

Lord Dunther led her to Sir Murith, who had raised a flag. It was a dirty red tapestry on a simple pole pushed into the ground. Yet it shined like a majestic banner as the sun was lowering into the red of an evening sky. Dunther then motioned for the other girls to come forward. Some were reluctant. Others walked up and stood by Loranna, leading the rest to follow. They cowered together below the banner. Mothers wavered, wanting to rush up and take their daughters back, but were held back by the fathers, who feared the knights.

As the sun set, it caused worn armour to gleam as if new. Lord Dunther stood with Sir Murith, Lord Tahnwhithe, and Sir Gorham, shoulder to shoulder, facing the girls and the banner. Then unexpectedly, they each bowed on one knee for a long silent moment. The girls were stunned and then hugged each other and cried. Mothers rushed forward. Fathers cried tears of pride. Something took place that day that had never happened in the history of the peoples of the West.

No king or peasant, no emperor or warlord, no brigand or bandit, no wizard or cleric, no sage or seer had ever heard of such a thing. Even the people who stood before these knights, the weary and dirty peasants, the mothers and fathers of these few girls, did not quite understand what happened.

Abedeyan licked his dry lips and leaned on his rake, knowing full well that a legend was taking shape before his eyes.

As the seasons passed and in times of peace when they spoke of this moment, when the minstrel sang the song, "Honor at the Field," all knew that royal knights had bestowed the highest praise imaginable on a few peasant girls.

As quietly as they had bowed, the knights rose and turned to get back on their horses. As the sun set, they were wary, thinking there could be more goblin stragglers to dispense with that night. Lord Dunther swore under his breath that as long as he was alive, no farmer, no man, no woman and no child of this land would be hurt by those foul creatures. So the knights rode off on the hunt.

Days turned into weeks with no goblin or ratkin sightings. It was amazing for all to see, especially for several dozen minstrels and a collection of traveling merchants who came to observe for themselves what happened in the forgotten Westfold. They had never encountered anything like this. All came, migrating to where great stories are to be seen and heard.

Like other visitors, the troubadours were fascinated by the tale of the battle and traded performances for every story local people would tell them. At night crowds celebrated with singing and dancing at the farms, in the castle or outside of it surrounded by makeshift tents. That summer was an endless festival. As the tales spread, many more visitors came to hear what had transpired — a small kingdom had defied the great evil witch!

Alfred and the knights were told of great troubles in distant lands. A merchant from Telehistine, a renowned seaport, told them that some of Gorbogal's forces were there now, laying siege to its outer kingdoms. He subtly remarked that if it wasn't for this distraction, Gorbogal would have easily overrun the Westfold. Dunther rebuked the assertion. Alfred merely nodded in acceptance.

After a long thoughtful pause, Alfred looked seriously at the merchant and said "We are all in this together. Only united may we defeat her."

The merchant had been hired to learn about this small remote area for the merchants of Telehistine. He was not a spy looking for weakness in the castle's defenses or devising a devious trap to destroy its walls. He just did not disclose that he was in direct communication with the hardened Merchant Lords of Telehistine. He was sent to assess this new ruler, to see if they should begin a dialogue to work together. The few words King Alfred spoke were enough. "Thank you, your majesty," the merchant said. "I will send word that there is interest in exploring an alliance." With that, he bowed and left.

King Alfred felt encouraged by all that was happening and how the people were at one with each other. There was the constant clatter of hammers and saws and the voices of team leaders and workers. Many repairs were under way in the castle, it's towers and the King's Hall. Many craftsmen and tradesmen scattered throughout the lands were flocking to the small keep to find work. Alfred felt a sense of pride in the rebuilding and growing of the kingdom.

Constantly looming in the back of his mind was his concern that another confrontation with Gorbogal was brewing. He knew that the four knights, the children with bows and spears, and the peasants were not going to be enough. Yet somehow, he was able to remain at peace.

He looked around and was amazed at all that was going on. Dunther was now busy instructing Cory and the other boys in combat. Loranna and the girls continued honing their archery skills. Broggia and Boggin were busy smelting goblin metal, scooping out impurities to create stronger metal and hammering out pieces of armour and arms. They were all busy rebuilding and preparing.

Alfred visited Verboden, who was still healing the many wounded. All were in good spirits. Verboden seemed at ease in the ward of the wounded. Alfred came to talk to all the boys and girls, peasants and ex-bandits to see how they were getting on. All hailed the king as best they could with their bandages, coughs, pained ribs and dry throats. It took Alfred and Verboden a while to settle them down.

Alfred and Verboden sat on a bench in Verboden's small chapel for a quiet moment.

"Will Tirnalth return?" Alfred finally asked.

"Yes, he will."

"When?"

"Oh, I don't know for sure. I think he was reading and studying his many tomes and scrolls, preparing for the worst."

"Was?"

"Oh… well, right now I'm quite sure he's in his great

librarium of tomes and scrolls, his great hall of books. I do not believe he is reading, though. I suspect he is dancing around like a crazy hooligan."

Verboden turned toward Alfred with a great and very rare smile. Alfred could not help but smile back. Both could hear a faint whooping and hollering, a joyous ruckus echoing in the magical hall far, far away.

At night as all were resting, Alfred felt safe hearing the sound of Captain Hedor's guards walking the walls. When he slept, he often dreamed of his mother. He wondered how she was doing in that small apartment and if she was still alone. He tried to remember when he saw her last.

Yes, she had to let him go. She sat beside him in bed and gave him a fated farewell, and just like that, in an instant, he was back here.

He wanted to see her again but was unsure how. He tried to will it, expecting each morning to awaken in the apartment. Instead, he woke up in his castle bed. As the cool days of autumn came, he had many meetings and discussions about the kingdom and about repairs and improvements in the Keep. He made many decisions. When he would have quiet moments, as King Alfred and as a boy amongst friends, he thought of her. As time passed and he kept waking up in his chilly castle bed, his disappointment grew. He worried that he might never be able to return and how that would impact his mother.

As his dreams of her increased, so did his distress. He knew he had to find a way to return to her.

One day, Alfred was walking on the castle wall with

Loranna. He found comfort in her presence and sought it more often as time passed. On this occasion he was unusually downcast.

"You seem sad today. What is troubling you?"

"I miss my mom. I worry about how she is doing since I've been gone."

Loranna wore an earthy wool dress and a cloak. It was a chilly night of fall. The battle had changed her internally and externally. She was young in age but now seemed and looked older, like a woman. She looked close at him. "You should go. You should see her."

"But how? I don't know how?"

"I'll let you go. I want you to go."

And with that, Alfred was gone before her eyes.

Chapter Thirty Five

Alfred Returns Home

Alfred ran from his room into his mother's arms. She was sitting in a chair and sewing. She dropped everything and hugged him tightly, tears streaming down her face.

"Mom, mom I missed you!"

"I missed you too."

"How long was I gone?"

She looked deep into his eyes. "Only moments, but it felt like a lifetime," she said. And she wept.

Alfred held her.

"Then we battled the ratkins as long as we could. They kept coming, and eventually we directed them up into the Great Hall. Loranna and the other girls fired tons of arrows and killed even more. I was stuck in the small corridors down in the stinking dungeon. The knights and all of us fought a whole mess of ratkins. When it was over, we had to freaking help clear them out."

Alfred was hunched over, munching on sweet cereal in a bowl of cold pasteurized milk.

"I know, I know. You've told me so many times," his mother said, filling the bowl again.

"Just keep it coming! There were so many dead ratkins, mom. You wouldn't believe it! I even said to Abedeyan: 'Hey, let's just burn the whole hall,' but he smacked me on the head."

"That Abedeyan, he always was an old bugger."

"You knew him!!!"

His mother fell silent. It was now in the open between them that she came from that land. Somehow she had put it so far back in her mind and heart that actually acknowledging it was painful. And it almost seemed like a dream. Something in her did not want to face the grief and loss from long ago.

"Mom, they need you."

"Haven't they taken enough from me already? I've come this far only to find that they are taking my son too? It is not a game, Alfred! You could die there! You could die the most horrible death!"

Alfred looked down at his scrumptious bowl of modern sweet cereal. He put his spoon down and wiped his milky mouth. "Lord Dunther and the knights came up to us when we were piling the dead goblins. He gathered Loranna and the other girls around. Then he placed a pole in the ground with a red cloth on it."

Alfred paused, seeing a wrinkle of confusion in his mother's face.

"It was weird. The knights stood there and saluted Loranna and the other girls. They were so scared, all of them hugging each other. You wouldn't believe it. Then the knights went down on one knee and were silent. It was pretty cool, mom. Turns out, Dunther is a nice guy. He even told me some stuff about... well... about you. He said that he was sorry."

His mother sat in a chair next to Alfred. She did not know what to do with her hands. She tried to restrain herself, to hold her head up, but again the tears flowed. She finally stood up. "Oh, I do too much crying over the past! I see death and war everywhere, even on the news here. All lands are in struggle, and all people are at war." Her anger seemed to strengthen her, steadying teary emotions.

"Well here, aren't the wars about man versus man? I mean, there, you have witches and goblins and dead guys on giant vultures. You know, man is barely hanging on there. They needed outside help. Not that I'm all powerful like Gorbogal or that dark god but..."

His mother looked at him. "What do you know of the Dark One? And Gorbogal? Tell me, Alfred."

"Well, I think she is your sister? Ooh, then that means she's my aunt!?"

His mother gasped, "I should not have asked that..." She grew angry and began to pace around the room. "Dunther! He told you much, didn't he?"

"Well, yeah."

"It is his way of getting back at me, knowing he has our son!"

"Our son?"

She suddenly turned away. He could tell she was unnerved by his question. "Well, I mean, yes, our son, your father and I. Your father served under Lord Dunther."

"Yeah, I know."

"Well, Dunther had it out for us. Perhaps he is getting his revenge through you?"

"Mom! Please! He was plowing farmer's crops, for crying out loud. I don't think this is the same Dunther you knew!"

"Plowing? Crops?"

"Yes. And like I told you, he bowed to peasant girls. Heck, they saved his life in battle. He is plowing crops, playing with the kids and interacting with the farmers and peasants. A lot can happen in twelve years of famine and distress to change a knight, mom."

Alfred tilted the bowl to get every drop of sweetened milk.

His mother seemed confused. She tossed her head in disbelief, with too many thoughts, too many memories. She shook her head to clear it of past memories. Then she looked at Alfred. His mouth was bulging with sweet cereal, and milk was dripping out. She almost smiled.

"Well, I gotta go to school! Ooh, and I might stop off at the library tonight. I want to get some more books on agriculture, castle defenses, military tactics—you know, the typical stuff any growing boy wants to read."

Just before Alfred left, he looked at his mother sitting

there silent, smiling to herself. "What are you thinking about, mom?"

She turned and blinked. At first, she thought she wouldn't say anything. But then, as she saw how alive Alfred looked, she reconsidered. "Your father," she said softly. "I'm thinking of your father."

Alfred smiled and then left.

He hurried down the apartment steps with his backpack on, ready for school. He could easily have carried five times the weight with all he had been through. Out on the street, other kids were walking along, nodding and greeting each other, as they did every morning. Alfred had changed. He was walking with a happy, strong willed gait, ready for anything.

He was so preoccupied that he slammed into Wooly, who was coming out of his shop. Both fell back as if each had hit a brick wall. And both tumbled, landing on all fours, ready to get up. Alfred had been trained by the knights to do this instinctively. Wooly's face suddenly seemed familiar to Alfred, and he didn't know why, especially given all the scars on it. Oddly, Wooly was solid and took the fall well, recovering just as Alfred did.

"I'm sorry, Wooly. I was distracted."

"No harm."

For a moment, they looked at each other, puzzled. The sounds of the street snapped them back to focus on what they were doing. They stood and dusted off.

They saluted each other as knights would and continued on their separate ways.

A few blocks later, Alfred had a thought and turned back to see if Wooly was still there. He was gone. Alfred figured he could ask him later. He turned back and headed to school, his mind churning with all that he wanted to learn before his next journey back to the Northern Kingdom and the land of the Westfold.

So ends the first book of Alfred the Boy King.

Next Up:

Alfred

And the
Underworld

Volume Two

Made in the USA
Columbia, SC
03 May 2017